Planet of the Orange-red Sun

Series Volume 8

The Aliens Return

Planet of the Orange-red Sun Series

Volume 8
The Aliens Return

by Vic Broquard

http://www.Broquard-ebooks.com
Broquard eBooks
103 Timberlane
East Peoria, IL 61611
author@Broquard-eBooks.com

Artwork by Crooked Willow Studios.

For Morgan and L. Ron Hubbard

Table of Contents

Part I Periods of Organization

Chapter 1 Investigations
Chapter 2 Unexpected Changes
Chapter 3 Just Your Average Working Girl
Chapter 4 Actions and Reactions
Chapter 5 Meetings
Chapter 6 Milk Factory
Chapter 7 Resolutions
Chapter 8 Arrivals
Chapter 9 Educating Lena
Chapter 10 Adventures
Chapter 11 Surprises

Part II The Return

Chapter 12 Decisions and Actions
Chapter 13 Reactions
Chapter 14 Demands
Chapter 15 Treachery Among the Wasps
Chapter 16 Terror
Chapter 17 On the Trail
Chapter 18 Other Plans
Chapter 19 The Return of the Aliens
Chapter 20 Confrontations
Chapter 21 Politics
Chapter 22 Acceptance
Chapter 23 Of Dust and Loss
Chapter 24 In the Land of Ice and Snow
Chapter 25 Finding a Senator

Part I Periods of Organization

Chapter 1 Investigations

"Official Inquiry 3276598 re Senate President Carlos Amandos is now in-session. Sector ID Minister Lena Squire presiding," the tall, thin black woman of thirty-five spoke in a stern voice, one that seldom anyone ever questioned. Rumors abounded about those who did — they simply vanished without a trace. True, her real age was closer to one hundred twenty, but no one dared mention that detail. She kept her thick hair cropped close to her scalp, but there was no mistaking her sex. She wore a white silk blouse, a grey silk skirt, black nylons, and black patent, low, practical heels. A blaster was strapped to her thin waist. Those who knew her sensed she was more than a little annoyed at having to come to Caltran on Beltzar-4, when elsewhere there was a war being fought.

"Now then, Mr. Roberto Amandos, state your full name and relationship to the apparent-deceased Carlos Amandos. Just a formality, your DNA is on file. I assure you I checked *long* before I came here," she ordered.

A very nervous Roberto stood before the court. "Roberto Amandos, eldest son of the missing Carlos Amandos."

"Good. Proceed. Tell the court about that day when Senate President Carlos Amandos apparently disappeared," she ordered.

"Well, dad's shuttle landed, and I received notification of that from the automated pilot computer on his ship. Yes, that was routine. He always let me know when he landed at the estate. You see, I am — er was in charge of its maintenance staff. He would let me know when he was expected — usually during the Senate breaks, and I would alert the staff to prepare for his arrival. Well, I dropped by around six that evening to visit my father and mother."

"Good. Tell the court exactly what you saw and what you did then," Lena barked sharply.

"I saw the shuttle was gone."

"Is that unusual?" she interrupted him.

2

"Well, yes and no. Sometimes he kept it there, if he had plans to return to the city. I saw the shuttle was gone and headed to the front door. Both large doors were wide open."

"Is that unusual?" she interrupted him again.

"Yes. Dad never leaves the doors open like that. I knew something was amiss. I went inside and called out. I heard no answer except a garbled woman's voice."

"I see. Did you recognize that voice?" she asked pointedly.

"No, Your Honor. I walked into the hall that opens into the front room. I found the strange woman trying to sit up on the sofa. She looked — well, different."

She again interrupted him. "Please note, Roberto, we have sworn testimony from four business men that Senator Carlos had four telepaths present at meetings he held last fall. They described the three women in great detail. Describe this strange woman in detail."

"Well, she was a woman, that much I am certain. She was naked, except for a pipe corset, hose, and those ballerina style boots. Her waist was at least as small as dad's three new telepaths. She had the largest breasts I've ever seen, at least this big around," he gestured. "She had very long hair, which I later saw almost touched her ankles. She could not talk properly, because she wore these gold disks in her lips. I think the lips were slit and stretched to hold these disks that were a foot across. My ULAT box, which I then turned on, kept saying 'Error. Unknown speech.' So I turned it off. She was quite helpless, and she had no arms at all, not a trace. She also had these golden neck rings that kept her head immobile. I believe she was probably around fourteen, just a young teenaged girl, really. I ignored her and went on inside. I found mother asleep in her ball gown on her bed."

"Is that unusual?" Lena again interrupted him.

"Yes, she never does that. I couldn't wake her. Then I panicked. I raced from room to room. All dad's servants were also unconscious, as well as two security guards. Dad was nowhere to be seen."

"What about the four telepaths?" Lena asked, pointedly.

"Not a trace of them. Their rooms were empty. Clothes,

hairbrushes — everything gone. Even old blind Hernando was gone; his few possessions were not there either."

"I see. For the record, did you ever see these three new women telepaths?"

"Well, yes, Your Honor. They looked like the young teen I found lying on the couch."

"Exactly like her?"

"Yes, but they were perhaps eighteen, no arms, monster breasts, tiny waists, ballet style boots, very long black hair. This new teen's hair was brown and slightly curly. There is no way the teen that I found was one of the three new telepaths that dad had hired, Your Honor. Of that, I am absolutely positive. This teen did not have any telepathic ability or she would have communicated with me. I then raced through every room in the house, including dad's two locked offices."

"Locked? How secure were they?" Lena barked.

"Security Level 10, Your Honor. Dad told me they were un-crackable. A thief would have to break the door down to get inside. Anyway, I opened them and found all dad's extensive communication and computers were gone, as well as dad's medical machines. Vanished without a trace. The doors were intact as were the locks. I had a security man check on them both. Neither had been tampered with, Your Honor."

"So how do you explain the missing four telepaths, all your father's equipment, and the unconscious personnel?" Lena asked bitingly.

"Er, I cannot, Your Honor. It is a complete mystery. I know dad's computer and comm system were there three days before his arrival. I got relay messages from it, but not after it disappeared. I have no explanation. I summoned the doctors, of course, and sent the security guards at the gates to search the grounds for the missing people and equipment. I did get a report that dad's shuttle did take off before I arrived. Nothing was found on the grounds."

"Fine. Now, did the doctors find what had happened to them? Did you trace the shuttle?" she inquired, though she already knew the answer to the latter. That's partly why she had become involved in this matter.

"The doctors only surmised they had all been somehow

stunned. None knew what had happened. They arrived home, and the next thing they knew, the doctors were reviving them. I had a hard time tracing the shuttle. That cost funds. That's when I discovered dad's huge bank accounts were drained of everything, except one credit in each one! Someone has robbed him of millions of credits."

"Yes, we'll get to that. Go on. What did you do with the strange woman, and what about the shuttle trace?" she asked.

"Well, since the teen was unable to communicate and was in hysterics, I sent her to the Nursing Home. She obviously needed constant care. She could not even walk without someone holding on to her. That's the last I saw of her. The shuttle had flown back to the spaceport. I have ascertained that dad, for unknown reasons, had ordered his four telepaths to be taken to the spaceport. Lord knows why he did that. That's all I know. About the missing credits?" he asked what meant everything to him. His long expected inheritance had evaporated.

"Yes, I have followed his bank transfers. They are all legal and came from his own computer, so there is no doubt he intended to transfer the funds. However, we've been entirely unable to trace them to their final destination. That alone, in a time of war, is highly suspicious! Do you know of any nefarious dealings Senator Carlos might have had with our enemies?"

His face flushed. "No! No! Dad would never do anything like that!" he protested wildly.

"Okay, you may step down. I call Agent Ramierz." One of her field agents rose.

"My report speaks for itself," he began. "We traced the shuttle and the four passengers, the telepaths, to the spaceport. There, they were taken to Bay 5, per the orders of Senator Carlos. After that, they were taken elsewhere, but I found nothing but a totally confusing trail. Someone went to a great deal of difficulty hiding just where these four telepaths were taken. It is my belief they were ultimately taken to an unused repair docking station, from which an unscheduled deep space transport later took off. However, I have been unable to verify that is actually where they were actually taken.

It does make sense, thought because the transport is unidentified. Further, it jumped-launched into hyper-drive, as it was being challenged by the port authority. Destination: unknown. Likewise, the bank routing trace yielded no final destination for the billions of credits. Only Senator Carlos knows where they ended up."

"We did a thorough search for Senator Carlos. He has simply vanished without a trace. There is no way he could have been with the four telepaths; they were totally helpless, a blind man and three armless women — all verified by the workers. The only possibility is he might have been inside one of their packing crates, but that is a very remote possibility. It is also possible his body was disintegrated entirely by whoever raided his estate and stole his equipment. I tend to believe is a more remote possibility, personally."

"Yes, it is also possible his equipment may have been in those crates accompanying the four telepaths. That scenario is more likely than his person or body being stored in one of the crates. It remains a mystery why he sent his telepaths away and his money."

"Were you able to get anything out of that strange young teen?" Lena asked.

"No. She is as Roberto described, hysterical and completely helpless. Per policy, in times of war, everyone must work towards winning the war. She has been donated to Praline's Escort Service, where she can at least perform such services as wealthy men might desire."

"What is your summary, then?" she asked formally.

"Senate President Carlos Amandos obviously has had some illegal, nefarious dealings, most likely with our enemies, and has somehow gone off-world, probably joining the Federation of Planets. Per your requests, all his security codes have been canceled. Alerts for his ID card use have been issued to every planet in the Imperium. If he so much as opens a door with his card, we will know about it. However, it's been six months now, and we've received no such notice. That alone tells me he must not be anywhere within the Imperium. No one can go that long without using their ID card! It's hard to avoid using it at least once a day."

"Thank you. Okay then, the verdict of this court is that Senate President Carlos Amandos has consorted with the enemy in a time of war. As such, his property and possessions are hereby confiscated and a warrant for his arrest is hereby issued, alive or dead." She pounded a gavel on her desk, sinking the last hopes of Roberto. He had hoped at least to inherit his father's estate. Now he had nothing at all. His many businesses had already been closed down.

After everyone filed out but her agent, she said, "Okay Agent Ramierz, you are with me. Have you found our telepath?"

"Yes, I had to pull in some big favors with a business man, but I have him. When?"

"Now. Let's use your shuttle. Less questions," Lena stated dryly. "Come on. I want to question her myself. Just who is this mysterious teen? How did she get involved in this mess? Have you verified the three women that Carlos had as his telepaths were indeed Senator Isabella Valen from Tierra and her two wives?"

"Yes, that is beyond doubt, just as what he did to those women. Honestly, boss, from all reports from his servants, the three women looked just like that strange teenager. Suspicious. Why did he do that to the senator and her wives?"

"Telepaths are exceedingly rare. In his line of work, you can go far if you have them working for you. He fixed them up so they could not talk or escape on their own. Clever of him, but totally illegal. My god, if Senator Isabella is still alive, she could bring a huge lawsuit against him and the Imperium. She could easily settle for several billion credits, which we dare not spend in this time of all-out war. We need the funds to win this battle."

They reached his shuttle. She stepped inside and sat down beside an older man. "Are you the telepath? Can you send and receive?"

Yes, both. What is the assignment, he sent her, rather surprising her. Lena was good at concealing any and all facial expressions. Still, he read the surprise in her mind and smiled.

"Good. I need to question a young teen, who is unable to speak in any known language the ULAT can translate. I will feed you the questions, and you telepathically send me her replies. I do not want you speaking aloud under *any* circumstance. If you *ever* tell anyone what you may learn on this little outing, I will have you sentenced to *death*. Do I make myself clear? This is a delicate matter of Imperium security. In times of war, I have no recourse but to issue the death sentence, if you so much as breath a word of what we discuss. Clear?"

Yes, Sector ID Minister!

A half hour later, the three stepped out before the Escort Service. Agent Ramierz had already sent word to the proprietor to have the woman available for questioning. As the three walked into the red light establishment, the manager nodded and motioned for them to follow him. "She really is completely helpless, but I assure you she is earning her keep, as we all must do in times of war."

"Yes, yes." Lena said curtly. He opened the door to a private room. "If you have any surveillance equipment in this room, eliminate it immediately. If anything which transpires in this room every gets out, I will sentence you to death. Understand?" He nodded nervously and hastily left them alone. Lena took out a small electronic device, a Scrambler. Even if he had a video or audio system spying on this room, her device would jam its signals.

Now she got her first look at the teen. She was just as described. She sat rigidly erect, her neck held motionless by a series of neck rings. Her shoulders were bare; her arms had been removed from their sockets. She had huge lip plates, drooping down towards her massive bosom. Lena had never seen ones as large as these. They were larger than the poor woman's head. She wore a red satin gown, but Lena could see from the incredibly tiny waist that she wore a pipe corset. Her feet were pointed downward; toe shoes forced her to walk on the tips of her toes. Indeed, here was a most helpless woman, whose only use was to perform in bed. Well, at least she could do that much, Lena thought.

"Okay, ask her what her name is?" Lena said as soon as they were seated across from the teen.

Senator Carlos Amandos! The telepath looked very

surprised.

"Who did this to you?" Lena asked.

She got a very lengthy story! A half hour later, the telepath finished relaying the teen's story along with a desperate plea for help. *Can you read me?* She asked her telepath.

Yes.

Good, tell him this. What you did to Senator Isabella Valen and her two wives is beyond inhumane. All your bank accounts and business accounts have been mysteriously drained of all their credits. Do you know anything about that? The reply was as she expected, he had no idea and looked horrified, if she read his eyes right.

Good. Tell him this. If Senator Isabella Valen is still alive, she can sue the Imperium for billions of credits and be awarded them. Hence, this is my final judgment. I have already issued an arrest warrant for high treason on Senator President Carlos Amandos, dead or alive. As far as I am concerned, you can stay just as you are now. Poetic justice is served. Just know that if you should ever regain your former identity, you will be hunted down and executed. Enjoy your prostitution. We must all do our part in times of war.

The woman begged and cried, all unintelligibly, but Lena was not moved in the slightest. She rose ending the meeting. Once in the shuttle, she reminded the telepath never to breathe a word of what he'd just heard. The sweat trickling down his temples told her he knew she meant it. If he were not an incredibly valuable telepath, she would have had him shot right now. Then, there would be no possibility of any of this ever being leaked out. The telepath also picked this up, which is why he was sweating.

"Well, are you satisfied?" Agent Ramierz asked.

"Yes, silly teen got in the way. She's doing well where she is at now. Case closed. Let's go home." *God, I hope Senator Isabella Valen doesn't show up. Good lord, the trouble she could cause is enormous. If only he'd not been the Senate President!*

Chapter 2 Unexpected Changes

Konrad Burkhardt and his wife Neva returned to his home world, where they spent the first six months after the spaceport on Plateau Grado was closed down. They used the medical machines to repair their lips. Once they arrived, Neva insisted on buying a whole new wardrobe, one that would make her appear to be a "great lady." He was madly in love with her and went along with her desires. Now she wore satin ball gowns all the time. This was actually quite acceptable to him, because the two became "celebrities." He was now the most famous governor in the Imperium. As a result, hardly a week went by without their being invited to another elegant party in his honor.

Between these social gatherings, he took her on a tour of the sights of his home world. She was fascinated with each and every little detail. He began to see his own world with new, fresh eyes. So yes, they had a most enjoyable six months there.

However, since both were now known telepaths, he soon received a visit from his Sector ID Minister. "We must all do our parts in times of war, Governor Konrad. I need you and your wife to visit many of the outer planets of the Imperium. Hobnob with the leaders there. I want you both to look for traitors, enemy spies, and such. Neva, you take the women; Konrad, you take the men. Here is your first planet."

Both groaned, but had no choice in the matter. For the next three years, they traveled to dozens of such planets. At least, they were able to ferret out two spies, so Konrad as satisfied he had done something worthwhile. Both he and Neva hated every day of this new life. However, she was wise enough to play along, for she was learning a great deal about the Imperium and how it worked. No longer was she the innocent social gadfly, the barmaid turned "great lady." Ambition rose within her.

Their extensive movement between many distant planets on the edge of the Imperium took them into several different official sectors. Hence, the two met with three other

Sector ID Ministers. While Konrad saw this as boring and a waste of time, Neva had other ideas. Having seen just how valuable the Imperium considered its working telepaths, she used her additional *mentales* gifts to probe the minds of these new ministers.

As she expected, some viewed her with great suspicions, believing no state secret was safe around them. One went so far as to change every last security code the moment the two left his presence! While all of them viewed her with awe and respect, several, however, had financial dealings with telepaths. Her light probe told her so. It was these ministers she chose to explore further, risking a deeper probe of their minds while they were asleep.

Once she met a person and lightly brushed his or her mind, at a later date, she could make telepathic contact with them, as long as they were not too far away. Distance was always a factor for her. Through these Sector ID Ministers, she began to learn far more facts than she was supposed to know. First, there were thirty-five of these Sector ID Ministers, one for each of the sectors of space that formed the vast Imperium. Some sectors were larger than others were. Their boundaries were more political than anything else, except for those at the edges of the Imperium.

More importantly, these ministers reported to one of six Imperium Legates. These Legates formed the High Council that ruled and controlled the Imperium. The High Council itself reported to the President of the Imperium, who in turn had a Vice-president beneath him. While the Senate theoretically made the laws of the Imperium, she learned in fact that the High Council and the President sometimes overruled the Senate. Officially, they could do just that in times of war, but over the millennia, the various Presidents and High Council members had stepped in on several occasions to nullify a new law here and there, laws that might hinder the powers of either themselves personally or businesses in which they had vested interests.

Neva had met many different men on these new worlds she and Konrad visited. Observant, she also noticed men of power were often quite alike, just as the men were at the old bar where she grew up serving them. Sex, money, power, though some were after fame. This trifecta combination lay behind their motives. She knew that to control one these men, she only needed to play to the proper one of these, the one that the man held uppermost. With poor Konrad, it had been sex. He cared little for money or power and the fame that came with it. True, he was enjoying the fame he'd earned as being the foremost successful governor in modern times, but being the best governor was not part of the trifecta. Rather it had been sex. She reflected on how Nadja had played the card of helping him achieve his goal as top governor. Look where that had gotten her, she thought. Nadja was altruistic, having failed to make any real use of her marriage to Konrad. *Well, I have!*

Neva knew it was time for her to move upwards, perhaps even towards the President himself. From the various Sector ID Ministers, she learned that the six Legates and the President resided on Baltzar-4 in the capital city of Caltran, but that these powerful men had many businesses scattered among many other worlds. They all had offices on Proxima Prime, where the Senate was located. The Sector ID Minister over that planet was one Lena Squire, a hard-nosed, no nonsense woman, who had her own way of handling situations. From thoughts extracted from her current Sector ID Minister here on one edge of the Imperium space not far from where the massive war was being fought, Gnak Booud, she learned Lena often played by her own "rule book." Well so did Gnak, for that matter. To get to the Legates, her current objective, she would need somehow to use Gnak Booud and not Lena, who was in charge of security around Proxima Prime.

She was patient and finally was rewarded. He had summoned her to his battle cruiser to receive her latest report in person. Walking was still rather tricky for her, since she insisted on still wearing her toe shoes. In her form-fitting satin gown, her extreme curves and heels never failed to attract attention towards her. And that was the whole point, one of the trifecta points.

As she made her slow, careful walk into his office onboard the massive ship, she sensed his eyes staring at her.

Perfect, she thought. "Welcome Mrs. Burkhardt," the forty year old short man said in a rather high voice. Her ULAT box translated for her and for him. He wore one of the recyclable synthetic unisex cat suits with a blaster strapped to his side. His eyes were piercing and coal black. She sensed a very keen mind and acted accordingly. She took a seat across from him.

"Thank you for seeing me in person this time, Sector ID Minister Booud," she replied demurely.

"I am not sure why this report is more important than the others you have filed, but I am listening," he said stiffly. She proceeded to give him the details of the spy she'd uncovered. He took a couple of notes, which she thought was favorable.

"He is clearly a spy intent upon sabotaging the war efforts. He ought to meet an untimely death," she explained. "While I know you could arrange such, I also know there would need to be a formal autopsy done. We both know that could reveal poison or other suspicious means, which in turn would give away the fact we know what he is up to, giving our enemies a head's up alert. That's why I wanted to see you in person."

He looked up at her and met her eyes. She did not flinch, as so many others did when his eyes drilled theirs. She sensed he was impressed with this. "You see, while I am a telepath, I am actually far, far more than that. Konrad, well, he's just a telepath, Class V, as we all are. Yet, I have far more, shall we say, 'useful' gifts. For example, did you know a thought of mine can kill? I can dispose of this spy, and any autopsy will reveal he died of 'natural causes.'"

His eyes opened slightly wider. "Do go on," he said lowering his voice, watching her closely.

"Yes, right from where I am sitting now, I can slay him, and no one will have the slightest clue he didn't die from anything but natural causes. Yet, even this simple thing is only a small part of my repertoire. I have many abilities that are wholly unknown to even my silly husband." She took this opportunity to place some distance between herself and Konrad.

"Do go on. What form might some of these other

abilities take, Mrs. Burkhardt?" he inquired.

"Neva, please, just Neva between you and me. I would not like all these widely known. Someone might want to take advantage of me," she replied coyly. "I can see you would like proof. Let's see. Do you value that chair over there? It's not flammable is it?"

"No, it's just a chair, and it isn't flammable. Why?" he looked at her curiously.

"Well, how about a little ball of fire? That ought to be a convincer," she replied.

"That's impossible, Neva."

She focused and poof! A three-foot in diameter ball of flames erupted over the chair. She extinguished it after a few seconds, noticing how this demonstration registered in Gnak's mind. Neva smiled coyly; it had just the right effect.

"How did you do that? Can it last longer? Can it be larger in size? I didn't see you doing anything. Can you do that again?" he asked very much interested, keenly so, she sensed from his mind. She duplicated it, allowing it to burn slightly longer before extinguishing it.

"Like I said, I am a woman of many talents."

"That's unreal! So you are serious about thinking a thought and having our spy die of natural causes?" he asked.

"Precisely so. I know if I were running this show, I would do just that. No one would be the wiser. Plus, it would not reveal we were on to this spy," she answered.

"I see. Of course, there must be something in this for you, right?" he came right out with it.

"Of course. I can see that we see eye to eye, Sector ID Minister."

"Okay, you have my permission to terminate this spy. Right now. From here. If I find out this has happened just as you've said, then we can talk about what it is that you desire, Neva," he replied coyly.

She focused for a minute. He stared at her, looking for any outward sign, but saw nothing unusual at all, except she seemed to be thinking about something. She looked up, "There, it is done. The spy has just died. You may check on him at any time. I will return after you are convinced I am telling you the truth." He nodded, and she left.

The next morning, she received a personal summons back to meet with the minister. Two armed men knocked on her door and escorted her to Gnak, who met her in the same room as before. After making sure she was comfortably seated, he sat down. She noticed a distinct change in his attitude towards her and knew she had him. "Well, you were right. He was found dead. The doctors pronounced his time of death around the time we were speaking yesterday. Natural causes. Heart failure. Who would have thought such a thing was even possible!"

"I know. Awesome, isn't it? My true potential is not being used in the slightest with these routine, simpleton telepathic assignments. I can be far more useful to those above you, don't you think?" She planted the notion of what she really wanted, re-enforcing it with a subtle mental push into his mind.

"The Legates?" he asked curiously.

"Precisely."

"I see. But what about your husband, Konrad?"

"He can continue with these simple assignments. He is good at them, but hardly any more than that. I am most willing to relocate to Beltzar-4 or Proxima Prime, and discuss how I may be of far, far better service to those in power," she suggested.

He grinned, "Any you think I can make that happen, do you?" He was halfway teasing her, but she knew he was thinking along those lines himself.

"Certainly you can. What do you suppose a Legate would do for you, if you brought me to him and I proved my worth?" she hinted not so subtlety.

He grinned. "Okay, Neva. Pack your bags. I'll have you on the next transport ship to Beltzar-4 sometime tomorrow morning. I'll make up some excuse for your husband. Plausible deniability."

"I'm sure you'll be well rewarded, Sector ID Minister. I'll make sure the Legates know it was *you* who recognized my potential and sent me to them," she replied coyly. He returned her grin, and she sensed from his thoughts that he certainly would be rewarded, either way, whether or not she proved worthwhile.

"I don't like us to be separated like this," Konrad moaned, when he learned the minister was transferring her to Beltzar-4 and not himself.

"I know, dear, but we all must do what we can for the war effort. I'm sure there's a very good reason that they need me there. I want to do my part too, dear, just as you do. Perhaps it'll be a short assignment, don't you think?" she softened the blow.

"Well, I certainly hope so. I'll try to speak to Gnak when I can. Maybe I can get him to send me there too, once I get done here. I'll miss you so, dearest Neva," he replied, more like a wounded cat, she thought. He helped her pack her many clothes into four shipping crates. Two armed men arrived at ten the next morning to escort her to the spaceport. She touched their minds and knew they were ordered to make sure she got on that flight.

When the transport ship landed several days later, an escort of six armed guards swarmed around her, as she very carefully stepped off the ship. She intentionally offered her hand to one of the men, using him for support. "Ma'am, we're to take you to a secure facility. Your things will be brought there later on. This way," he said briskly. She slipped her arm around his, intent upon using him to help her keep her balance, and yet walk seductively in her toe shoes. The six men did notice them — her nylon covered legs, and huge bosom.

An hour later, she arrived at a hundred-story skyscraper, which she gazed upon in awe. The security guard pressed the button for the top floor, and she knew this would be a very formal meeting with the Legate. But which one, she wondered?

Plush. She had no other word to describe what the huge office looked like, as she stepped out of the elevator, her arm still clinging to the guard. Walking on the soft carpet was challenging in her shoes. The walls, though a plastic polymer, were decorated with fine paintings, which she didn't appreciate. A formal fountain gushed water out of a demon's mouth, while colored lights alternated, giving the scene a surreal effect. She was led into a business conference room, replete with a water pitcher, glasses, sterile but expensive furniture, and more of the rather exotic paintings. These consisted of several nude women in various seductive poses, and she knew one of her trifecta was already met.

Two men, dressed in the finest suits she'd seen, rose as she entered. Both were a light black and probably a silk derivative, she guessed. One man was tall and thin; the other shorter, but both were well-muscled for middle aged men. She sensed very bright and sharp minds with a high IQ. She also sensed immense power coming from these two men. Purposely, she allowed the two men to eye-scan her form briefly, before taking a seat across from the two.

"Welcome Neva Burkhardt. I am Legate Herman Mels. This is Legate Daag Taal. Sector ID Minister Gnak Booud referred you to us. Time is precious, so let's get down to business, shall we? Oh, this office is electronically protected against all forms of eavesdropping. What is said in here remains in here. Understood?" His voice was cold and business-like.

Legate Daag spoke up, "So Gnak says you can kill a person with a mere thought? Is this so? He claims the autopsy showed the man died of natural causes. How do you explain this?"

"Of course. That's the whole point of an assassination, isn't it? Leave no trace behind that would indicate anything other than natural causes. Of course, a thought can kill. How silly. No, I keep forgetting you are not *mentales* gifted as I am. While I am in your designation a Class V telepath, that is the most minuscule of my mental abilities, Legates, the tiniest."

Both men smiled, when they duplicated her thought of leaving no trace, but both looked slightly worried when they heard the rest. "While we appreciate Sector ID Minister Booud's appraisal, you must realize we need to see proof of your skills and perhaps a catalogue of just what all you are able to do," Legate Herman stated businesslike.

"Well, if you have someone who needs to die, all I need to do is to meet with them once. I presume you would like a small demonstration too. I would expect nothing less from such powerful men as yourselves. So Legate Herman, you make those big spaceships with all the guns, cruisers? No, battle cruisers. And you, Legate Daag, your companies supply the big guns for the war effort."

"How did you know that?" Legate Herman asked. "No, you probably just looked us up on the Net."

"No, I just read your minds. I've been stuck on that transport ship for days. Besides, I didn't know who the Legates actually were, not until you introduced yourselves. I can pull whatever I like out of your minds though, but it isn't pleasant for you if I were to do that."

"This I got to see. Okay, Neva, tell me what I was doing last night? That isn't on the Net. And as you say, you were on the transport ship at the time," Legate Daag challenged her.

"As you request, Legate Daag." She focused and probed his mind. She knew he would be trying to keep it from her, which was only human nature. Hence, it was very visible to her. "Oh, you went to a fancy theater with a blonde escort woman, who is not your wife. Kathleen is the name she used, but that isn't her real name. She wore a satin dress, light blue. Too bad she doesn't have larger breasts; she could look really sexy if she did. You sat in seats 5 and 6 up front. Hum, you must have special seats, but that would make sense, since you are a Legate."

"Stop! Enough. I believe you," a flushed Legate Daag ordered, somewhat annoyed at the seemingly ease with which she extracted the data.

"Well, we have a prisoner who needs to be executed. I'll have him brought here so you can, as you say, meet him. Then, you may use your powers to kill him," Legate Herman spoke up dryly.

"Do you want me to kill him right here in this room?" she asked demurely, as if this was but a trivial matter.

The two men looked at each other, and then smiled. "Sure, why not. As long as it isn't messy," Legate Herman answered.

A few minutes later, armed guards led a man in chains into the room. "Barrack, you have been sentenced to death. Any last words?" Legate Herman asked.

"You filthy beasts! You'll get what's coming to you," Barrack cursed them, fighting against his chains and the two men who held his arms securely. Neva focused and stopped the man's heart. As the two Legates watched, Barrack slumped lifelessly, held up by the two guards.

"Okay, take him out and dispose of the body," Legate Herman ordered. A minute later, he looked at Neva and said, "Impressive, Neva. Very impressive. I do believe there is a place for you here on Beltzar-4. Sector ID Minister Booud mentioned you can create balls of fire?"

"Oh yes. Simple matter. I made one on one of his chairs that wouldn't catch on fire. Do you want a demonstration of that too?" she asked.

"Not in here! There are valuable paintings on the walls," Legate Daag countered.

"We will take Booud's word about that. Now then, is it possible for you to force another to do something they might not otherwise do?" asked Legate Herman.

"Oh sure. It is not very polite to do that, but it's possible. Of course, out there, one ought to have a very good reason to be forcing another to do something they might not want to be doing," she replied demurely. "Ethics and all that."

"I see. How about a simple, harmless demonstration. Make Legate Daag take off his pants right now."

"Hey, that's not funny!" he exclaimed. "Make him do it too," he countered. She sensed the rising antagonism between these two men. In some ways, they were rivals, she thought.

"Okay. Give me a minute here." Neither man saw her hidden germanium crystal glowing for a brief instant. Both men fought hard to keep from removing their pants, but her will won out. "Nice legs," she teased them.

Rather embarrassed, both men hastily put their pants back on. "Excellent, Neva. Amazing even. So, I do believe we can work together. What is it that you desire?"

"Well, I would like a fancy estate with a garden and fountains. Oh, and a few servants to take care of it all. I sure don't want to be cleaning house, if you know what I mean. I'd like to be escorted to all the fancy affairs and the social things, like the theater. I've never seen such things. I suppose I need to purchase more fitting clothing. I've no idea what the elegant women wear here on Baltzar-4. Some guidance would be nice. I always want to look my very best," she replied.

"Okay, then I believe we can work out a mutually agreeable situation here. Give us a few days to make the arrangements. In the meantime, you will be staying in the penthouse suite, where all the top dignitaries stay when visiting here. My secretary will accompany you, and she can help you pick out your new clothing. She has a tasteful eye," Legate Herman stated businesslike. She picked up he was having an affair with her as well and smiled.

After she left with the twenty-five year old Hanna, Legate Herman said, "Now that was scary! I didn't see her doing a damn thing, yet he died right before our eyes! That woman's pure, raw power. We sure can use her."

"Yes, indeed so. Pretty good trick making us take our pants off. But what about making our competitors accept deals they never would sign off on? Now that gives us an even better edge. Still, she's one scary woman. With that kind of power, she could take over the Imperium, Herman. Damn. What's to prevent her from taking over our 'businesses?' Tell me that one. How do we control her? Surely, she isn't interested only in having an estate and servants as she says."

"We should reward old Booud rather handsomely on this one. Think of what could've happened if he had sent her to President Snarry instead of us? She could well unravel our business enterprises and bankrupt us!" Herman pointed out the obvious.

"Right. And she still could. If we cross her in any way, she'll have our butts. We've got our hands on the most powerful telepath ever, but how do we protect ourselves from her? Answer me that one. I can think of all sorts of projects to use her on, but how do we control her when she can readily control us! My pants! Man, I couldn't help myself!" Daag exclaimed, growing more and more worried.

"Old Senate President Carlos, wherever he's gone too, had the right idea with his telepaths. Damn, Minister Lena has probably already worked out what he did to those three new telepaths Carlos was bragging about. Do we dare do something like that to this one? Hell, this woman could easily kill us if we did, quite unlike those that Carlos found," Herman replied, growing more and more worried.

"I know. We've the most powerful telepath ever to surface, but she's also the most dangerous person in the whole damn Imperium! We have to temper that power somehow, Herman. If we don't, she'll turn on us one day, mark my words," Daag replied nervously.

"She could be made more helpless, if we had her arms removed. I've an idea how we could convince her to have that done. Still, I don't know how we could get her to wear that neck brace thing that Carlos put on his. She has to see the person, so we don't dare blind her. Probably wouldn't do us much good either."

"Say, he had his wearing those monstrous lip ornaments things. You know, like that one escort, which has been seen around the city at night. If she wore those, she couldn't be understood when she talked," Daag suggested.

"With telepathy, she probably doesn't need to talk. We could kill her voice box too. Would that stop her from turning on us? I doubt it. We could threaten to harm her husband, but clearly she doesn't much care about him anymore or she would not be here," Herman theorized.

"Quite true. She's obviously looking to gain more power and prestige, or she would not have revealed herself to Minister Gnak, as she did. She is sexy looking and probably doesn't have much money. A governor doesn't make all that much, even if he's really successful. I think I know a way to convince her to lose her voice. If she's caught, no one can force her to speak and reveal anything. She might buy that. Hobble her physically and silence her, but with *her* agreement to *have* that done. Then, she won't come after us in retaliation. Still, I can't see how we can really protect ourselves from her, if she wants to go after us," Daag pointed out.

"Points taken. We could introduce her to that exotic escort with the lip things and the neck rings. We could claim this is the very latest style, the vanguard for the fashion world here on Baltzar-4. Get her to agree to have the alterations done. As much as she seems to want to appear well-dressed, she might go for it. Then, she would be physically helpless, but such would not impact her powerful mental abilities, I don't think," Herman thought aloud.

"True, but we would need more than one such example to show her. Besides, she can probably read that woman's mind and want nothing to do with it," Daag countered. "We've an impossible dilemma on our hands, that's for damned sure! We can use her talents, no question of that, but how the devil do we protect ourselves from her?"

"I wonder if there are more like her out there somewhere?" Herman mused. "Anyway, we've got a couple of days to figure this one out. We could always inject a poison in her and then feed her the antidote regularly. If anything happens to us, the antidote delivery stops, and she dies. Do you suppose she'd buy that as a safeguard?"

"If she did, she'd be a fool," Daag replied, "and that, she does *not* seem to be. When we put her under for the modifications, we could use some of the psych's brainwashing on her. In fact, we could make her crave sex and such, turn her into a corporate escort as a cover. In fact, let's go see just how well that is working. Psych man Donatello has been working on new methods. If those are half of what he claims, then maybe that combined with the physical restraints will do the trick for us. Come on; we've some investigation of our own to do."

Legate Herman replied, "Aye, that's perhaps the easiest thing in the world to do. The top three escort services in Caltran are using my services to 'enhance' their top models. My latest behavior mods are working well, quite stable. Plus, there is Case 10392. This man was vehemently against the late Senate President Carlos Amandos. As such, he had to be altered by Doctor Donatello. Come with me, and I'll introduce you to him."

They found the doctor, who led them to a locked room. As soon as the "patient" saw the doctor entering, he called out, "Ah, Doctor Donatello, have you found my idol yet? Surely, after all this time, you have found Senator Carlos. He's the very best senate leader the Imperium has ever had." Both Legates proceeded to question the prisoner at length, finding him intelligent and quite aware, but without the slightest trace of animosity towards the late senator. He'd gone as far as attempting to assassinate him, before he was apprehended and turned over to the psychs for appropriate behavior modifications.

"Okay, here's what we need done, Doctor Donatello," Legate Daag explained in detail, once they were back in the secure, spy-free office.

"Oh that's hardly worth my time, but I'll do it. One hundred percent guarantee that the modifications will be wholly effective. Her loyalty will never be in doubt," Doctor Donatello replied.

Just then, Herman received a text message from his secretary. "I've got to go to Blooms. Slight fashion detail, but I know just how to handle it." He grinned wickedly.

"Oh thank you for coming," Neva said coyly, when Legate Herman, accompanied by his six bodyguards, appeared in the most elegant fashion boutique in Caltran. "It's my choice of shoes that's the problem. She's been showing me all these tall platform styles. Do all elegant women wear them?"

"Why yes, some of our women wish to appear somewhat larger than life," Herman explained. "But I do see your problem." Her feet were modified so she could only wear the toe shoes found on Tierra and in the Ataro System. Here, three vastly different styles were available. Besides the toe shoes and the tall platforms, the third style were takeoffs of the ballerina en pointe slippers, called ballet boots. Hence, the fashion dilemma — three choices. Of course, the ballet boots were supposed to be confined to bedroom fun times. "Might I suggest you wear shoes that are *most* fashionable, as befitting the elegant young woman that you are?" the Legate suggested.

"Back home, these toe shoes are the height of fashion, but I have to have a pair of mule toe shoes by my bed. So with these others, I will appear even taller, but can I even stand on my toes?" she asked. Now that she was more or less on her own, she would not have Konrad around to lift her into the bath or to the toilet at night. It was always a pain to have to fumble around for her mules in the dark. It was either that or crawl, and she never did that!

Legate Herman answered coyly, "If the elegant women of Caltran can manage these, I'm sure that you could as well. You do want to be the height of fashion, right?"

"Most definitely. I aim to be as well dressed as the most elegant women of Caltran. Thank you, Legate Herman," she replied batting her eyes a little, much to the annoyance of his secretary.

"Good. I'll arrange for the modification right now. Meantime, you and my secretary begin picking out the new styles, which will match your new gowns. I take it you've found gowns to your liking?" he asked.

"Excellent. Remember, money is no object. We've been working on our arrangements. We ought to know more in a few days." His secretary gave him a quick dirty look, but went along with him. He left the women and made the arrangements for her feet to be modified further. A short while later, he stopped by Praline's Escort Service, where he met privately with Elmer Praline.

"So she's working out?" he asked, referring to the exotic woman they were calling Esmeralda, since no one could understand a word she said.

"Oh yes. Initially, she was always protesting and crying. Keep this between you and me, but I made use of the psych's behavior modification program. Now, she has become one of my top models, always in demand. In fact, so much so, that many of the former top models have been begging me for similar modifications. I've been hesitant, the expense, you see. I have to have someone looking after Esmeralda all the time she's not out on a date, to say nothing of the cost to have these modifications done."

"I see. Perhaps you and I could make a deal. I've a young woman I wish to bring by here and show off how terrific your top models actually look. Suppose I paid to have, say, another six of your top models, who want these modifications done. In return, you can show them off to my young woman; convince her that this is the latest in high fashion. Let's limit the mods to their arms and breasts for now."

"Now that's a deal I can't refuse! Indeed, in many ways, Esmeralda actually *is* setting the fashion stage. I've had many inquiries from 'respectable women' asking about her. Breasts like hers are found on all women on one of those newly discovered, but Closed Worlds. One of the senator's wives has them. I wouldn't be surprised to see more women sporting them in the near future. Another senator's wife wears the neck rings, I'm told. How soon were you planning on making this happen?" Elmer asked.

"Can we do it today and give the six women a couple of days to get adjusted?" Herman asked. After a bit more discussion, they shook hands. The Legate then made a series of phone calls, arranging everything, including giving Psychman Donatella more work to do.

"Oh! These are really hard to walk in!" Neva exclaimed. She had just had the minor procedure done on her feet there at Blooms. Her feet had been fused into a permanent en pointe position. Now her toes pointed straight down to the floor. In fact, she could not move her toes at all. Her soles were barely an inch square, but her added spiked heel height added another two inches to her height, allowing her gowns to be even longer. The look gave the appearance of having very tiny feet indeed. However, the heels of these new boots were further back from her toes, giving her more balancing ability than her former toe shoes, whose spike was essentially right behind the back of her toes. Certainly, walking would be challenging, if not hard on her knees.

"You do look most elegant in them. I would say these are a far better choice than those four inch platforms. So many women stumble in them and break an ankle or leg, usually at the most inopportune times," the secretary explained. She chatted on about women she knew who took stumbles in the platforms and had broken many bones. Hence, Neva felt secure she'd made the proper choice. In fact, Neva felt quite satisfied with her many purchases. She'd seen the total of her order, close to ten thousand credits. None of this came out of her pocket, pleasing her even more.

That done, they took her to her new penthouse suite. She'd never seen such luxury before, and it rather swelled her head for a time. Additionally, Legate Herman brought her a personal assistant to help her with dressing and such things.

"This is your new personal assistant, Marjorie Wells. She's twenty-five," he explained. Marjorie had blue eyes and shoulder length, wavy brown hair. She was rather homely, but dressed well, Neva thought. After the introduction, Herman explained, "Personal assistants are not allowed to speak. She's had her voice removed, before she began her career as a personal assistant. I assure you she makes a good salary and loves the work." Marjorie nodded appreciatively. He lowered his voice to Neva, and whispered, "Make sure she doesn't find out about your telepathy." Neva agreed. In a louder voice, he added, "When Marjorie needs to tell you something, she'll write on her pad for you. I trust you can read Imperial Standard?"

"Of course. Who doesn't?" Neva replied coyly. She didn't want him to think a primitive from Ashford-5 was illiterate! That would never do. He and his secretary then left.

After they had gone, Marjorie wrote, "Bath time? Luxurious."

"Sure, I've not had a real bath in absolutely ages! Let's!" She soaked for over two hours, chatting with Marjorie, who listened intently to her tales of gallivanting about many worlds. Once out and dried off, Marjorie got her back into a new pipe corset she'd just purchased today. Unlike the ones she had been wearing, this one was somewhat tighter on her, but more importantly, it had a good deal of steel in it, severely restricting her movements while wearing it. Since this was what all the fashionable women were wearing, she decided it was just a matter of getting used to it.

The next day, Marjorie helped her put on one of her new outfits. Neva was appalled at just how many parts it involved. The hoop skirt billowed out twelve feet around her. Only with difficulty could she pull it back enough to see her feet. Marjorie wrote, "Much practice."

"Yes, I can see that. And I am out of breath. This corset's a bit too tight I expect. Anyway, I'm starving. We need to get breakfast."

She wrote, "Order in. They deliver." Marjorie showed her the menu and pointed out some suggestions, which Neva took. Their breakfast cost Herman a hundred credits, but she didn't mind in the slightest. She knew he had to be loaded.

Two days later, Legates Herman and Daag again met with her in private. "We've found an ideal estate for you, out in the country a ways, but not far. Very, very expensive, I might add. Formal gardens, swimming pool; you name it, this place has it. A wealthy senator once owned it. Very plush. Very much in demand, but we outbid the others for you. Now then, we'll give it to you along with the needed servants to maintain it, but we need something from you to show your good faith. It's something that'll greatly aid you in performing your *work'* for us." He placed a coy emphasis on that word. She grinned.

"If you'll come with us, we want to show you the most elegant women in Caltran, the top models, the fashion setters. If you agree to these minor modifications to turn you into a top model as well, then we'll give the deed to the estate to you immediately. You'll receive a handsome salary each month, whether or not we've made any use of your unique skills. You can live your life of elegance and luxury, and no one will suspect anything at all."

"I do need your arm. I'm not very used to these new heels and this gown," she said, taking Herman's arm. He graciously escorted her to his shuttle, while Daag and a dozen security men followed behind them. A short while later, they entered Elmer Praline's establishment. As agreed, he had his six new top models waiting for them. All six were extremely excited to be able to model for the two Legates!

"Oh my!" Neva exclaimed, as she saw the six elegantly dressed women. Each wore a gown similar to hers, but their shoulders were bare, revealing the absence of arms. Their bosoms were much larger than her own were, which she thought highly unusual, before she remembered Konrad telling her about that strange new world he'd governed for a short time.

One young woman spoke up, "We're really the *top* models around Caltran! Men go nuts with us. Everyone looks *our* way; we're the *center* of attention everywhere we go. Besides, we each have our own personal assistant." She chatted gaily for a time, while the others continued to interrupt, adding their own words of praise. Neva didn't believe them and gently touched their minds. To her amazement, she found they were being wholly sincere in all they were saying! At last, she was convinced these women were telling her the truth. That was one of her gifts; she didn't detect any falsehoods, but then she'd never come across psych men's behavior modification either.

After spending a half hour with the models, allowing them to chat away and convince Neva, the group returned to their top floor office to hash out their agreement. "Here's the deed. It's yours, as soon as you sign your contract with us. In our *special* line of work, we need you to be a *top* model. That'll *distract* our 'businessmen' sufficiently to enable you to do your work without raising suspicions. However, we *do* need a concession on your part. After all, we've gone to a *huge* expense setting you up in this estate, to say nothing of the clothing, which still must be purchased. We need to *safeguard* you from *inquisitive* others. Under *no* circumstances do we want others to discover you are in fact a telepath — let alone all the *other* skills you possess," Herman explained.

"I agree. It's wise not to let others know about me and my gifts. But what concessions do you have in mind?" she asked.

"We want to eliminate your voice for now. That way, if you cannot speak, no one can *force* you to divulge your skills or that you work for us. The business world is quite ruthless, Neva. Some men will get you drunk to get you to talk. Others less kind will slip you a truth drug to get you to spill everything. If you can't speak, *no one* can ever do that to you. In a way, this is as much to safeguard *you,* as it is to *protect* our quite substantial investment in you. Your monthly salary will be ten thousand credits, whether we've an assignment for you that month or not. That is in excess to the salaries of the estate support personnel, which we'll be paying out of our pockets. Marjorie will continue on as your personal assistant, by the way. She's taken a liking to you, I might add. You sure *do* turn heads, Neva. With these modifications, there's *no limit* to how far you can go with us."

"Well, I guess I can agree to it. It seems a bit drastic. Is it reversible?" she asked. *I'm certain unscrupulous men might just try to do that to me — drug me and force me to spill everything. If I can't speak, they won't try. Only another telepath could get it out of me, and they're very rare indeed, from all I've seen.*

"Oh yes, it's reversible. Okay, sign here, and the deed is yours. We should get started today. We've a major deal coming up in a couple of weeks, but we want you accustomed to the changes. By the way, Marjorie will take you to see all the many sights during the daytime. Whenever there is a *special* event, either Daag or I will escort you to those. You do dance, don't you?"

"Well, I don't know your dances, but I can learn them. Does Marjorie know them? Wait, but how will I communicate my needs to Marjorie?" Neva asked, slightly confused.

Daag played his role well. "You can use your telepathy with her, since she cannot speak and reveal it."

Neva bought that. It didn't occur to her that someone could just as easily force Marjorie to write out what she knew about Neva. She signed the contract and took possession of her new estate. Next, she accompanied the two men down to a slightly lower floor, where they had a state-of-the-art medical facility. Before she knew what was happening, she was unconscious. The doctor removed her arms under the watchful eyes of the two Legates. With these two men, the doctor didn't even consider asking questions! He then altered her vocal cords, and finally enlarged her bosom three-fold. Once he'd finished his work, a dressmaker began her work, altering Neva's current gown's top. Meanwhile, the psych man, Donatello, whose own behavior had been modified, placed headphones over her head and played his recording several times, over and over for nearly a half hour.

Unconsciously, she recorded his message. "You're very, very happy with your new life. You're on the leading edge of fashion. Your body is hypersensitive to sexual urges. Your breasts are extremely sensitive to touch. Even the slightest touch on your breasts will turn on a strong sexual urge. You need to have sex or be pleasured at least twice a day. You crave sexual pleasure and must have it daily. You will always obey Legate Herman Mels and Legate Daag Taal. You'll never betray them, not even under duress. You'll be faithful to the two Legates and always do as they ask of you. Your new life could not be any finer. You'll find great pleasure in your new life. You'll be very happy with everything and never complain about anything."

When the seamstress finished altering Neva's top, with the nurses' help, they got it back on her. After Donatello was satisfied, he removed the headphones, nodded to the two Legates, and left. Since Neva hadn't seen him here, she would suspect nothing, even if she by chance saw him again. Now the doctor revived Neva.

She stirred and felt funny. Her breasts seemed to weigh a ton. She tried to touch them, receiving a shock. She had no arms any longer. For a second, she panicked and tried to call out, but her voice was entirely gone. "Here, let me help you sit up. Take it easy for a minute until you get your stability back. Anesthesia takes a few minutes to wear off completely. You'll be fine," a nurse told her. She looked rather panic-stricken at the two Legates. Both men smiled kindly. Then, the behavior modifications kicked in. She too smiled at them and placed in their minds, *Thank you. I'm feeling really very happy with all this.*

A few minutes later, Marjorie entered and offered Neva her arms, helping steady her on her feet. Legate Herman said, "Well done, Neva. This is the beginning of a very beautiful and profitable relationship between you and us. Marjorie will now escort you to your new estate. I do hope you'll truly enjoy its incredible luxury. We'll be in touch later on, after you get used to things."

Thanks. I don't know what else to say. This is so wonderful. I'm so happy. I'll be ready when you need me. Both men smiled, and they left.

Oh! Walking is so hard now. I can't see my feet. I am a top model now. Everyone will be looking at us. Please, you must keep a secure hold of me. I don't dare fall down. Oh god! I am having an orgasm as we walk! I am so hypersensitive now. Please, you must pleasure me when we get to the estate!

She paused to write, but Neva sent to her, *Just think what you want to say, and I'll pick it up.*

30

Okay. They trained me to be able to care for your needs. I know how to give you great pleasure, but you need to pleasure me too. I'll show you how tonight. I'm always supposed to be with you, unless you are away on an assignment with the bosses. Isn't this exciting? We have a multi-million credit estate! I can't wait to see it! She too had been unknowingly slightly modified by Doctor Donatello.

Just outside the skyscraper, they found a shuttle clearly marked "Lady Neva Burkhardt." Their pilot was an older man, who opened the door for them. "Welcome, My Lady. I'm your pilot, Hans. Let me lift you both inside." He did just that. "I know neither of you can speak, but that's okay with me. Marjorie can write me notes on where you wish to be taken. I've a small room on your estate. Shall we go there now?" Neva nodded vigorously and smiled broadly. She had her own shuttle! How absolutely wonderful. Great ladies must have their own shuttles!

When she arrived, she mouthed, "Wow!" over and over. Marjorie didn't need telepathy to know what she was thinking. The estate had green grass, almost unheard of on Beltzar-4. The U-shaped main estate building was huge, and they carefully made their way through the wide double doors, designed for two women wearing such billowing gowns. Inside, her new staff stood waiting to present themselves to the two.

"I'm your cook, Ilse. This is your maid, Mattie. This is your gardener, Joshua." The three were also some ten years older than Neva, friendly enough. She added, "Marjorie will write us notes about what you desire. First things first, I've got a fine lunch prepared. After that, Mattie wants to take you on a tour of the estate, and then, if you are up to it, Joshua wants to show you the formal gardens. This has got to be the finest place any of us have ever worked! I just know we're all going to love taking good care of you both! Now follow me to the dining room. Pheasant under glass, with a special sauce of my own making — it's sure to please you both." She chatted away, as she led the two into the huge dining room, just to their left there at the bottom of the U.

Marjorie helped Neva get seated and then sat beside

31

her. Neva saw at once she was completely helpless, but Marjorie began to feed her, and she again relaxed. The meal was as mouth-watering as Ilse suggested. After lunch, Mattie gave them the big tour. Further down the bottom of the U hallway, they saw the fully equipped kitchen. Then, they turned ninety degrees and headed down the left wing. The first room was the master bedroom, huge and plush, with a king sized bed, satin sheets, and a very large wall to wall walk-in closet, designed to hold many of their billowing dresses. Already those they had purchased had been carefully brought here and arranged by Mattie. Of note, the dressmaker had already modified these dresses earlier, since Herman had anticipated that Neva would sign the contract. The many other guest rooms were empty.

They returned to the bottom of the U and headed on past the entrance hall to the spacious living room. The right wing held the four servant's quarters, but most of the many rooms there were empty. Then, the two stepped out onto the paved courtyard. Lawn chairs, as well as regular tables and chairs, surrounded a swimming pool. Just beyond the pool were the formal gardens. Walking on the gravel in her new ballet shoes was extremely difficult. Neva kept trying to move her arms to keep her balance, but they weren't there. Quickly, she became utterly dependent upon Marjorie, knowing she couldn't possibly walk here by herself. Yet, happiness flooded through her mind. The fragrances were intoxicating; the gardens were simply beautiful and well maintained.

Oh god, I need pleasuring, Marjorie! I can't take any more of this. Please! Neva begged her assistant, as they made their painstakingly slow way back to the courtyard. *These flowers — they're turning me on!*

I have to get us out of these gowns. Hold still, I'm hurrying, Marjorie thought, hoping Neva would somehow magically hear her. Neva's frustration only escalated; for some unknown reason, she just had to be pleasured. She could not ever remember having such a powerful urge before, but her mind could think of nothing else, especially since she found herself helpless to do anything about it. She mostly fell back on their new bed as soon as Marjorie got her out of the hoop skirt.

A few minutes later, she sighed in relief, totally relaxed and satisfied.

I don't know what came over me, Marjorie. I've never felt this way before. I don't understand what's happening to me.

Marjorie wrote a short note. "I have a way for you to do me. Watch." She opened one of her bags and brought out a device that fit in Neva's mouth. Marjorie demonstrated how Neva could use it, fastening it over her head and into her mouth. A while later, Marjorie felt fully satisfied as well. After freeing Neva from the pleasure-giving device, the two women lay beside each other on their bed. She wrote, "Thank you." Neva smiled and tried to roll over to snuggle, but her huge breasts prevented it. Instead, Marjorie snuggled against her.

As she lay there contented for the moment, Neva began to ponder what had come over her and why. She knew she was frustrated with her physical condition, but yet somehow she felt *totally* happy, indeed contented. *Strange, why should I feel happy?* She had no answer for the moment.

Her life had definitely taken a strange turn, but she still felt empowered. Certainly, both Legates were sexually oriented; both were heavily into ultimate power; both men had money to spend on her. For now, she was satisfied, if only she could prove herself valuable to these two, then perhaps, she could move on up the power ladder. Neva decided she needed to meet this President Snarry Knoschy.

Chapter 3 Just Your Average Working Girl

For several days, Neva didn't leave her new estate. She was mentally confused. On one hand, she knew she was utterly helpless, wholly dependent upon Marjorie for everything. Yet at the same time, she felt utterly elated and happier than she'd ever felt in her life. Then, there were these inexplicable and incredible sexual urges, desires so strong she nearly went berserk when they came over her. In fact, Marjorie had merely brushed against her monster breasts, triggering another bout. Inexplicable. Was her body always this sensitive, and had she always suppressed these urges? She didn't think so, but what else could explain it? Combine all this with having to learn how to live like she now was, barely able to walk and little else, Neva was in a rather confused state.

After five days, Marjorie suggested they go do some shopping and then visit the museum. She made a list of "great things to see" for Neva. Marjorie put numbers beside each, indicating the order of importance she attached to them. She loved to spend hours roaming the museum. Although utterly frightened of going out into the world as she was, Neva also felt elated to have an opportunity show off her fashion-setting body. *I guess I'm always going to be stuck with this duality,* she thought. *I'm scared to death to leave the house, but I'm extremely happy and proud to be seen by everyone. I don't get it, but we need more gowns.*

The shopping trip turned out to be absolutely terrifying for Neva, while at the same time, it was extremely pleasing and satisfying. She felt like a goddess. Top fashion model didn't quite seem to fit; goddess did. Yet, she was utterly terrified of her complete helplessness. Try as she might, she couldn't see her feet over her bosom, though Marjorie did pull her hoop skirt back. Walking on her unseen toes was a nightmare; yet she felt utterly happy doing so. Neva was very confused, but her face smiled continuously. They added another dozen complete outfits to their wardrobe before heading to the museum. Here, she saw just how much Marjorie loved to look at the sights, reading each plaque or framed description. Soon, she got caught up in reading along with her. *We must come here often,* she sent, in spite of her throbbing feet.

For another week, the two took daily trips into the large city, visiting many sights. Some were famous ones, like the Senate. They took a tour of the Presidential Skyscraper, though only the lower historical floors were open on the guided tours. After these two weeks, Neva was still running on a heavy duality. From the moment she woke until she fell asleep, she was both terrified of her physical condition and utterly elated and happy with her new life. The confusion did not let up. The only relief she had was briefly after Marjorie pleasured her, in the morning and at night. Even that seemed somehow strange to her. She craved it, but she'd never craved such before.

The following Monday, Legate Herman dropped by to chat with Neva. "How's everything going for you? Just fine?" She nodded vigorously. "That's very good indeed. We have an assignment for you tonight. A businessman will be meeting with us later this morning. I'll introduce you to him, and he'll escort you to the theater tonight. After that, he'll take you up to his suite. After he pleasures you, he'll be very receptive to your suggestion. I need you to convince him to sign the contract first thing the following morning. After you have satisfied him and convinced him to sign, you may leave. Marjorie will be outside the suite waiting to bring you back here to your home. Any questions?"

She shook her head no. Then, she sent, *What ought I wear?*

"I think a red satin pencil gown would be most appropriate and easier for you to handle. He'll know how to handle you and your needs. I'll see to that." She nodded and gave him a big smile. He smiled back.

Right after supper, a security guard for Herman picked up the two women from their estate. He took them into the city and to a very fancy skyscraper, the Hasta Hotel. They got off the elevator somewhere in the middle of this imposing building. There, she was presented to a middle-aged businessman. "Ah, just as promised, a real beauty! And you really have no voice?" he asked. Neva shook her head no. Again, the duality confusion swamped her. Yet, she smiled and moved closer to him. He put his arm around her thin waist, and they headed off to the theater. He was kind enough to walk slowly enough for her to walk somewhat gracefully on her toes.

She didn't grasp much of the subtly of the play; Imperium humor eluded her, especially in her present mental state. The man wanted to snuggle with her, but his touch had her body crying out for sexual gratification, impossible in the crowded theater. Sometime later, she found herself back at his hotel room. Though quite nice, it was not luxurious or extravagant by her standards. She pressed her body into his, doing her best to encourage him to hurry up and get her dress off her. If only that craving would die down, she thought. Finally, she got her much needed relief.

As they laid back, she remembered her assignment and touched his mind. Ah, he was supposed to sign a contract to deliver ten thousand d-guns to the army. Part of her had to know why he was hesitant to sign. Then, she saw that if he did, his company stood to take a substantial loss, selling them at below market prices. Well, the war needed guns, she rationalized. She placed the command to sign the contract without hesitation into his mind, convincing him the war needed his guns, and that he was doing his part in the war effort. As he fell asleep, she rose and stood there helplessly, unable to get her gown back on, let alone open the door to leave. She reached out and sensed Marjorie just outside the door. Relief! An hour later, the two women were soaking in their large bathtub. Later, just before she drifted into a peaceful sleep, she thought, *Well, that wasn't so hard.*

Days turned into weeks. Neva's duality confusion slowly began to lessen, primarily due to her growing more accustomed to her new lifestyle and Marjorie's constant assistance. The Legates continued to make use of her services, often on contract negotiations, which gave them a competitive edge, although an unfair one. Then, she got another assignment, quite unusual.

"The man in the next room has stolen corporate plans for an improved d-gun. We've put him through our advanced interrogation techniques, but he hasn't revealed their location. We need those plans back. Can you find this out for us?" Legate Daag asked Neva. He'd sent two security men to bring her to the military headquarters, where the prisoner was being held.

Sure, if I've some idea of what they physically look like, I probably can scour his mind and find out, Neva suggested, growing more interested. *This is different. I can show them what I can **really** do this time,* she thought. They showed her an image of one.

She was led into another room, where she took a seat across a table from the man. Two security men stood on either side of her, but the man looked to be in bad shape. He'd been beaten, tortured, and even mind probed, she discovered, as she lightly touched his mind. She focused, and her crystal hidden beneath her blouse began to glow with a pale blue light. The man fought hard from thinking about the plans, throwing up an effort worthy of interrogation techniques. She then saw images of the man getting anti-interrogation training and realized this was what had prevented them from obtaining the location. *Well, this won't stop me,* she thought and focused harder.

Now she pulled up images of his theft. He was indeed quite clever, she noted. Somehow, he had obtained the retinal scan of an authorized man, using that to gain access to the secured vault. He took the plans from their locked drawer. She noted he'd used some kind of electronic device to crack the safe's combination and wondered what that was. *Strange, we don't have any communications equipment or computers at our estate. How strange. Oh, I can't use them if I had them. Makes sense, but I feel kind of cut off. Oh, I am happy about that! Focus, Neva.*

A bit later, she saw the man leaving with the plans taped to his chest. He fought hard to keep her from seeing anymore of his images, though he didn't really know she was seeing them. It was just his training that kept him from even recalling those memories. Then, she saw what she wanted. He'd slipped them into an empty pipe, twisting a cap onto either end. He laid it in a pile of other such pipes. This one had a tiny orange dot on one end. She smiled and broke the connection.

Neva very carefully rose and turned to face the door, hoping the security men would open it for her. Thankfully, they did so. Legate Daag was just outside, waiting for her. "Well? Nod if you got it."

She did as asked. Then, she placed the image sequence into his mind. He smiled. *I can do lots more than this. This was child's play, Legate Daag.*

"Amazing. We'll talk more later. Jacques, see that she gets safely home to her estate. You, come with me," Legate Daag ordered.

That evening, Legate Daag took her out to a three-dimensional holographic movie. To her surprise, the theater was empty, except for themselves and a number of security men posted around the exits. "Okay, this is a secure location. We have a small problem. Is it possible for you to figure out just how much a person might know about some activity of ours? But without alerting him to the fact you have figured it out? Am I making sense to you?" he asked cautiously. "If the person discovers you are probing him, it could be quite dangerous for your well-being."

Neva thought for a moment. Anyone would be aware they were recalling those memories in question. If they also knew she was a telepath, they would be highly suspicious of that, especially if they were not intending to remember those images just when she was pulling them up. She guessed she could install a mental block of her tinkering, but that was not an optimum way of going about this. Now if he were sleeping, then she could probe away, and the man would only think he was dreaming, if he was even aware of it.

If I can be sleeping with him, after he goes to sleep, I can safely search through his memories. I'd have to know what I am looking for though.

"Hum, interesting. I'll get back to you on this one, Neva. Let's watch this show; it's in three-dimensions." She picked up his unspoken thoughts. He was afraid he would have to reveal too much of his operations to her in order for her to extract the information from President Snarry Knoschy! She smiled involuntarily. *Moving up the ladder,* she thought, pleased with how things were going.

She heard nothing more for several days. Then, Legate Herman dropped by. "I have a small assignment for you this afternoon. I'll be meeting with Senator Halan Bilks. He and I will discuss some things. I need to know if he is telling me the truth or if he is withholding facts or ideas from me. Can you do this?"

Sure. When? Should I wear my red pencil gown?

"I'll have someone pick you up around one. No, wear a blue one. This is a formal meeting," he replied. She picked up his thought that there wouldn't be any sexual aspect in this meeting for her. She pursed her lips.

Around two, the security guard escorted her into a meeting room in the hundred story skyscraper. The room was a small conference room on the ninety-eighth floor. Shortly, Legate Herman entered and dismissed the guard. He smiled and said, "The senator will be here shortly. You will be my 'escort,' and we are supposedly on our way to the theater. Ah, here he comes now."

Senator Halan was fifty-five with distinguished grey streaks through his freshly cut brown hair. He wore a perfect suit, not a crease was amiss; she sensed he was a perfectionist. "Afternoon, senator. Ignore my escort. She can't speak. Glad you could visit me. I know how busy both our schedules are. We're on our way to a play. So I'll get right to it. What do you think of the chances of the new appropriations bill being passed? I've heard many worlds are protesting the increased taxes to support our war effort."

"Yes, well, it is going to be close. There is a strong block against it, led by the Ataro System. Their emperor believes this war is getting out of hand, and that we should search for ways to bring about a lasting peace. They've got quite a few senators backing them. Right now, I'd say it can still pass, but not by very much at all." He discussed more details. Then, the two rose and shook hands, and Senator Halan departed.

Legate Herman looked at Neva. *He is telling you the truth. I detected no hesitance to withhold anything. Are people really getting worried about losing the war? That's scary.*

"Very good, Neva. We just need more funds to build more battle cruisers and guns. In time, we can defeat this Federation of Planets. Okay, the guard will escort you home. Thanks."

On the long ride home, Neva began thinking. Surely, the mighty Imperium wasn't losing the war — or was it? She vowed to try to find out all she could about this ongoing war that was seemingly without end. With Marjorie's aid, she began watching the news on their lone big screen. She also listened to her servants, when they chatted about the war. Sometimes, she gave them a little mental nudge to chat about it. She got the distinct impression the war was not going well.

She didn't hear back on the Legate's request to probe the president's mind, much to her annoyance. A month after he made that suggestion, he returned with a very worried look on his face. After sitting down in her bedroom so they would not be overheard, he explained. "Something serious has come up. One of our generals has just lost a very significant battle, and President Snarry Knoschy is hauling his ass here to Beltzar-4 personally to interrogate him about what went so very wrong. This is critical. It is against the law to electronic mind probe an active general, so President Snarry cannot do that. Yet, some of us have our doubts about this general and his actions in the field. He might be working for the enemy, but we have to find out."

Where do I come in?

"That's just it. If you were present during the meeting with the president, you could tell us if he is lying or covering up his complete incompetence. The president simply has to know what the true situation is. I hate to do this, but Legate Daag and I agree. It is time to alert President Snarry to your unique abilities. If we are right, he will insist you sit in on this meeting and immediately alert him to any discrepancies or lies this general might say in reply to his questions. We'll at least get President Snarry to classify you and your skill as Top

Secret Level 10. That ought to keep nearly everyone else from discovering your identity and abilities. We'll present this to President Snarry tonight. Expect to hear from us in the morning. If President Snarry wants you present, wear a light blue pencil gown. Not those huge hoops skirts. Questions?"

She shook her head no, and he left at once. Neva sensed he felt as though he were on a major tipping point. The ball could fall on either side, good or bad for both Legates.

Anticipating the call, she had Marjorie dress her in her favorite sky blue satin pencil gown with matching knee high ballet boots. After breakfast, she had her brush out her long hair. If nothing else, she wanted to look her best. This might be her only shot at getting to President Snarry, and she was determined to make the most of the opportunity, if it came.

Late morning, a heavy security force arrived. Their captain merely said, "Neva, you are to come with us now. She didn't wait for Marjorie to help her rise. She lunged up, wobbling slightly catching her balance, once more cursing her loss of arms and yet feeling totally happy about it. At least the captain had the good sense to put his arm around her thin waist, as they headed out of the double doors of her estate. On the lawn was a large shuttle, marked in the presidential colors of yellow and green. Recognizing the colors, she took as deep a breath as she could, knowing this was the most important meeting yet!

An hour later, the captain led her into a plush side office called the Blue Waiting Room. She saw all six Legates sitting around an oval table, plus another man, perhaps forty, she guessed. He wore a very nicely made brown tweed suit with a yellow and green sash around his waist. "President Snarry, allow me to introduce you to Mrs. Neva Burkhardt, our extraordinary telepath. Her skills are just enormous, but remember, she cannot speak."

President Snarry smiled and said warmly, "Welcome, Neva. I'm very pleased to meet you. I wish it were under better circumstances than these. You look stunning, very fashionable. Forgive me, but I do need to test you for myself. Might I ask what it is I don't want you to know about me?"

Neva flushed. She was on the spot. Focusing, she gently

touched his mind. Like everyone around her, he was head blind. Quickly, she saw what he was mentally trying to withhold from her. She sent, *You find me highly attractive and want to take me to bed, but your wife would object. Perhaps, we can find a way around that detail.* She tossed out that suggestion. It was one of her trifecta, sex. He probably wasn't into money; he was the president, after all.

He flushed. "My god! She picked that up in seconds! You two are right. This is the find of the century, maybe the millennia! Okay, Neva, have you been briefed on what we are about to do?" She nodded. "Okay then. Let's get this over with. I hate having to grill one of our distinguished generals." He rose, and the Legates did likewise.

Neva lunged to her feet, wobbling a little, but Legate Herman quickly came to her side and slipped his arm around her, steadying her. They entered the next room, the Octagonal Office. The general in his dress uniform sat on one of the eight sides, but jumped to attention the moment President Snarry entered, followed by the Legates and Neva.

President Snarry asked many heated questions about how such a key battle could have been lost. Sweating, the general did his best to answer them. For a while, all went well. Then, she detected something the general was hesitant to disclose. She sent, *President Snarry, ask him about the thermal exchangers. There might be something amiss there.* He could not help but glance across the octagon table at her, but he followed her lead. "So what is up with the thermal exchanges on the battle cruisers?"

The general startled. "Well, Mr. President, I haven't had time to do a thorough review of them. Just before they lost power and were blown out of the sky, I got some reports from the battle cruisers that their thermal exchangers malfunctioned, forcing a loss of shields. If those failed, then that would explain the loss of so many of our brave men and cruisers. Yet, I don't see how those could have failed, unless they were sabotaged or perhaps they were improperly installed or had manufacturing flaws in them."

He's telling you the truth.

President Snarry asked other pointed questions, even

alluding to the possibility the general was a Federation spy or sympathizer. At last, since Neva didn't detect anything amiss in his many answers, President Snarry said, "Well, general, you've satisfied me. I shall order an immediate thorough inspection of all battle cruiser's thermal exchangers. Let's hope that we find something. Everyone will soon know of this stunning defeat. You know the population as well as I do, general. They'll want to lay the blame on someone. That'd be you, unless something comes up on these exchangers." He saluted, resigned to his fate, and the meeting broke up. Neva was quickly escorted back to her home without so much as a thank you.

A week later, Neva was again summoned rather mysteriously to the Presidential Office. She found President Snarry in the Green Room, sitting on a soft leather sofa. "Ah, here you are at last, Neva. I wanted to personally thank you. We found defective thermal exchangers on another ten of our precious battle cruisers. Your actions have saved countless lives and a vast sum of money, assuming we had to replace those cruisers. An investigation is underway to discover just how those defective exchangers got onboard the cruisers. Oh, please, do sit beside me."

Neva tossed her hair to one side, carefully stepped to the couch, and did as he asked. He turned to her. "You are an amazing young woman, highly attractive. It must be hard for you to be away from your husband for such a long time." She sensed what he really wanted to ask. Neva grinned, leaned over, and gave him a passionate kiss. Of course, that electrified her. Waves of sexual cravings flooded over her body. He responded, as she had hoped. "We won't be disturbed in here," he whispered.

An hour later, he helped her get her gown straightened out. "Would you mind if I saw you again? I've never had such pleasure before. Incredible. You are one fabulously sexy woman!"

I know. I loved it too. Let's get together often. He smiled and agreed. After that, he saw her at least once each week, usually on a Wednesday afternoon. Neva felt sure she was making a very indelible impression on him, which was her goal.

Chapter 4 Actions and Reactions

Emperor Kino Sango carefully paced around his holographic three-dimensional model of the entire galaxy, a marvel of technology. The many planets that formed the Imperium were shown as red dots, with the largest dot being right here, Ataro Prime. He ruled the Ataro Empire of the Twelve Sacred Planets of the Wasp from his palace, some thirty-six planets in all. The Imperium stretched from close to the central hub, where it was founded millennia ago, outward along one spiral arm to the rim. Close to the rim lay Ashford-5 and several other recently discovered but now abandoned new worlds. The war was not going well.

The vast Imperium was divided up into thirty-five sectors. The Ataro System was halfway between the outer rim of this spiral arm and the central hub, where the Imperium was ruled from Baltzar-4 and Proxima Prime. His system was in Arm Sector 14. Early in the war with the Federation of Planets, the Imperium was forced to abandon Rim Sector 15. Those planetary systems were shown in brown, indicating losses. The Federation of Planets was based two-thirds of the way down the second spiral arm, a very long distance from the Imperium heartland. However, the two empires had encountered each other there in the outer rim, where the two rim arms nearly encircled or wrapped onto each other.

Over the past few years, the Federation of Planets had been slowly sweeping down the Imperium's arm. What caused Emperor Kino to study the display this morning was the terrible defeat, in which ten battle cruisers were lost in Arm Sector 20, just six sectors from the Ataro System. Here in their system, the emperors and empresses had established an incredible record of over two millennia without any wars. Emperor Kino was determined to keep the record spotless. He had to take action and soon.

"Emperor Kino," an aide interrupted his train of thought, "Senator Amago has the video conference call set up. Remember, there is a five minute delay in transmissions between here and there."

"Yes, of course. Help me to my seat, please," the emperor requested. Walking on his toes and constrained by his pipe corset and lack of arms, he needed the supporting arms of his aides. Seated on his throne, he looked at the large video screen and waited.

Shortly the screen played the first transmission. "Emperor Kino, Senator Amago here. I have the conference call setup. Here is President Snarry Knoschy. He has agreed to speak with you. President, go ahead." He stepped back and the president stepped forward into full view.

"Greetings Emperor Kino Sango. It is an honor and pleasure to speak directly with you. To what do I owe this honor? Senator Amago was most insistent. Over."

"Direct and to the point," Emperor Kino whispered to his aide. "Welcome President Snarry. Thank you for taking my call. It concerns the war being fought with the Federation of Planets. I have my three-dimensional galaxy hologram up as you can see. The planets we've lost are shown in brown. Sorry, I cannot point to them. As you can see, with this recent loss, it is clear to me the enemy is systematically moving down our spiral arm. Further, they are only a few sectors from my Ataro System. This has me very worried. Over."

After a long delay, the screen animated. "Yes. We've traced that loss of ten precious battle cruisers to faulty thermal exchangers. When they failed, they caused a chain reaction, causing the loss of the entire ship's protective energy shield. I have had all our cruisers inspected, and they found many more defective exchangers. Repairs have already begun. I have the situation under control now. Over."

"That is good. Sabotage, perhaps? I would look into that aspect. Why I called is simple. As you know, we are a peaceful race with a long history of locating and handling the root causes of conflicts, thereby eliminating such costly wars. I'm calling today to ask your permission to send forth a delegation from the Ataro System to conduct meetings with this Federation of Planets, in hopes that the root causes can be discovered and handled, ending the war. Over."

He looked at his aide and added off-camera, "Now we

shall see how he responds to this request. I hope I'll get his permission. Things will be far simpler if I do, but we are going to do it no matter what he says. I'll not have a war here within our system, Imperium or no Imperium." His aide smiled, and both men waited patiently.

The reply came over ten minutes later, indicating there must have been a considerable amount of hasty discussion there on Baltzar-4. "Perhaps this is a wise move, Emperor Kino. While I cannot publically condone such a trip, I intend to support your efforts. To that end, I'll be sending a small group of my people to you, ambassadors to represent me in absentia. I'll expedite their trip, as soon as I can get them organized and briefed. Will this be acceptable to you, Emperor Kino? Over."

Emperor Kino smiled. "Ah, yes. Most. We'll await the arrival of your ambassadors. While I do not need them, they'll be useful in discovering the source of this great conflict. Let us know their numbers and when we may expect their arrival. Send the data via our senator, please. Thank you for placing trust in me. That is all. Over and out."

He turned to his aide, "Well, that went better than I had anticipated."

"Ah yes. You carry a good deal of influence within the Imperium. It is time that such is utilized. May I draw your bath now?" he asked. Emperor Kino nodded.

Sector ID Minister Lena Squire presided over the Hub Sector 1, guaranteeing the safety of Baltzar-4, Proxima Prime, and many other planets at the very heart of the Imperium. Lena had not gotten her position by being nice or pretty or even social. The tall, thin black woman of thirty-five spoke in a stern, unquestioning voice. Rumors suggested she had killed those who opposed her, but there was never any real proof — they simply vanished without a trace. Her real age was closer to one hundred twenty. During her long career, she had made periodic use of the rejuvenation machines. Her thick hair, cropped close to her scalp, added to her no nonsense appearance, but there was no mistaking her sex. She always wore a white silk blouse, a grey silk skirt, black nylons, and black patent, low, practical heels, but a blaster was strapped to her waist.

Lena never forgot a detail, and just now, she had far too many loose details that did not fit into a larger puzzle. The whole affair with the late Senate President Carlos Amandos still was unfinished business, as far as she was concerned. She had enough evidence to convict him of massive crimes against Senator Isabella Valen and her two wives. Only problem: the three women had vanished, along with the senator. Well, she now knew just where and what the senator had become, and how that had happened. While others would have long forgotten this business, Lena kept the files open. During her long career, she'd learned no unresolved case is ever truly closed until all the parties are found and handled.

As Sector ID Minister, one of her self-appointed tasks was to monitor all new arrivals on Baltzar-4 and Proxima Prime. Since both the president and many influential senators had their private estates on Baltzar-4, Lena did not want any "bad accidents" or sabotage to happen on this world, let alone Proxima Prime, where they all met for work. The repercussions would be enormous. One of the reasons she'd held onto her post for so long was that she was extremely good at her job of ensuring the overall safety of everyone on Baltzar-4 and the other nearby worlds of this Hub Sector 1, which consisted of the entire globular cluster of stars, a very compact formation here near the center of the galaxy.

Thus, the very day that Neva Burkhardt climbed onboard the deep space transport to begin her journey to Beltzar-4 from her location with her husband in a rim sector, Lena knew she was coming, just not why. She *always* wanted to know the "why" of any significant personnel transfers, though sometimes she was not privy to that information. She knew of Governor Konrad Burkhardt and his recent fame as the "best governor of the century." She also knew he had a new wife. Nadja and Konrad's divorce was on file in the Imperium database. She also knew he'd taken a local Ashford-5 wife. That alone was suspicious because top secret documents stated that Ashford-5 was home to many, many telepaths.

As a result, upon hearing the unprecedented transfer of

48

Konrad's wife to Baltzar-4 while he remained on the distant rim, she began to dig deeper into what was known about this Closed World. She came across a highly classified document that said, "Ashford-5 telepaths can be identified by their eye color: yellow with brown speckles." She smiled and ordered her computer to bring up all known images of Konrad and Neva Burkhardt.

Most of the images were unusable for her purposes. Then, she found a perfect one; the two were posing for publicity shots just after he received his governor's award. "Bingo!" Lena whispered to herself, blowing up the image with quick, precise motions of her fingers on the screen. She studied their eyes and smiled. Both had the distinctive yellow eyes. She rummaged through older images of Konrad and found another one. In this one, his eyes were definitely not yellow. She sat back and pondered this significant detail. Prior to going to Ashford-5, he had normal eyes. Now he had the marks of one of their telepaths. Could Konrad have somehow picked up telepathic abilities during his stay on Ashford-5? If so, she thought, the ramifications would be enormous. By all studies, one was born with such a gift. No one got it mid-life. Yet he had.

Again, she made use of her top security clearance to dig into more recent details about Konrad Burkhardt and his wife's assignments. Clearly, he was not being used as a governor. Before long, she discovered the interesting fact that both were now classified as Class V telepaths! "Well, isn't this interesting!" she sat back and pondered the ramifications of this discovery.

"As long as I'm looking at images, Computer, bring up all images of Senator Isabella Valen," she barked her orders. "She came from Ashford-5 as their senator. I wonder if she too is a telepath. She ought to be, since Senator Carlos used her as one. If so, things are making far more sense." Two hours later, she had the confirmation of eye color she needed. Again she sat back to ponder.

"So Senate President Carlos must have known or discovered that Senator Isabella was a telepath. Then, we lost the outer rim fuel refinery and abandoned Ashford-5, effectively forcing Senator Isabella to remain there on Proxima Prim, unable to return to her home world. According to the time line from my investigation, Senator Isabella accompanied him to his estate outside Caltran on Beltzar-4 during their fall break. After that, she and her wives were brutally crippled. Further, I know his old telepath, this Hernando fellow, was with him at several business meetings during that break as were Isabella and her wives. It is obvious he stole the women to become his slave telepaths. By crippling them so badly, he guaranteed they could not speak to others or escape. Good god, they could barely walk, if his servants are to be believed."

"So now we have the Burkhardts in the same situation. Until now, both were undoubtedly being used as telepaths out on the rim, hunting for spies. Wise move. We need all the Intel we can get. But, now she alone is being moved here! Separating husband and wife? No sense. Something is going on, and I am not being informed! Well, that can only mean someone is playing dirty. Not while Lena is on the job. I'll watch, wait, and gather more data."

Not long after that, her computer popped up an alert message. When she tracked it, she was amazed. Long ago, she had placed a "Watch Notice" on the late Senator Carlos' estate. She knew the Amandos back accounts had all been drained, and that the bank had taken possession of the multi-million credit estate, where it had remained unowned for some time now. Her alert notified her of any legal transfer of ownership. She quickly scanned for the recent deed transfer. Imagine her surprise when she read the name of the new owner: Neva Burkhardt. She dug deeper into the transaction. It was in her name only, not Konrad's. Strange. She checked the woman's bank account. Until recently, it held a reasonable sum, with most expenditures going to women's apparel stores. Now new funds were being deposited into it on a monthly basis, very significant amounts. A pay off? A bribe? Payment for services rendered?

Lena could not let this one go. Not after, she saw a recent image of Neva Burkhardt! She, too, had lost her arms and had similar massive breasts as had Senator Isabella Valen! She kicked into high gear, launching her own private, top secret investigation into the source of those monthly funds being deposited into Neva's account. At first, they seemed untraceable! That only convinced Lena something underhanded was going on, and she persisted.

It took her nearly a month to unravel the actual origin of these devious and mysterious funds being deposited into Neva's account. When the names finally appeared, Lena sat back and groaned. Legates Daag Taal and Herman Mels were alternately depositing the funds! "So this conspiracy goes higher than I ever imagined! What the devil are these two Legates doing with her? Why am I being kept out of the loop? It cannot be for Imperium Security reasons!"

Thus, she began covertly monitoring Neva Burkhardt's activities. It took a little time for her field agents to quietly track down what had happened to Neva. A few months later, one reported the psych Donatello was involved, that Neva had been briefly treated by him. Now, she began to assimilate a more complete picture of Neva. The poor woman was horribly mutilated and wholly helpless. Yet, she seemed utterly happy about her life, completely incongruous with her physical situation. The intense depression, remorse, grief — they were simply not present, according to the field agents, who were covertly monitoring Neva, when she was out in the public view. The psych must have illegally used Behavior Modification on her! Lena continued to build her case against the two high ranking Legates.

Then came the most shocking report yet! Neva had been summoned to assist President Snarry Knoschy! Her agents reported she had been present when the President interviewed the disgraced general, who had suffered the worst defeat yet in their long war with the Federation of Planets. This was too much for Lena. "The President no less. Does he know or not? Is he part of this conspiracy or is he a victim too? Just how much of this does he know? Is he behind the two Legates? My god, have I ever stumbled upon a big one!"

That the President began to have an affair with Neva was the last straw. Lena had to act. She requested and received a top security, private meeting with President Snarry Knoschy. "Welcome, Sector ID Minister Lena Squire. We've not spoken for some time. What is up with this private meeting? It must be extremely critical, considering the protocol you've invoked. Imperium Security at risk? Surely, this isn't that bad, whatever it is."

Lena didn't answer, but activated her many handheld devices, following the precisely outlined protocols. "There, no eavesdropping, no recordings of this meeting are possible. All electronics are scrambled. What is said between us remains between us per Protocol 52," she said sternly.

"Yes, yes, but what is all this about?" he asked growing more worried by the minute. His aides had not reported anything suspicious of late. Had they missed something critical? If so, he'd hang them for leaving him at the mercy of this intelligence woman.

"Mr. President, this involves Imperium Security in a rather big way. This woman you have been using and seeing, Neva Burkhardt. She is actually a telepath." He did not look surprised, and she began outlining all she had uncovered. When she pointed out the mutilations done to her body and that the psych Donatello had been used, he grimaced quite visibly. She knew now he had not known this part. Lena was methodical and took an hour to lay out every last detail she'd uncovered, including the sordid details of Senator Isabella Valen's rather similar abduction and mutilations.

President Snarry sat back in his overstuffed chair and ran his hands through his hair, clearly disturbed and emotionally upset. "She is such a fine woman. Good god, what have they done? Well, I must apologize for not having brought you into this situation earlier. I ought to have had you present from the onset. I make no excuses for myself or my conduct with her. She is the most fascinating, charming, and sexiest woman I've ever met. But that's beside the point. Yes, she is at least a Class V telepath. It goes far beyond that, I'm afraid, far, far beyond that."

He told her all he knew about her and her impressive skills. "I believe we should summon Legates Daag and Herman here and hear their justifications in this matter. Clearly, such mutilations and misuse of a woman cannot be tolerated. Still, we are at war, and this betrayal at the highest levels can only undermine the war efforts."

"War or no war, these two men have grossly abused the sacred powers invested in their high office, Mr. President. Protocols must be followed," Lena replied sternly. No way was she about to let these men off the hook for their crimes.

Two very embarrassed Legates listened to Lena's outline of their crimes against Neva Burkhardt. Per protocol, they were required to listen without interruption, as Lena presented her case before them and President Snarry Knoschy. Finally, they were allowed to make the case in their own defense. Both men knew this was a critical point. If they could not convince either Lena or President Snarry, they would be in very serious legal troubles, which would cost them everything.

Legate Daag spoke first. Solemnly, he began, "Mr. President, everything Sector ID Minister Lena Squire has stated is correct. However, what is missing is the vital reason we acted as we have done. You see, this woman presents simultaneously both the greatest possible threat to Imperium Security, our very stability, and the greatest potential for good for us all. She is no mere telepath. Heavens, if she were just another telepath like her husband, we would have been quite content to let her help the war effort with her husband out there on the rim, where telepaths are ferreting out traitors daily. No, there is far more to this woman than mere mind reading skills!"

"She possesses vast, untapped and hardly explored abilities. First, one thought from her can outright kill a person! We know, she's done just that for us!" He outlined their testing on condemned traitors. Lena looked very sober, and Legate Daag knew he was scoring points with her. "She can cause fires to erupt out of nowhere." They outlined this and the other skills that they had discovered this woman possessed.

Legate Herman added, "So you see, we've no idea what other incredible skills this woman possesses. We can't get her to give us the full picture of just what all she can do. Instead, we present her with an assignment, and she then tells us if she can figure out a way to accomplish it. In so doing, we've been compiling lists of what she can do. I'm terrified of her, to be honest, Sector ID Minister. If she's on the loose and uncontrolled, think of the damage she can do! Why, she could easily force President Snarry to do whatever she chooses! Once she has met someone, thereafter, she can kill him with a mere thought! None of us in the Imperium is safe from her! You see, this situation is the most serious threat to Imperium Security we have ever faced!"

Legate Daag smoothed everything over. "You see, that is one reason Legate Herman and I have limited her acquaintances. If she knows someone, that person is forever in danger of being murdered by Neva with just a thought of hers. We have kept her from meeting the other Legates for this very reason, to preserve their lives, as well as yourself, Sector ID Minister Lena. It was only the impossible situation with the general, which forced us to bring her to your acquaintance, Mr. President. We didn't want to do that, putting your life at risk, but the situation was most critical. Once again she proved valuable discovering the true problem with the heat exchangers."

"We also attempted to limit her ability to move around," Legate Herman added. "Yes, Lena is correct; we adopted some of the methods, which we suspect Senate President Carlos did to limit Senator Isabella's movements and physical actions. Yet, we took pity on her and also used the psych Donatello to modify her behavior so she would believe she was extremely happy with her physical restraints. We gave her precisely what she wanted, Lena. She wanted the late Senator's estate. We are covering the servant's salaries and giving her a generous monthly salary. Keep her happy and contented, and we keep the enormous threat she poses at bay, while we also make use of her incredible and unexplored skills to benefit the Imperium."

Legate Daag decided to force a decision at this point. "So, there you have it. I believe any court of law will side with us in this matter. Allowing Neva to wander around the Imperium, possessing the kind of powers she has, is tantamount to allowing the Federation of Planets to win this war and subjugate us all."

President Snarry sighed and looked at Lena. She gave him a slight nod. He answered, "Very well, Legates. It's my opinion based on your statements that you acted with the Imperium's survival as your motives. While I cannot personally condone the physical mutilations done to the poor woman, let alone the illegal Behavior Modifications on her, the circumstances warrant taking some kind of defensive measures. Good lord, gentlemen, I don't know what I'd have done in your shoes, excepting perhaps outright killing her, which is even worse. My god, what are we facing here with this woman? Lena? Ideas? Thoughts?"

"Damn you two for not bringing this to my attention at the very beginning! You've wasted my precious time and efforts in tracking all this down. Still, I see your point. If she can kill anyone without leaving the slightest trace just by thinking him or her dead, this is of monumental significance. None of us are safe, nor can we ever be safe again, once she has met us. I will point out that *your* lives will be worthless, *if* she discovers you've modified her mental state and behavior. We all know the psych's behavior modifications sometimes wear off in time. Lord help you both if and when that should happen. The only possibility I can see for us is somehow to have her located a vast distance from us. Out of range, I believe that is the proper term. You've said that she's said she has to be at least on the same planet as the person who she is to kill or bend to her will. So ultimately, we need to get her consent to be a very long way from President Snarry and you Legates."

President Snarry grimaced. "Er, right now, that could well be a problem. She is smitten with me, that much I can tell. What am I going to tell my wife?"

Lena smirked, "That's your problem. You should be more careful who you bed. Let's get back to the more serious problems we're facing here. Correct me if I misunderstand, we want to keep her happy, while we make use of her enormous skills?"

Legate Daag nodded. "Precisely, Lena. I would have loved to put her into the science labs and have them study her, catalog all her skills, and such. But we dare not do anything remotely like that. She would simply kill us all and escape the lab. Lord knows what kind of a rampage she would then undertake."

"We have put a new protocol in place," Legate Herman added. "If Daag, me, or Snarry here should die mysteriously, the security guards will be given orders to have her immediately executed by any means available. I don't know what else we can do to protect ourselves and yet make use of her."

Lena bit her lip in thought. "Has anyone researched what this woman's plans, desires, and wishes might be? Her overall goals? Power, money, material goods, sex? Everyone has goals, wants, and needs. What are hers?"

"We gave her what she said she wanted, the estate and clothes," Legate Herman replied.

"Not good enough. Let's look at this from her point of view, and see if we can reconstruct her actual motives. She began by being a literal nobody on an backwards, primitive planet Ashford-5. What did she do next? She managed to marry the most important person on that world, Governor Konrad Burkhardt. Next, she goes off-world with him. I find that detail key. She would be going beyond her own primitive world into the vast civilized Imperium. Clearly, she has goals far beyond those of a primitive bumpkin. Now, she positions herself into extremely valuable situations using her telepathic skills. This too is key, for certainly Senator Isabella Valen and her wives also had telepathic skills, and yet they never, ever mentioned them during her time here as a senator. Neva is using her skills very publically, but *only* before those in power."

She continued her analysis. "So what does she do next? Who has more power than Governor Konrad? Your Sector ID Minister, that's who. Did she not use him to get to those in power above him? Yes, she used him to get to you two Legates. I'll bet my position on that one, gentlemen. You've been used, *had*, as the expression goes, conned, duped." Both Legates looked crestfallen. Put this way, they both felt utterly used and foolish old men.

"So she endeared herself to you men, obtaining a multi-million dollar estate, certainly the finest here in Caltran. Plus, she has a substantial monthly income doing virtually nothing at all. True, she must be seeing her horrific physical mutilation as a detriment, but the behavior modification has also probably played into her goals too, keeping her happy about it. So what does she do next? She goes after your boss, Legates. She's clearly seduced President Snarry here. Lord knows, tomorrow, she might demand he divorce his wife and marry her! This woman's ultimate goal is one of *power*, gentlemen, simply ultimate power, not sex, not wealth, not fancy estates, but ultimate *power*. Boys, you have played *right* into this woman's hands. My, she is the most impressive woman that I've ever heard of. Good for her."

"But — but — what do we do now? Is she really going to force me to divorce my wife and marry her?" President Snarry asked, rather terrified of this now obvious prospect.

Lena laughed, "Well, you've made your bed. Now you have to sleep in it." He flushed red. "Okay, sorry. I couldn't resist that one. Clearly, gentlemen, we have a problem far worse than the war with the Federation of Planets! As long as she remains married to Konrad, you are safe, Mr. President. And as long as that behavior modification holds, you are safe too, Legates. God help you if it wears off, though. We need to find a plausible way to have her desire to be a very long distance from here, that's for sure."

"Until we can find a way to do that, I suggest it's business as usual with her. Continue to utilize her skills, as situations arise. Mr. President, continue with your affair with her and just focus on thinking about how good the sex is. Meanwhile, keep your eyes open for some way to get her off-world!" Lena pointed out. "Also, keep a close watch on each other. Be on the lookout for some behavior or decision you feel that the others would not normally be making. It could be a sure sign she is forcing one of you to do something she desires, overriding his will."

After more discussion, the meeting broke up. On her way back to her battle cruiser, Lena thought, "Men! Leave it to men to screw it up. They can't keep it in their pants! I sure would not want to be in Snarry's pants right now." She chuckled to herself.

Once more, time passed. Then one day, President received a request for a private video conference with Emperor Kino Sango of the Ataro Empire. He knew the old man and their strange customs. Considering this system was extremely wealthy and wielded quite a lot of political power, he agreed to take the private call.

President Snarry didn't like what Emperor Kino was proposing, tantamount to near treason. Still he had a point; the war was going badly. He didn't see the Imperium winning anytime soon. Then, he had an idea. He knew this Wasp Culture well. Emperor Kino had a lot riding on ending the war before it reached his Ataro Empire. He'd go ahead with his "thing" whether or not he agreed with the emperor. That he could potentially send someone along with him was his bright idea. "Get Sector ID Minister Lena on a private line immediately! No, I am not going to reply just yet. Let him wait. Get her now!"

Shortly, he was chatting with her on a secure line. She agreed, pointing out the emperor had no arms as well. It would be a good match. He smiled, problem woman solved, at least temporarily. He pressed the reply button and said, "Perhaps this is a wise move, Emperor Kino. While I cannot publically condone such a trip, I intend to support your efforts. To that end, I'll be sending a small group of my people to you, ambassadors to represent me in absentia. I'll expedite their trip as soon, as I can get them organized and briefed. Will this be acceptable to you, Emperor Kino? Over." He grinned broadly.

An hour later, Snarry met with Daag, Herman, and Lena, outlining his agreement and what it meant. All three agreed with him; this was a perfect solution. It would buy them considerable time. Besides, any number of "accidents" might befall Neva before she could return here. Now President Snarry had to present his case to Neva and convince her to go on this trip for him. He headed for her fancy estate, accompanied by a dozen security men.

"So that's the plan, Neva. I am desperate! This war is not going well at all. I can't think of a more important mission for you to undertake, bringing peace and an end to this war with the Federation. If you will do this for me and the Imperium, I'll owe you a very big favor, a very big one. Oh yes, I'll be sending along one of my top Sector ID Ministers to look after your security, as well as the emperor's. Will you do it?" The two were sitting on her couch in the living room. Marjorie was sitting across from them in a chair in case she was needed. Neva nodded towards Marjorie. "Oh, certainly, Marjorie must go with you. You must have your personal assistant with you at all times!"

But do I dare reveal I am a telepath? If I don't, how will I be able to tell this emperor anything I find out?

"Of course, you must take him into our confidence. Just don't let on you can do more than telepathy, unless the circumstances warrant it."

Okay. I'll do it for you, but can we have one last romp in bed before I go? I do so need a good sexual partner like you.

An hour later, the slightly flushed Snarry left to make further arrangements. Marjorie had her hands full packing their bags. They would bring along pencil style gowns, not the huge hoop skirt styles, for those would be wholly impractical on this mission.

The next day, a security detachment arrived to escort the two women to the spaceport. There, Legates Daag and Herman, along with President Snarry, met them. The dark skinned woman stood at attention. "Neva, this is Sector ID Minister Lena Squire. She'll assume responsibility for your total security on this long trip. Place your full trust in her and do whatever she tells you to do. She's the very best at what she does. Okay, then off you three go. I wish you all the very best of luck." Neva nodded, moved slowly up to him, and gave him one final passionate kiss, before carefully walking to the entrance ramp. Both other women hastened to her side to help her up and into the deep space transport ship.

As the ship lifted off, the three men breathed a huge sigh of relief. For now, their problem was solved. They could only hope it would remain solved and not reappear, especially President Snarry.

Chapter 5 Meetings

Emperor Kino Sango met the incoming deep space transport carrying President Snarry Knoschy's ambassadors. He had some misgivings about having others coming along with him, those who did not understand the basic principles upon which the Ataro System used to resolve conflicts. He anticipated they would cause more trouble than help, but politically, he didn't dare refuse the President on this one. The Imperium was at war, and what he was doing could well be viewed by some as treasonous. His aide kept a steadying arm around him. Standing was challenging for him, as were most physical actions.

"Welcome ambassadors. I am Emperor Kino Sango," he said formally, as the three women stepped carefully down. As Lena and Marjorie mostly lifted Neva down, his eyes blinked, taken quite by surprise.

"Welcome from President Snarry Knoschy. I am Sector ID Minister Lena Squire. I'm afraid these two cannot speak. This is our telepath Neva Burkhardt and her personal assistant Marjorie. I'm in charge of our security, and I guess I do the speaking for these two women," Lena said, her voice no less stern.

"Excellent. I am honored," he bowed to Neva, showing her a deep respect, rather surprising both her and Lena. "Seldom do we find others beyond Ataro, who accept such physical restrictions to temper their great powers." Neva didn't understand what he meant, but returned his stiff bow. She saw that he too wore a very restrictive pipe corset, perhaps even smaller than hers. His toe shoes looked just like the ones she used to wear back on Ashford-5. She suspected the design had come from these people. "We must wait just a few minutes for Queen Altha, who will be joining us on this trip. I dare not bring the empress, for if something happens to me, she must reign in my place, per our system of government. Ah, I hear another transport coming. If you will follow me, the ground crew will transfer your things to my ship. Let us greet Queen

Altha." His aide continued to keep him balanced, as they walked the short distance to the next landing bay, where Queen Altha and her personal assistant were just disembarking. Lena and Marjorie did the same with Neva.

Lena didn't say anything, but certainly had many thoughts, none good. This promised to be one doomed trip. The emperor, the queen, and Neva were all armless. All wore these impossible-to-walk-in shoes and could scarcely breathe in their overly tight pipe corsets. Lena frowned, but thought at least Neva cut an incredible figure with her massive bosom. She shook her head in dismay. *What have I gotten myself into this time? How can I possibly protect three totally helpless people?* She felt exasperation rising by the minute, especially as Queen Altha soon struck up a conversation with Neva and herself.

As the deep space transport entered hyper-drive, Queen Altha began, "So Neva cannot speak. How very strange. Couldn't your medical facilities repair her vocal cords? It must be horrible to be unable to speak, especially since we are so helpless. I guess your assistant must have to pay close attention to pick up your needs, Neva."

How do I answer this one? Lena cleared her throat, "We've only just met, Queen Altha. I'm not familiar with Neva's physical situation. Marjorie must be a very good care giver. Neva is a Class V telepath, though, so that must help her tremendously, I expect."

"Oh, a telpath. Well, that changes everything! Indeed, you have a way of communicating then. I was so worried about you, Neva," Queen Altha expressed her relief, settling down in her seat for the long day. "We've some unfortunate souls who are unable to speak on my world. They use hand signs to communicate. I am fairly good at reading their signs. I have to; it comes with my job, you see. So tell me, Neva, don't you agree that those of us who wield great powers simply must have severe physical restraints upon ourselves so we are not tempted to abuse the immense powers invested in ourselves? This is the way it has always been in the Ataro System for millennia now, and it has worked to perfection. The emperor over there wields even more power than I do. I can only control one planet, while he handles all thirty-six. Our word is law you see, so with this kind of power, we have to be physically restrained. What can I possibly do with money or possessions, eh?" she grinned and shrugged her shoulders.

I am envious, Queen Altha. I want real power too. The top models in Caltran have no arms and big breasts. I am emulating them; everyone notices us; we attract everyone's attention wherever we go. Our bodies are so sexy and hypersensitive to touch! But I had to make a concession to lose my voice. You see, they didn't want others discovering I am a telepath. Evil men could torture me to get me to speak and reveal things. This way, they can't do that, but I'm really happy about everything. They gave me my own very fancy estate outside Caltran, where Marjorie and I live when we're not on an assignment.

Queen Altha frowned; she'd heard something that raised her curiosity. "So they gave you your own estate, if you lost your arms, got your breasts altered, and lost your voice? Payment for your services?"

Why yes, they did, as payment for my services, you see. I'm so happy. So now I'm a top model and get to work for the Legates and the President, who I think is falling in love with me. I suppose when this mission is over, he'll want to marry me.

"Wait a second, Neva," Queen Altha broke in. "You have always been a telepath?"

Sure, since I was eighteen.

"And you wanted power?"

Of course. Don't tell anyone, but way back then, I was a lowly barmaid. Now, I'm the President of the Imperium's lover!

"I see. So who were these men who helped you become a top model?"

Legates Herman and Daag. They helped me gain so much power. I'm so happy now. They took time from their busy schedules to take me to visit with the top models on Caltran, you see. Six of them. They too were very happy being like this. She shrugged her shoulders and wiggled her bosom slightly, but quickly wished she hadn't done that. Neva felt powerful sensations electrifying her body, but this wasn't an opportune time to have Marjorie pleasure her, leaving her feeling a little frustrated.

"And they also asked for a concession with your voice too?"

Well, yes. It makes sense. I can't be tortured into revealing anything.

"That's silly, Neva, if you don't mind my saying so. They could torture you and make you tell them what they want to know via telepathy, just like you are chatting with us now," Queen Altha pointed out. "I think those two took advantage of you, Neva. I have immense powers, and thus must also have these awful restrictions with my body. I can't say I am happy about my physical limitations, though. I live with them, because I have overpowering goals and purposes to rule and lead my whole world."

But I'm truly so very happy, and my body now needs to be pleasured so very often. It craves it now, though it didn't used to do that. How strange. Neva's face looked a bit puzzled.

"I don't get it, Neva. How can you be so happy like this? We are utterly dependent on our personal assistants for nearly everything. It's a restriction I accept so I know that I can never accidentally abuse the immense powers my people have entrusted me with. Happy is not how I would describe my viewpoint. Satisfying, contented, pleased — that's how I feel, not giddy happy," Queen Altha countered and pointed out.

Neva looked very confused. Suddenly, she heard a man's voice in her mind, saying, "You're very, very happy with your new life. You're on the leading edge of fashion. Your body is hypersensitive to sexual urges. Your breasts are extremely sensitive to touch. Even the slightest touch on your breasts will turn on a strong sexual urge. You need to have sex or be pleasured at least twice a day. You crave sexual pleasure and must have it daily. You'll always obey Legate Herman Mels and Legate Daag Taal. You'll never betray them, not even under duress. You'll be faithful to the two Legates and always do as they ask of you. Your new life could not be any finer. You'll find great pleasure in your new life. You'll be very happy with everything and never complain about anything."

Unfortunately, she still had her mental contacts with Marjorie, Lena, and Queen Altha. They also heard the voice.

"Oh my god! That's a psych man's script! That's Behavioral Modification! It's totally and highly illegal! When I get back, I'll launch an investigation, and see that psych is uncovered and punished for his unethical, immoral, and illegal behavioral modifications on you, Neva!" Lena said in a surge of anger and hostility. "God damn those Legates. What were they thinking?" Lena had to make this outburst and declaration, because Queen Altha had just heard this. If she didn't, then the queen's suspicions would fall onto her next!

Neva began crying. *What's happening to me? I feel so weird. I'm truly helpless like this. I'm supposed to be a top model. They said so. I saw the six top models with my own eyes.*

"Look, Neva," Lena pointed out, "you and Marjorie have been around Caltran. How many women have you seen that look the way you look?"

Only those six, Neva admitted, still sobbing, though soundlessly.

Lena pointed out, "Right. Top models? Not likely. Well, maybe top escort models, I'll give them that, women who hire out for a night. No, Neva, you were setup; they simply took advantage of you. But why? Now that's the more intriguing question. Telepaths are a very rare commodity in the Imperium, highly sought after, highly prized. I know in the past, powerful men and women have done the most heinous actions to get telepaths to work solely for them." She felt a little sympathy for Neva, but not too much. *How stupid has this young woman been to have fallen for that trickery?*

But they gave me a multi-million credit estate. I have the deed. They were so sincere, Neva protested slightly, fighting to keep that man's voice from repeating its words yet again in her mind.

"Yes, they gave you what you wanted as payment. Dangle a banana in front of a monkey, and it'll do what you want. I'm sorry, Neva, but they have cleverly manipulated you," Lena didn't hold back. *She's got to learn the truth, if she's ever going to have any chance of breaking down that psych man's behavioral modification.*

But why would they do that? What's a monkey? What's a banana?

Queen Altha spoke up, "I can answer that one, Neva, and I don't even know these men who did it. Fear. They were terrified of you and what you can do. Yet, they greatly needed your telepathic skills."

Lena added, "A money is an animal found on some worlds in a tropical environment. A banana is a soft fruit with a yellow skin. She's right about fear. People fear what they don't understand, especially in your case." She knew she wasn't lying about this point, not remotely! The three men were absolutely terrified of Neva.

Well, I've helped them uncover several traitors and even sort out what actually happened with the bad heat exchangers and the loss of ten battle cruisers.

"Of course, you've been invaluable to them. Yet, Neva, they're terrified of you. What would you do, if you found yourself absolutely terrified of someone? Wouldn't you do everything in your power to keep that person somehow under your control and at bay?" Queen Altha asked gently.

Well, sure.

"Right. So they made you into a totally helpless, dependent person so they can more easily control you physically," Queen Altha evaluated.

"I agree with Queen Altha," Lena added her stern voice to the soft queen's. "They got you into a position where you're dependent upon them and are easily controlled. The psych man's behavior modifications were intended to make you always feel happy and contented about the whole physical mutilation thing, remaining forever their pawn, under their total control. Bastards!" Her vitriolic words cut deep into Neva's mind. She knew Lena was right.

I've been a complete fool! Now I'm ruined. This voice in my head won't shut up. I got to have sex soon. I can't stand it much longer. Her rubbed her legs together tightly, fighting off the nearly overwhelming urges.

Come on Neva. Let's get you to our quarters for a few minutes, Marjorie volunteered. Neva didn't hesitate, allowing her assistant to help her get to her feet gracefully.

After she left, Queen Altha said softly, "That's horrible. Will she be all right? Will she ever recover from this behavior modification?"

"I surely don't know. That's the whole point of the psych modifications — to permanently alter a person's behavior. Still, I'll do all in my power to get some justice for her," Lena said sternly.

"You must. I'll leave that to you. For now, we have to focus on how to contact the Federation of Planets," Queen Altha pointed out, bringing their attention back onto their true mission. "Perhaps I ought to have kept my big mouth shut."

"No, it has brought this crime to our attention, and maybe Neva will have learned something from it all, poor woman," Lena replied. Now she relaxed, the queen was washing her hands of this mess. Lena considered herself phenomenally lucky Neva hadn't sensed or detected her small role in this mess. She changed the topic at long last, "So how are we going to get to the people you need to talk to within the Federation?"

"I can answer that one," Emperor Kino spoke up. He'd overheard them and explained, "Once we get out to the war zone, we'll begin broadcasting our request for a meeting on all frequencies and in many languages. We should be there within two days. Since the Imperium has lost the outer quarter of this spiral arm, we'll have to refuel wherever we can still find an outpost that hasn't been destroyed. I expect we'll have an answer by the time we reach the very rim of this arm at the outermost edge of the galaxy. I have a theory about this whole mess with the Federation."

"Please, go on," Lena encouraged him, greatly desirous to hear his take on the conflict.

"Well, as you know, Sector ID Minister, for centuries now, the Imperium has been slowly expanding out from the central hub of the galaxy down this arm. The Federation of Planets operates mostly out of the other arm of the galaxy. Only within the past few centuries have our two civilizations been in contact with each other out there on the rim, where the two filamentary arms partially overlap each other. As you know, they have been conducting this war by sweeping down our arm from the outermost planets, such as Ashford-5, towards the central hub. In my vast experience in settling conflicts, the solution, the cause lies out there in the rim area of our spiral arm or perhaps theirs, at the very edge of the galaxy, where the first contacts between our two civilizations were made. Out there lies the culprit or culprits, who I aim to flush out."

Lena smiled. *This emperor is observant; I'll give him that much.* "That makes sense. I just hope we can meet with the right people."

"Oh, I am sure we can, in time," he replied confidently.

Days passed. A week later, they had already refueled twice and were in the vicinity of the Ashford-5 system. The emperor preferred to keep their fuel topped off. He had no idea how far they had to go, and he wanted to make darn sure they did not run out of fuel.

Neva recovered somewhat from her terrible shock and revelations. Still, the darn voice in her head continued to dictate to her, but now she didn't feel so happy about her life. Worse, she could not do anything about the overwhelming sexual urges she felt several times each day.

Lena listened to the message the emperor was sending out and gave her approval to it. "This is Emperor Kino Sango of the Ataro System, Imperium. We wish to meet formally with representatives of the Federation of Planets about our ongoing war. Together, we must put an end to this costly war. Please advise and respond. We are traveling in an unarmed deep space transport ship."

"Well, we're leaving the last of our explored suns here in the outer rim," Emperor Kino told everyone on their eighth day out. "Now, we fly aimlessly further out and hope someone responds. Of course, we'll not use more than half of our fuel supply. If nothing comes of this, we must be able to get back to that last refueling station. Too bad that Ashford-5's refinery was destroyed. If we could refuel back there, we could've extended our range significantly."

Lena relaxed. *At least he is not on a total suicide*

mission. We can return. In some ways, I hope we do just that soon. Should know in about a week, that would be the point of no return. "Excellent, emperor," she replied in her stern voice.

Two days later, the emperor received a formal reply. "Emperor Kino Sango. This is Federation Captain Schmidt. Land at the base on Gamelon-3. Sending coordinates. One of my representatives will meet you and escort you to my ship. Try anything and your ship will be blasted from space. Over."

His personal assistant, who also could not speak, flipped the microphone switch, and the emperor replied, "Acknowledged receipt of coordinates. We'll be there in six hours. Thank you, captain. I look forward to our meeting. Out."

"Well, they didn't blast us. That's something," Lena commented dryly. "Remember, I'm here to protect us all. Don't do anything foolish, please." He smiled.

Before long, they watched the blue-green world of Gamelon-3 growing larger. The transport homed in on the base coordinates, all on automatic. Lena was relieved, in that they would have more than enough fuel to return home. Now, she took stock of her weapons. Her d-gun was strapped to her waist as always. She had a concealed small gun strapped to her right leg and a dagger on her left leg. A small needle knife acted as a hairpin, though her short hair really didn't need such things. Adrenaline flowed; she was ready for anything.

After his assistant opened the ship's bay door, Lena stepped down first, followed by the emperor and his personal assistant, then Queen Altha and hers. Neva and Marjorie brought up the rear. The planet had a rather foul smell, and the lighting was rather dim, but this was a spaceport, after all. A dozen d-gun armed men stood at attention around the party, as they disembarked. Two men then approached, and both men could not conceal their shock and surprise at the physical appearance of the three.

"I am Lieutenant Jones. This is Lugar Domes, the ruler of the Gamelons," the uniformed man spoke.

"I'm Emperor Kino Sango. Queen Altha, Neva Burkhardt, and our guard, Lena. Neither my personal assistant nor Neva and her personal assistant can speak. I'm pleased to meet you."

"I see. Okay then, if you will follow us. I have some refreshments waiting. It'll be an hour before I get word from Captain Schmidt. This way." He allowed Lugar to lead the party across the darkened concrete to a tall building, the control center, Lena assumed.

Once inside, they could better see their hosts. Those from Gamelon-3 were all very short humans, barely five feet. Six of the locals along with Lugar were in the room. The lieutenant, on the other hand, stood six-five, lean and fit. His complexion was white, contrasting with the light brown of the Gamelon men. A brew similar to coffee was served. Lena watched these smaller stature men, as they stared at the three, who needed the help of their assistants to sip the hot coffee. *Well,* she thought, *they probably haven't ever seen such helpless people before. I hope this goes well.*

They chatted pleasantly for a few minutes, before the lieutenant and Lugar excused themselves to make the communications connection to Captain Schmidt. The remaining six men stared intently at Neva and Queen Altha, and to a lesser extent to Lena and Marjorie. They mostly ignored the emperor and his assistant, though he continued to chat about the coffee and how it was similar to that on his world.

Shortly, the two leaders returned. "Okay, Emperor Kino, here's how this is going to go. I'll take you and your personal assistant to rendezvous with Captain Schmidt. The women will remain here on Gamelon-3 as an insurance policy against any trickery or deceit on your part. We should get going now."

"But Queen Altha wishes to help with the negotiations, and Neva is the Imperium president's ambassador," Emperor Kino countered.

"That may well be, but I have my orders. If you want to meet with Captain Schmidt, then the women stay here as security. If anything happens, they'll be executed. Understood?"

"Okay then. So be it. I don't like it, and this is a diplomatic snub of the Imperium president. Still, we need to talk and that takes precedence. Lena, watch over them please. I'll be all right," he replied, turning to face Lena.

She wanted to refuse flatly this arrangement. Everything in her training told her this was not a wise move. Still, she saw the intensity in the man's eyes and knew he would out-vote her if she protested. This was, after all, his venture. While she couldn't protect him, at least, she could protect his queen and Neva. Instead of venting her mind, she merely nodded to the emperor.

"This way, emperor," the lieutenant said. The three men rose and left the room.

"Well, it's suppertime here. If you would care to join me for dinner, I'll have some comfortable rooms prepared for you while we dine," Lugar said. Lena picked up a coy or covert feeling emanating from the man, but could not discern what he intended other than what was said. They rose and followed him out of the room. They walked through long halls and rode the elevators twice before entering a well-lit dining room. The aroma of freshly baked bread wetted their appetites.

After getting seated, Lena asked, "Are your wives going to be joining us?"

Lugar gave her a rather strange look. "Not at this time," he answered. Again, she sensed he had something that he wasn't saying. She had no way to alert Neva to probe his mind without speaking openly, and instead focused on eating. At least, the food was flavorful, though quite exotic to their palettes. They ate with little conversation, which again Lena found unusual. She did try to start a conversation several times, but only Lugar answered her, and then only with the briefest "yes" or "no" replies. Frustrated, she gave up all attempts at being pleasant. Besides, being pleasant was not in her nature.

Later, they were shown to two rooms that were extremely bare, but did have a large bed in them. Lugar said, "These are your rooms. I'll send someone by in the morning to bring you to breakfast." His tone was still rather cold, Lena thought, but had no choice but to accept his pledge. "Guards will be posted in the hall, so don't try anything," he added. Lena nodded, and they entered the rooms. Lena went with

Neva and Marjorie, leaving Queen Altha and her assistant to deal with the second bedroom.

A bit later, Lena crawled in beside the two women, smiling as Marjorie had to pleasure Neva, who was again craving such. She didn't comment on it, though, pretending to fall asleep. She had her d-gun at her side and didn't sleep. Rather, she was on guard, ready for anything. Soon, she heard the two women beside her sleeping peacefully, and she relaxed a little. Now, she began pondering just how far she could press this Lugar. Surely, they had better accommodations than this sparse room. She resolved to ask about it in the morning.

Then, she heard a faint hissing sound and carefully sat back up. She detected an unfamiliar odor. Gas. They were being attacked! She got out of bed. An unexpected dizziness swept over her head and body. She noticed her d-gun had hit the floor. *Clumsy,* she thought, but in trying to pick it up, she fell onto the cold floor herself. Then all went black. Lena didn't even have the chance to curse herself for having been caught in a trap!

Chapter 6 Milk Factory

Lena's hardy constitution kicked in. She was the first to waken from the gassing. Her body felt all wrong. She couldn't move. She blinked and opened her eyes. What she saw totally shocked her. She gagged reflexively. Neva was on her right side; Queen Altha, her left. Their two assistants were in front of them. They were in some kind of huge mechanical room, along with hundreds of other women, or rather what was left of them!

This was a nightmare beyond description. All the women's arms were absent. Their breasts were enormous; hers protruded over a foot in front of her chest, larger than basketballs. A metal brace surrounded her chest and was attached to two secure metal arms holding her body upright and slightly forward. Her feet ached. She could see all the women were naked, except their feet, which were enclosed in knee high boots, which kept their feet in the ballet en pointe position just touching the ground, exactly like those Neva wore. However, both legs were spread far apart with ankle chains holding them securely there. She was able to move them a few inches in a vain attempt to ease her throbbing feet.

Two giant suction cups were secure over her massive nipples. She saw two tubes, one small, one larger coming from the other women's privates, and presumed she had them in her as well. Her mouth was forced open with some kind of plug in it. A tube ran out from it and upwards. Her skin felt very funny, like it was covered in something, but she could see that none of the women was wearing any clothing. Try as she might, she couldn't get the mouth plug out of her mouth. She tried to make noises to rouse the others, but she discovered she had no voice! Gradually, the light seemed to brighten, and far off, she heard a door open.

She sensed the panic coming from her companions, as they too woke to find themselves horribly trapped. Then, the sneering face of Lugar appeared, standing before them. Several other nearby women turned their heads to look at him too. "Well, awake at last. I hope you don't mind joining the other women of Gamelon-3. Women here are keeping our men alive by producing the elixir of life, nourishing milk. When you are hungry, suck in on the tube. Wholesome liquids will flow. It contains a special ingredient that will help you lactate readily. Tubes carry your excrement away to be recycled into fertilizer for our crops, which we men carefully tend and convert into your nourishing food."

"This whole operation is done automatically. Twice a day, you'll be milked dry, so make sure you suck in as much liquid as you can. During the milking times, the devices will activate, giving you a most pleasureful time. They'll also activate three times during the day as well, so that you don't get bored. Also, your skin has been partially plasticized. Sweat can flow out through your plastic skin, but no microbes can enter into your body. In fact, you are mostly hermetically sealed, except through you nose. Once a day, the showers turn on and wash you all off, so don't worry about hygiene. We keep this milking farm very sterile, so nothing interferes with the milk making process."

"You will be spending the rest of your lives making the life-giving milk that sustains the men of Gamelon-3. If you are lucky, one of these days, a man may choose to breed with you and help create more men and more women for the milking machines — though I don't know if anyone will want to breed with the black woman, but you never know. Oh yes, forget about talking. Your voice boxes have been altered, though we didn't need to do that to Neva and Marjorie. Well, it is time for your first milking. I'll leave you to enjoy the pleasures. Relax and enjoy the milking process, as do all the women of Gamelon-3."

He turned and left. Lena wanted to cry out in protest, but couldn't. If her eyes were been blasters, she'd of disintegrated Lugar on the spot! Suddenly, she felt a sucking pressure on her right breast, and then it alternated between each one. At the same time, she felt the mechanical contraption exciting her and then the plunging thrusts. This was too much to bear, and she broke down, sobbing silently to herself. She did observe her thin milk beginning to flow through the two tubes, heading upwards and out of sight. How long the process took, she didn't know. She only wanted it to stop!

At last, the automated process ended. A warm, gentle water spray drenched her and the other women — the promised shower. Then, a warm, dry air blew over her strange-feeling skin. A while later, she felt ravishingly hungry and had no choice but to begin sucking. A tasty liquid soon seeped into her mouth. She swallowed and continued until she felt full. Lena also noticed pure water was interspersed at uniform intervals with the liquid food. She stopped after taking a final drink of water from her tube.

Now she tried to move. The supporting metal arms kept her upper body quite rigidly in place. Yet, she could move her feet a few inches, but not enough to relieve the terrible cramping pains in her toes. Then, the pain subsided, and she guessed some kind of painkiller had been part of her "meal." She gave them credit for that much. She looked at the other women and realized this was set up much like a factory. From the little that she could see, there must be hundreds of other women in here with her. They too were moving their feet a little.

Then, the lights dimmed down, and the pleasure-giving mechanical devices began working yet again. She wanted to cry out, "Stop! I can't take it anymore!" Only silence came. Then, mercifully, it ceased. Her body had relaxed of its own accord, and she moved her head about and saw many of the other women had closed their eyes. It must be naptime. She sighed and closed hers too. Now, her back ached, trying to support the massive weight of her new bosom. She hoped the painkillers would be stronger. *Maybe if I eat more next time,* she thought. *No, this is utter insanity!*

Next to her, Neva fought to keep from losing her mind! Slowly, she too began to take in what had happened to them all. Yet, all this was too much for her to understand. Until the sex devices began working, she believed she was having the worst nightmare of her life! Then, her mind finally began working once more, as she felt the surge of satisfaction electrifying her whole body. *This cannot be a dream! What is this place? Milk factory? Why? What are they doing to all their women?*

She began to relax and expand her awareness outward. Her germanium crystal was gone, and, for a moment, she cursed, but then realized somehow, she was easily able to utilize her *mentales* gifts. She sensed the other nearby women were all more or less in a complete apathy. Some of them had been here for over twenty years, though they found keeping track of the days nearly impossible. Several had given birth, while they were attacked to these devices. Their babies were taken away by the men. She sensed most of the females were brought back when they reached puberty. That would account for the widely diverging ages of the women that she could just barely see around her.

Worse, she sensed many of the women were contented — that they were somehow giving the elixir of life to the men of Gamelon-3! That notion startled her, and she moved her awareness easily out beyond the milk factory. It didn't register she should not be able to do this without the added power increase from her germanium crystal. The world outside was bathed in the yellow light of daytime. She focused her attention and began seeing what was going on.

She only saw men. Quite a few were working in the fields, fertilizing and hoeing weeds. Neva looked in vain for an adult woman, but found none at all, only men. Further expanding her zone of awareness, she spotted a city and hovered above it. Below her, she saw factories building spaceships and all manner of other equipment. This was not a primitive culture, she noted, anticipating seeing a world like Ashford-5. No, it seemed more like Caltran, except the only females she saw were little girls. Hovercraft provided the main transportation vehicles. The sky was filled with them. She also spotted the spaceport and their deep spaceship, right where they had landed, some fifty miles from where she now was in this underground milk factory.

Just then, she spotted a transport ship that had just landed. What got her attention was the fact that armed guards were escorting a dozen captured women off of the ship. From their clothing, she guessed they had been taken from distant, more primitive worlds. Certainly, these women did not look like the others here in the milk factory. Their skin colors were white to yellow, quite unlike that of the local Gamelon-3 population. Curious, she kept her attention on these terrified women. They were pushed onto a waiting hover car and brought here. Neva continued to spy on them.

They were led into a room and then gassed, much as she guessed had happened to herself last night. She watched closely and saw the men then stripped the women. One by one, they were placed into some kind of full-body machine that enclosed their bodies. After a time, the machine opened back up. Now the women's skin looked different somehow. Their arms were gone; their breasts, enormous balls. Men now picked them up and carried them into the factory. Fortunately, they were being placed in front of her. She watched, as they fastened the metal collar around their chests and hooked them into the metal arm bars, which then held their bodies upright. They put the ballet style boots on their feet and chained them spread-eagle to the sides of the container.

Next, she watched, as they began inserting the tubes and fastened their mouths around the contraption, hooking it up to the food delivery tubes. Then, they adjusted the pleasure-giving devices. Finally, they hooked up the breast pumps and the new additions were ready to go. It took them about an hour per woman. Around her, she sensed the other women were rousing, relieving themselves, and then sucking in their lunch. She did so as well, but continued watching the men, as they hooked the twelve new women up to the milking machines.

Finally, it dawned on Neva just what this all meant. *I'm being turned into a human cow!* She had become a human cow, whose sole purpose in life was to make milk! *Well, I don't think so! At least now, I know how to get myself out of this contraption. Oh!* The pleasure-giving devices activated once more, and Neva forgot about all else for a time. *At least they got this part right,* she mused.

Later the lights dimmed, and she chose to go exploring once more. As she became aware of the outside world once again, where it was late afternoon, it finally dawned on her.

How can I do all this without my germanium crystal? She knew without its amplification, she simply didn't have this much *mentales* power. The barmaid in her kicked in. *There must be a reason. Could they be feeding us psi-powder? No, then everyone here would become telepaths, and I'm the only one. That much I know for sure. Wait. I sense a source of real power here, but where?*

This time, she sent her awareness downward. Suddenly, she knew! Then, it dawned on her what this was all about, well the war anyway. Lying below the surface of the planet was one giant germanium psi-crystal! The amplification it gave her *mentales* gifts was staggering beyond her comprehension! She felt she could well blow up the entire world.

Just then, the milking machine began operations. Once more, she felt the alternating suctions on her breasts and felt her milk flowing out and into the tubes. The pleasure devices then started up, sending her into a fit of ecstasy. For a time, she couldn't think of anything at all, lost in the pleasurable sensations flooding her body. It felt so good to be relieved of the milk her breasts had been building up all afternoon. For a moment, she entertained the thought perhaps they should be milked more frequently.

She didn't realize just when the alternating suctions ended. Neva only knew pleasure at the moment. Then, that device too ceased, and she found she was starving. Her back ached from trying to support the massive weight of her bosom. Greedily, she began sucking in the liquid food, praying it also contained a painkiller. Wiggling her back was not helping relieve the pain.

A bit later, Lugar entered the factory and stood before the new arrivals. He went through the same explanation he'd given Neva's group earlier. Then, he stepped before Neva and Lena. "I checked and your milk is starting to flow very nicely indeed. Keep up the good work. You are saving many men's lives here on Gamelon-3. Without your milk, we men would all die."

He sighed. "We need far more women to sustain the number of men in our population now. We've exceeded the capacity of milk production from our women. We've had no choice but to go off-world, and kidnap women from other worlds. We just added another dozen this afternoon. If we Gamelons are going to survive, we must add at least another five hundred women to our milk factories. Either that or start killing off some of the men and boys. It takes around fifteen years to breed another milk woman, but you already know that."

"You see, we were doing just fine until a few years back. It's all your damned Imperium's fault. They came here and wanted to take over our world — something about a large fuel deposit or something. Well, we were already a lowly member of the Federation of Planets, but we've managed to keep our 'problem' to ourselves. We couldn't let the Imperium land here. Now with the war raging, we are able to help ourselves to women of other worlds, as you've just seen. We anticipate in another two months, we'll have added enough women to sustain us once more. Of course, you women could always help out more by having more female babies. This fifty-fifty ratio is not working at all well. Well, I'm tired of talking to myself. I got to go. I'm overdue for my elixir of life dose. See you all another time, perhaps. Oh, do be sure to eat lots. Your breasts demand it, if you haven't noticed."

Neva had thought she was full, but his parting shot made her feel ravenously hungry once more. She began sucking in the liquid food once more. Oh how she wanted to massage her breasts, which were aching. She sent soothing waves to them, and to her surprise, she found they were craving more food, as if she were nursing! She continued to suck in food until she thought her stomach would burst.

Later, the lights dimmed down signifying nightfall. Again, the pleasure-giving devices activated. She could hear their low humming sounds echoing from the many hundreds of women around her. Neva soon forgot about all else, as usual.

When the devices shut down, she was totally relaxed. Now able to think again, she realized what she had learned would be critical for the emperor to know. Perhaps, these Gamelons had somehow started this devastating war. Ordinarily, she knew her telepathy range was limited to the world she was on, but she was "sitting" on the largest germanium crystal ever. Will it be strong enough for me to reach him? *Won't know unless I try.* She focused and began reaching out, searching for the unique tiny wavelength that was characteristic of Emperor Kino. Each person has their own special frequency, that she already knew from her training back on Tierra. That seemed like another lifetime to her, just now.

She was as shocked as the emperor was, when she actually made the telepathic connection to him. He was in flight to wherever the captain's battle cruiser was located. *Emperor Kino! I have tons of news. Most is horrific. We have been kidnaped and are being tortured. Let me send you some images, and I'll explain everything!* She lost track of time, but Emperor Kino didn't. She'd talked with him for nearly an hour!

Hang in there a while, Neva. You may well have given me what I need to end this war. I'll get that handled first, and then see about rescuing you. Can you survive for a while?

Survive? Yes, we are being milk cows forever, unless you can rescue us or I can do it somehow. I'll stay in touch, and let you know if I find out anything more. Good luck. I am beginning to see what you mean by someone behind the scenes actively promoting the war.

When Neva returned her awareness to her body, she found it was asleep. She too dozed. The next morning was an exact duplicate of the previous one. Everything in the milk factory was on automatic, and nothing could go wrong. This morning, her breasts ached, craving to be relieved of the massive quantity of milk they'd produced during the night. She was only too eager to hear the suction pumps beginning again. Beside her, she sensed many other's relief as well. Rather, she waited for the pleasure devices to begin. *Ah. Perfection,* she thought. Later after eating all she could for breakfast, she made contact with her companions.

Hi everyone. Are you doing all right? Neva thought this was rather a lame way to begin. Obviously, none of them was all right. *Still, what else could I say,* she asked herself.

Tell me this is just an awful nightmare! Lena fairly

screamed back in her mind.

This can't be real, can it? Marjorie replied morosely, but with some faint hope that it wasn't.

We are as good as dead, but can you somehow get word to my emperor? Tell him what Lugar has told us. He's probably the cause of the war, Queen Altha thought, as she duplicated Neva's thoughts in her mind, all the while wondering how she could be understanding Neva. She no longer had her ULAT box, but then she remembered Neva couldn't speak anyway. The queen was very confused.

Already done, Queen Altha. I reached him a bit ago, told him about what's happened to us, and what Lugar told us. He also believes Gamelon-3 is somehow behind the war. I asked him to rescue us, if he can. Lena, this is very real, that I am certain of.

Neva felt the intense waves of Lena's emotional loss, as her thoughts formed. *Then, kill me right now, Neva. I beg you; put me out of my misery. I have failed to protect you. I should have detected the trap and saved us. No one should be tortured like this. I hope they all die! Go ahead. Do whatever you do. Put me out of my misery. I can't take this. Rescue? Ha. We're all going to be totally helpless, even if we are rescued. I can't live like this. So go ahead. Kill me somehow. I'm ready.*

Neva was torn between two conflicting counter-thoughts. Her instant reaction was to say something like: Now you too will be a top fashion model and very happy too. But that was the male voice in her head responding. In opposition to that thought was the idea that Lena was right. She should kill Lena; put the horse with the broken leg down. Even if a rescue came, Lena's career and life would be over, even if somehow she could get her voice back. Force-counter-force. Neva faced a growing problem and didn't reply straightaway.

Marjorie added her pleas for a quick death too. *Neva, I can't help you any more, even if we are rescued. I have no credits to hire a personal assistant for me, so put me down when you put Lena down.*

Neva? I am hearing Lena and Marjorie's thoughts too. How is this possible? Queen Altha thought, hoping Neva would hear her. She had never experienced telepathic communication before. The novelty of it temporarily made her forget the horrific situation she and they were in. *I feel so close to everyone.*

Telepathic rapport. I've hooked us all together.

So that's why I can feel their emotions too? Queen Altha asked, growing more fascinated with the intense experience. Deep down, she was relieved to have something to think about instead of what she was facing.

Right. Our minds are open to each other, our feelings too. Thoughts are just ideas, concepts, not words. If they were merely words, we couldn't understand each other without the ULAT boxes. I was going to tell Lena that her life isn't over if we get rescued. We can get by somehow. Lena, Marjorie, you are both welcome to come and live at my estate on Caltran, when we get rescued. I've plenty of credits to hire personal assistants for us all. Besides, I was happy, even if I was behavior modified somehow. I felt happy, I think. Oh, I don't know. I am too confused right now.

Queen Altha asked, *Is there something we can do to free ourselves? I don't know what. I can only move my feet a little bit and turn my head slightly. Can you actually use thoughts to kill these men? Would that help any? How will the emperor find us in here? Where is this place?*

Neva sent them all some images of what she'd seen before, orienting them as to where this milk factory was located. *Oh hell! They'll never find this place! It's miles from the landing base and underground,* Lena protested. *Come on; put me out of my misery! This is beyond hopeless.*

Not necessarily, Lena. I can guide them to us. That's easy enough. Yes, I can kill Lugar and any others who are here.

Queen Altha thought quickly. *Wait on that one. I think we need them to keep our bodies alive until my emperor comes for us. My breasts are definitely lactating like mad — reminds me of nursing my boy. Even if we can somehow get out of this milking machine, it's going to take some time before we dry up again. But these are so huge. I guess they must really think they need mother's milk here. I don't understand that at all. Do you think Lugar is lying about their need for our milk? I've never heard of such a thing, but then this is an alien world.*

No, I didn't get any sense he was lying. Sorry. I've not had any children yet. So if I can get us down from here, our breasts are going to still produce milk? Neva asked.

Yes, for quite some days, I am afraid. Takes a while finally to dry up. At least, my nipples aren't being bitten, she tried for a small bit of levity, but it was missed by the other three who had not had any children yet.

Good god! Not again! Lena fairly screamed. The pleasuring devices activated, once again indicating it was lunch time. *Make it stop! Oh God, no, let it go.* Lena was again swept up in the overwhelming sensations flooding her lower body. *This is utter madness!* Neva lost her concentration. The rapport ended abruptly, but the others hardly even noticed the loss of their rapport..

Totally contented, Neva barely noticed the machine had stopped. Now, she felt quite hungry again. Greedily, she sucked in the liquid food, ignoring what possible drugs she might be ingesting. She just knew she had to eat or rather drink, and a rather large amount she finally noticed, though she had no way really to tell the volume of the liquid she swallowed. She ate until she felt full and sucked in some water, rinsing her mouth with it before swallowing it. Sex-eating-thought. Now her mind began to think once more. *How strange. After sex, I get the munchies. After eating, I get to thinking about things. Strange pattern. I wonder why I never noticed it before? No matter. What can I do to rescue us?*

Neva didn't have the gift of telekinesis, which would have been most useful in this situation. Her gifts tended towards controlling others. With the incredible power amplification she could utilize, she knew she could dominate even Lugar, forcing him to do whatever she asked him to do. Just what ought she make him do? Release them? That would be easy, but then what? Where would they go? If he was right and there were no women in this society, they would be in danger of being gassed again, just as soon as they went to sleep, finding themselves right back here hooked up to these machines. Besides, without personal assistants, they would all be completely helpless.

Instead, she decided to explore the outside world of Gamelon-3 further. Perhaps, this was an isolated pocket of men. Maybe there were women and a proper civilization elsewhere on the planet. She focused and was delighted to see the ease with which she could tap into the immense magnification powers of the mammoth germanium crystal that lay buried beneath the surface. Time flew by rapidly. Without warning, Neva was pulled summarily back into her body. Once more, the alternating suction pumps were milking her monster breasts. The pleasure devices had already activated and that's what completely broke her concentration. *I have to get me one of these devices,* she thought, as it finally stopped, leaving her exhausted, but starving once more. Greedily, she sucked in her supper. As she finished eating as much as she could, she became aware of others entering the factory floor.

Turning her head, she saw men bringing in another half-dozen unconscious women, whose bodies looked like all the others in here. She watched closely, as they methodically hooked these new additions up to the machines. From the empty stations, she estimated this facility or floor, if there was only one, could hold at least twenty-five more women. Although she couldn't see behind her, she looked that way from one of the workers' eyes, forcing him to look up and out over the floor of milking stations. She held onto the mental image and counted. All told, she tallied one hundred seventy-five women in this milking facility or on this floor.

She tried to sense if there were minds below, as in a sub-floor, but found none. She extended her probe in four other directions. Still no more collection of minds. Neva then concluded this must be the entire facility. She resolved to take a good look at whatever was above ground, and then to see if she could find other similar structures. Just how many of these hideous facilities did they have on Gamelon-3? Somehow, she thought she needed to know that answer. The workers finished connecting up the new arrivals and left, at which point, she got distracted again. The warm, gentle shower came down on the whole area, washing away any sweat and probably disinfecting everything as well. Then, the warm, dry air followed, which she found refreshing. The lights then dimmed, and their nighttime pleasuring began once more. When it finished, she drifted into sleep.

The lights in the milk factory turned on, once more rousing Neva. Her breasts felt heavy and sore, weighted down by the rather large amount of milk her body had produced. Thus, like all the women, she was greatly relieved when she again felt the dual, alternating suction pumps beginning to pull gently on her breasts. As usual, the pleasuring devices began shortly thereafter, much to her satisfaction. If nothing else, it kept her mind off her almost unbearable situation. She was hardly aware of the cessation of both. Then, her hunger kicked in, and she began sucking in breakfast rapidly. Full at last, she began to think once more.

This is crazy. Sex-eat-think, one comes right after the other. I wonder why? Neva didn't get time to ponder this further. Lugar walked in and stood before them, a clipboard in hand. "Well, ladies, good news. You are up to the standard milk output per day. Each of you is producing a half gallon. Nicely done, ladies. You are doing your part to keep many Gamelon men alive. We thank you."

Neva wanted to know more about what this was all about and gently nudged Lugar's mind, encouraging him to explain in greater detail. "Well, you are aliens, so I guess now you are fully producing members of our society, I ought to tell you a bit more about all this. You see, it all began over three and a half centuries ago, shortly after we began exploring other worlds around our sun. Apparently, our quarantine procedures were faulty back then, and a strange virus was unleashed upon Gamelon-3. Men sickened and died relatively quickly. Our top scientists and medical doctors simply could not find any cure. Strangely, the virus only affected the men of Gamelon. Not a single woman ever died from the virus. That's when by fortuitous chance, serendipity if you prefer, we discovered a mother's milk kept all nursing baby boys from contracting the virus."

"With half of the men on Gamelon already dead, the doctors were desperate to try anything to keep all humanity from dying out. Experiments were done, so our history books say, and the doctors proved that by drinking mother's milk, those who came down with the virus recovered. Once taken off the milk, they quickly sickened once more. So you see, the only way the men of our world could survive was to daily continue to drink the elixir of life, as it soon became called by the common man. Of course, that meant a huge supply would be needed."

"Our doctors launched a massive program. They produced a enzyme that caused any woman's breasts to begin producing milk, even though they had not just given birth. Volunteers were sought — women to save our world. While many did so, they were not enough. Soon, our ancestors realized that, if humanity were to survive, we would have to adapt. Calculations proved that even, if all our women were producing, the amount would be wholly insufficient to maintain our civilization. More research was undertaken. Fortuitously, one of our long range craft encountered the ships of the Federation of Planets, and they brought back a medical machine."

"That was the breakthrough that saved Gamelon from extinction, you see. Our doctors and scientists were able to use some of that technology to enlarge women's breasts, which eventually enabled each woman to produce a half gallon of the elixir of life. Of course, the women began to have physical problems with the heavy weight of their breasts. Plus, infections developed along with other sanitary problems and pains. Two hundred and fifty years ago, our top researchers hit upon a more humane process, one we are still using today with all of you. Your bodies are kept free from all infections and pains. Plus, you are given a significant amount of pleasureful stimulation to compensate for the uncomfortableness you must be experiencing daily."

"Our scientists and medical staff guarantee me that they have done everything possible to ensure you live long, healthy lives with proper nutrition and wholly free of pain, infections, diseases, and such things. Voices were eliminated, because women were getting themselves into choking problems while trying to talk. Arms were removed because they continually interfered with the apparatus. Movement was restricted, so the equipment could operate efficiently without harming your bodies. The plastic skin solved the hygiene barrier, preventing illness and allowing us to give you a daily, cleansing bath. Plus, everything that can be done to give you some pleasure for your noble sacrifices has been done as well. All went well for several hundred years, until our overall population became too great once more."

"My father told me a story of those dark times. With all our women producing at maximum, there was still not enough to support our thriving population. He said, 'Lugar, it comes down to this. Either I kill you to reduce the number of mouths to feed or we find more women volunteers from other worlds. Son, I can't kill you. Nor can I ask any other father to kill their sons.' I am glad I wasn't facing that awful dilemma. That's when we began seeking out volunteers from other worlds. Of course, few cared about the fate of us Gamelons. What choice did we have? I ask you that? You women are the saviors of Gamelon. For that, we are eternally grateful. Now, I really must be going. We are expecting the arrival of more women later today, and I must get prepared for their transformations."

He paused partway out, turned back, and added, "Oh, don't worry. When or if anyone comes back for you, we'll tell them that you went for a hike and met with an unfortunate accident. We have these giant tigers that love to dine on humans. We found only your shoes left behind. So don't worry about that." He turned back and left the factory floor.

Neva focused and contacted Emperor Kino. *I've got more on the story here on Gamelon-3.* She proceeded to relay to him what she'd just heard.

Are you sure you're all right? he asked.

Not really, but we are alive and desperate for a rescue. I'm sure they'll keep us alive for many years, but this is almost an intolerable life. Do hurry. They're kidnaping many other women from other worlds, adding them to their milk factories. Bring along a bunch of doctors and medical machines, that's for sure!

Chapter 7 Resolutions

"So Captain Schmidt, I rest my case. If these Gamelon-3 folks have been doing just what I've said, then that would explain why our two empires are at war — over nothing basically. I know; we both have committed atrocities on each other in the name of war. Yet, if this is the cause, I know our president will be most willing to sign a peace treaty with the Federation of Planets. This galaxy is more than large enough for both of us," Emperor Kino summarized. He'd finished outlining in detail just who the behind-the-scenes person was that had incited both sides to go to war with each other. His biggest problem was not having Sector ID Minister Lena with him to handle the long distance communications with the president.

The delay in communications back and forth at this extreme distance was nearly two hours. Still, he had persisted. The Legates and President Snarry had done their homework. Indeed, near the start of the war, their outposts had received all manner of dire predictions of the Federation of Planets. The rumors the Gamelons had spread included ones that claimed the Federation was about to take over all their planetary systems on the outer rim, that they were about to launch a preemptive strike on their fuel refinery on Ashford-5, that they were planning to sweep down this arm and take out the entire Imperium, and that they had five thousand battle cruisers, and more. The Gamelons had been very persistent in spreading rumors into the right ears. Over five years, they had totally convinced the Sector ID Ministers of the seriousness of the threat. That they'd once tried to attack the fuel refinery on Ashford-5 really aided their illusion. Convinced the Federation was about to attack them, the Imperium had launched a surprise attack on the Federation's fuel refinery planet, Rimon-F. Of course, then the Federation had little choice but to launch the devastating raid on Ashford-5's refinery, destroying the entire moon along with the factory.

In order for the Imperium to carry out their previous attacks on Federation bases and planets, their battle cruisers had to cut across the spiral arms, a highly unusual and dangerous move. They had no means of refueling so far from their sectors, which is why the Imperium forces had so quickly abandoned Rimon-F, once destroying the refineries there. The two empires used quite different fuels in their space fleets.

At this point in time, President Snarry was convinced the Gamelons had intentionally setup the Imperium. He even went so far as to suggest that world be destroyed, something Captain Schmidt was hesitant to do. "We need actual proof, verification what you are telling us is, in fact, true," the hard-nosed battle cruiser captain countered. "No one is that stupid — to turn all their women into, as you say, milk cows. I just cannot believe it. However, if this is true, then we must take action. Mind you, if this is a trap or turns out to be false, I have no choice but to arrest you."

"Of course, captain. I would suggest you land with a sizeable force. Undoubtedly, they'll resist discovery of their inhuman crimes. As you have said, no one has ever been aware of this situation on Gamelon-3. They've hidden it from both our forces for a very long time. If threatened, they may well attack your ships and ground forces," Emperor Kino advised.

"No need to tell me how to do my job," he barked. "The guard will take you back to your quarters now. It'll take us a week to get to Gamelon-3, so sit back and relax," Captain Schmidt ordered. Once the emperor was gone, he barked a slew of orders. Shortly, the giant ship veered away from the Federation formation and dropped into hyper-drive.

They are on their way here to see for themselves, Neva sent to her group, once more forming a Mind Link between them. *Emperor Kino has been able to convince the Federation and the Imperium these Gamelons are behind the war. This Captain Schmidt and the emperor are on their way here. He says it will be a week before they arrive. Hang in there everyone. Help is on the way.*

Queen Altha relaxed; she was pleased and satisfied. Her personal assistant didn't respond, she'd fallen into the sub-apathy emotional tone band, having given up all hope. Marjorie sighed; she too was in apathy, unable to cope with her hideous imprisonment. Lena was still fighting it. She shook her head violently this way and that, straining to break out of the bonds that held her. That is, to un-connect the two steel bars on either side of her that held her body rigidly in place. No other movement was possible for these women.

I can't take it anymore! Kill me. I beg you; kill me! I don't want the world to see what's become of me! God, I'm a Sector ID Minister, for heaven's sake. No, I'm not that any longer. Now I'm a vegetable — a helpless milk cow. Please, Neva, please put me out of my misery. I can't live like this.

Sure you can, Queen Altha thought. *Look, I and all we queens do just fine. We bear even more power than you do, Lena. If we can manage, so can you. Don't give up.*

I don't want to be a helpless woman, dependent on a personal assistant. Good god, woman, death is far better! Kill me please, Neva. Have a heart, for god's sake!

Maybe later, Lena. We have to be here when they arrive. We have to make sure they see what these debased Gamelon men have done to us. We need to get justice, not only for ourselves, but also for all these other women they've kidnaped. It's only a week. Neva focused, and sent soothing emotional waves over Lena's body and mind. She slipped into rapport with the angry woman, and quickly drained the anger from her, allowing her body to relax.

Queen Altha began to ponder Lena's situation, but had to stop. The dual suction pumps began again, followed by the pleasure devices. That totally broke her concentration. She relaxed and allowed the machines to do what they were designed to do. Later, like the others, she felt like she hadn't eaten in a week, and sucked in the liquid food, swallowing gulps. until she was able to slow down some. Full, she then found she could think clearly once more. She felt obligated somehow to help Lena — not now, of course, but later, once they had been rescued.

She could take her under her wing and train her, as if she were to become an Ataro queen. No, she thought, that would not suit Lena. She was a fighter, a leader, head of an intelligence-gathering network. She would never be satisfied being an arbitrator of disputes, Queen Altha realized. *So what can I do for her?* She continued to think.

After a time, she reflected upon Queen Isabella Valen, who she had trained. This outsider had been the first person ever to come to the Ataro Empire requesting to learn their unique ways. She had been Queen Altha's finest student and had returned to her world of Ashford-5 to see if she could implement the Ataro's ways. Now Queen Isabella was also a fighter, the same kind of temperament. Like Lena, she never took anything lying down. Perhaps, she could convince Queen Isabella to help rehabilitate Lena. She vowed to inquire, as soon as she could. Of course, everything depended upon her regaining her voice somehow. That thought snuffed out her ability to think clearly. Grief seeped into her mind.

The next thing she was really aware of was the dimming of the lights, indicating night was coming. Shortly, the pleasure devices began operating once more. For once, she welcomed it, because it took her own mind off her own situation. No voice, no queen! Was her life totally ruined as well?

Three days later, Neva knew something had gone very wrong with both Marjorie and the queen's personal assistant. Each day after breakfast, when her mind had finally risen above sex and eating, she was able to think clearly, Neva made contact with the emperor and then with her small group. This day, she was unable to contact the two women! She focused harder and expanded outward. Still nothing. She turned her head to try to see the two women, but could not. Queen Altha and Lena blocked her view on either side. Instead, she refocused and pervaded Marjorie's body. It was alive and breathing, but Marjorie was nowhere to be found.

What's happened to them? Queen Altha wailed silently in her mind.

I don't know. Both were below apathy. They couldn't take this torture. I think they thought they had died and left somehow. I am not sure, but they are nowhere to be found. I don't understand this, Queen Altha. I wish I knew. I'll keep trying.

Oh, so I can kill myself by going below apathy? How do you do that? inquired Lena, emboldened by this sudden discovery. *Wait, their bodies are still alive? How can that be?*

I can see Marjorie; she's breathing. How come she isn't responding? She's right there. I don't get it.

Neither do I. Neva had reached the limits of her knowledge. She chose not to answer Lena's first question.

Queen Altha suggested, *Perhaps we are spirits after all. The religious priests insist we are spirits or beings or souls. Perhaps, her soul left her body behind. Mind you, I'm not well-studied in such matters.* They chatted about this unexpected development, giving the three pause to think.

Okay, I see you. You are close. Keep walking ahead. It is below that building with the metal tanks. There must be a doorway. The battle cruiser had finally arrived above Gamelon-3. Captain Schmidt and Emperor Kino, accompanied by a hundred battle-armored soldiers landed at the base in six smaller transports. Lugar had protested their coming, but Gamelon's small fleet was no match for a single battle cruiser. When he learned what they wanted to see, he denied any knowledge of such things. Captain Schmidt ignored his protests, commandeering a number of local shuttles and forcing Lugar to come with them. Neva provided the directions to Emperor Kino, who relayed them on to the captain. They landed at a large parking area not far from the milk factory, though there were quite a number of other factories and buildings in the area. It was a commercial center.

"This is highly illegal. You are violating our rights. You can't go in there," Lugar continued to protest. Captain Schmidt motioned to one of his men, who smiled and placed Lugar in a vice grip. The door was locked.

"Open this door, Lugar, or we will blast it down," Captain Schmidt barked. From all the man's protests, he knew they were hiding something here, but he highly doubted it would be the women the emperor had suggested. No, bootleg guns or perhaps outlawed drugs. Those would be more like it. The Gamelons were known to traffic in most things illegal within the Federation of Planets.

"But you won't understand," Lugar whined, but was greeted with a cold, impassioned stare. He opened the lock. The men saw a lot of cylinders and mechanical apparatus.

However, a stairs lead to a sub-floor. "No, please, I beg you. Don't go down there. This is sacred to us Gamelons." Captain Schmidt ignored him, and headed down the steps. The emperor's personal assistant very carefully helped him down the stairs, and both were passed by the other men.

"Oh my god! What in the name of hell is this? Emperor! You were right. Lugar, I should blow your entire world to smithereens!" shouted the captain.

"Oh my!" Emperor Kino whispered. "It's worse than I imagined, captain. I must find my people who were kidnaped while I was en route to your ship." He and his assistant began walking further into the room, following the central path. On either side, five milking stations held five women, some of which turned their heads to see what was going on. The two walked nearly the length of the floor before they came to the more recent additions, just behind them were their people.

"Queen Altha. Ambassador Neva. Sector ID Minister Lena. We're here. Hang in there, while we sort this out and find a way to set you all free. Are these all women from other planets?" Neva nodded. That fact was rather obvious; their differing skin colors, facial features, and taller stature demarcated them as not native Gamelons.

"My god, this is beyond imagination," Captain Schmidt exclaimed, joining Emperor Kino. "These your women?"

"Yes, Ambassador Neva Burkhardt, President Snarry's personal ambassador to you, my Queen Neva, and one of our Sector ID Ministers, Lena, and their assistants. Now do you believe me?"

"Of course. We'll get to the bottom of this. Wait, what's that noise?" he asked. They had arrived at milking time. The men watched in horrified amazement, as the machines milked the women while sexually gratifying them. "We're going to need a whole lot of doctors and a whole lot more men," he whispered.

"But you don't understand," Lugar wailed.

"Okay, Lugar. What is this all about?" Captain Schmidt barked. Lugar had no choice but to fully explain. Slowly, both leaders began to understand the situation. There were hundreds of these milking plants scattered around the planet.

However, this one was dedicated to those women who were not native Gamelons. They didn't trust the milk these women produced. In case it did not have the same curative properties, they didn't want to mix it in with that produced by their own women.

When he finished, Captain Lugar ordered, "Lugar, you will immediately send word to all your space fleets that any captured women are to be returned to their home worlds at once. Now then, how do we undo these women here, those of the emperor's?"

"Of course. I'll send it right away. But there is no way to undo them. You cannot disconnect them, not until they die. Their breasts are producing milk at peak levels. They have to be milked two or three times each day."

"What do you mean they cannot be undone? Fix up their voices and fix up their breasts right now," he demanded.

"But we can't. We have no idea how to do that. We don't even know how to get their plastic skin covering off them. We've never had to do that before," Lugar wailed helplessly. "We need their milk to stay alive. The virus will kill all men in a week!"

"Are you saying your doctors and scientists cannot undo any of this?" Captain Schmidt asked incredulously. Lugar nodded vigorously.

Captain Schmidt ran his hands through his hair, quite exasperated. "Looks like we have a huge problem here, Emperor Kino. We best return to the battle cruiser and send for help. I suppose you would prefer to bring some of your Imperium doctors here?"

"Quite right. We both should pool our best doctors and medical machines. Plus, we should alert our leaders of this. Can you take some video of what we've found here and send that along? A movie is worth a million words with top leaders," Emperor Kino suggested. He turned to Queen Altha and added, "Hang in there a little longer. We'll bring our very best doctors here as soon as possible." She nodded. Lena cried, humiliated beyond all words.

Emperor Kino dropped by each day, trying to sound encouraging to the women, but Neva noticed he timed his visits carefully. He always came after they had been milked and fed, when they were at least able to think more clearly. Two more endless weeks passed before teams of doctors and scientists arrived from the Federation of Planets and from the Imperium. Finally, Neva saw bustling activity both day and night. First, they took samples of everything and observed the process the Gamelons used to turn women into their private milk cows.

With so many different modifications, they decided to split into teams, each one researching the cure for one specific detail. One doctor explained to the women, "First thing we'll be doing is modifying the enzymes in your liquid diets so you naturally stop lactating and dry up. That way, we can safely disconnect that part of the machine."

A week later, the one hundred seventy-six women finally ceased their massive milk production. To their great relief, the suction pumps were disconnected. Next, the researchers asked, if they should leave the pleasure devices operational, while they worked on the rest of the mess. Most all nodded affirmatively. In a way, this was a wise move, for it kept the women more or less relaxed. The daily showers also kept the researchers at bay for a few hours, proving to be only a minor nuisance for them.

Another week passed before they had a cure to undo the partial plastic skin conversion. They invented a solution to dissolve it and put that into the shower water. This time when the drying air began to flow, Neva's skin felt normal at long last. Things progressed rapidly after this point. Neva and her four companions were gently taken down from their mountings and carried directly to waiting medical machines.

Finally, the doctors could get a complete picture of what had been done to their bodies. At the emperor's insistence, they set to work on repairing their damaged voice boxes. If the women could talk, that would go a very long way. They could once more communicate their needs to the researchers and doctors. It took the team of doctors nearly two days to work out just how to repair the damaged voice boxes. In the meantime, they began reducing the women's breasts, gradually that is. Without the women being able to communicate how it was going, they opted to proceed with extreme caution.

Neva eavesdropped on their rather heated discussions over solutions to the voice box problems. At last, the team of doctors reached a consensus. One explained, "In order to ensure your voices return to normal, we are also going to rejuvenate your bodies physically at the same time. We calculate this will give you all the best chances for a full recovery of your voices. You will have fourteen year old bodies once more. Okay?" Neva nodded.

The doctors placed her in the machine, which totally enclosed her body. Then, she fell unconscious. When she awoke, she was lying in a bed covered with warm bedding. A doctor examined her eyes with a light and then asked, "How do you feel? Can you talk?"

Neva tried. "Can you hear me? Oh! It worked! I can talk at last. Thank you, thank you!"

"Excellent, excellent, Ambassador Burkhardt! Well done. By the way, we have adjusted the other women's breast sizes more or less to fit the clothing they wore when they arrived here. We found your spare clothes in your deep space transport. In your case, we were a bit baffled. Your breasts used to be rather large. We kept them that way, but we can always reduce them some more, if you prefer. We just didn't know."

"Can you make them like normal women's breasts, please? I don't want those monsters. I've had enough of breasts to last me a lifetime! Maybe I can have someone alter my dresses," Neva replied. She ignored the male voice in her head. After what she'd been through, she discovered she had some power over the psych's implanted behavior modifications. Some, but not all. She knew she still craved sexual sensations.

The doctor worked on her a little longer before releasing her into the care of the emperor and a couple of nurses, who had come with the medial staff. "What about Marjorie?" she asked, as the doctor finished her last alterations. "I know nothing can be done about my loss of arms, but what about her? I've not seen her much these past few days."

His face turned grim. "I'm terribly sorry about her. Both she and the queen's assistant didn't make it. We are not sure what happened, but they died during their long stay in the machine. The machines were keeping their physical bodies alive, pumping milk, but they had already passed away. I'm afraid we're finding many others who have also perished but whose bodies are being artificially kept alive producing milk. Honestly, Ambassador Neva, we've never seen anything remotely like this before."

He went on, "But there's a brighter side to this whole affair. We've also done extensive gene testing on the men of Gamelon-3. Yes, in their distant past, they did contract a virulent virus, and, yes, their women developed antibodies that fought off the infection. So originally, they were right in consuming their women's milk. Via it, they received the proper antibodies, just as normal babies receive such from their mothers. However, and this is very important, their own bodies have long ago begun producing the same antibody."

"What does that mean?" she asked, sensing what he was about to tell her.

"All this was unneeded. The men have been immune to the virus for at least two centuries now, as far as we can determine from the extensive gene study we've done. All this has been wholly unnecessary. Worse, they have no normal women left in their society, only some young girls."

"Can you undo some of them like you have for us?" Neva asked. "That would be the only humane thing to do."

The doctor smiled, "Ambassador, we are discussing that with the Federation's president and our own President Snarry, as we speak. Lugar has already been begging us to do that. I am sure some kind of arrangement can be made. If not, the Gamelons may well face extinction this time. Come on; let's get you dressed and out of here. Fresh air will do you good."

When the nurse entered to help her dress, she noticed her feet were different — flexible again. The nurse noticed her looking at her feet. "I hope we did the right thing. Queen Altha insisted on still being able to wear her fancy toe shoes. Plus, the emperor was most insistent. So we guessed you would like yours done that way too. Did we guess right?"

Neva smiled. "Thanks. Yes, I liked them. Hard to walk, but quite sexy and elegant. Are you going to be my assistant until we get back to Caltran?" She nodded.

A bit later, the nurse led her to a sunny porch, where Queen Altha and Lena were sitting basking in the warm sunlight. "Ah there you are at last. Come join us, Neva," Queen Altha said cheerily. From her tone, one would not have guessed the ordeal she'd just been through. Neva felt alive and mostly free from the behavior modifications. However, she noticed Lena was not. She looked morose. Her face was downcast. Melancholia had set in strongly.

Lena barked, "Here we all are, but look at us! We are useless now, helpless baggage, dependent on others for everything. Neva, you should have killed me back then. Can you do it now, please? I can't live like this. I don't know how you two get by, but I sure can't," Lena added, with a deep sigh.

Neva focused and sent calming waves over Lena's body, watching her body relax. "Has anyone found my necklace with the big blue crystal in it?" she asked. The nurse had and went off to fetch it. Neva relaxed. As long as she was still on Gamelon-3, she could use the buried giant crystal to amplify her powers, but if she lost her personal crystal, then she would have no choice but to return to Tierra and try to get another from one of the towers there. *That* she did not want to do. If she never returned there, she'd be happy.

"So have you heard? The war is over now. Officially. The two presidents signed a peace treaty," Queen Altha chatted. "Each party will be staying within their own spiral arm now, but they've agreed to cooperate, and will soon send ambassadors to each other's capital cities. Isn't that good news? We've ended the war. Peace at last. Neva, we couldn't have done it without you! Getting the facts of what was going on here on Gamelon-3 to Emperor Kino was the breakthrough he needed. You and he are Imperium heroes now."

Lena grumbled. "Right. Neva returns the hero, and I return utterly helpless and out of the only job I ever wanted, and completely helpless to boot. Fine reward for me, eh?"

"About that, Lena. I know someone who might be able

really to help you out. They have had a lot of experience helping women, who have lost their arms and such, learn to live independently, or so I'm told. If they are willing, would you at least give them a try?" Queen Altha asked. Neva focused. If Lena refused, she would override her and force her to consent!

"Well, are you sure they could help? Honestly, we are completely useless to everyone," Lena griped.

"It is worth a try, Lena. If you could regain some independence, that'd be terrific. I suppose you could return to Ataro and learn to be a queen for us, if you would prefer that. Of course, you would have to get your waist drastically reduced and your feet altered like ours."

"No thanks! I'll give them a try," Lena replied. Then, she realized she'd just been played by Queen Altha. By asking her that, she'd readily consented to try this other, as yet unknown, approach.

"You said that on purpose, didn't you?" Lena asked sternly, using her old voice pattern.

Queen Altha smiled. "Yes. If you'll excuse me, I'll make that call now. Back in a while with good news, I hope."

At noon, their nurse brought a tray of food out onto the porch. "Looks like I get to feed you. I've got hot tea at long last. I sure had to do some digging in the ship's galley to find it. Hope you appreciate it," she chatted. While they were eating, Queen Altha rejoined them.

"Well, that took some doing. Just getting to a long distance comm channel was a bit of a challenge. Okay, got some news everyone. We are heading home tomorrow. President Snarry wants you to meet with him as soon as you arrive on Caltran. He's sending a new personal assistant for you, Neva, and she'll rendezvous with us when we get to Ataro. Lena, we'll be dropping you off with Queen Isabella Valen, as we pass by Ashford-5."

"What? Ashford-5? We don't even have a base there any longer. We abandoned it years ago, after they blew up our fuel refinery," Lena protested.

"Yes, but Queen Isabella promised me she would personally see you get all the training you can handle and a full round of their special therapy, whatever that entails. She says you'll be back to battery in no time, but I think she's exaggerating a little, if you ask me."

"So she has a long distance comm set? How can that be? Our technology isn't supposed to be in the hands of the primitive worlds," Lena asked.

"I surely don't know. Probably she brought it there when she returned from the Senate on Caltran. You can ask her though. Right now, I'm famished."

Chapter 8 Arrivals

It was early May 1290 on Tierra. The first of the baby boomers had turned fourteen, having been born in 1276, when a hugely disproportionate number twins were born. Nadja and Diego had been running the only school on Tierra, the one built by the aliens before they had abandoned Tierra. Many hoped they would never return. Her gift with languages proved useful to her, and she'd just graduated her first class of young people. Some twenty hand-picked fourteen year olds just completed her eight year educational program. It had blossomed, and she now had sixty others in a mixed-grades type of school, far more than she could easily handle. She depended upon Diego rather heavily. Both were looking for other potential teachers to lend a hand, so the small, pilot program could be expanded. Her graduating class consisted of young adults from all three sectors of Tierra, including the Easterlings. She had turned forty-two, but she looked vibrant, even though she still wore the enormous lip plates.

Queen Isabella was thirty and also doing well in her role as the supreme justice for all the kingdoms. Her revolutionary political changes were working out well thus far. The kingdoms all elected their own leaders, called rey or reina. Their elected senators had done a fairly decent job of establishing individual kingdom laws. While they varied a little between the many kingdoms, on the whole, she was satisfied with them, just as she was satisfied with the arrangements she had made with her first-born daughter, Amy, who had turned fourteen.

After the birth of Gabriella, she decided Amy would become her successor. She and Hernando discussed this at length, and he convinced her. "Look, if done at an early age, she can adapt far better than you did. Far less trauma, don't you think?" She could only agree with that, and they went ahead and had Amy's arms removed and her feet altered so she could wear only the toe shoes like Isabella wore. Why? Isabella already made arrangements to send Amy off to Queen

Altha for her official training. Thus, Amy's body had to meet the requirements the Ataro System demanded of their queens and emperor. At only a year and a half old, the surgery was done by Inez using her medical machine at Elegant Fashions Inc. Thus, Amy grew up without them and, at fourteen, had adjusted very well indeed, considering.

Amy Valen Gervasi had company, though, the infamous Gang of Eight, part of the graduating class of 1290. When she enrolled in Nadja's school at age six, Jan Bellweather had joined her. Among those "in the know," Amy and Jan were simply continuing their previous lifetime relationship. Once they had been emperor and empress of Tierra, a failed attempt to bring law and order between the kingdoms. Amy vowed to get it right this time around and had gone along with her mother's wishes. Jan was one of Bart and Anita's twins; he still was the communications expert for the Underground.

The others in the Gang of Eight were Bernardo Valen Gervasi, who was Amy's twin brother; Adrianna del Baldo, who was Nadja's son; Henry and Nita Valen Franks, who were Inez's unexpected twins — she was now fifty-eight; Drina Blackwater, who was one of Lord Emilio and Anita's twins and also a katalyein who kept Amy company as she also had no arms; and Ben Blackwater, who was one Ken and Crystal's twins. The Gang of Eight were known for their constant playfulness, and harmless, but sometimes educational pranks.

For example, one day when Nadja was giving them a verbal test, she called upon Drina and Nita to answer one problem. Both did so, but spoke in the click language of Agon-3. Nadja had been the one, who had first studied that language, providing the learning discs for the Imperium. The Gang of Eight spent the previous evening using the computer and the discs to pick up that language. Of course, the whole class began giggling, and only Nadja could understand their answers.

Another time, Drina and Amy concocted an experiment they demonstrated for the class. Using their feet, they added the liquids together only to produce a huge geyser of foam that shot up three feet into the air. This one was "educational" or so they claimed, but they had to clean up the mess they made.

Their friends helped them with that, though.

As the gang grew older, their pranks became commonplace. At least once a week, they'd devised some new "educational" feature. However, the last couple of years, they began to take a romantic interest in each other. Pranks took a back seat to their hormones. Of course, Amy and Jan was a pair. Henry and Adrianna were dating now, as were Ben and Drina. Nita chose not to date just yet. She was helping her mother and older sister out with Elegant Fashions Inc, fully intending to devote her life to designing clothing as well. Bernardo had taken up fighter training and was something of a school "protector." Exchange City was home to some of the more disreputable people on Tierra, mostly from the half-breeds — the tag applied to the offspring of aliens and local men and women. Bernardo made sure none of the sixty-some students were ever bothered or bullied by the seedier elements of the city.

At supper, Queen Isabella announced, "Amy, Jan, we are going to be hosting a new arrival here. I want you all to look after her as much as possible." Hernando held another bite up for her to eat.

Amy put her fork down with her foot, somewhat annoyed with this sudden news. "What? How come we are just now finding out about it? Who is she?"

"This is going to take some explaining, dear. I just got a comm network call from Queen Altha. We had a long talk. It seems they have ended the alien's war. Of course, she and the emperor of Ataro had a good deal of help from Neva Valen Burkhardt, of all people. Anyway, she and the other women were captured and tortured. One of her companions is a Sector ID Minister, Lena Squire. She lost her arms, in addition to suffering unspeakable tortures. In order to fix them all up, they had to use the old rejuvenation machines, and their bodies are now the same age as yours, fourteen. Anyway, Lena will be coming here. We're to help her recover. Apparently, she's a basket case, according to Queen Altha. She used to be a very powerful woman, but has been reduced to being utterly helpless. She is loaded with traumas as well, so we've quite a challenge ahead of us."

"Mom! A Sector ID Minister? That cannot be a good idea!" Amy barked. "There's no telling what she'll learn about us. Our secrets will not be safe with her around."

"She has a point," Jan broke in, supporting her.

Bernardo spoke up, "I'll look after her mom and keep her out of trouble."

"Thanks son. That might be wise. Amy, you must show her how to do things with your feet. You and Drina can share those duties."

"Sure thing," Drina replied. "She must be feeling really bad. I wonder how old she really is?"

"What're we supposed to do about our *mentales* gifts? Keep them a secret from her?" asked Adrianna. The Gang of Eight often dined with Queen Isabella. While Nita and Henry lived a short distance away at Elegant Fashions Inc, they were often a common sight at the supper table there in the Imperial Castle.

"If she's a Sector ID Minister, she must be aware many of us on Tierra have the gift. So don't try to hide it," Isabella ordered. "Sip of tea, dear," she suggested to Hernando, who smiled and lifted a spoon of tea up to her mouth. With her enormous lip plates, this was the only way that she could drink. Everything was made awkward by the neck rings that made her head immobile. Actually, her neck vertebrae had been fused, and the rings protected her neck, should she take a fall. Still, she had endured it for fourteen years, but she could never have managed without the constant support of Hernando, who still doted on her, and she, him.

Drina spoke up. "Have you contacted the Underground to set up therapy sessions for her? If not, I can do that for you."

"Would you dear? That would be helpful. Tell them to expect a very serious trauma case," Isabella replied. "Now then, I want you all to promise me you'll help this Lena learn to do well on her own. She must have been a very independent and powerful woman, before she was captured and tortured. Since Neva, Queen Altha, and Lena have been responsible for ending the war, we owe it to Lena to try our best to salvage her life."

"But what if she finds out things she shouldn't know about us and the Underground?" Ben asked, growing a bit worried.

Isabella sighed. "Kids, if she does, then before she leaves here, I'll do a Mind Wipe on her. I hate to do things like that, but I will, *if* she finds out things she shouldn't know. Will that be acceptable?"

"Sure mom," Amy replied. That her mother was willing to go to that extreme to protect them was enough to satisfy her and the others.

"Amy and Drina, when she comes, I'll have her stay in your room. That way, you can show her how to do thing in private. I think that'll work out better, don't you?"

"As long as Jan and I can have some private times," Amy replied. The others giggled; they knew what that meant. With so many around the castle, finding private moments was challenging.

Isabella grinned, but it wasn't visible, but her emotion was detected by the eight kids, who smiled back. She added, "She should be here in two days. That should give my staff time to get your room fixed up for a third teen. And yes, that means you'll be getting a wider bed, Amy, Drina." Both teens giggled. "Also, *no* pranks on Lena. She's in a *very* fragile state right now," she added sternly, hoping they'd at least obey this request.

As the deep space transport dropped out of hyperspace above Ashford-5, Queen Altha explained, "I can't get over the fact we are all fourteen again — so young. Anyway, Lena, you'll be staying with Queen Isabella Valen Gervasi. She has twins that are fourteen too. Actually, she told me she's got eight of them, who are always hanging out at her place, the Imperial Castle. So you'll have plenty of company your own physical age, that is. Gosh, it's so weird being as old as I am and yet with such a young body!"

"Tell me about it! I've now got to relive all those years as a helpless cripple, unable to do a damned thing for myself. I still think Neva should have obeyed me and just killed me when I begged her," Lena replied testily. "Maybe I can find a way on this planet. Do they have cliffs I can jump off of?"

Neva countered, "Lena, with a personal assistant, it really isn't as bad as you are making it out to be. Without one, then yes, I'd agree with you. Still, personal assistants are easy to find. You're now young and quite attractive too, if I do say so myself."

"I've never been much on men. You should know that by now. Who cares about being attractive? Certainly not me. It's only what you can *do* in this world that matters, and I can't *do* a god damned thing now," she grumbled once more. As the ship began its descent, in her mind, Lena began reviewing all she knew about Ashford-5. There were an alarming number of telepaths on this world. Yellow eyes. Yes, that was their identifying characteristic. Neva had them. She decided she'd keep her eyes open and learn all that she could about this mysterious, Closed World. If nothing else, she might gain valuable intelligence for the Imperium. Then again, why bother, she thought. No one will pay any attention to me any longer, not a helpless cripple.

The ship settled down onto the long deserted spaceport. Giant dust clouds rose around the ship, the first to land in some fourteen years. Over the intercom, the pilot's voice explained, "We'll be waiting for the dust to settle before disembarking." A half hour later, the door finally opened, and a security man disembarked. Lena watched from a window, knowing full well the protocol he was following. Disengage security locks; check for security breaches. If all went well, according to Queen Altha, he'd retrieve one of the electric shuttle vehicles. Apparently, this Imperial Castle was located on the southeast corner of this vast plateau.

What Lena couldn't shake off was how strange this world seemed to her senses. It was nearly noon, if the dim, orange-red sun's position could be believed. So dim, she thought. How can any plant grow in such light? The air was filled with many strange scents. Trees? She thought she could smell resinous trees, such as pines. She could see the dark, tall mountains both to the north and south of the plateau; some still had snow covers on their peaks. The eerie silence was also a bit foreboding. Perhaps, she thought, I'd feel better if this was a working spaceport. I'm being stranded here.

Almost as if reading her thoughts, Queen Altha suggested, "If things don't work out for you here, Lena, just have Queen Isabella give me a call. I can send a transport to come pick you up. I'm sure the Imperium will be returning here soon. Come on. I'm going to go with you. I want to see Queen Isabella too. We've not seen each other in over fourteen years. She was my best student, you know, and the first outsider ever to come to the Ataro System to learn our administrative ways. Did you want to come along too, Neva?"

"No thanks. I'll wait here for you. I'm a cosmopolitan woman now, not a backward primitive," she replied. Queen Altha merely smiled. The nurse-turned-assistant helped both women down the ramp, especially the queen, who could barely walk in her toe shoes. Once inside the small electric car, she pointed out their destination to the security guard, and they set off at a rapid pace. A dust cloud followed them, as they headed as straight as possible for the southeast corner. Soon, the tall tower and then the castle appeared on the horizon followed by Exchange City's Admin Building, which was mostly occupied by Elegant Fashions Inc.

At the edge of the spaceport, the security guard had to step out to deactivate the perimeter barrier. They drove onto the wide road that led into the city, but turned left at the first corner and a few hundred feet beyond that, entered the main gates of the castle. Not surprising, Queen Isabella and her group were standing in the main courtyard waiting for them. Queen Altha remembered years ago how difficult it'd been to take Queen Isabella by surprise and smiled at those pleasant memories.

After being helped out of the car, she grinned broadly and walked carefully up to her former student. "It's so very good to see you again, Queen Isabella. You look like you haven't aged a bit." The two women pressed their bodies into each other. Lena gasped at the sight. Queen Isabella looked pretty much like what she'd imagined from the descriptions she'd uncovered during her investigation of the senator's disappearance back on Caltran. It was just the stark reality of her appearance that so shocked her.

While she'd anticipated the woman's lack of arms, the neck rings made her almost immobile. She also wore the pipe corset and impossible toe shoes that Queen Altha insisted on wearing. But the gigantic lip plates gave her face a very strange appearance indeed. Lena began listening to the exchange; they were speaking Imperium Standard. For a moment, she regretted no longer having her ULAT box around her waist. How was she ever going to communicate with these people?

"I'm so very glad to see you again, Queen Altha. You're so much younger looking. Fourteen again. You could be one of my kids. And this must be our guest, Lena Squire. Forgive us, Lena; Queen Altha and I haven't seen each other in ages. I'm Queen Isabella Valen Gervasi, though you might be more familiar with my former title of Senator Isabella. This is my husband, Hernando. This is Nadja del Baldo and her husband Diego. Nadja is our resident Imperium linguist and now our first school teacher. She was married to Governor Konrad Burkhardt, when she first came to Tierra. This is Inez Franks, who runs Elegant Fashions Inc in the old Admin Building next door."

Lena saw both Queen Isabella and Inez were very well dressed. Formal pod-silk, satin gowns, black nylon hose, patent leather shoes — both would blend in with the most sophisticated crowds on Caltran! Even Hernando in his pod-silk suit would fit right in as well. Queen Isabella continued the introductions. "And this is the infamous Gang of Eight, our teens. Well some are our children, and the rest are Nadja's and Inez's and some friends of ours. They went to school together and have been staying here with us. My twins, Amy and Bernardo. Come on you two, nod for her or something. You know I can't point you out," she pleasantly chastised the playful duo.

Amy took a step forward and back; Bernardo waved a hand. Lena noticed Amy also had no arms and was wearing similar toe shoes as her mother. She also must be wearing a pipe corset, for her waist seemed way too small compared to the others. "My younger daughter, Gabriella." She waved rather bashfully. "Amy's constant companion, Jan Bellweather. Adrianna, Nadja's daughter. Nita, Inez's daughter and her twin brother, Henry. Drina Bolivar and Ben Blackwater, close family friends." Lena also saw Drina had no arms either, but unlike Amy, she wasn't wearing a corset or the nasty toe shoes. She wore flats. What struck Lena the most, as she tried hard to begin to match a face with a name, was every one of these people had yellow eyes with brown speckles! They were all telepaths!

"Yes, Lena, all telepaths. We all have the *mentales* gifts. We can talk more about that later on," Queen Isabella said, as if reading her thoughts. "You'll be rooming with Amy and Drina, who can help you learn how they do things. However, I've assigned Bernardo to be your personal trainer. He'll be responsible for your well-being, while you are with us. You can depend upon him with your life. Now then, let's go inside. I've had some refreshments prepared, and I know Queen Altha and I have a lot to discuss, and you, Lena, probably have quite a number of questions for us as well. Oh yes, I forgot. Welcome to Tierra or Ashford-5 as you call our world."

That brought a slight smile to Lena's face. *Questions? You bet I have!* For a moment, Lena forgot about her physical situation. Now, she had the chance to meet directly with Senator Isabella and discover just how they'd been miraculously rescued from the clutches of Senate President Carlos, who she knew was now that pathetic escort woman. She also realized he looked exactly like Queen Isabella, that is, with all the physical restraints.

"I should not really stay very long. Everyone's waiting for me to return," Queen Altha explained, as they all sat down at the huge oak table in the Great Hall. Lena felt dwarfed in this room, which could hold many hundreds of people at one time. The two quickly began chatting about official progress of her implementation of the Ataro system of administration, none of which Lena could follow.

Sensing that, Drina and Amy, who sat beside her, talked with her. "So Lena, you are a Sector ID Minister? What sector, if that isn't classified information?" Amy asked. "We're quite knowledgeable about some things, you see."

"Hub Sector 1, which includes Baltzar-4, Proxima Prime, and the other nearby worlds, the heart of the

Imperium." She sighed; she'd spent her life working her way to the very pinnacle of ID Minister postings, and now she'd lost that forever.

"Wow. Impressive. We're pleased to have you here with us for a while," Amy replied cordially.

"Like this, use your toes," Drina whispered, showing her how to help herself to the tea.

"Sorry, got these shoes on, and I can't get them off," Lena whispered back.

"No problem, allow me," Bernardo whispered. "I've had a lot of practice with helping mom. You aren't going to get those darn lip plates are you?"

Lena cracked a smile, "Good lord no! They're awful. You can barely understand her. My god. I just realized you're all speaking Imperium Standard."

Drina giggled. "Of course. We're all multilingual here. Have to be. You see, there are three different languages spoken on Tierra. There's the Easterlings dialect, Midlands where we are now, and Westerlings. Plus, most all the lords, ladies, and nobles — the wealthier ones that is — all wear those lip plates. Even my mom and dad. So we have to be able to understand the lip plate wearers, which is almost like three more dialects. And then there's the Imperium Standard, which we've learned so we can communicate with the aliens — er, the Rigels, who used to run the spaceport. Plus, we've been around Nadja and Adrianna far too long. You know she's the best linguist in the Imperium, don't you? Well, anyway, she's got volumes of other languages. We sometimes learn some of those too. The strange click languages are most fascinating. One time we all learned the click language of Agon-3 and began answering Nadja's classroom questions in Agon. It brought laughs to the whole class. We're kind of mischievous, aren't we, Amy?"

Amy laughed. "Yes, but Lena, mom's made us all promise not to pick on you or tease you while you're here. So Bernardo, no tricking of Lena here."

"What? Me? Trick anybody? Why, that's never, ever happened, sis," Bernardo replied, feigning a serious mien. The teens all laughed, bringing an involuntary smile to Lena's face.

"Seriously, Lena, you'll find we know quite a lot, far

more than you might think," Jan spoke up from the other side of Amy. "We know the Imperium thinks we're a primitive society. While that may be so, we like it that way, but that doesn't mean we're ignorant. You may be surprised at what all we do know about the world."

Lena asked, "So how many telepaths are there on Ashford-5, er Tierra? I've always wondered that. All of you are, that much I can see from your eyes."

Drina giggled. "Lots. Actually, Rafaela is the authority on the numbers, but I'd guess one in twenty has the *mentales* gift. Some of them work in the towers. We call this gift *mentales*, but really it's a mental psi power, because it goes far beyond simple telepathy. In fact, telepathy is the smallest part of our special gifts, which we all try to use to help our world do better. Some of us work in one of the many towers. They're called *Círculo de la Torres*. Each tower has one or more circles called *Círculo de mentes*. A Circle usually has nine members plus a Regulator, who monitors the physical bodies the others, while they were working as a unified whole. We've got two full Circles here in the Imperial Tower. They work for Queen Isabella and the Justice or Supreme Court."

"Incredible. What kind of powers do you have?" Lena asked. She knew Neva could kill with a single thought, at least that was what her investigations had suggested.

"Centuries ago, Marisol compiled a big list of the many different forms the gifts can take," Drina chatted. "But since then, more have to be added. Rafaela's the expert on that. Me, I am very rare and special. I am a katalyein." From Lena's blank stare, she knew she had to explain further. "You see, sometimes when a young person reaches puberty and their *mentales* gifts should blossom, they have severe mental blocks, preventing it from happening. Those blockages cause them to get the Verge Sickness, which if untreated, causes a high fever and a sure death. Normal treatment often fails in the worst cases. That's where we katalyein come in, you see."

Lena didn't, and she explained further. "We are a catalyst telepath. We have the gift to be able to disintegrate that mental block and cure them, allowing their inherent *mentales* gifts to blossom. Without us, they'd die within a week at most. But katalyein are very rare, found mostly in the greater Brom area, where I come from and where we'll be going in a while. All katalyein are women and are born without arms, you see. In Brom, if you see a woman without arms, she's very likely a katalyein. People come from all over Tierra to get our help before it is too late. My mom's one too. I inherited it from her or so Rafaela says."

"She's right. She's already saved one boy here in Exchange City, who came down with the Verge Sickness," Bernardo pointed out. "Now you have to watch out for Amy and Jan. Those two have *really* powerful *mentales* gifts!"

Both Amy and Jan flushed. "You're just jealous, that's all," Amy countered, teasingly. All the kids laughed. "Don't worry, Lena, Bernardo's got strong gifts too. That's why mom assigned him to you. He's the best fighter among us all. Everyone on Tierra uses swords and daggers. All other distance type weapons have long been outlawed by the Blackwater Ultimatum centuries ago. If you want to settle a dispute with another, both must have close contact and an equal chance. Things like d-guns are totally forbidden. Bows and arrows are only used for hunting. It's a serious crime to use a bow to harm someone; the penalties are quite steep. Of course, Drina and I can't use a sword, but Bernardo is a hot shot with one. You should be quite safe with him around. Plus, he's pretty good with physical combat styles. Oh, I think your term for that is martial arts."

Lena sighed. "Before now, I'd have been interested in checking out your style, Bernardo. Now even that has been taken from me." Her deep sense of loss was felt by all and a hush followed.

Queen Altha's chat with Isabella broke the silence. "Okay then, I must really be going. I look forward to your visit this winter. I'll have everything prepared for Amy and Jan. If she is as good as you are, she ought to be finished with her training within months."

"Thanks, I really do appreciate all you've done for us. If something comes up to delay us, I'll let you know," Queen Isabella replied. Queen Alta and the nurse arose, and Hernando escorted them out to the waiting electric vehicle.

She turned to the teens. "Okay kids, why don't you go do something, and let Lena and I have a private chat. When we're done, Amy and Drina can help get her settled in."

"Cards?" Drina suggested, as the teens got up to leave. Several agreed with her idea, and they headed off chatting among themselves. Soon, the two were alone.

"Well, Lena, I suspect you've many questions to ask. I'll be up front with you. I've left orders no one will lie to you or twist the truth. Will that be satisfactory?" Queen Isabella asked, hoping this was a good way to begin, and to get Lena to open up a little. Of course, she desperately needed therapy, but that would have to come a bit later.

"Kind of you. Okay. Then, you'll really answer my questions?" Lena asked.

"Absolutely. What would you like to know?" she asked, suspecting much.

"Well, I'll be frank. I've done quite a lot of investigation into your abduction back on Caltran. I know most of what Senate President Carlos did to you and your two wives. Which reminds me, what happened to those two young women?"

"They couldn't stand to live like I'm forced to live. They died and have new bodies. They're Amy and Jan now," she replied.

Lena gave her a funny look, but went on. "I know he kidnaped you and your wives and did all this to you, keeping you as slave telepaths. I also know all of you were mysteriously rescued somehow. I 'borrowed' another telepath and interrogated that escort woman, who was found in the estate home after you left. I know she's somehow Carlos, but no one else does. I've kept that to myself. She's living the life of an escort woman, a lady of the night. She hates it, but can't do anything about it. She, like me, is totally helpless now."

"Serves him right for what he did to us. He fused our neck vertebrae. We have to wear these neck rings to protect our necks. One small fall and I'd break my neck and die. The rings protect me from that. I'll give him that much credit. The medical machines can't repair that damage."

"I wondered about that. So that's why you're still wearing the rings. Makes sense, but that must make your physical situation almost intolerable," she replied.

"Very nearly so. I depend utterly on Hernando. He's a god-send."

"Well, you've a powerful case, Queen Isabella. You could ask the Imperium for substantial damages and receive them. Anyway, what I want to know is just how you managed that incredible escape? How did you get off-world? How did you get to the Ataro System?" Lena asked what she most wanted to know, but was never able to figure out.

"Amy and Jan's doing. Jan suspected trouble might come and purchased us a deep space transport ship ahead of time, concealing it well. She was able to use her *mentales* gifts to break into the senator's computer room, where he also had the medical machines. She made all the arrangements. When the senator and his wife returned, I stunned everyone, as they entered. Amy and Jan used his machines on him. Jan so wanted him to experience what he'd done to us, you see. She planted fake orders with the shuttle, and it took us into the city. Personally, I got totally lost after that — one crazy move after another. Many hours later, we got to Jan's new ship, and she and Amy flew it out of there. Even though it was fully fueled, we could only get about halfway home and had to stop somewhere. I decided to give the Ataro System a try, and Queen Altha was quite receptive of my learning their system of administration. When I finally passed all her tests, Jan and Amy flew us home. If you want more details about all Jan's crazy moves, you'll have to ask her."

"But I don't understand. Jan and Amy — they were just as you are now. No arms, neck rings, lip plates, corset, toe shoes. How could they have done any of that?" Lena asked. At first, she didn't believe a word Isabella was telling her. However, she remembered Drina mentioning their gifts went far beyond mere telepathy.

"Telekinesis is part of it. Those two are quite powerful in that arena. Me, that's not part of my skill set. Each *mentales* gifted has their own capabilities. There's quite an extensive list of the manifestations that have surfaced among us. Does that help a bit?"

"Yes. So would you like to file a claim? You could easily

get several million credits in compensation, senator."

"I suppose so. Funds can be useful."

"I'll somehow see that gets done, but I don't know how just now. Say, is that deep space transport still around?" Lena asked, tying up loose ends.

"Yes, we intend to use it, when we really do need to go to another planet, like this winter to visit Queen Altha. Getting fuel is a problem though. I'm sorry, but we stole fuel from the abandoned spaceport. When or if they ever come back, we fully intend to pay for what we took."

"Heck, they probably will not even miss it."

"Sorry, I am smiling, but of course you can't see it."

"What is with those huge lip plates anyway? I'd have thought you'd have gotten your lips repaired. Oh, you don't have the medical machines here. I forgot," Lena amended her question hastily.

"Oh yes. We do have quite a few of them. Jan brought back some of the very latest models, but that's fourteen plus years ago now. Here on Tierra, the lords, ladies, and wealthier class are very fashion conscious. These lip plates are one of the currently 'in' things. You'll find many wearing them. It's rather a status symbol these days. At least, if you see someone wearing them, you know they are important in some way. However, some of the younger new lords and ladies have yet to adopt them."

"I see. Good tip. Does everyone speak Imperium Standard?" Lena asked.

Isabella laughed. "Heavens no. Only a few of us do. Nadja has prepared some computer language learning discs for you. There are three dialects spoken on Tierra. Easterlings, Midlands, and Westerlings. However, right here, we're at the border of the Midlands and the Westerlings. There are very few Easterlings around here. That sector is thousands of miles to the east. So focus on Midlands first and then Westerlings. We'll have you speaking enough to get by in a few days. Thanks to Nadja, language will not be a barrier for you."

"That's a relief. I always depended on my ULAT box, but now I couldn't turn it on if I had to." She sighed, but there was a distinctive catch in her breath, indicative of a great feeling of loss and grief.

"My turn. Do you have any clothes with you?"

"No, just what I am wearing. We lost everything mostly."

"Figured. Well, Inez has volunteered to outfit you at no cost. You'll be a walking advertisement for her wares. I'll send you, Drina, and Amy over there in a bit. You'll share a room with those two. Honestly, Drina can really teach you how to do a great many things for yourself. Amy often cheats and uses her telekinetic powers, which Drina doesn't have. But Drina always teases her about using them. Kind of funny in a way."

Isabella continued, "I'm going to have those two work with you in the mornings. In the afternoons, Bernardo will take over. Our first objective is to get you a bit more functional. Then, I'll send you up to Brom, where you can get your therapy sessions and more training. You'll love Brom — at least in the summertime. In the harsh winters, they get something like twenty feet of snow up there."

"Got a map? What's this therapy thing everyone keeps mentioning? I'm fine, really. Helpless, but fine," Lena asked and insisted.

"Forgive me. I forgot. This way. Over here is a map of our world. Crap, I can't point. Oh, I'll use my nose. We are here. Plateau Grado. Southeast corner. These are the Goza Mountains, which divide the Westerlings over here from the Midlands here. Because of our ancient climate shift, the breadbasket lands are way down south here. Way over here is the Buku Hills, which separates the Midlands from the Easterlings. Brom is way up north here. We call this city Exchange City, because the aliens used to deliver the iron and gold to us here. Our people also traded furs and such with the aliens as well. It's kind of like a melting pot. There are quite a few mixed men and women here. You know, sex never sleeps. Bernardo will keep you away from those women, though. Does this help orient you a bit?"

"Yes, quite a lot. About this therapy?" Lena reminded Queen Isabella.

"We'd best sit again. Long story. How do I explain it? Benjamina, some of the Brom katalyein, and others including

Rafaela, invented it. It's the most remarkable thing. It erases the emotional trauma a person has suffered. It erases physical pain and unconsciousness times as well, but most importantly, nearly everyone discovers they are truly an immortal spiritual being in the process. Quite remarkable. You'll just have to wait and experience it for yourself."

She went on, "Fourteen years ago, just after Benjamina passed away and got a new baby body over in the Easterlings, they built a large building, where they give therapy sessions now. It's called the Trauma and Spiritual Rehabilitation Center. However, I must warn you. Some of the therapy givers have very strange physical bodies. Oh this is going to be so hard to explain," Isabella sighed.

"Go on, I'm listening," Lena hinted, growing a bit more curious. Had they stolen or kidnaped others, like the men of Gamelon-3?

"Well, in ancient times, Tierra used to have a pantheon of gods and goddesses. Five — a pentagram. The five were or are very powerful spiritual beings, which do not need to have or use a human body as we do. Anyway, Lysandra is the Goddess of Life and Death. She looks after the welfare of women, though for her aid, she always extracts a sacrifice from those women she helps. Then there is Calder, the God of Waters. He used to be worshiped by those who make use of the oceans and rivers. Wystan is the God of Battles and Warriors. He's the men's god, and he loves to create conflict and strife so that men fight and he can watch and enjoy. Ariana is the Goddess of Fertility. No one has really seen her, but we all know she has been having quite an effect on us all. Alleric is at the top of their pentagram, all powerful, but he appears to be seldom mixing in our affairs."

"Now some years ago, Wystan disappeared and hasn't been seen since. Calder modified young women's bodies, turning them into his priestesses and giving them the power to heal the sick and injured, along with blessing ships. When he disappeared from Tierra, all those powers he was giving to his Daughters of the Seas vanished, leaving those women far more helpless than even I am. You see, they have no arms and only one very strange leg. All that they are physically able to do is

116

hop. Benjamina gathered them all up, rescuing them from a certain death. She trained them to deliver her therapy, and those women have become some of the very best therapy givers on Tierra. You are likely to have one of them assisting you. They are called mermaids for short, because their strange bodies look somewhat like such a mythical creature."

"When the war came here and the aliens blew up your refinery on one of our moons, that moon literally exploded. We believe Alleric somehow put it back together and saved our world from being annihilated. Then, Ariana struck with her fertility enhancements. My goodness, fourteen years ago, we had a baby boom! Never has so many twins been born in one year. It is amazing. Plus, the men grew breasts and actually shared the nursing duties. Now things are back to normal, though I still appreciated what the men endured. So things have been a little strange around here."

"All this is truly rather hard to believe," Lena admitted. She didn't believe much of all this. "So you worship these as your gods?"

"Well, actually no. In ancient times, there was something called the Church of God, but that's been more or less extinct for centuries. There's no organized religion on Tierra. Women in very desperate need sometimes pray to Lysandra, but few are willing to pay the price of her intervention on their behalf. No one I know of has ever seen the fertility god. Or Alleric for that matter. Certainly no one prays to them," Queen Isabella explained, but realized Lena didn't believe much of what she was saying.

"Well, I've taken up far too much of your time. Let's get you to your room and then over to Elegant Fashions Inc to get you some descent clothes. I'd suggest you at least get one or two fancy outfits. We do have parties and formal occasions here. At those times, you'll want to be dressed up for sure. Follow Inez's suggestions and you can't go wrong. Ah, here come Amy and Drina now." Lena suspected Isabella had summoned them via telepathy. How else could they arrive at just the right moment?

"Hi. Come on; we're going to show you around the castle and where our room's at," Drina said cheerily. "It's easy to get lost around here, but just ask anyone you come across. They can direct you. It took me a couple of weeks to figure it all out. The only place you can't get into will be the actual tower proper. They are doing useful work there and don't want to be disturbed. You'll see. Come on."

A short while later, the three teens accompanied by Bernardo headed over to Elegant Fashions Inc. Drina chatted, "I'm going to get me a new gown to wow Ben with at the next dance. I do look good in cherry red. You should get one too, Amy. Jan'll appreciate it."

"Oh she can't keep her hands off me as it is," Amy teased Drina. Both laughed.

Bernardo just said, "Ignore those two."

"Do all the women have incredibly long hair here?" Lena asked. She had quietly noticed Isabella's fell to her ankles, a rich, wavy black. Amy's was also long and wavy, reaching her knees. Drina's was also black, slightly wavy, and falling to her knees as well. Now that she thought about it, thus far, all the women she'd seen had very long tresses. Hers was dramatically shorter, but it had grown some since her imprisonment. Hers fell to her shoulders, but she was unable to cut it short herself. The men kept theirs cut just above their shoulders.

Drina explained, "We women like long hair. Over in the Easterlings, both the men and women believe they'll lose part of their life energy, if they should ever cut their hair. Men wear theirs in a single braid, while the women have two braids. Often, their hair nearly touches the floor. Around here in the Midlands, women trim theirs to about the middle of their backs, but the Westerlings women let theirs just grow as long as it wants." She then added, "Don't worry. Amy and I will show you how to brush out your hair. We help each other with it at night."

"Hi Inez. We're here. Need everything for Lena here," Amy announced gaily, as the three stepped out of the elevator on the top floor.

"Mom's napping at the moment. I'm Lilly, her eldest. Nita," she called out. "They're here, front and center please," she called out. "Okay, Lena, let's get you properly measured first. Then, we can go over your likes and dislikes. We've a big catalog of styles from which to choose."

Nita poked her head out of a side room. "Hi'y'all. We've worked out some suggestions for you, Lena. Isabella was quite specific. You're to have some day dresses like Drina and Amy are wearing, simple for you to put on and take off. Then, you are to have some fine leathers for outside adventures and horse riding. Plus, you just *have* to have some fancy gowns for the balls and such. That's where you have a wide variety of choices." Lilly finished her measurements, and the teens headed over to a desk, where Nita paged through the catalogue. Bernardo looked over the men's suits, and then sat down for a nap. He knew from past experiences the teens would be here probably until suppertime. He was just thankful he didn't have a girlfriend just yet. Time enough for such things later on. Besides, girlfriends were obviously *very* expensive.

"How do you make satin?" Lena asked, admiring some of the fancy gowns.

Lilly explained, "Some of the material we import, but that's pretty well dried up, since the aliens abandoned the spaceport. We make our own from pod silk imported from the northern lands and from silk worms in the far south. The second floor is tied up with fabric construction. Farmers bring in wagon loads of pod silk from time to time."

Lena acquired two leather outfits, a waterproof leather cloak that Drina insisted she must have, and four cotton day dresses. She also got a goodly selection of undergarments and four pairs of easy to don flats, just like Drina's. Back in her own world, Lena very seldom went to formal affairs, and when she did, she always wore her dress Imperium uniform. Now, she had to dress more feminine. She was floored with the myriad designs of the gowns.

Drina explained, "You see, when I dress up in these and don the heels for Ben, he knows I am giving up most of my independence for him. He then has to be my assistant in all things, since I can't use my feet any longer. In your case, Bernardo will fill that role for now — Isabella's orders. So you can splurge and get a couple of these that meet your fancy.

Nita, what would look the best on Lena? Ones like mine? Strapless perhaps?"

Nita countered, "No! Lena ought not to take such daring chances, Drina! You know what you're doing. She should go with anything but strapless gowns." In the end, Lena took a bright yellow satin gown and a light blue one. Both came with matching six inch oxford style heels, which more than daunted her. She also had a good pair of hiking boots, but why they insisted on those she didn't know. Nita added, "Later on, you can get winter boots and coats."

Poor Bernardo. He felt more like a packhorse carting the load back home, even though it was only a very short distance. He deposited the pile in their room and left the three to deal with the clothes. Thus began the education of Lena Squire.

Chapter 9 Educating Lena

"Like this. You have to use your feet and teeth. That's what the strings are for, so we can pull them up. That is, unless you want to cheat like Amy does," Drina teased Amy. They were showing Lena how she could dress herself. "I know; it's hard at first, but you'll catch on. We've had years of practice. At least I have. Amy cheats a lot. One day that's going to plague you, Amy. Mark my words."

"You should show her our limbering exercises," Amy countered. "Lena, you have to be able to touch your nose with your toes, if ever you're going to be able to scratch your nose." Lena tried unsuccessfully. "We'll practice the limbering exercises each morning. In no time, you'll loosen up. Your body is quite young now. That's a real benefit. You'll see."

"These straps and strings are a real godsend," Lena admitted, having managed to wiggle into her own panties and her new day dress by herself.

"Yes, incredible. Inez invented them for us katalyein. Oh, that's the dinner gong. Slip on your shoes. Time to eat," Drina explained.

"You look good," Bernardo complimented Lena, as he took his place at her side at the large table. "Let me know what you want and how much to dish out. Don't mind Amy and Drina yet. Give yourself some time to practice. Drina's actually pretty good at most things. She has different ways of doing things than the rest of us. It just takes her a lot longer to do things and more patience than I have. I'll admit that."

"Like this," Drina showed Lena how to use the fork and spoon with her toes. "Have the guys cut up your meat thought. Using a knife's a bit too dangerous for us."

"I need to be more limber," Lena justified this evening, content to let Bernardo feed her. The friendly meal passed without ceremony or incident. Lena did note it took Queen Isabella far longer to finish than even Drina. Her lip plates and inability to move her head without pivoting her whole body slowed her down, but Hernando was a model of patience, she observed.

After dinner, Adrianna suggested, "Anyone for a game of cards before bed?"

"I'm in," her boyfriend Henry called out. At once, the others echoed him. "Come on, Lena. You have to play too," he insisted.

"But I can't hold the cards, let alone deal," Lena protested, thinking they were crazy for even asking her. Why won't they just let me die or something?

"Hey, that's never stopped Drina or Amy," he countered. "Come on. It's fun." Soon, the nine gathered in what Lena thought must be a study. A large table surrounded by chairs occupied the center of the room. While the fellows seated the ladies, Henry got the deck of cards and shuffled them. Lean quickly caught on to the game; it was a variation of poker. Though she seldom played, she did know the rules. She often watched her junior officers playing.

Jan spoke up, "Okay gang. Remember. No cheating and looking at our hands." Turning to Lena, she added, "Sometimes they use their gifts to look out of our eyes at our own cards. That's cheating."

"Yes, but I don't have any hands for them to look at," Drina punned, bringing chuckles to the other's faces. Even Lena cracked a brief smile. "Hold them with your toes like I do. It's kind of hard to pick them up, but just take a peek and remember which is which." Lena watched, as Drina used her foot to slide a card close to the edge, where she could then lift one corner up with her toes, taking a brief peek at it. She struggled and managed to emulate her, then relaxed. They used wooden chips for their betting. Drina asked for three cards, sliding the ones she didn't want towards the dealer with a foot. Lena asked for two and awkwardly slid her two over as well, growing a bit more confident.

Several rounds of betting later, everyone had finally folded except Bernardo and Lena. He studied her face, "So you think you can beat what I have, do you?"

"I've beaten *far* older men," Lena couldn't help but tease him back a little. "You should respect your elders, young man." He laughed. He raised her, and she finally called his bluff. "Well, I'll be damned; she was bluffing!"

"Yes, but she won the pot, and that's the whole point," Amy teased him. All roared with laughter.

Lena added, "I've had a hundred twenty years to master my bluff, fellow." More laughter followed.

Just then, Queen Isabella came into the room. "I hate to break up your game, but we've a busy day tomorrow, and those two have to help Lena prepare for bed. So get cracking."

"See you all in the morning," Nita called out, as she headed next door.

"C'ya," Henry added, following his sister.

"Back around nine, 'cause I got some chores to do for mom," Adrianna explained, as she too left for home. At the door, she turned and reminded Amy, "Don't forget to plug Lena into the language discs tonight." Amy smiled.

A bit later in their room, the two began to show Lena how they accomplished routine actions before bed. Before long, Lena was doing her best to help Drina brush out Amy's hair and vice versa. Drina then showed her how limber Lena needed to get. "Yes, you have to have enough flexibility and leg control to get your feet behind your head like this. In fact, I used to sleep some like this just to stretch the muscles out more. Come on; we'll help you get there."

In the morning, Drina put Lena through a whole series of limbering up exercises. Then, they put it to use dressing themselves and brushing their hair before heading down to a help yourself type breakfast. Their cook had plenty of choices available. "Who are all these other people?" Lena whispered to Amy.

"They are the *mentales* gifted who work in the tower. That is, the morning shift. Come on. I'll introduce you to them." She did just that. Lena was a bit awed, for she was surrounded by another ten telepaths. After that group of folks finished, a number of grounds keepers and castle staff entered, and Lena was introduced to them as well. She relaxed a little; none of these had the distinctive yellow eyes. However, she soon learned why everyone was staring at her. Nowhere on Tierra was there anyone who had black skin. She felt relieved that they were not staring at her gross deformity.

"My home world is a hot one. We all have dark skins to protect us from the harsh rays of our sun," she explained, but realized she would have to repeat this fact many times in the future. She soon realized another reason why women preferred long hair. There was no central heating, and the castle rooms got quite chilly after the fires went out during the night. Now, she grasped why Amy and Drina slept with their hair over their top sides, a bit of extra warmth. Slowly, she began to see reason for the way things were done on this world.

The language discs were helping. Even this first day, she was able to pick up what some of the folks were saying over breakfast. Unlike the teens and the adults she'd met yesterday, the castle staff did not speak Imperium Standard, but Midlands. She vowed to make sure the learning disc was activated each night. After breakfast, the two teens took turns working with Lena, making her use her toes to work with the silverware and drinking mugs, along with many other smaller actions.

After lunch, Bernardo took charge. "Okay, Lena, let's get you into your boots. It's time for some real exercise." Lena didn't know what he meant precisely, but allowed him to tie her new boots on her feet. Dressed in her new leather outfit, she looked much as he did. They headed out of the main castle doors and into the crowded streets of Exchange City. The air was still a bit chilly, but the leather kept her warm. She also noticed many others wore similar apparel, though many were nowhere near as finely made as hers. Many strange smells drifted on the air, as they walked along. Bernardo was being helpful, pointing out the origins of some of them as they passed by.

"There, that shop's cooking rabbit stew. You're smelling the herbs they use in it. Pretty tasty, but she overcharges for her stew, if you ask me." Before long, they reached the southeastern edge of the city. Here, they paused for a minute. Stretching out for miles before her was a green valley, cradled between two distant rocky ridge lines. The valley ran off into the distance as far as she could see.

"Impressive. Where I come from, the whole darn planet

has been covered in steel and concrete, even the oceans too. This is really spectacular, Bernardo."

"Valleys like these cover all these western Midlands. You are in the high foothills of the Goza Mountains out there. This high up, there are only a few paths across those razor ridges. A hundred miles down there, the ridges become hills and are easily crossed. Lots of sheep and cattle farms are in many of these valley systems. Okay. So you are supposed to be a hot shot fighter type. Time for a run. Don't worry. I'll not let you take a fall. You set the pace. Head off out there; anywhere your heart desires to run."

"But I might take a nasty tumble. How'll I keep my balance?" Lena asked growing worried.

"Like I said. Trust me. I'll not let that happen. Come on. Are you chicken or something?" he taunted her.

Damn you. No, I'm terrified! Lena glared at him. He gave her a push. Nearly unwillingly, she began to jog carefully. "Come on. Are you lazy or just wholly out of shape? I thought you hot shot Sector ID Ministers were fit." Oh, that got a response. She was furious and began to run all-out. Suddenly, she lost her footing. Lena knew she would have tumbled, but she felt a force pulling her back upright. She turned and saw Bernardo grinning. "Told you. I have your back. Now, let get some exercise, lazy." She smiled back and began running again.

After going for a couple of miles, she felt invigorated but out of breath. "Sorry. Haven't run. This much. In a long time. Feels great out here. So beautiful."

"Yes, it is that. Come on; let's head for that line shack shelter over there. Going to rain shortly. We don't want to get soaked. Won't last long. Rains very frequently on Tierra, at least around here." They jogged to the small shack. It was crude, but protected them.

"Who built it? It's out in the middle of nowhere," she asked.

"Locals. When they have the spare time, they put these up here and there around the countryside for emergencies. Mostly, they're for winter snow emergencies. Blizzards are common around here. If you get caught in a whiteout, you've pretty much had it. That's why these shacks are here. They lay in a bit of firewood and some dried food for emergencies. Of course, if you use any of it, later, you're supposed to replace what you've used so others will have it when they need it," he explained.

Just then, the sky darkened and a giant lightning bolt flashed, striking a tall peak. The peal of thunder shook the small shanty, startling Lena. "Is it safe?" she asked timidly.

"Sure. Lightning usually strikes the peaks, rarely anything lower this close to them. Here comes the rain." Sheets poured down for a few minutes, before letting up. A half hour later, the dull orange-red sun reappeared, and the two jogged back into the city. As they walked through the streets, he said, "Okay, tomorrow afternoon, we'll test your fighting skills. I have to see what you can do, and what you want to be able to do. I take it you're quite skilled."

"Hey, that was *then*. Now, I'm a *helpless* cripple. Don't expect much at all. If this were *last* year, why, I'd take your pants off you. We're highly skilled fighters." She sighed, recalling what was, versus what had become of her. Wisely, he let it be.

After supper, for a while, the Gang of Eight got together for more games. After that, Drina and Amy helped Lena to a bath. The tub was a bronze one, and servants brought in hot water for them. The two insisted Lena wash herself as much as possible, but they helped dry her off.

The next afternoon, Bernardo took her into a basement room that was filled with pads. "Okay, here's our dummy punching bag." Roughly humanoid in shape, the bag hung suspended from the ceiling by a thick rope. "Let's see what you can do."

"Not much at all, I'm afraid. My fighting days are gone *now* for sure," she replied morosely.

"Oh come *off* it! I didn't figure you for a *wimpy* girl! Let's see your circle kick."

Infuriated, she let loose and nearly fell down. "Here, try it like this." Bernardo held his arms behind his back and delivered a solid circle kick to the dummy. Then, insisted she try it. He was merciless, cajoling her, pushing her, needling her — anything to get her to break loose and have at it. "Okay, imagine that's the body of that Lugar fellow you've been talking about. Get even with him!" That did it; she kicked it as hard as she could, and would have fallen down, if Bernardo hadn't used his telekinetic skills to keep her on her feet.

She noticed the stone around his neck glowed with a pale blue light whenever he was preventing her from falling. "Thanks, but why's your stone glowing?" she asked.

"It is my germanium crystal. It's attuned only to me, and it amplifies my *mentales* powers at least a hundred fold. We all have a limited reservoir of psi energies we can use without eating and sleeping to recover. The crystals enable us to do far more with less of our own energies. That's all. Now that was a good kick. Let's see you do that again, but without falling down."

"Hey, once was enough. I'm done," she challenged him.

"You aren't done, until you can take me out in a real fight," he countered.

"But that's impossible!"

"No it isn't. You just need lots more practice. You need to make far better use of the resources you possess. Agility and cunning, for two. Plus, you need to observe your opponent and find his weak spot, before he or she finds yours. We'll work on that part later. Now back to kicking," he ordered.

An hour later, he again adjusted her kick. "Look Lena, you're kicking him in his abdomen, which he'll very likely be protecting. For a clean kill, you need to strike him in his neck, snapping it. Either that or his head, which will likely amount to the same thing. Higher. Aim higher."

"But I can't reach that high without falling down," she whined.

"You reach. Leave the falling down to me," he insisted.

Later when they finished for the afternoon, he explained, "Around here, you'll likely be facing men with swords. So we'll have to get you well versed in dealing with that aspect. You know, avoid their strikes, and yet take them out. I'll save that one for later though. Don't want to get you all bruised up too soon."

"Ha. I'm already bruised and sore as the devil, but I did

get in some good kicks, didn't I?" she asked.

"Yes, you've improved considerably from that first kick. Come on; let's get a bath. Tomorrow, we nine are going for a horse ride in the valley."

"Horse? I've never been on one of those animals, though I've seen pictures of them. Wait, I can't do that! Are you teasing me or something? Even Drina can't do that. You need arms to hold the leather things."

"Are you kidding me? Of course Amy and Drina ride. They're good at it, and love it. Drina can't get enough of it. We tie the reins to a wooden block, which she holds in her mouth. You'll see."

"I get it. Horses must be your main form of transportation on this world. You do have roads to follow, don't you?" she asked, again growing curious. She'd forgotten about this aspect of more primitive worlds.

"True, the average person uses horses, carriages, and wagons. There aren't any roads. Who needs them? Well, there's the one small road built by the aliens across Plateau Grado, so they can bring their vehicles into Exchange City. They extended it to Valen over in the Westerlings side. No, there are some well-traveled tracks, especially leading into this city from the north, south, and east. But really, one just heads off in the desired direction mostly, except around these foothills, where the ridges are mostly impassible."

He went on, "However, ourselves, we usually teleport to where we need to go. That's one of the remarkable abilities of a tower's Circle. They combine their powers into their leader, who's called a capo or capa, depending on their sex. He or she then does the actual teleporting. I won't lie to you. Sometimes, we use our own Imperium made teleport machines."

"What? You have such technology here on Tierra? Those things are supposed to be not allowed." Lena took offense, thinking of the Closed World policy.

Bernardo countered. "Those who brought them here were allowed to do so. They had dual citizenship, and were allowed to bring whatever they desired. I admit, very few people know about those teleport machines."

"Well, yes, that's a glitch in the policy. But wait. Those

machines take electricity, and you don't have any power generators here," Lena countered.

Bernardo smiled. "Oh yes a few do, but we make better use of solar power, though our sun is poor producer of it. Perhaps, we can get a tour when we are in Brom."

"This planet is full of surprises. Next thing you'll be telling me is that you have quite a few of our medical machines too."

"Well, we do." Lena gave a huff, and let it go at that.

The next afternoon, the gang wore their leathers and walked to the stables, where the castle staff had their horses waiting for them. "So this is a real live horse," Lena said, rather daunted by the size of the mare Bernardo said would be hers.

Bernardo smiled, "It's not a mechanical one, though I suppose you have robot horses where you come from."

"What?" Lena looked confused. She saw his teasing grin, and realized he was spoofing her, and she grinned back. "No, don't be silly, but I can't ride this beast even if I had arms. It's too big. I'll fall off or something. There's no steering shaft."

"No there isn't. Not the last time I checked," Bernardo said playfully. "Okay, quick lesson. Always mount from the left side of the horse. Watch how Drina does it. Yes, someone will hold the reins for you, just as we do for Drina and Amy. See how she leans over as she gets up? You hold the reins in your teeth. Bite down on that wooden block to which the reins are tied. Don't try to mount like Amy does."

Drina immediately called out, talking through her teeth now holding her reins securely, "She cheats."

"But I have to cheat, Drina," Amy protested. "With these toe boots and corset, I don't have a choice." As Lena watched, Amy's body magically floated up, over, and then came down upon the saddle. The crystal around her neck glowed in a pale blue light, but it vanished, when she bit down on the wooden block Jan held up for her. Lena was amazed.

Bernardo whispered, "Don't worry. I won't let you fall." Lena took a deep breath, lifted her left foot up ,and got it into the stirrup. Then, she lunged as Drina had. She needed all her powerful leg muscles, but managed to get up and into the saddle. At least, she didn't need someone to get her hair repositioned as did Drina. "Well done," he complimented her and began explaining about neck reining and how to control the mare. He knew Lena was nearly petrified, but not because of her lack of arms this time. She'd never been around an animal quite this large before.

They paired up and headed out of the Imperial Castle's main gates, turning right and leaving the southern edge of Exchange City fairly soon. Once more, they were out on the vast green valley to the south and east of the city, where she had been running. Before long, they broke into a canter. When they finally returned to the castle some three hours later, Lena was beaming. "That was scary, but incredibly fun! Such freedom. Exhilarating even, but my legs are mush," Lena commented, as soon as she'd dismounted.

"Glad you like to ride," Drina exclaimed. "Back home, mom hardly ever lets me get out and ride like that. The adults keep trying to tell me I can't do it, but, of course, I can ride. You, Amy, and I — we kept up just fine. I wish people wouldn't keep telling us that we can't do things, just because we aren't like them."

"Right," Lena replied mechanically. For the first time, she sensed a little bitterness in Drina's emotions. So others keep holding her back, she thought. Well, she doesn't have arms. They probably are worried about her safety, she justified, as if she were Drina's mother. She had flashes of her teen years, something like ninety years ago. Her parents kept telling her women couldn't join the ID Division nor could a woman ever become one of their Sector ID Ministers. She recalled how badly that had hurt her and just how much it had steeled her will to prove them wrong. Lena found herself telling Drina, "Hey, don't ever let someone tell you that you can't do something. If you set your mind to it, somehow, you can find a way to make it happen."

Drina looked at Lena with rather surprised eyes. "Hey, did you hear her? She's on my side. Way to go, Lena. That's what I keep trying to tell people. If I set my mind to it, I'll find a way; just give me lots more time to figure out how. Thanks Lena, you're all right."

Lena grinned. "Yea, my folks kept telling me there was no way I could ever become a Sector ID Minister, because I was female, and there were no females in those top positions. Ha. I busted my ass for close to fifteen years, but I made it into that division and worked harder than anyone else. I had to be twice as good as my male peers, but I got there eventually. Drina, your parents are just trying to be protective of their little daughter, like you'll be one day with yours. Still, parents need to allow their children the freedom to try and to fail or succeed on their own. That's what I think, though I've never had any children of my own," she admitted.

Amy asked, "You never got married? A hundred twenty years old?"

Lena laughed, "No, my career was everything to me. I had to be the best Sector ID Minister ever. That's what I am. That's what I do. Protect others. I was damn good too. Shit, then I failed Neva and Queen Altha!" Her brief gaiety vanished instantly. Her single failure once more overwhelmed her.

Bernardo broke the awkward silence. "Well, we'll have to go riding more frequently. Maybe we can talk mom into letting us ride to Brom later on. Won't that be fun — a month out on the trail!" That brought everyone's spirits up, excepting Lena's. However, she was curious.

During the next two weeks, Lena was pushed hard, both by Amy and Drina, and even more so by Bernardo. Just as she was about to master one thing, he kept on raising the level higher, frustrating her. She needed the daily baths; her muscles were being stretched and battered at the same time. Still, she knew she was making some progress. At least, she didn't have to have Bernardo feeding her all the time now. Their occasional afternoon rides quickly became the highlight of her days. Lena took to riding as a native of Tierra might.

Lena didn't realize it, but this was what Queen Isabella was waiting for — Lena had to be able at least to care for her own basic needs around the castle. That evening, she announced, "Okay, tomorrow you all get to go to Brom for an extended stay. I want you to all promise me that you'll be on your *best* behavior. No tricks or I'll have Maricela send you all packing, excepting Lena, of course."

"Yahoo. Thanks mom. We promise," Amy declared.

"Hey, Lena can meet my family and relatives now," Jan exclaimed enthusiastically.

Queen Isabella explained, "Yes she can. Nadja and Diego are going with you. They want to visit their friends in Brom too; plus she and Diego want to make plans for their annual summer excursion." Looking at Lena, she added, "Nadja teaches school here in the winters, but she travels around Tierra during the summer, making her language recordings or studies. Diego accompanies her and uses his gifts to heal the sick and injured they find on their travels, and he gives them musical concerts."

"Hey, someone mention travel?" They turned around to see Nadja, Diego, and Hidalgo walking into their large living room. Hidalgo, Adrianna's twin brother, wasn't part of the Gang of Eight as she was. Rather, he was as monomaniac about music as his father was. Already he had mastered his father's flutes, guitars, and citerns. At this point in time, the father and son act was quite famous in Exchange City. Hidalgo was planning to go along with the two this summer, entertaining the locals with his father. Plus, he was working on inventing some new musical instruments. He had no time for the silly pranks of the Gang of Eight.

"Hi, yes, just explaining to them tomorrow they're all going up to Brom with you folks," Queen Isabella pointed out. "I've told them to be on their best behavior, for what that's worth."

Nadja laughed. "I don't think I can box their ears, if they pull another prank, Isabella. They're too big now." The gang giggled.

Bernardo spoke up, "Mom. Can we ride our horses up to Brom? Lena loves riding, and we'd have a great time getting there. Please? We'll be on our *best* behavior."

"Not this time, Bernardo. Lena needs her therapy as soon as possible. Already, I've delayed it a couple of weeks," she replied. Bernardo looked crestfallen, and she hastily added, "But I don't see why you can't take a trip *after* she's finished with her therapy sessions."

Nadja suggested, "Say, why don't you all tag along with

us when we go up to Hilliard Heights later this summer? First, we have to catch up on things around Brom. She can get her therapy while we're doing that. Diego and I want to visit Hilliard Heights this summer. Don't see any reason you can't tag along with us. Of course, you might get really bored, while I'm doing my linguistic studies up there. Will that be all right with you, Isabella? Hernando?"

"Please mom," Bernardo begged.

After Hernando nodded his assent to her, Isabella replied, "Well, all right. But you have to let Lena get her therapy first. But *no* pranks. I'll contact Venerada Maricela and tell her not to allow you to go on the trip, if you eight cause her any troubles. Now you all should go pack, so Nadja and we adults can chat a bit."

"Thanks mom!" Bernardo gushed. He and the others dashed off before she could change her mind.

Lena hung back though. She considered herself an adult. At one hundred and twenty, she more than qualified, though her body was now only fourteen. Nadja suggested, "Lena, stick around. I can see you want to chat." Hidalgo and Diego headed off with Hernando to study the large map of the Midlands. They'd never been that far north.

Lena moved over to a sofa and sat down across from Nadja. "Well, I kind of did want to talk to you," she admitted, as she studied the forty-two year old Imperium linguist. "How come you got stranded here when the spaceport closed? Didn't Governor Burkhardt let you know about the closing? That you'd be stranded here? I hope you don't mind my prying, but I'm, er was a Sector ID Minister." Even Nadja could sense the suppressed grief Lena held back, but she knew the woman was still searching for answers.

"Oh yes, Konrad did let me know well ahead of time they were abandoning the base. He offered me a ride on the last shuttle when I hadn't left earlier. No, I'm here because I want to be here on Tierra. Honestly, this is now my home. At first, I was doing what I've always craved to do — be the first linguist to study a telepathic society. Well, I'm still doing that, though I doubt I'll ever publish my findings. I've grown to love this world and its people, Lena. I really don't know how to say what I truly feel about this place. Out there, technology dominates everything. Don't get me wrong, the technology is fantastic and has allowed not only me to do my work easily, but also to live well. But there's something that's missing out there that this planet has in abundance. Humanity. True, there are bad apples in every barrel. Lord knows, this world has seen some really rotten ones, before the baby boom a while back. But the people of this civilization have something no other planet in the galaxy has. Widespread telepathy may have something to do with it, but there's far more. You'll begin to see what I mean when you have finished your therapy. I owe my undying support to this world now, and I'll never leave here. We can talk more after you are done with your therapy. Until then, I just don't know how to communicate how I feel about this world and its people. There just aren't words for it."

"Accepted. I really don't need this therapy. I'm perfectly fine, just mostly crippled," Lena insisted. "Thanks for being honest with me. I just had to make sure you weren't rudely abandoned on Tierra when the spaceport was abandoned, Nadja. After all, you've become a famous linguist in our times. I just can't stop being the ID Minister, you see, even though we both know that position is no longer mine. I've lost that forever now." She shrugged her empty shoulders punctuating that finality. She thought, *I so wish Neva had just killed me when she had the opportunity. My life's ruined, gone in the wind, forever lost, and I've to face living this dismal lifetime anew.*

Nadja sensed what Lena wasn't saying and decided to let it be. "So we're going to ride up to Hilliard Heights later this summer. Of course, we'll be stopping in all the small villages and such, so I can sample their regional dialects, while Diego handles any sick or injured. Then, Diego and Hidalgo will play for them. I hope you won't be too bored with the journey."

Lena felt the pangs of her immense loss. Nadja's change of topic wasn't helping, so she took her leave, saying, "Thanks. I best go see to packing for tomorrow. Amy and Drina will be wondering what's keeping me. Good to see you again, Nadja." She lunged to her feet and headed off to her room, fighting watering eyes. No way was she going to let them see her bawl! Not her, not a Sector ID Minister. *But I'm not one now, not any longer! Not ever again!* She fought hard to keep her eyes from watering, pausing before her room to wipe them awkwardly on her shoulders before entering.

"Oh hi. Come pack. Amy's cheating again," Drina called out. She was sitting on the floor, using her feet to stuff her nicely folded clothes into several bags. Nearby, Amy was too, only she was using her telekinetic skills to do the same thing. Amy laughed. "Mark my words, Amy, one of these days you'll regret not practicing properly."

"You're just jealous because you don't have telekinetic abilities, Drina," Amy countered.

"Maybe a little, Amy," Drina admitted, "but the more you practice doing things, the easier they become for us to do. You know that."

"But I can't bend much at my waist, and these feet of mine are a royal pain," Amy defended herself.

"Why did you lose your arms and have your waist and feet altered in the first place?" Lena asked.

"Oh mom did it when I was about one and a half years old. The idea is I'd have a long time to adjust before she sent me off to Ataro to be trained by Queen Altha. I'll be taking over here for mom when she retires. We owe it to her to do that as soon as possible. God, have you seen how horrible life is for her? Jan and I were just like her, but then you know that, don't you? We simply couldn't take living as she's been forced to live, so we dumped those bodies and got these new ones. Still, I did agree to take over here for Isabella, as soon as possible, so don't worry about me. I'm supposed to go to Ataro and get trained properly this winter. Jan will come with me."

"Yes, I've heard that. I still don't buy into their crazy notions about ultimate power having to have ultimate physical restrictions. I got into lengthy discussions with the emperor and Queen Altha over this. I just don't see why they need to have such horribly crippled bodies just so they can rule," Lena said, glad for a topic change. She sat down and tried to pack her things as best she could, emulating Drina's motions.

Amy replied, "Well, you have to agree it is damned near

impossible for the emperor and queens to abuse their powers. They are harder than normal to corrupt. But just between you and me, and don't ever tell mom this, but they can still become corrupted. Fame and egos. While money and such things are not remote temptations, fame and importance could well be used to corrupt them, though it apparently hasn't happened in over two thousand years in that Ataro System."

She went on, "Here on Tierra, mom's trying a system of checks and balances on the powers of those who rule. So far, it is working out, but they've only had fourteen years to get it going, terribly short amount of time."

"Tell me about it," Lena asked. "Say, do you have history books? I'd love to read up on the history of Tierra." She then wished she'd kept her mouth shut. *How the hell can I read a book now? No hands to hold it!*

Both Drina and Amy laughed. Amy answered, "We don't have those. No one has ever written that stuff down. It's all verbally told somewhat. I know quite a bit, since I was there, but I have big gaps in what I know. Mostly, the earlier days are just legends."

Drina added, "Some of the towers do have some ancient scrolls that talk about some things, like the Nuclear that was detonated on old Bettingham."

The two began to relate what history they knew of Tierra. Lena listened fascinated for hours, even while they lay in bed long after they ought to have been sleeping. Lena found much to be simply unbelievable, the stuff of legends. Well, she decided, that was what history was, legends made up to explain events to the liking of the teller. It was not like her own official reports, which were entirely factually based on raw observations. These were primitive peoples, she recalled.

The next morning, Lena complained, "I can't carry these two big bags." She and Drina had the same problem, though Amy merely floated hers along using her powers.

"Don't worry, that's why I'm here," Bernardo called out, coming to the rescue of the two.

"Thanks," Lena said, as he picked up her pair and Drina's too.

"Thanks," Drina added. "Come on. We don't want to be

late for the teleport. Who is doing it? Do you know, Bernardo?"

"I think the Underground is. We have too much stuff and too many people for the tower. I don't think Venerada Maricela wants to waste her Circle's power on us," he replied.

They gathered in Isabella's living room. After saying their goodbyes, Isabella and Hernando left the room. Nadja ordered, "Okay, we're all set. I'll let Bart know we are ready. Stand by."

Jan, who was standing beside Amy, whispered to Lena, "Bart's my dad. He's an expert with the teleport machine. I think he's going to deposit us on Brom Tower's teleport pad. We're staying in the tower's manor house as Venerada Maricela's guests. Don't worry, I'll take us all down, so you can meet dad and the others of the Underground. I know they want to meet you, Lena."

Just then, half of the group and their bags vanished from sight. A minute later, the rest did as well. Lena found herself standing on a small raised stone platform in a strange room. Already the first group had stepped off the pad, making room for Lena and the second batch. She saw a middle aged, armless woman standing before her.

"Welcome, Lena Squire to Brom Tower. I'm your host, Venerada Maricela Wait. My twins, Casilda and Beltran, and my younger son, Carlos. Kids, you'll be staying in the guest rooms on the first floor. First things first, Lena, Amy, you'll be staying with Casilda. Drina, your folks want you to spend time with them. So everyone, follow my kids to your rooms and get settled in. After that, we'll meet for lunch, and I'll give Lena, and anyone else who wants it, a tour of the tower. After that, I know the other parents want to meet Lena too, so the rest of the afternoon you can monopolize Lena. However, tomorrow first thing, she gets her much needed therapy. Questions? Good. Oh yes. Gang of Eight — you are to be on your *best* behavior — Queen Isabella's orders, not mine," she hinted. The eight giggled, but Lena wondered what that was all about.

As they followed Casilda, the fourteen year old girl said, "Mom's under orders to report any pranks to Queen Isabella, but as long as she doesn't *see* them, she *can't* report them.

That's what mom meant, Lena. She doesn't mind them having a little harmless fun, as long as it doesn't affect the Circles and their work. So you're really a hundred twenty years old, Lena?"

"Yes, I am. I'm still getting used to being fourteen again, though obviously from time to time, I took some years off. Never anything this drastic though. So you're a katalyein too, like Drina?" she asked, guessing as much. She did look an awful lot like her mother.

She giggled, "Yes, but Drina gets to do *so* much more than I do. Anita, that's her mother, allowed her to go off to Nadja's school and live like ordinary people, while I'm stuck here in this tower. Drina tells me a lot of what she's been doing. Oh how I wish they'd let me live life as she is."

Lena began to see that Casilda was being "protected" by her parents, perhaps overly so, but then perhaps not. After all, she was as crippled as Lena was, totally helpless, dependent upon others for so much. However, she also felt the conflicting attitude that, like Drina, Casilda should have the freedom to choose her own path in life. Lena's mind became confused once more.

"Here's my room. They've brought in another couple of low chest of drawers for you two to use. As you know, we can more easily use low ones with our feet. Those two are for you. Take your pick. At least, I have a large enough bed. Sorry Amy. I tried to get mom to put you and Jan into a private room, but she insisted Jan should stay with her parents this time."

"No problem, Casilda. We already figured that would happen. We'll probably get married this winter, just before we have to leave for the Ataro System," Amy replied.

"Here, I'll help you some, Lena," Casilda sat down to help Lena unpack her clothes and put them into the bottom drawer. "I'm glad you are both staying with me. I'd love to hear stories of what the world out there is like. As you know, Amy, I don't get many chances to get out much. Mom's so overly protective of me that it hurts sometimes." She chatted away and soon their clothes were stowed.

"At least, dad does take me out with him to see his eagles. Dad raises, trains, and captures eagles, Lena. I have some skills from him, but I just wish I had arms so I could hold and train them too, but I don't. Beltran does, and he's taking after dad though. Amy, you already know where everything is around here. Let's show Lena."

Next, Lena got an extensive tour of the huge Brom Tower complex. She was very impressed with the scale of the operation, including the two mammoth manor houses adjoining the tower. From the tower's observation deck on the roof, she got a terrific view of Brom Castle and the city that butted up tightly against the tall Goza Mountains. To her, it seemed as if they built the city up every conceivable valley and gorge of the mountainside. Then, she saw what truly impressed her.

Venerada Maricela explained, "One of the Circles is helping with the construction of more stone buildings for Brom. Over there, you can see the stone quarry," she nodded with her head in the direction. "The Circle is cutting out the stones. You can see the dust from their cutting. Watch. They've finished cutting out another stone." As Lena watched the light grey dust settled. To her astonishment, the giant stone rose up in the air, floated from the quarry over the entire sprawling city to the site of the new construction on the south of the city, where it was carefully laid in place. Maricela explained how the Circle was doing this, but in simple terms for Lena's sake. She was very much impressed.

"So all these stone buildings — they were not made by stone cutters and the like? They were made by the Circle?" she asked.

"Yes, that's right. One of the things the towers do for the people of our kingdom is to help with the construction of new buildings. With our help, the construction times are drastically shortened. We use stone around here because such dwellings are warmer in the long, cold winters," Venerada Maricela explained, and then continued her tour. "Brom has really grown over the years. There are about thirty thousand people living here now. Over there is our new Senate building, and there is the new Trauma and Spiritual Rehab Center, where you'll be getting your therapy starting tomorrow. Don't worry; there are underground tunnels, connecting the tower here to the center. Has to be, considering often the winter snow depth exceeds twenty feet."

Lena noticed Maricela seemed not to have much of a problem with her giant lip plates, which drooped down onto her chest. So many had these, and she began to notice and wondered why they were so fashionable. Life with them must be awful, she thought.

After reaching the first floor once more, Jan led them down into the basement and into the tunnel system. "These tunnels can be a maze. If you notice the painted signs and follow them, you can't get too lost. You'll eventually end up somewhere. Lena, the red arrows lead to the Rehab Center where you'll be going tomorrow. The brown ones lead to the Underground, where we're headed. Follow me. They all want to meet you, Lena, but don't be surprised at what all you are going to see. Not everyone on Tierra is technically challenged."

Before long, she entered a huge chamber filled with all manner of electronic equipment, more than was on her own battle cruiser! Fourteen adults and a host of teens gathered around. Jan introduced them all to Lena, going slowly. "These are our leaders, Ken and Crystal Blackwater." Lena noticed he appeared to be in his early forties. None of these people had the lip plates, but many of the women had the small waists, indicative of the pipe corsets. "These are my folks, Bart and Anita Bellweather. He's our resident electronics man, takes after me," Jan added, causing the room to chuckle some. Evidently, Lena surmised, they somehow believed Jan was this Jan of legends. She continued with the many other introductions of the adults, pointing out their areas of specialties, medical and therapy. Lena was lost with all the children, and she began to see there really must have been a baby boom. So many were nearly the same ages and so many sets of twins.

Ken then introduced two late arrivals. "Lena, this is Rafaela and Andres Bolivar. She knows more about the *mentales* gifts than anyone on Tierra except Benjamina, my mother. Well, she passed away some years ago, but now has a new body over in the Easterlings. She's still in touch with us from time to time and is working on her therapy over there."

"Pleased to meet you, Sector ID Minister Lena Squire,"

140

Rafaela said formally, rather surprising Lena. Rafaela and Andres were in their middle sixties. Age was taking its toll on both of them, she noted. Grey streaks predominated in their hair.

"Thanks. I have many questions for you then. But forget the formal title, I'm no longer qualified to hold that position. Not now. Not as I am," Lena's suppressed grief rose once more and was sensed by all here.

"Yes, we should talk soon, Lena. I too have some very important questions for you. But I know Ken wants to give you a tour first. Ken, I'll be waiting in med lab four. Bring Lena to me when you finish up, will you dear?" Rafaela asked.

"Sure thing. Lena, as you can see, we have a very sophisticated comm network here," Ken began.

"Ah, so when Queen Altha said she was able to contact Queen Isabella," Lena began to ask.

Bart finished her question. "Right. I picked up her call, since the aliens have abandoned Tierra. I relayed it to Isabella." He boasted, "There isn't any place in the universe I can't reach from here."

Lena had an idea. "Say, if that's so, can you make a call for me? I want to get Isabella her rightful compensation from the Imperium for what Senate President Carlos did to her and her wives. The Imperium should pay her several tens of millions of credits in compensation, but I need to file the proper form. Shit, I can't even fill it out."

"Hey, no problem. I can fix up a voice-activated system for you in a jiffy. Point me to the form, and we'll get it filed," Bart promised. She watched over his shoulders while she called out directions. Soon, he had downloaded the proper form. Bart commented, "Oh this is simple. Heck, I can fill it out while Ken's showing you around. When you're done, you can check it over, and we can send it in." Lena smiled and agreed.

"Now, here are our four fully equipped medical labs, each with a pair of medical machines in them. Two have rejuvenation machines as well, but they hardly ever get used," Misty proudly explained. These were her "babies."

"But I don't understand. Where do you get the power to

operate all this equipment? Where do you get the supply of stem cells the machines need?" Lena asked.

Ken answered for Bart, who was busily typing, "Solar cells and a battery system. We really do need a better power generator, but those would too easily be discovered by the aliens at the spaceport. We prefer to be wholly unknown to those, no offence Lena."

"None taken. So the Rigels don't know this place exists?"

"Nope. It is heavily shielded and far underground. The solar panels are disguised. They have no idea we are here, and we have to keep it that way. Even the other rulers of Tierra don't know that we exist. Only a handful like, Maricela and the current leaders of Brom Castle, know of us. It's for our own safety as much as anything. In the past, others have tried to have us assassinated. Power hungry fellows, you see."

"Yes, I understand that only too darn well," Lena replied, thinking of the two Legates and President Snarry.

"We stay behind the scenes and do everything we can to maintain peace and prosperity across all of Tierra. That's our purpose, and we've been at it quite some time, centuries in fact. Amy and Jan first began the Underground a long time ago, after they retired as emperor and empress," Ken explained. Again, Lena didn't quite believe this. Much was probably legends.

"Oh, I best get you to Rafaela. She wants to talk with you; about what, I'm not sure. Whatever Rafaela wants, she gets. She knows more than I *ever* will. Come on; she's back in Med Lab Four," Ken said, and led her there. Meanwhile, the other teens headed off with all the other Underground teens to chat and exchange stories and news, all talking at once, bringing a smile to Lena and Ken's faces. He added, "Jan's not been here all winter, and they all seem to have a lot to catch up on. Kids."

"Hi, have a seat, Lena. I guess we should begin by letting you ask your questions first," Rafaela began, offering her a seat. She dismissed Ken and Crystal. Andres stayed in the background by the door, ensuring their privacy.

"Everyone has yellow eyes with brown speckles. All are

telepaths? This *mentales*?" Lena asked.

"Yes, the *mentales* gifts are far more than mere telepathy. That's the tiniest part of our gifts."

"So I am beginning to see. So why do you all want Tierra to remain a Closed World? Surely with these kinds of power, you could all become the most powerful people out there in the vast Imperium?" Lena asked, thinking of Neva and her rise to power.

"We are quite content to live here. We've no need, or rather very little need, of such technology that's out there. You've seen how we can cut stone from the mountainside and construct buildings. We don't need the Imperium's fancy machines. Yet, there is no denying we could use electricity and central heating, things like that. Still, for the most part, we who have this precious gift prefer to use it to help those of Tierra who don't have it. We aren't interested in controlling whole worlds. Don't get me wrong, there are always some who would desire nothing more than to do just that. Bad apples are in every barrel," Rafaela answered.

She went on, "If we opened up Tierra, many would be tempted to do just that. Honestly, Lena, what would the Imperium do if one of us used our skills to take over one of your worlds? Short of assassination, they simply couldn't stop some of us. A few even have the ability to kill with their minds. Of course, you already know that. Neva is one, right?"

Lena smiled. "You read my mind. Yes, she is one, but I couldn't get her to kill me. Like this, I'm totally useless, a pathetic excuse for a human. I ought to be just put out of my misery. I begged and begged her to do it. Obviously, the perverse woman didn't."

"I understand how you feel. In my youth, Andres and I had an unfortunate experience and lost our arms. Life was dreadful after that." She waved her arms and added, "The goddess Lysandra gave us back arms though. Rather a miracle." Lena didn't believe her.

"So how do people get this *mentales* gift thing? I assume it is inherited?" Lena asked.

"Yes, it is frequently inherited, passed along in genes. However, it doesn't always breed true. In the distant past, they launched into a massive interbreeding program, trying to create children, who would have specific abilities, particularly those of the katalyein. That nearly led to the doom of us all. Thank god, we were able to get that eliminated. But I haven't answered you fully. How did we first get the gifts? Long story."

"I've all the time in the world now. Not much else I can do except listen," Lena complained bitterly.

"Many centuries ago, the alien's refinery on Plateau Grado blew up. The severity of that explosion knocked Tierra off its axis. The poles shifted, and the planet wobbled daily. The horrific climate change very nearly made the human population here extinct. However, the explosion tossed an enormous amount of germanium crystal dust over the planet. It got into our bodies directly and via the food that was grown and eaten. It altered the size of our pituitary glands, which are directly responsible for the psi powers we have, the *mentales* gifts, as we call them."

"Some of us believe this was again a gift from one or more of the five gods and goddesses of Tierra to somehow save us humans. Benjamina and I have done extensive testing, and have been able to take a normal person and give them the *mentales* gifts. What I'm about to tell you must never leave this room." Lena agreed. "We took pity on Nadja, after someone tried to assassinate her and she lost both of her arms. She had about six inches left of each. I fed her the proper amounts in her food, and she developed the *mentales* gifts she has today. Of course later for reasons we don't know, the goddess Lysandra also restored her arms."

"That's hard to believe, but I'll not say anything. Did you do this to Konrad too?"

"No. We did not, though we suspect someone else discovered how to do it and did it to him. Why? We still don't know, but it wasn't the Underground."

"So when a person gets the gift, it's pot luck? They get whatever skills they get?" Lena asked.

"Yes, but I've proven that usually the gifts take the form most needed by the person. Drina's dad, for example, has devoted his life to the eagles, which are used for hunting. Hence, his gifts lay in that arena. Nadja's gift was primarily telekinesis, making up for her lack of arms. Again, what I'm about to say must not leave this room. Anyone, who has the *mentales* gifts with the proper training and practice, can develop any one of the skills that were cataloged centuries ago by Marisol. Amy and Jan are prime examples of this. What they can do never ceases to amaze me. Again, that alone makes many of us terrified of Tierra becoming an open world. Some of us could go out there and take over the whole Imperium! Damn scary!"

"They are a bit precocious," Lena admitted, still not believing what Rafaela was saying, not completely. However, she was right about their taking over the Imperium. Damn scary. "But hasn't the Imperium tried making telepaths using the dust too?"

"We believe so, but that was a long time in the past. We believe they failed. It's possible the dust only has this effect here on Tierra. Just like with women's breasts. If you stay here long enough, yours will become as big as mine are. All women here have melons, but at least they're not the monsters Senator Carlos gave Isabella and her wives or you, as I understand what happened to you and the others on Gamelon-3."

"I've had all the boobs I ever want," Lena admitted. "Can I ask you more questions later when I think of them?"

"Sure. Now that you are done, I've some for you. Lena, I'm sixty-six, and my body is failing me. Andres too. However, my research and work here is not finished. As you probably have heard, I'm considered the expert in such matters. Jamie and Luisa have been following in my footsteps, but they still haven't got it all down pat. I promised Benjamina that I would see it through to the end, but my body is giving out on me. I've talked with her, telepathically that is, since she is thousands of miles east of here now. Anyway, until now, no one has ever used the rejuvenation machine. We prefer to live normal lifetimes. Only right now, we, that is, Andres and me, are considering using it, so we can continue with the research without having to undergo the delay inherent in having a baby body grow up. Plus, we're not sure in our next lives that we'd be able to remember everything we know now. We're not Amy,

Jan, or Benjamina."

Rafaela finally asked her question. "So what can you tell me about the rejuvenation machine and its effects on your body, mind, and memory when you use it?"

"I'm not a medical doctor, but I know something about it. Apparently, our bodies have cells with genes and DNA in them. The genes are always being copied and replicated. Over time, mutations develop. Usually, they are corrected, but not always. Some of them have extra information on their strands. These also get duplicated and eventually corrupt the DNA strands, which accounts for the body beginning to fail to rebuild itself. As I understand it, in about seven years, every cell in our bodies has been replaced with new ones. Hence, the failures accumulate, like your grey hair. The rejuvenation machine replaces your cells with new ones built from fresh stem cells. Depending on the number of years you are trying to take off, the process can take many hours to complete."

"As far as memory goes, I've never found anything amiss afterwards," she added remembering her secondary question.

"Okay. Another thing. You see, in the past, Andres and I lost our arms. If we rejuvenate our bodies to that age, will our arms still be there or will the process rebuild us as we were back then?"

"I have no idea about that one. No guesses on that. Sorry," Lena replied honestly.

"Okay then. I guess Andres and I will try it. I have to say the whole Underground has been pushing us to go ahead and do it. Kids. They just don't believe in themselves enough. Ken urged Benjamina to do it, but she refused. I don't have the luxury. Everyone is depending upon me, and Andres, to a lesser extent, to continue my research. Even Josh in the tower has been pressuring me to do it. So I guess we'll give it a try. I was going to do your therapy myself, Lena, but I've assigned someone else to do it. I'll tell you up front, Gracia was once in the same situation you find yourself now. She was the top fighter in her city, wholly unusual for a woman. She could beat any man in her city in a fight. Then, she lost her arms and so much more. It devastated her, much as it has you. In a way, she can empathize with your unique situation far better than I can. Her skills with Benjamina's therapy are as good as mine are, in my opinion, but she doesn't think so. Anyway, I just want you to know that you'll be given the very best therapy giver we have, short of sending you over to Benjamina in the Easterlings."

"I'm fine, really," Lena countered mechanically. She knew she wasn't fine, but no one could give her back her arms, so what was the point of therapy anyway? None that she could see.

"Well, I've monopolized you long enough. The kids all want to keep on showing you around. Thanks for being so frank with me. Andres and I will see about the rejuvenation now. Perhaps tomorrow you'll see a very youthful me," she grinned. Lena smiled too.

"Say, do you want someone to watch over the rejuvenation machine's setup? I've used it many times," Lena volunteered.

"Would you? That would make us feel far more comfortable about this whole thing," Rafaela asked.

A bit later, Misty led the two into Med Labs One and Two. Both Rafaela and Andres stripped and laid down in the machine. "Okay, press the Close button. Your whole body will be covered by the machine. Soon, it'll put you to sleep," Lena explained while Misty worked the controls. "When you wake up, you'll be twenty-one again." Misty watched as the anesthetic was injected into both of them, verified they were unconscious, and that their vital signs were normal.

"Okay, now set the dial to the number of years to rejuvenate," Lena said.

"Okay, forty-five years. Press the Go button?" Misty asked. Lena nodded, and she did so. "Here goes nothing. Oh look. It says processing will take eight hours. Well, that's useful. I don't have to sit here wondering when it'll be done."

"Right. I'll leave you to it. That's all there is to it. Of course, it's going to use up quite a lot of your stem cells," Lena pointed out.

"We know. I wish Jan had brought more back with her. Maybe we can sneak some more in here when the Rigels reopen the spaceport. If not, maybe Queen Isabella can get some when she goes to the Ataro System," Misty suggested.

A bit later, Lena returned to Bart. He had the form filled out. Lena checked it over. She then had him enter her ID number and name. "Now, we just have to have someone file it and follow up on the funds delivery. I know, maybe Queen Altha could do that. Can you possibly contact her, Bart?" she asked, suspecting this was beyond him.

"Coming up. There'll be a three minute delay at this distance. Within ten minutes, she had a video link with Queen Altha, who looked terribly grim. "Hi Queen Altha. I've filled out a monetary compensation claim form for Queen Isabella and her late two wives. The Imperium should compensate her for what Senator Carlos did to her. Could you possibly send this in for me? If they approve the funds, could you somehow get them to her? I simply can't, not anymore. Over."

"Glad to do that for her. It is only just. By the way, something tragic has just happened here. I don't know who to even tell this to." Queen Altha looked like she would break down and start crying any second. Somehow, she held it together and continued. "Yesterday, the transport ship from President Snarry arrived, bringing Neva's new assistant. We said goodbye, and she boarded it. After the transport took off, something terrible happened to it. It just blew up! They're all dead. I'm so very sorry. We don't know what happened. An accident, perhaps. Over."

"Oh my god! Neva? Dead?" Lena gasped. At once, her ID Minister mind started working overtime. It couldn't have been an accident. Transports just don't blow up. Besides, it had gotten there safely. Why blow up after takeoff? Lena calmed her voice and replied, "Queen Altha. I suspect sabotage. I think someone planted a bomb on that ship to assassinate Neva. Have your people take sample readings in the area of the explosion. Look for traces of alenite-hydrocarbons. That would be my guess about the explosive used. How many were onboard. Over."

"Sabotage? Yes, yes! That makes sense. I'll get my security team on it right away. Neva, her new personal assistant, a pilot, and navigator. Four, I believe. Who could have wanted to kill Neva? She ended the war no less? She is, er was, a hero. Over."

"I can think of three. Legates Daag and Herman, and President Snarry. Those three were terrified of Neva and what she could potentially do, particularly the Legates. But a thorough investigation ought to be undertaken. If you find signs of an explosion, contact your Sector ID Minister. Contact me, if you do not get proper handling of this. My god, Neva dead. I can't believe it. Over."

"Okay. We're on it. Over and out." Queen Altha signed off.

Lena looked grimly at Bart. Then, she grimaced. "God damn. If only I weren't a helpless cripple! I'd be all over that investigation like a bull dog!"

"What's a bull dog?" Bart asked. "Never mind. I get it. I'll stay in touch with her and follow up on it. I'll let you know what happens. Sorry about Neva."

More sober now, Lena's tour continued with the Gang of Eight, along with Casilda, who refused to be parted from Drina, taking her through the public parts of Brom Castle. Then, they headed out onto the streets of Brom proper, stopping for a snack at one of Brom's finest pubs. Lena suspected this was an opportunity for Casilda actually to get out of the tower and into the city. She was right.

At breakfast the next morning, Venerada Maricela insisted Lena eat a lot of protein for breakfast and a goodly amount at that. However, the news making the rounds of the tables was what had happened to Andres and Rafaela. "Have you heard, they used the rejuvenation machine? It worked too well. They are back to being twenty-one again, but their bodies are just like what they were back then. They've lost their arms again!" Jan pointed out.

"Oh no! Really? She asked me about that. I didn't have any answer. I didn't know. Please, I need to see her," Lena replied. "I have to apologize! This must be horrid for her!"

Venerada Maricela replied, "I'll take you there, when I take you to the therapy room as soon as we finish breakfast. Don't worry about her. She and Andres lived very well like that for many years. Both are quite experienced in getting by, and I doubt very much if it'll be more than a minor annoyance to her incredibly valuable research. At least, we now know a bit more about the rejuvenation machine and its process. Benjamina was afraid something like that would happen too. That's partly why she didn't want to use it. For one thing, she'd likely end up being a male again. She was born male, but Lysandra came to her assistance once and that was what the goddess required for her intervention, turning him into a her."

Again, Lena didn't know what to make of all this. Of course, the newest medical machines could easily alter one's sex. Perhaps, that was what had been done in this case. Soon, she followed Venerada Maricela through the confusing tunnel system to Rafaela's quarters. Others were in the process of rearranging everything for her, putting their clothes into bottom drawers and such.

"Oh hi Lena. It worked. We're twenty-one again! Side-effects though," she laughed.

"I am so sorry, Rafaela, Andres, I didn't know. This is awful!" Lena gushed.

"Oh nothing major, dear. We're both quite used to this. Back to writing with our toes again. Benjamina was really afraid of this side-effect. She didn't want to have her male body back again — far too confusing for everyone she claimed. I can see her point. Things are confusing enough. Jan and the others are kind enough to rearrange things for us, getting them back low to the ground so we can reach them. Good luck with your therapy session. Gracia is waiting for her, Maricela."

Hastily, she led Lena back down the halls and through the doors of the Rehab Center. "Notice you can open the doors just by pushing against them. Further, the tunnel comes out on this main floor of the center. You are in Room One; that's the one Gracia always uses. She's really good, you know. Rafaela is pulling out all the stops for you!"

She pushed open the door, and Lena got her first look at Gracia. She was shocked. Gracia was a fifty year old mermaid. Like the other Westerlings, she had wavy, long black hair and bushy eyebrows. Her hair fell to her knee, rich and thick. She had an oval face and no trace of arms. Her face looked radiant, and Lena sensed that in spite of everything, Gracia was highly intelligent and vibrant. She hopped on her leg over to meet Lena. "Gracia. This is Lena Squire. Lena, Gracia. About the best we can do for a hug is a push." Smiling, Gracia hopped a little closer and pushed lightly into Lena, who smiled.

"Please to meet you, Gracia. Rafaela speaks highly of you. I've never seen someone like you before. I'm sorry if I'm staring."

Gracia laughed. "I'd stare too! Without using my *mentales* gifts, about all I can do is hop. Come on; have a seat. Let's begin. We can chat about things at lunchtime." She deftly hopped back to her chair, swung her hair around to her front side and sat down. Lena took her seat, and Maricela left them alone.

"I really don't need any therapy," Lena began.

"Thanks okay. I was once a powerful fighter, breaking new ground for us women. Then, all this happened to me. I was crushed! My whole world came to an end," Gracia explained.

"Yes, that's the way I feel too. My world's come to an end. I spent my whole life, some hundred twenty years, working my way up to the prestigious Sector ID Minister post over the central sector of the Imperium no less. Now I'm nothing at all, a helpless cripple," Lena replied, her grief coming to the forefront.

"So close your eyes. Let's go back to the first moment when you realized you'd lost it all and become a helpless cripple," Gracia cleverly ordered. Lena's therapy began.

Chapter 10 Adventures

"I've never cried so much in my entire life combined!" Lena said over lunch with Gracia. Together, they had stopped for lunch. She'd watched Gracia, as she gracefully hopped along to their lunchroom at one end of the Rehab Center. There, a local cook dished out their food and took it to a table for them, Gracia hopping all the way. Lena was amazed Gracia could even keep her balance.

Now, she saw Gracia had no choice but to use telekinetic skills to feed herself, while she struggled to use her toes as Drina and Amy had taught her. "Sorry, I'm so pathetic. I'm not Drina."

"Hey, it takes time to learn new ways to do things. At least, you've far more mobility than I do. All I can do is hop, and touch the center of my head or the back of my head. My foot can't even touch my ears. No lateral movement at all. I'm dependent on the bots, my *mentales* gifts, and my loving husband too. In fact, I can't really survive outside this area. I'd never make it up there in Brom proper." The two chatted while they ate. Gracia gave her plenty of time to eat, going slower herself so as not to seem to be pressuring Lena to hurry. After using the restroom, she hopped back to her room again.

By suppertime, Lena was experiencing the pain that went along with her recovery processes in the medical machines. The next day, she began experiencing the trauma the medical machines had done to her body while she was unconscious. Again, the pains were severe, and she cried a lot before the pains began to subside.

The third day the pains had mostly gone, but now she was fighting against the enforced sexual stimulus she'd endured countless times, along with her intense feelings of total helplessness. Gracia suspected these feelings would be the actual thread that led to earlier material, upon which all this pain and loss was hung. The milk episode didn't erase fully, but Gracia didn't expect that it would. She was just glad it had only taken two whole days to partially reduce. She'd expected she might need a week of slug, slug going. After going through the sexual stimulus and intense feelings all morning, she pressed Lena for something that happened to her earlier in time.

Before long, Lena was going through her teens and twenties. Way back then, she'd had similar intense feelings and a revulsion of sexual feelings. Naturally, those didn't erase either, and Gracia pushed for earlier and earlier times. She then ran smack into a prenatal experience her mother had while carrying her. Her father had tried to insist on having intercourse, but her mother vehemently refused. The argument led to her mother being struck, and the blow had knocked the developing Lena unconscious. After ten times through that one, Lena still felt bad, and Gracia continued to ask her for something even earlier.

"How can there be anything earlier?" Lena protested.

"Do you see any images there? Pictures? Masses?" Gracia hinted.

"Oh, there's this silly picture I sometimes see. But it's nothing."

"Well, let's take a look at it, shall we?" Gracia gently nudged her into it.

"I see a young woman. Wait, I sort of feel it's me," Lena said. Then, she got the full blast of its contents. She was a teen who had been forcibly raped. The man held her down, tied her arms to either side of her own bed, and then tied each of her legs to either side. She felt completely and utterly helpless to stop him. An hour later, Lena was laughing hard. "No wonder I hate sex and feel so helpless!" Gracia quietly ended that day's session.

As Lena rose, she suddenly exclaimed, "Oh my god! I've lived before! That was me in an earlier life! Oh my god!" Gracia merely smiled and led her out of the room, telling her to report back in the morning for more. She knew from vast experience Lena needed the rest of the day to enjoy her huge success.

"So how's it going with Lena? I saw her laughing her head off in the hall," Rafaela asked. She'd come to chat with Gracia.

The mermaid smiled, "She's encountered a past life. I'm not through with her yet. I want to track down any residual side somatics from her horrific milking episode. God, did they really do all that to those poor women on Gamelon-3?" she asked.

"Yes, and those men were behind starting the war between the Federation and the Imperium. They used the war as a cover to kidnap more women from abandoned Imperium worlds to add to their milk factories. Hideous," Rafaela replied.

Gracia was quite thorough. She made darn sure she erased all the trauma chains that had been tied together into one during Lena's horrid experience on Gamelon-3. She found five more smaller threads, each of which also ended in a past life trauma situation. Then, she tackled other minor traumas Lena had experienced during her long hundred twenty year lifetime. A few broken bones were handled, but little else. After two weeks of therapy, she pronounced Lena finished with the basic therapy.

"Congratulations Lena, we're done. What you've had, we call Basic Therapy, which handles the obvious traumas one's incurred in his or her lifetime. So we are done, and you can get on with whatever you want to do next. However, if you are interested in more, we have Advanced Therapy available, but that you can get at any time later on," Gracia explained.

"How can I ever thank you enough, Gracia? You've literally saved my life! I feel so alive now. Still can hardly do a damned thing, but who cares? I'll get by somehow. If you can, I sure as hell can. Say, I'd really like to see where you live and meet your husband. He must be a really fine man."

"Sure. It's early enough that I can fix supper for a change. Let's get Jan to tag along, so you don't get lost finding your way back," Gracia suggested.

"You can cook?" Lena asked quite startled.

Gracia laughed, "Sort of. You'll see. The bots do it really. Come on. I've let Jan know. Follow me. I'll hop along at your speed. I can hop really fast if I have to," she teased. Lena smiled and followed her down the long maze of hallways.

At last she caught on. "We're following the black circles,

right?"

Still hopping along, Gracia replied, "Yes, so we don't get ourselves lost either. Here we go. Inside this doorway, you are entering our artificial world called Madiera. I'm told it's really inside some giant spaceship that landed here many years ago. Welcome to Madiera, home to us mermaids."

Lena saw a whole world or rather a self-sustaining town-like setup, complete with sky and real grass. She saw many other mermaid women hopping along the streets, as well as countless children, some of whom were also young mermaids. However, not all the female children were like Gracia, only a handful. "The robots that run this place have modified our recessive genes, so that our daughters are born normally. There are still a few like us around, but in another generation, this horrible body form will be history, thank god. Come on; it's this way to my quadraplex." When she reached her front door, she said, "Open door." It opened for her.

Bit by bit, Lena began to see all the automated devices that made a good life possible for these women. She found Diego to be very handsome and quite charming. Of course, Gracia had to show her how she fixed meals by ordering them via the bots, which cooked it. She demonstrated how the mechanical devices worked that allowed her to carry things to and from the table and elsewhere. "See, I operate it with my foot and toes. Marvelous invention. I can actually use these mechanical arms to use the silverware to feed myself."

Just then, Jan showed up. "Hi y'all. Sorry I'm late. Doing a little something for Rafaela. What's for supper? Thanks for having me Gracia. I hear Lena is done with her therapy now." She sat down in the chair that Diego hastily produced for her. The perfect gentlemen, Lena thought.

"Yes, she's done. Now, you all can go on your trip north. Yes, we've all heard about it, Jan," she teased the teen. Jan flushed a little.

"I can't believe how wonderful I feel now," Lena added. "Still can't do much of anything, but what the heck. I'm really alive and that's what counts, isn't it?"

"Absolutely, Miss Squire," Diego replied politely, but enthusiastically. "That's what counts in the end. Isn't Gracia here the best darn woman in the entire universe? I knew that from the first moment I ever laid eyes on her." Gracia blushed this time. They chatted and continued to dine on a steak dinner.

After dinner, Gracia showed Lena more of her bots. Over tea, Jan explained about the arrival of Alpha and Beta and this ship. On their way home, she took Lena up into the control room to show her the two robots. Lena was very impressed with the incredible level of technological sophistication nearly everywhere. Much to Jan's disappointment, she had no idea of the actual planet of origin of this ship or its original women. Jan had rather hoped Lena would recognized something here and be able to fill in blanks.

On their long walk back, Jan said, "Okay, tomorrow we pack up. We are going by horse up north to Hilliard Heights. This is going to be great fun. Drina has actually gotten Maricela to allow Casilda to come with us! Amazing. Usually, they make the katalyein ride in carriages or wagons, if they *ever* let them go on a trip without using teleportation. I think you've had an influence on Maricela. Anyhow, Casilda thinks so. First thing in the morning, Bernardo will be by to help you and Casilda pack. Nadja will be riding in a wagon along with her recording gear and all our food and tents. I guess if Casilda or you get tired of riding, you can ride in the wagon with her. This will be a blast." Jan was quite excited, Lena could see that much.

The next morning, Lena did her best to wiggle into her leathers, using her teeth and head to pull up her pants. Casilda, she noticed, was having as much trouble as she was getting into hers and relaxed a little. Amy was cheating, of course, and she came to the aid of the other two, fastening their belts for them. Each had a bag of their trail clothes and one bag with their fancier outfits, just in case an occasion arose. Bernardo and Beltran, Casilda's twin, knocked and entered, ready to carry their bags down for them. Beltran grumbled, "I don't like you going off like this sis. You are fragile."

Casilda almost broke down. Lena stepped in, "Hey, give her a chance to experience life a little, Beltran. She may have a hard time with things, but allow her the opportunity to see the world a little bit." He flushed and apologized to his sister. Casilda gave Lena an appreciative look. So few stood up for her, Lena realized.

Outside, the small party was getting organized. Jan introduced their two guides. "Lena, these are two Sisterhood members. Mary Tribe e Hays is our guide, and her free mate Jean Hays e Tribe is our fighter-protector." Both women were twenty-four with short brown hair and dressed in leather trail clothing. Except for their melon sized bosoms, they looked much like the men. Both carried short swords and daggers, she noted.

"Pleased to meet you. Can I ask what's a free mate and what's with the e and the last names?" Lena asked.

It brought a smile to Mary's face. She replied, "I'll tell you that, if you'll tell me what happened to your skin. It's so black! Did you get burned or something?"

Now Lena smiled. "The planet of my birth is a very hot one. We all have dark skin to prevent having our skins burned when we're outside," Lena answered.

"Hey, I thought all the aliens were grey," Jean called out, checking the cinching of all the horses.

Lena laughed. "Only those from Rigel-3. There's all manner of skin colors out there among the stars."

Mary chuckled, "Okay, okay. We're free mates. We chose to marry, and we take pride in our mothers and use their names. Mine was Tribe. Jean's was Hays. When we marry, we put the e, between the last names, like the Westerlings' 'and,' I think. We best get going. Lot of ground to cover, if we're to make Crooked Creek by nightfall." She and Jean swung themselves into their saddles.

Both were obviously pros at this, Lena noted. She needed Bernardo's help mounting. Soon, she saw that Casilda, Drina, and Amy also needed help and forgot about how awkward she looked trying to mount. She bit down on her wooden block to which her reins were tied and fell into line beside Bernardo, who insisted on riding behind the two Sisterhood women. Lena noted the boyfriends rode beside their girlfriends, namely Henry and Adrianna and Ben and

Drina. Of course, Jan was next to Amy; they were inseparable. Beltran rode beside his sister, Casilda. Then came Hidalgo beside Nita. Diego drove the wagon and Nadja sat beside him, but the wagon was rather loaded with bags, food supplies, musical instruments, and camping gear.

Jean and Mary set a reasonable pace, considering they had four armless women on this trip. Neither quite knew what to expect from the four. Would they be able to keep up? This was one reason Bernardo wanted to ride right behind them, to convince the two Sisterhood women they could keep up.

Soon, Lena could tell they were traveling on what must be a trail of sorts. Bernardo picked up her thoughts and chatted. "Yes, this is a trail, right Mary?"

"Yes, it is a northern track, well-traveled." Then for Lena's benefit mostly, she began explaining as they went along. "Main route north here by the mountains. Notice the dense resinous pine forests. The sap is used for oil; the wood makes for nice fires. Of course, we have many fire patrols out here. Lightning strikes start them. If all hands don't get the fires put out, the forest blazes can well wipe out farmsteads and even towns. Over on your right, you can see the nut trees. They provide us our nut flour for baking and pod silk for your satin gowns."

"What's pod silk," Lena asked through clenched teeth.

"I'm told that long ago, the nut trees didn't have the pods. But when the Great Climate Shift came centuries ago, the nut trees adapted to the daily cold and snowy summer by developing those pods. Tonight, if some nut trees are near us, you can see the pods closing over the fruit, protecting the developing nuts. It's summer, but nights are still quite cold this far north. Locals harvest both the nuts and the pods. Once a year, we take wagonloads of the silk to market. I think someone in Brom takes them on down to Elegant Fashions Inc."

"Wild animals?" Lena called out. The terrain looked void of inhabitants, something she'd never seen before.

"Lots. Around here, the only ones you have to worry about are the big cats, the Montaña beasts." She described them in detail.

However, Diego yelled up towards the front of the line, "Don't worry about them. I have my flute handy. One note drives them away. They can't stand that sound." Lena didn't believe him, though. The cats sounded horrible.

"Then, there are bears and wolves, but they won't bother us. Our party is too large for them. No poisonous snakes up here," Mary added.

An hour later, they spotted a man out working among some nut-type trees. Mary spoke up, "That's old Wilbur. He's working on domesticating another variety of nut tree. Hope he's successful."

Later on, they passed an ore mine from which copper was mined. They saw two wagons loaded with the ore and three more waiting to be filled. As they rode past, they spotted a miner coming out of a tunnel. He waived, and Mary replied in kind. Lena began to notice how friendly everyone was, strangely different from the worlds, which she had overseen.

Around four as the orange-red sun sank behind the tall mountains to their left, they came upon a large farmstead. The manor house was built of grey stone, quarried from the mountainside close by. A very large corral housed horses and reindeer. Sheep were grazing on the grass within a nearby pasture surrounded by a low stone wall. Picturesque. A large grove of nut trees grew to their right. Smoke curled skyward from a chimney. Mary announced, "Crooked Creek. An extended family lives here. We'll pay them ten silvers to put us up for the night. Let me go make the arrangements first. Old Hank is expecting us."

While the others dismounted, she headed on up to the wooden door. Bernardo insisted on lifting Lena off her horse. "Why?" she asked. As her feet hit the ground, she added, "Oh! They are mush! Thanks, Bernardo." The others took a hint from Bernardo and lifted Casilda, Drina, and Amy down as well. Amy nearly fell down, though.

She grumbled, "Jan, these heels are almost impossible to walk in out here." Jan replied, but Lena couldn't hear what Jan said though, but guessed it wasn't complimentary.

A nut tree was not too far distant. "Come on, Lena. Let's go see if the pod are closing."

"Hey, I want to see them too," Casilda called out. "Beltran, help me please."

"Wait for us; we want to see them too," Drina added. She and Ben followed the four.

"Now that's interesting," Lena commented, watching the large pods slowly closing over the tiny nut that one day would be quite large at harvest time.

"Neat. I've never seen the pods before. Cool indeed," Casilda added.

Just then, Mary came out of the manor house. An older man tagged along side of her. She called out, "Diego. We can use your services. Hank's wife, Ann, took a bad fall yesterday and broke her leg. Can you help her?"

"Sure thing. That's why I'm along. Coming. Dear, can you manage the wagon?" Diego asked, then added, "Hidalgo, help your mom." He followed Mary back inside, while Hank helped them get their horses into his spare corral and unsaddled. He provided hay and grain for them as well.

Once inside, they saw Diego was tending to the older woman. Several other women introduced themselves along with their husbands and a host of children. Julie said, "Come on in. Supper is about ready. Rabbit stew, cheese, greens, and freshly baked nut break will be ready in a few more minutes. Josh, you lead them to the wash basins and take them to the dining room." She glanced worriedly at her mother, however, before scampering back into the kitchen, but not without staring at the four armless women.

The extended family had around thirty members, including the children and several sets of twins around the same age as the Gang of Eight. Three wooden tables served the large group. Hank and Diego were the last to arrive, carrying Ann between them. She looked better than before or so Hank claimed. "I'll finish up on her after supper," Diego explained.

Over dinner, Nadja explained to them she was a linguist and was traveling Tierra studying everyone's language so she and others could learn to speak their language better. She then asked if it was okay if she recorded some of what they were saying. They really didn't know what she was talking about, but agreed. Lena knew how she was doing it though. She wore an ear-microphone, which relayed the sounds she heard to her portable recorder computer in the other room.

Some thirty watched as Lena bit into the freshly baked bread. They were also watching Drina, Amy, and Casilda as well. "Oh my! This is incredibly good tasting bread. I swear this is the best bread that I've ever encountered," Lena commented after swallowing her first bite.

"Nut flour bread. My own recipe, Annie baked it, since I went and broke my leg," Ann quickly explained.

"Incredible bread. I could eat the whole loaf!" Lena added, bring a smile to both Ann and Annie's faces. The ice broken, the large group began chatting away. Meanwhile, Lena gobbled up more of the bread.

One of their teen boys asked her, "How come you lost your arms? Are you one of them tower women too — that can do the helpful magic stuff?"

Lena laughed. "Heavens no. Some wicked men cut them off and tortured me, but thankfully, I was rescued. Casilda and Drina here are your tower women, who do wonderful things to help others. Not me." Of course, they all looked at Drina and Casilda with awestruck eyes. She was pleased to have diverted their attention off herself.

After the meal, many hands helped with the dishes, while Diego worked more on Ann's leg. Unable to be of any use, Lena chose to sit and watch, as did Drina, Amy, and Casilda. Drina made a telepathic rapport connection to Lena. *I'm joining you with us and with Diego so you can see firsthand what he is doing. Just don't bother him; bother me.*

Lena had never felt such a powerful and intimate bond before and was breathless for a moment before her body finally inhaled. *Are those her cells?* She asked Drina.

Yes. Diego has the healing gift. He's mending her break, one cell at a time. If he has enough time and doesn't run out of energy, he might get the whole bone healed up. Pretty neat, isn't it? I wish I could do that, but I can't.

Lena watched in utter amazement. Ann's break was healing right before her own eyes, and there was no medical machine in sight. Normally, in her world, she'd just put the leg into the medical machine and have the break healed in a few minutes. Here, the man was doing it all with his own mind and will power. It also shocked her that Diego could actually see such tiny cells!

Finally, he broke the connection with Ann. "Not fully healed, but you can put your weight on it. You should be careful with it for another couple of weeks, Ann."

"Thank you, Diego. Thank you. That was a miracle. You tower folk are welcome here anytime," Ann replied, standing and testing her leg. "Almost good as new, Hank!"

"Come, Hidalgo, bring out the guitars; it's music time," Diego called out. Hidalgo unwrapped the two instruments. "Gather round; time for some fun. You can dance, if you've a mind to." He and his son began playing dance duets. Soon, Hank and several others began clapping time, and Diego broke into song. His voice added a wonderful contrast to their strumming sounds. Several of the extended family did just that. Recognizing a local dance tune, they began dancing around the dining room, dodging the chairs and tables.

Before long, Jan put her arms around Amy and they joined in. Quickly, so did Ben and Drina, and Henry and Adrianna. Bernardo pulled Lena up to her feet. "Come on; you're not going to be left out."

"But I don't know how to dance," Lena protested.

"Who cares. Fake it," he whispered. He kept both his arms around her waist, just as Jan was doing with Amy. He swung her around and around. Lena kept glancing at the others, trying to figure out what she should be doing, but soon realized they were all just improvising and having fun. An hour later, Diego and Hidalgo ended. Both were pooped, as were the dancers.

Annie led Lena and the others to one of their guest bedrooms that sported two beds, nicely made. Two gorgeous quilts covered them. "Wow! Look at this quilt! Fantastic. Did you make these?" Lena asked.

Annie flushed, "Yes, miss. My sister made the other one. We make all our blankets."

"Well, I've never seen such a beautiful quilt before. The flower baskets look so real. I hate to even sleep on it," Lena added.

Annie giggled. "You're supposed to sleep on it and keep warm. These guest rooms get quite cold at night. That's why we make them."

"Do you ever sell any of your quilts? If so, I'd love to buy some. This one is fabulous. Oh crap. I don't have any local coins," Lena suddenly realized she had no way to pay for anything on this world!

"Hey, I can cover it until we can get your funds here," Amy spoke up.

Annie was very pleased to sell the quilt to Lena, but Lena insisted on paying her twice what she asked for it. "So much hand work and such tiny stitches. I've just got to give you more than that," Lena insisted. Thus, the next morning, Annie folded her quilt up and stowed it in a small bag for Lena. Annie was very pleased this strange alien had taken such a fancy to her artistic creation. When they headed off northward the following morning, the whole extended family waved goodbye to the group.

Lena did take note of the nearby nut trees. Already the pods were opening up, something she found rather amazing. She wondered if other botanists knew of such things and made a note to herself to ask one day. Then, she realized she'd not ever likely be able to do such a thing any longer. That life was closed to her now. Soberly, she rode on, following the two Sisterhood women, thankful her facial expressions were hidden by her tight grip on the wooden block with her reins.

Again, they passed through dense pine forests, teaming with small wildlife and wild flowers. Periodically, off to their right, they spotted more groves of nut trees. Lena rightly concluded there was probably a farmstead not far from them. The ground was rocky, quite unlike that green, sloping pasture by Exchange City. She was now a thousand miles further north along the very edge of the Goza. This much she recalled from the map at Isabella's.

Twice, they crossed a babbling brook, whose waters came from the still melting snow on the very tops of the mountains. Harsh country, but beautiful, Lena thought as she rode along, a bit more subdued today. She estimated they had to ride some five hundred miles. Mary had suggested they try to make fifty miles each day, so Lena estimated they'd spend ten days on the trail.

After a time, Mary wanted to break the monotony of the ride. She turned to Lena and said, "Isn't this county just incredible? Beautiful lands. Can you see why some of us just love to live up here, far from the maddening civilized farmlands of the south. Jean and I love it up here, especially being out of doors. I tried to be a shop keeper once, didn't last a month." Jean laughed and confirmed Mary's statement.

"It is very different from what I've always been around," Lena replied. Images of the steel and plastic of her battle cruiser came unbidden into her mind. She'd spent over a half a century within that sterile metal cage, like some bird with clipped wings. She could and did move around, but only occasionally dropping down to concrete, steel, and glass buildings, hardly much different. Out here, there was life and beauty. She breathed deeply and sighed. What have I missed?

Early afternoon, dark storm clouds gathered. Quickly, they donned their rain cloaks. Bernardo hastily put Lena's over her and fastened it around her neck. "Going to storm soon. Don't worry. The mare shouldn't spook," he explained. He did pivot in his saddle to make sure that everyone was covered. A sharp flash of lightning startled Lena. A loud peal of thunder caused her to jerk and drop her wooden block. Smiling, Bernardo leaned over and grabbed it, holding it up for her to take back again. She mouthed a thank you.

"Going to be a big one," he yelled. More lightning struck, and the downpour began in earnest. They plodded onwards. Then lightning struck not far ahead of them, temporarily blinding them so brilliant was its flash. After blinking several times, Lena sensed something was wrong. Perhaps it was because Mary and Jean reined in causing her to pull back on her reins.

Then, she smelled smoke and looked up. The strike had started a fire on a resinous pine just ahead of them. "We have to put it out!" yelled Mary.

Everyone dismounted. Bernardo yelled above the noise of thunder and lashing rains, "Fire. If we don't put it out, it can spread and burn down massive acres of pine and farmsteads too. Come on; you can help." Quickly, Jean raced to the wagon and grabbed several shovels, handing them to the men. Bernardo gathered the four together. "Okay, you four are to stamp out any embers on the ground. We're going to fight the fire with the shovels. Got it?" Amy yelled that they had. Quickly, Diego, Hidalgo, Ben, and Henry took the shovels and began tossing dirt onto the fallen, blazing tree. Nadja and Mary gathered up the horses, tying them to the wagon.

Amy, Jan, Drina, Casilda, and Lena began stomping the fires that sprang up among the thick bed of needles. For a time, Lena thought this was hopeless. The heavy resins only seemed to fuel the fire like an accelerant. Coughing from the thick smoke, they kept at it, thankful for the heavy rain, which helped. None noticed when the rains stopped, and the orange-red sun popped out again.

Suddenly, two gliders swooped down from the now blue sky. Lena spotted them and pointed them out to the others. "Look. What are those?" she yelled.

"Thank god, help has arrived. Those are the fire gliders from Brom," Mary yelled. They circled around and landed in a small clearing. Soon, four young men and two women came rushing up, carrying axes and shovels.

"Hi ya. Doing our job for us, eh?" their leader called out. "I'm Tom. Fire patrol. We spotted this strike during the storm, but we couldn't get the gliders up until it passed. Thanks for nearly putting it out for us. By now, we expected to have to call in more gliders. There are two further ahead of you."

"You're welcome," Mary replied. "We saw the strike and stopped to put it out as best we could."

"Thanks. We'll take over now." The group backed off and allowed the six to do their work.

"Well done," Mary complimented everyone. To Lena, she explained, "You see out here in the north country, fires are commonplace. We've got Fire Patrol Stations at Brom and at Hilliard Heights. They are constantly manned, looking for fires breaking out. When spotted, they send out these three man-gliders to try to snuff them out before they become a major blaze."

"What happens if they get too big?" Lena asked.

Mary answered, while dusting herself off. "Then, they call an all-hands and gather everyone within twenty miles or more to come lend a hand fighting it. Sometimes, they bring in folks from Brom, who have a special ability to snuff out fires. They are rather strange women, but they sure can snuff out a fire. I once saw one doing that. It was more like magic. She just stood there, kind of like you are, Lena. The fire was a veritable raging inferno, and then the fire just went out. Just like that. Poof. No fire. Strange. Well, we've lost a lot of time. Let's get going. I know a place where we can camp out tonight."

An hour later, Mary reined in beside another bubbling brook. Off to their right was a large grassy patch where they pitched camp. Two-man pup tents went up, compliments of the boys. Meanwhile, Mary gathered stones to make a campfire, while Jean gathered up firewood for cooking. The four had very little they could do and mostly watched the others. "Okay, so who is the cook on this trip?" Mary asked, looking from person to person.

"That'd be me," Diego called out. He'd finished hobbling the horses to a tether line. "Give me a minute. Why don't the rest of you wash off the smoke?"

Mary looked at Nadja, who laughed. "Don't look at me. I've never cooked a thing in my life!" For once, Lena felt comfortable. She wasn't the only woman who had never cooked meals. All the teen girls had rather funny expressions on their faces. Lena didn't need telepathy to know they didn't cook either.

"What a bunch we are," Lena laughed. "None of us women can cook." That brought laughter all around.

"Well, we can, but we thought that we'd ask first," Mary pointed out. "Tower folk. Bunch of lazy women." More laughs followed.

"Well, I have a good excuse," Drina justified, raising her shoulders. Casilda added her "me too" to Drina's comment. Amy didn't say anything.

"I just push a button," Lena added her laughter to that of the others, causing them to laugh all the harder.

"Fine bunch we have here, Jean," Mary joked and went to help Diego out.

As they sat around the campfire eating their supper, Diego explained, "I've always been my own cook. Before I met my angel here, I rode over the countryside of the Westerlings and had no choice but to cook up whatever I had at hand. I don't mind. Besides, Nadja's work is too important for her to waste a lot of time cooking."

"Dad's a good cook," Adrianna spoke up. "I'm just learning from him now. I know, I should have learned that a long time ago. Don't worry, Henry, I'll have it down by the time we get married. I won't let you starve."

Drina spoke up hastily, "Ben, we'll just hire us a cook. Okay?" He laughed.

"Okay, tonight, I want someone with arms to sleep with one who hasn't. Safety. We're out in the wilderness," Jean got serious.

"I'll sleep with Amy," Jan volunteered instantly. Everyone laughed again.

Nadja spoke up, "No monkey business in your tent." Amy flushed, but everyone else roared with laughter.

Adrianna volunteered to sleep with Drina, while Nita took Casilda. "Hey, mom put me in charge of Lena. So I'll be with her." Bernardo spoke up.

"Well, I don't know if that's a good idea," Nadja suggested. "I can sleep with Lena."

"Oh, that's okay with me, Nadja. If he tries anything, I'll kick him where it hurts," Lena countered. "I'm not shy." Again, the teens all laughed heartily at Bernardo's expense. He flushed.

He helped her into the tent and got her situated on the wool blankets and then squeezed in beside her. She asked, "Is this necessary? Is there danger out here?"

"Jean's being cautious and probably wise. Nothing is likely to happen, but if something does come up, it's smart to have one of us handy. Wolf or bear might get nosy or something, but not likely. We best get some sleep," he replied.

Lena hadn't slept this close to a man in her hundred twenty years. It felt strange to her. He fell asleep quickly, and, for quite some time, she listened to the night sounds and his easy breathing. She felt his body heat helping keep her warm.

The last thing she remembered was thinking that this was rather pleasant. Then, she heard the dinner gong.

Diego had pancakes waiting for them. "Oh, I slept on a boulder," she complained. "My backside." Bernardo began rubbing her back. "Lower. Yes, there. Ah. Great. Thanks." He smiled and got her shoes on for her and then helped her get out of the confines of the small pup tent. Both stretched in the early morning, chilly dawn.

Lena was a little frustrated, unable to really do anything to help out while camp was broken, gear stowed, and the horses readied. She was used to doing her part, often far more, onboard her battle cruiser. Now, she was reduced to being baggage. Glancing surreptitiously at Casilda and Drina, she saw they were also a little bothered by similar feelings.

She soon forgot about that. They mounted up and rode north with the low orange-red sun just over their right shoulders, bringing new rays of hope to the great trees. Never had she seen so many trees before. The planets she patrolled only had scattered trees on some luxury estates. The air smelled so fresh and clean, full of exotic fragrances, at least they were foreign to her, quiet unlike the odors of oil and metal that had surrounded her for so many years. As they rode along in silence, the chatter of birds caught her attention. Then, she spotted great hawks circling high overhead. Lena wondered if they could see her. If so, what did they think of her invading their forest? *Invader, yes, in a way that is what I am, an invader.*

Midmorning, they passed another farmstead. Mary pointed out, if it had not been for the fire, here's where they would have spent the night. They rode on, silence prevailed, but now Lena noticed their two guides seemed to prefer it this way. Both women were also looking at the world around them. She smiled and did likewise.

Some distance ahead, she thought she saw someone coming towards them. *Good, Mary and Jean see them too.* As if in response, they picked up speed before reining in before the woman who was on foot. She was frantically waving her arms. Lena was close enough to both see and hear the woman. "Help me. Please, help me. It's John, please."

Lena was shocked. The woman didn't have any hands. She wore a warm leather dress, somewhat similar to her own outfit, except she had pants instead of a skirt. Brown leather moccasins covered her feet. She was frantic and out of breath from running. She heard Jean call out, "It's okay. We're here. What's wrong, Martha? Catch your breath." The group halted before the woman, who bent over gasping for breath.

After a minute, she began talking rapidly. Lena guessed she was probably in her mid-twenties. "It's Phil. He's in bad trouble. Hank's back at the house with him. We don't know what to do. Sent me for help. Please, you must come. Help us."

"Of course, Martha. Give me your arm. Up you come," Jean's strong arm latched onto her arm, and she swung the woman up and behind her on her horse. Lena now realized just how muscular Jean really was beneath her loose fitting leather top. Jean led them at a canter, but Martha said little, holding on tightly, her arms around Jean's waist. A few miles later, they arrived at another stone-built farmstead. The quaint cottage was built from loose stones gathered and mortared together. It was rather large with a thatched roof. Smoke curled from its chimney, and there were a number of outbuildings. As they rode up, another handless woman and a man stepped out, followed by five children, the oldest was barely five.

"Thank god! Jean, Mary, we need help!" the man called out urgently.

"We're here, Bill. What's the matter with Hank?" Jean asked worriedly. She lowered Martha to the ground, while everyone dismounted and gathered around the three adults. Lena noticed several were looking at her, but at her skin color, not her shoulders. It dawned on her they were not surprised to see armless women, but rather one whose skin was black.

"It's Hank. He's in a trance, and we can't get him out of it. Come, you have to see him." Bill led the group inside. There in their kitchen, Hank sat on a chair staring into an irregular, blue crystal, which was emitting a soft glow.

Amy spoke up at once. "Where did he get that crystal?" Jean and Mary backed off. This was not something they could handle; Lena picked that up from their unusual facial expressions, as the two Sisterhood women glanced at each other, then Amy. Both backed away, joining the two wives.

Bill explained, "Two days ago, we were plowing the east field, going to try to raise some tubers this season. Hank dug that rock up. He kept it because he said it was pretty. We woke up this morning and found him like this. He's just staring into the thing and it's glowing. It wasn't glowing before when we found it. I've tried everything I can think of to break the spell. Can you help him?"

Amy looked at Jan and then replied, "I think so. Get everyone back a ways. Jan, take a look. You thinking what I'm thinking?"

"What's wrong with him?" Drina asked. "Is that a giant crystal? Like ours?"

"It has to be," Casilda added her thoughts.

"It told him he ought to go to Brom Tower," Martha wailed. "His eyes turned yellow. I told him to go, but he kept telling me it wasn't necessary. Is he going to die?" She pulled a five year old boy and a three year old girl in close to her body, comforting them with her arms.

Amy looked up. Turning to Martha, she asked, "When did his eyes change color, Martha?"

"About a month ago. He seemed all right at the time. Is he dying? It's all my fault. I should have insisted that he go to Brom," Martha wailed.

"He wouldn't leave you and the birds, Martha. You know that," Bill put in. "Can anything be done for him? Is it too late now? It's not contagious, is it? We're not in danger, are we?"

"Not contagious, whatever is going on," Amy put them a little at ease. She thought for a minute and then spoke up, "Okay. Mary, Jean, take the families outside. Leave us alone for a while. Lena, you can stay. Gang, gather around. Drina, Casilda, gently, gently see if he has a mental block in place. Do not under *any* circumstances try to remove it; just gently see if he has a block. If there is one and you try to remove it, you might be killed too."

Cautiously, the two teens moved up close, and Lena watched them carefully, but could see them doing nothing really. Whatever they did, it was mental, she concluded. The small crystals they always wore around their necks did glow pale blue, like this enormous rock was glowing, but only for a brief instant. Both back up. Drina spoke with a trace of fear in her voice, "No blocks. Amy, what does this mean?" Casilda nodded her agreement.

"That's a break. Lena, you have visible proof of our cardinal rule. An untrained telepath is both a danger to himself and to others. Hank here has recently gotten the *mentales* gifts. Martha is right. He should have gone to Brom Tower at once for a couple weeks of training. He didn't. Yes, that is a monster-sized crystal, like the ones we all wear."

Lena put it together. "So that crystal is amplifying something a thousandfold more than your crystals?"

"Observant, Lena. Precisely. Only he hasn't learned to control his gifts, and it's now controlling him."

"Can anything be done for him? Is he as good as dead?" Lena asked worriedly.

"Don't know. For sure if we hadn't come along," Amy answered solemnly.

"But we don't have a clue what to do about it," Bernardo pointed out. "Do we try to get Rafaela teleported here?" Several others agreed with him. Lena quickly picked up only Amy and Jan really knew what to do with this situation.

Jan answered for Amy who was deep in thought. "It's beyond her knowledge too, Bernardo. Actually, Hank is in luck. Amy and I are about the only people on Tierra that have any chance of saving him. Fortuitous luck he has. No wait. Is that you Josh?" Her face went blank for a second, as if she too were deep in thought. Then, her face animated again. That was Josh. He was pointing us to Hank here. Clever man. Okay, where was I? Oh yes. Amy and I have dealt with these things, but gosh, that was over a century ago. I've lost track."

"Jan, let's focus together. We need to alter its resonance pattern. Yours or mine?" Amy asked.

"Yours, dear, you are stronger by a tad," Jan answered.

"Okay, then get into rapport with me. The rest of you, stand back in case this doesn't work, and the crystal explodes," Amy ordered. She and Jan slipped easily into rapport with each other. Together, they focused on the crystal itself, slowly aligning its resonance frequency from its own raw frequency to that of Amy's. Lena stared hard at the blue glow; she thought she could possibly see its glow alter slightly. Suddenly, Hank fell over, banging his head on the table. For him, the spell was broken. Amy and Jan slowly backed out and relaxed. "Whew that was dicey. Okay, Diego, carry him to a bed and check him out. Jan, find a bag for this crystal. No one touch it! For god's sake, don't touch it now. It might kill me!"

"I don't understand," Lena spoke up, as Diego dragged Hank out of the kitchen.

Amy tried to explain, "Hank focused on the crystal that just happened to be attuned to his own native emitting frequency. It overpowered him and sucked him into its power. I guess a way you could look at this is you are in a spaceship and you haven't a clue how to fly it and it is flying you around versus you controlling the ship making it fly where you want it to go. This crystal took over total control of Hank here."

"Makes sense, I suppose. So what did you do?" Lena asked. She saw Drina, Casilda, and several others were as keenly interested in this as she was.

"Jan and I joined together and attuned the crystal to my own personal frequency. Each person emits energy at their own unique frequency, a very tiny wavelength in your terms. Once its resonance frequency was changed, the contact with Hank was broken."

"So now it is attuned to you?" Lena asked. "If so, why would someone else touching it harm you?"

"I'd get a psychic shock. From a crystal this large, the shock might prove fatal to this body," Amy replied. "We can safely insulate it by putting it into a pod silk bag, if we have one this large. If not, we'll use whatever we can find for now."

"I see. Say, can't you then use it to amplify your own powers rather immensely?" Lena asked. Somehow, this all seemed logical to her now.

"Damn, Lena. You don't miss a trick," Amy answered with a broad grin, somewhat pleasing Lena. "Yes, I certainly could, but that kind of power we don't need on Tierra. Good lord. Centuries ago, it was crystals like these that very nearly exterminated mankind on Tierra. With these, one of us could melt stone! In fact, several towers were annihilated with stones such as these, countless lives were lost. If I recall right, been centuries now, but if I recall right, one of these stones was used to pull one of the Rigel's spaceships down from the sky, causing it to crash at their spaceport. You can see why we don't want this kind of power around. No one would be safe, not on any world."

"Holy crap! That's almost too wild to believe. I must check the records about this," her Sector ID Minister curiosity was roused.

"He'll be all right. Coming around now," Diego called out from another room. Amy sent Bernardo to fetch the others, just as Jan returned with a bag. Amy levitated the stone and slipped it into the bag, all without touching it, impressing the many teens.

The next few minutes, Martha and the others congregated around Hank's bed, talking furiously. At first, they were mad, but that soon changed to one of great relief and thankfulness. While this was going on, Amy contacted Bart and Rafaela. Shortly after that, Ken appeared beside Amy; Bart had teleported him. "Is this it?" he asked quietly.

Lena noticed his face was rather pale. This crystal was certainly causing quite a lot of worry, she thought. Amy nodded, and he picked up the sack as if it contained an explosive device, or so Lena believed. He and the bag vanished. Amy whispered, "Bart teleported them. He's coming back for Hank shortly." A few minutes later, Ken reappeared.

Amy and Ken joined Martha and her group around the bed on which Hank lay. He looked terribly pale. "Hi. I am Amy; this is Ken from Brom. You have had one very narrow escape. You should listen to Martha. She was right. You simply have to get yourself trained right now. Ken will take you to Brom Tower and see that happens quickly. You should be back in a couple of weeks. If you ever find another one of those large blue crystals, for heaven's sake don't touch it. Contact Brom Tower immediately. Let them dispose of it, unless you have a death wish." That last brought a trace of a smile to Hank's face. She added for Martha's benefit, "Hank should be just fine and back in just a couple of weeks."

After receiving many thank you's, Ken took hold of Hank's hand, supporting him. Bart teleported them to the tower's pad, where Venerada Maricela was waiting to get him into training at once. Meanwhile, Martha asked them, "I don't know how to thank all of you. Would you care for some tea and nut bread?"

Being polite, she replied, "Yes, if it is no bother." Martha flashed a smile. She and Bill's wife, Piper, headed off to the kitchen. Amy, Jan, and Lena followed them, while Nadja and Diego and the others chatted with Bill and the many children, easing their fears over what happened to Hank.

"So I take it you both are elementals?" Amy asked. Lena watched the two using their arms to carry a teapot onto the stove and a loaf of nut bread over to the table.

Martha smiled, "Earth. Piper is Air. Glad you noticed. We didn't know how to deal with that crystal thing. I just knew Hank ought to have gone to Brom Tower, but he was so worried about our falcons. He catches them and trains them. We just love it out here." Lena noticed both women went about their chores, using clever means in lieu of their hands. As they chatted, she understood just how much these two women truly enjoyed their lives out here in what Lena would call total wilderness. Once more, Lena devoured quite a lot of the nut bread. As always, Diego and Hidalgo gave the two families a short concert, before they left to continue their northward journey.

Two days later, the tall, imposing mountains receded further to the west and the track opened up onto rolling valleys of grasslands and stands of pines and nut trees. Now, Lena began seeing small herds of horses and reindeer. Bernardo explained Hilliard Heights raised and trained many horses and reindeer, the latter providing a lot of transportation here in the north country during the winters. "Snow depths can be twenty feet. Reindeer-power pulling sleighs are about the only way to get around, that and dog sleds." Lena couldn't imagine that much snow covering this idyllic setting. Soon, they spotted riders looking after some of the herds. Many were women dressed more like men. He explained they were

Sisterhood members. "Hilliard Heights is the heartland for the Sisterhood women, a safe haven for those battered women."

Mary overheard him, turned, and added, "All because of you men." Lena sensed bitter hatred in her voice. She began to assimilate what she'd heard of the Sisterhood, and she wondered what terrible things had happened to Mary and Jean. Well, it could not have been as bad as what she'd endured. Her own life was ruined utterly by men. Lena then realized, that for the grace of these people in the Underground, she too might well have become a Sisterhood woman, if they would even have a helpless cripple among them.

She asked, "Bernardo, is it safe here? I mean are there bandits around?"

He smiled, "Bandits are a nuisance in most kingdoms, but not up here in official Hilliard Heights country. My god, Lena. There are no better fighters on Tierra than these Sisterhood women. A man would have to be an utter fool to take one of them on!"

Jean turned in her saddle, a huge grin on her face. "You got that one right, buster!" Lena laughed and dropped her reins, forcing Bernardo to fetch the block for her.

Right on schedule, they arrived at Hilliard Heights. Lena was totally impressed with the town. The actual fortifications were up at the end of a valley system, almost as if carved out of the very face of a mountain. Over the centuries, an entire town had been built up around the entrance of the valley. Huge corrals dominated, some with horses, some with reindeer. Everywhere, she saw men and women tending the herds. Some were breaking them for riding; others were breaking them to pull wagons and sleighs. Women outnumbered the men three to one, she noted as they rode slowly into the town. They didn't stop though, but continued on up the steep, winding road towards the imposing fortifications and its huge manor house behind enormous lichen covered stone walls.

At last, they passed through a pair of mammoth wooden gates into the paved courtyard, where they were met by the Guild Mother herself. "Welcome to Hilliard Heights. I am Guild Mother Gina Hilliard. Good to see you again, Mary,

Jean. Come, dismount. Someone will take care of your horses. I've been expecting you. Rooms are prepared. We're honored to host the famous linguist at long last." She was thirty-five, short, and plump, but good natured.

Off to their left, sounds of sword practice echoed in this dead-end valley. Behind the impressive grey stone fortress, the sheer side of the mountain rose up blocking the afternoon sun completely. Nadja did the many introductions for the group. Gina then said, "Phillip is out training horses today. You can meet my husband at suppertime. Our kids, Trina and Jake, are over yonder getting their fighter training. You are welcome to join them if you desire. Our master sword woman is Ellen Bycombe e Wade. She's an extremely good teacher. Well, let's get you all settled in first, shall we? My, four katalyein!" she added, quite surprised.

Amy laughed. "Lena and I are not katalyein, but Drina and Casilda are, if you have any who need their attention." Gina's eyebrows rose a bit, but she didn't otherwise react.

"Right now, there are a couple of youngsters you could check out, if you don't mind," Gina replied. Quickly, other Sisterhood women escorted the rather large group to their new quarters. Lena, Amy, Casilda, and Drina found themselves sharing one large suite, but Nadja's family suite was right next door to theirs.

Lena had finished unpacking when Bernardo, Henry, Ben, and Hidalgo dropped by. Bernardo said, "Hey, Lena. We're off to watch the fighter training. Want to come along?" Curious, Lena agreed and headed out after the fellows. At the far southern edge of the courtyard, six boys and six girls were being trained by the forty year old sword master, Ellen Bycombe e Wade, a tall, well-muscled woman. She had her brown hair tied up in a bun, but wore similar leather clothing as Lena, who finally realized she was wearing rather traditional apparel for this world.

As they approached, the teens stopped their practice to look at the newcomers, staring at Lena's dark color. A broad, friendly smile on her face, Ellen walked over to the five. "You must be our guests from Brom. I'm sword master Ellen Bycombe e Wade." A fifteen year old teen walked up followed by a fourteen year old lad, insisting on being introduced as well. "Yes, this is Trina and this is Jake, Guild Mother Gina's teens."

Bernardo introduced Lena and the others. "So you've come to watch our practice?" Ellen asked.

"Sure. I've just started Lena on her training," Bernardo explained. "We need to continue sometime. Have you got any good moves?" he asked.

"Well, sport, why don't you pair off with the fellows? Let's see what you can do. Lena, you pair off with Trina here. She and Jake are still using wooden swords, as you can see. Hope you don't mind getting some bruises."

"Well, I've never fought against a sword before," Lena began to protest, thinking, *Are you blind woman? I don't have any arms. How the hell can I possibly fight Trina?*

As if anticipating her thoughts, Ellen explained, "Okay, Lena. What I want you to do is to avoid getting hit by Trina's wooden sword. Don't try to knock it out of her hands just yet. Let's see how you dodge first. Trina, take it easy on her, until we see how she does. The rest of you, action time. Jake, get these four some wooden swords please." Lena liked the way she took charge of her students and decided to play along. *The worst that can happen is I'll simply embarrass myself and get a few bruises,* she thought.

Lena crouched down, as she always did when sizing up an opponent. Trina circled her with determination. She tried to chop at Lena. She flung her arms up to help her back up, but they weren't there! She felt a grazing hit on her shoulder. Damn, she thought. Ellen asked, "You've never fought without your arms before, have you?" Lena shook her head no. "Thought so. It looked like you were trying to use your arms to help your body gain momentum to dodge. Try forgetting about using arms. Keep at it. Again, Trina."

Thus began a long workout for Lena. Soon she was dodging Trina's clearly broadcasted strikes. Ellen seemed to be everywhere around that practice field, handing out tips right and left. "Trina, you are signaling your every strike to Lena. That's why she sees it coming and gets out of your way. You have to stop telegraphing your strikes. Come on, you can do it.

Well done, Lena. Again."

"No Bernardo, you too are sending out signals to Pete, just like Trina is doing to Lena. Keep your free arm down. Don't use it to signal," she chided him.

An hour later, both Trina and Lena were sweating heavily. Trina did get in a few strikes, but not many. Ellen called a halt for the afternoon's practice, telling them all to report at one tomorrow. Trina, panting heavily, said, "Gosh, Lena, you are really good! I thought it would be a cinch to hit you all the time, but I keep missing most of the time."

"Thanks, Trina. I've never tried this before. Let me tell you, it's *really* scary. I keep trying to use my arms as I always used to do. It's so frustrating, you know."

"I can't imagine. I hope I didn't hurt you too badly. Come on; let's get washed up for supper. I'll lend you my hands if you need them," Trina volunteered.

"Mostly my pride got injured," Lena admitted. "Thanks. I don't know where anything is around here." She led Lena off, much to Bernardo's frustration. He was one mass of bruises. So were the other three.

Over supper in the Great Hall where at least a hundred assembled for the evening meal, Bernardo sat beside Lena, who sat beside her new friend Trina. "I ache all over. I have bruises on top of bruises. I guess, Lena, I'm not as good a fighter as I thought I was."

Trina laughed, "Silly boy, you are learning from the best there is. Ellen."

"Well, I can see I've a lot to learn then," he admitted humbly. Trina smiled and continued to attend to her new friend.

"More bread? Gosh, you sure do seem to like the ordinary nut bread. We don't get all that much wheat up here this time of year. Now come late fall, we do get in large loads from the southern breadbasket lands. But by this time of year, we've eaten it all and have to go back to nut flower," Trina explained.

"That's fine with me. This is the best bread I've ever had. I can't seem to get enough of it. I hope I don't look too piggish."

Trina giggled and cut her another slice. "You sure do use your feet well. I've been watching those other three. Amy is using her magic skills, isn't she? Not like you and the other katalyeins."

"No, Drina keeps telling Amy that she is cheating." Trina giggled again.

After another day on the practice field, Ellen called for a change. "Trina, you and Lena are now too evenly matched. You each know the other's moves by heart. So let's split you two up. Lena, you take on Bernardo. Henry, you take on Trina. Again, Lena, just try to avoid Bernardo's strikes. Okay, action."

Bernardo soon became frustrated. He'd only hit her once. Ellen broke them up, "Lena, well done. I see you know his moves too. Figures. Okay, Jake, you take Lena here. Bernardo, you take Jake's partner. Action."

Within two days, Lena had sparred with all the teens, rarely getting hit. "It hurts to get hit, so I'm avoiding them at all costs," Lena admitted to Ellen, who laughed.

"Good philosophy. If these were real swords, one hit could really spell your doom. Okay, back to Bernardo. Now, let's see if you can knock his sword out of his hand while not getting hit yourself. Action."

After another long week of practice, Lena was getting rather good at disarming her opponents. True, she had some nasty bruises on her legs, but she felt rather pleased she was dishing out far more than she received. The next day, things changed.

Ellen explained, "Okay, Lena, time for a change. I've rigged up this dummy. Your task is to knock its head off with your kicks. If you were in a real combat, you have to first disarm the sword and then take your opponent down. I assume you know enough to break his neck once the fellow is prone."

Lena smiled, "Yes, that's rather obvious. I don't need practice in breaking their necks." Now, she had to learn to stretch her kicks far higher. Just as soon as she was comfortable with one height, Ellen raised the dummy a few more inches.

"Look, some men are taller than others. You have to be

able to reach the necks of the taller men, unless you want to specialize in fighting only short fellows," Ellen teased her.

The following week, Ellen issued thick leather padding for the participants. "Okay, you are all ready for the real thing. I don't want any of you getting a nasty cut, so the padding."

Lena was again paired with her new friend, Trina. "Gosh, this is really scary!" Trina whispered. "We could really get hurt." As expected, everyone was far less dashing in their moves, far more conservative, bringing a smile to Ellen's face. She'd seen this hundreds of times. It was one thing to play with wooden swords and an entirely different matter facing an opponent who had a real sword.

Lena whispered, "Trina, look at the edge. These swords are so dull they couldn't cut nut bread. Stop worrying. The time to really worry is if and when she gives you a sharpened blade."

"Oh! You are right," Trina finally noticed that detail and launched into her moves. Unfortunately for the teens, the steel blades hurt far worse when they hit, in spite of the padding. Still, Ellen made them practice with these for another week.

"Okay everyone listen up. Today I am going to be testing you. Those that pass can move on to sharpened blades. Those that fail, you can chose to stop your training or take remedial training until you can pass. First, we have the luxury of having a non-sword fighter, Lena, with us. So your first challenge is to avoid losing your sword to Lena. In a real battle, if you lose or drop your sword, you are very like going to be dead. So this is really a matter of life and death. On the other hand, from Lena's point of view, her life depends on disarming you."

"But this isn't fair. Lena is over a hundred years old and has tons more experience than we do," one lad spoke up.

Ellen laughed, "So you only want to fight youngsters? Not adults? Is that it?" The lad crimsoned and shut up. "Action."

An hour later, Lena had faced all them and eventually had knocked the swords out of their hands, but had avoided breaking any of their arms. Ellen laughed and called out, "Lena is the only one who gets a pass on this one! Lena, would you like to offer any words of wisdom to these recruits?"

"You are all still telegraphing your strikes. Not anywhere as badly as before, but I'm still picking up when you are about to make a move and can counter it. Ellen's right about that. You need to be more devious — oh, I don't know, I've never held a sword in my life. Ellen, you explain it, please."

"She's right. The reason you are losing your swords is just that. You are signaling your next move to your opponent. In the real world of a fight, that's just what a good swordsman will be looking for — that's the weakness most fighters have. Only the very best fighters keep from signaling their moves. So let's all work on that some more. Lena, perhaps you can help me give them pointers on just how they are subtly signaling their next moves."

Another long week and they all finally passed, though Lena thankfully didn't have to take them on a second time. Now, Ellen gave them all sharpened swords. Everyone knew it was for real this time. A healer woman joined them, bringing along her bag of medical supplies, just in case of an accident. That really subdued them all, including Lena. Someone could get badly wounded and she knew it. *Yet, how else can they learn to fight properly,* she thought. *This is my test too. I still have to disarm them and avoid losing my legs in the process. Crap, if I lose a leg, I'll become more than helpless!* Even Lena was overly cautious at first.

"Now this *is* scary, Trina!" she whispered to Trina.

"I can't imagine facing me without a sword and especially without any arms, Lena. This must be terrifying to you," Trina whispered back, full of sympathy.

Lena steeled herself before replying, "If I should get attacked, I have to be able to defend myself somehow."

"I know. All we women feel this way. The atrocities some of the Sisters have undergone are frightening," Trina admitted.

When Diego joined the Sisterhood healer woman, Lena felt somewhat better. She'd seen him doing enough healing, and that alone allowed her to relax enough to put her attention where it belonged and not worry about getting her leg cut off by accident.

For two more weeks, the practice sessions invariable resulted in someone getting a nasty cut. Diego always worked his magic on the wounded, with the assistance of the Sisterhood healer. Even Lena took several nasty ones on her legs, battle scars she proudly announced, though with Diego's handiwork, she had to look hard even to see any signs of her cuts.

Here in the north lands, winters came early. Hence, they held their Fall Celebration on the last day of August. After this dance and party, Nadja told them they would all be heading back to Brom and then on to the Imperial Castle in Exchange City. "We don't want to be caught in any blizzards," she'd complained.

Trina hovered around Lena at all times now, best friends, she declared on more than one occasion. "So are you going to dress up for the big dance? Do you have any fancy gowns to wear? If not, I can try to find you one," Trina gaily asked.

"We brought some, but I've never worn them yet. I don't think I can dress myself in them," Lena admitted.

"Of course we can't," Drina butted in. "When we dress up, we give up our independence, and become dependent on our dates, you see. They know that too and look after our every need. It's really nice for a night, at least. Trina, you can help us all get dolled up for the party. Amy probably won't need the help. She always cheats and uses her skills."

"Do not!" Amy retorted.

"Do too!" Drina countered. Both began laughing.

"Sometimes," Amy admitted, as Jan walked in to help her get dressed up too.

"Okay, baths first," Jan announced.

Washing Lena's hair for her, Trina exclaimed, "Your hair is so different than mine. It's black, straight, and thick. But what I can't get over is how it shines and has a sort of reddish glow to it."

"Well, it's longer than I've ever worn it in my long life. Usually, I kept it almost as short as a man's. Easy to care for. Now that I can't care for it, it seems to have grown on its own,"

182

Lena replied good naturedly. It now reached the middle of her back. An hour later, Trina put the finishing touches on Lena and began helping Drina and Casilda with their gowns. Lena looked at herself in the mirror. She did look attractive, she thought. Her yellow satin gown was one of the pencil styles, fitting her budding curves well, but it covered her empty shoulders, as if her form never had arms. This way, no one would be staring at her empty sockets, which was why she'd chosen this style.

Her gown ended just below her knees, revealing the black nylons and her shiny patent heels. Oxford style, they were nicely tied in a double knot, so she didn't have to worry about the knots coming undone. However, she would be unable to slip them off. Further, their heel height was more than daunting to her, six inches. She felt extremely vulnerable and could barely walk. Yet, she knew well all the women wore these when they dressed up. Flats were out for formal occasions. At this point, she fully realized what Drina had meant about giving up their independence. Drina's words kept echoing in her mind: Take tiny steps. Make Bernardo hold you at all times.

Just as the teens were finally ready, Bernardo and the others knocked. "Wow! Lena, you are a knockout!" Bernardo exclaimed. He'd never seen her dressed up this fancy before. He wore an expensive suit, brown camel hair, she noted. He slipped his arm around her waist and carefully led her out, while Ben and Jan did the same with Drina and Amy. Hidalgo came to escort Casilda as well.

The Great Hall was packed. Diego was sitting with the musicians, lending his artistry to the dance as well. Shortly, Trina appeared, escorted by her boyfriend as well. Then the music began.

Bernardo put both his hands around her waist, pulled her close to him, and the two began to slow dance to the music. Around them, hundreds of others, old and young packed the hall. Lena noted the Great Hall was decked out in fall type colors. Banners and streamers of oranges, reds, and browns predominated.

During the long evening, Bernardo was the perfect

gentleman, Lena thought, caring for her needs almost without her asking. *Oh, he's reading my thoughts,* she concluded. Still, she felt somehow different. She liked being this close to him. Towards the end of the evening, she decided to do what she felt like doing. She gave him a brief, but passionate kiss. Soon, that turned into a much longer one. Lena felt electrified; her heart pounded. Somehow, she wanted more. All too soon, the music ended, and the party came to its conclusion.

Bernardo whispered, "According to Trina, now is when young couples steal away to dark corners. Want to?"

"Yes," she whispered back.

Much later, Bernardo finally dropped her off safely into her room. Casilda was already back, and Drina soon joined them. Since Jan wasn't around, Bernardo took their heels off and was about to help them out of their gowns when a flushed Trina popped in. "Okay, I'll take over, Bernardo. Thanks." He gave Lena a quick parting kiss and left. The teens giggled, but Lena had never felt so light before. They all chatted about the dance, while Trina got them out of their gowns and into their warm nightgowns.

"I know you are leaving in the morning, Lena. But please come back for visits when you can. I'll really miss you. You're the best friend I've ever had," Trina gushed.

"I'll try. Don't know when, but I'll try, Trina. I love it here."

She giggled, "You might not like it in the winter thought. Tons of snow. But then, we can go on sleigh rides. We can go sledding. Lots to do really, as long as you don't get caught in a blizzard."

"Sounds like fun. I'll just have to see."

The next day, Bart began a series of lengthy teleports. Rather than taking a gamble on the chilly weather, Nadja opted to return swiftly. They had too much equipment and baggage to have the new Circle at Hilliard Heights to teleport. She didn't want to place such a burden on them. Bart could easily handle their needs. After saying their goodbyes, Bart began the series of teleports, bringing everyone back to the Underground first.

Nadja and her family wanted to return to Exchange City

right away. After getting them all back to the Underground, Bart began the secondary teleports. However, Rafaela came walking up. "Amy, Jan, Lena, may I have some words with you before you go? It's important."

She led the trio into a side room where Ken and Crystal were waiting for them. After exchanging words about how their summer went, Ken explained. "Amy, we've been discovering more of those giant germanium crystals in fields around Brom. I've followed your advice and retrieved them without touching them. It looks like we do have a *serious* problem on our hands. These could well be scattered all over Tierra. Any advice? I know Queen Isabella is taking you both to the Ataro System soon, so I wanted to talk face to face, before you two leave. You are our experts in such things."

"You are doing it properly. Don't touch them. If someone gets locked up like Hank, the secret is to gradually go into rapport with the stone and attune its frequency to yours," Amy explained. "Gradually."

Jan added, "You probably should make an effort to find all the other rocks that landed. Don't know how, but that'd be wise." They chatted more, but really had little more to say. These giant crystals were dangerous. In the wrong hands — well they all rather not think about that possibility. After that, Jan and Amy left.

Lena had been sitting quietly listening to them, wondering why she was here. She knew nothing about such things. Now Rafaela turned to her. "Well, Lena, how did you like getting out in the wild? I hear you love the nut bread and even found several fancy quilts."

"Fabulous, really great. I made some new friends too. And believe it or not, I've got some fighting skills back. Well, at least I can more or less defend myself on this world where swords are the weapons," she replied. "So what am I doing here?"

Rafaela smiled. "Have you made any decisions about what you want to do with your life now? Any chance that you would like to stay on Tierra with us?"

Lena sighed. "Honestly, Rafaela, we both know I can't go back. They have already filled my position with a new

Sector ID Minister. I can't hope to get my old job back, and to be honest, I don't want it back. I really like Tierra, what I've seen of it. I don't know what I can actually do to support myself — job-wise, that is. I haven't really given the future that much thought. Why?"

"Would you like to stay on Tierra with us, like Nadja has?" Rafaela asked.

"Sure, I would like that. Only, somehow I have to find a place to live and find some kind of work I can do. At least, I can sort of take care of my own personal needs, more or less. I surely don't know what I can really do. I am still pretty much helpless, just like you are now. I'm still so sorry about that. I wish I had known more about the rejuvenation machine and how it works. I feel responsible for ruining your life and Andres too."

"Oh, think nothing of that. Our lives aren't ruined. Inconvenienced, yes. Ruined, no. Okay then, we of the Underground would like to offer you a job helping us maintain peace and order on Tierra, from the background naturally. You have much knowledge you can bring to bear to help us protect our world. Your help would be invaluable. What do you say?"

"Sure. Glad to contribute as I can."

"Excellent. Then, the next question is would you like to also have the *mentales* gifts that we all have?" Rafaela finally asked what she had wanted. All summer long, she and Ken had argued over whether or not to make her this offer. Her performance up in Hilliard Heights had been relayed to the two via Nadja. The only remaining barrier was would she want to leave Tierra now or would she desire to stay.

"Is that even possible? Well, if it is, sure I would love to have it. Who wouldn't?" Lena answered. *I — one of them too? I can't believe this is happening to me!*

"Sure it is. Okay then, I'll ask Bernardo to stick around a while longer. We'll move you two into a guest room down here and get started on it today. I think Bart wants to go over some interesting developments with you too. Say, do you really like the nut bread, made with nut flower, because we're low on wheat from the south?" Rafaela asked.

"Absolutely! It's the greatest. I've had wheat bread for a

hundred plus years. It just doesn't compare to the incredible taste of the nut breads. I'd have asked for their recipes, but as I am, I couldn't bake any. Why?"

Rafaela laughed. "Most of us are hooked on wheat bread and think the nut bread is a poor substitute." Lena laughed too. "Well, best go let Bernardo know that he's going to be sticking around for a while yet."

"Thank you, Rafaela. Thank you." Lena said meaning it from her heart.

After Lena left, Ken asked, "So are we going to try to create specific forms for her gifts or just let nature take her course?"

"In her case, I'm going to let nature do what it desires. I would predict telekinesis would be her strongest skill, but we will see," Rafaela replied.

Two weeks later, no one was more delighted than Lena, who found that she too had a powerful ability in telekinesis. She also could easily detect when someone was lying or withholding vital information. Lena also had a fair ability to Dominate Minds as well. Two weeks after that, she finished her tower training and received her own germanium crystal, attuned to her. Now, her powers were greatly amplified, pleasing her. As she often subsequently said, "Now I can cheat like Amy." Bernardo only laughed.

Chapter 11 Surprises

Neva de la Nieva met her new personal assistant at the spaceport outside Winiana, Winno-3, where Queen Altha held court. The queen personally escorted her to the port, where the deep space transport was waiting her. "President Snarry has personally sent this ship to bring you back to your estate. As I understand it," the queen continued, "he is planning a hero's banquet for you. Good luck and do watch yourself. There are those who will now be seeing your rise in power and influence over President Snarry as threatening. You are welcome to stay in the Ataro System with us. We would even be willing to train you as one of our queens, if you would desire to assist us."

"No, I want to get back home. Do you really think that some might threaten me? Well, I can take care of myself well enough," Neva declared.

"Okay then. Goodbye and thanks for everything, Neva. You are the best. Just watch your back. The Imperium out there can be vicious. They simply don't understand life like we do here." Queen Altha pressed her body into Neva's, the best she could do for a hug. Neva turned and made her slow, careful way across the tarmac to the waiting doors of the ship. Moving slowly, she got a good look at the ship. *Funny,* she thought, *they could have sent a newer ship. This one looks like a rust bucket. Ah well, home in a few days. That must be my new assistant waving to me.*

Her assistant was youthful, anything but pretty. Still, she had a nice personality, Neva thought, and she was kind, helping her into her seat. "Kind of an old transport. I thought it might be falling apart on the way here, but it flew just fine. The Imperium has lost an awful lot of ships during the war. You are now a hero, Mrs. Burkhardt, a real hero, but I don't know how you did it." She was interrupted by the captain calling out orders to buckle up, they were departing.

Neva sat back and watched the spaceport begin to recede. From above, she could see the city with its strange looking palaces that looked much like enormous wasps. Soon, even they grew smaller, and the planet's disk filled her view window. Quickly, the planet began shrinking rapidly. Neva's mind was not pondering the beautiful liftoff, but rather what Queen Altha had warned her about. Would others now see her as a threat? *Well, they ought to,* she thought, *I'm the president's lover. I aim to become his wife once we get back. How can he possibly not divorce her and marry the big war hero?*

Just then, a massive explosion tore the ship in half. In slow motion, Neva watched the bomb exploding, ripping the ship apart, aided by all the fuel that they were carrying, which ignited as well! Seconds seemed to move along as minutes to Neva, though later she wondered if perhaps her own thinking had somehow drastically sped up to keep pace with the explosion.

Bomb! Someone deliberately is assassinating me! Who? Help! Involuntarily, she felt across the vast space for that solid, massive germanium crystal beneath the surface of Gamelon-3. She felt its vast power flowing into herself. *Who is doing this?* Immediately, she thought of Legate Daag and Legate Herman. Aided by the enormous power from the giant crystal, she pervaded the minds of the two men half a galaxy away. Both were taking coffee in a conference room. She pulled through their recent memories, like watching a movie at high speed. She saw what she needed.

"Don't worry, President Snarry, the Neva problem is being handled as we speak," Legate Daag told him.

"Yes, we have that security hole plugged," Legate Herman added.

"I still say Neva could be very useful to us. I've planned a Hero's Banquet in her honor when she arrives," President Snarry reminded the two men.

He's not involved. Die! Neva focused and sent her decision across the vast space, even as the searing heat incinerated her fleshly body. Legates Herman and Daag grabbed their heads in excruciating pain. President Snarry asked what was wrong, and then panicked and summoned help.

Blinded and deafened, Neva found herself floating

above the blue-green world. Now, she was freezing in the intense cold of outer space! *What's happening to me? I've been assassinated. Those damned Legates! I hate men. They cannot be trusted. All men should be exterminated as the very vermin that they are! Hell, I am freezing. Got to get warm.* She floated downwards to the planet. Hovering several thousand feet above the spaceport she'd just left, she felt the relative warmth of the atmosphere and calmed down.

I am dead. No, how can I be dead? I am still here, still thinking, still seeing. I don't understand what is happening to me. My body is gone, that's for sure. I need a new one. Oh hell! Now what do I do? I have to get a new one. Wait! If I get one here, I won't have the powers any more. I need the mentales powers if I am going to exterminate the vermin of the universe. Tierra. I have to get back to Tierra. Where is it? I am lost. Oh hell. Now what?

I have to get my mentales back, so I have to find a way to get back to Tierra. But I don't know where it is now. Wait! I know. Queen Isabella is coming here soon. I can wait until she arrives and go back on her ship! That's the plan. Best hover down close to the spaceport. Don't want to miss her.

"Hi Lena. Welcome aboard the Underground Express," Bart welcomed her, as she walked into the comm center where he and Anita, his wife, and Lilly, their daughter, were monitoring the communications. He took the Imperium side, allowing Anita and Lilly to watch the daily chats between the many towers.

"Hi yourself. I'm back. You wanted to see me?" she asked, wondering if she really could somehow use her new skills to operate the equipment.

"Yes, let me put you through to Queen Altha. She has more news. You were right. Neva was assassinated!" Bart exclaimed and hastily made the long distance connection to the queen. It took nearly ten minutes before her grim-set face appeared on the video.

"Greetings again, Sector ID Minister Lena. I wanted to talk to you sooner, but this is just as well. You were right. Our investigators found traces of that explosive you suggested along with the remains of a timer. It was set to go off just after liftoff, once the transport cleared our atmosphere and before it jumped into hyper-space. Sabotage for sure. Four were killed, including Neva. We've identified part of her remains and given her a hero's funeral."

"There's more. We've learned at nearly the same time as the explosion, both Legates Daag Tall and Herman Mels died, while meeting with President Snarry Knoschy! Autopsies showed their brains had been liquefied by some, as yet unknown, method. The top leaders are quite spooked by this unexpected turn of events and have implemented an extensive investigation. Here, our own Sector ID Minister has been investigating the assassination, rather thoroughly, I might add. He has little choice, since the emperor himself has taken a highly personal interest in it."

"He's discovered an old scrap transport was used for this mission. Hence, it is clear to all that it was fully intended to be disintegrated. Much backtracking has been done over these past few months. Amazingly, he's traced this back to a conspiracy involving those same two Legates! While it is obviously impossible to question the dead men now, it seems clear they wanted Neva dead. The ID Minster's theory is they were terrified of the threat Neva posed for Imperium security, her being so intimate with President Snarry. By the way, he's been cleared of any wrong doing. All he knew is that he had a serious problem with Neva and her powers and that the Legates told him that it would be handled. Apparently, he had no idea they intended to assassinate her. No one can prove otherwise, but many of us do not believe him."

"Still unresolved is just how the two Legates were assassinated. Surely having one's brains liquefied counts as an assassination. I suspect we'll never know how that happened, despite the intensive research into the killings. Nevertheless, our emperor believes it was done by Neva. You see, he knows she was able to extend her telepathic ability across vast reaches of space to relay the news of Gamelon to him. As he says, 'What's to prevent her from reaching from here to the two Legates?' I don't know if that is possible, but he firmly believes Neva somehow got revenge on her two assassins."

"Following through all this, I had our Sector ID Minister take possession of Neva's assets on Beltzar-4 — namely her fancy estate and her bank account. Thus far, we've not found her next of kin, so Queen Isabella is now holding the deed and her bank account, as Neva's power of attorney. Plus, our ID Minister has filed a lawsuit for compensation from the Imperium for the Legates' illegal actions against Neva. Undoubtedly, the settlement will be a rather large one, since it's now been proved they were responsible for her assassination. Again, the funds will be forwarded to Queen Isabella on Neva's behalf. I don't know if she'll ever be able to find any of Neva's next of kin, though. Over."

"My god! The Legates? Well, I suspected them of many dirty dealings during the long war. I guess they got what was coming to them," Lena began her reply to the queen's lengthy message. "Well done, Queen Altha. If nothing else, Neva has her justice, if posthumously. I think having Queen Isabella oversee Neva's estate is a good idea. Thank you for handling it for me." She sighed and then added, "I've decided to stay on Tierra and make it my new home. I'll be resigning my post as ID Minister, but they've long ago installed my replacement, that's for sure. Perhaps, one day I can make the trip to visit you too. Oh yes, their therapy is just fantastic. I'm glad now Neva didn't do as I ordered and killed me. Life is hard, but I'm managing and have made some new friends, good ones, I think. Well, that's about all from here. Thanks again for everything you've done for us and for Neva. Over."

"Oh that's great news to hear, Lena. Congratulations. I look forward to having you here for a state visit. I know Queen Isabella will be coming shortly. I'm to train her daughter no less! Now if we could only get other worlds to follow her example, the Universe might become a safe place for everyone to thrive. Over and out."

Bart smiled, commenting, "Well, Neva's going to have a fortune, but I wonder if she has any heirs?"

Anita broke in, "No one knows where she came from originally. I think the wisest use will be to hang onto the estate until we get a new senator. Then, he or she can make good use of the estate and the funds. I wonder how soon the Imperium will be back to rebuild their fuel refinery?"

Bart explained, "Don't know, but I'm monitoring for any hints. We ought to know in plenty of time before they actually arrive."

Lena laughed. "Is there nothing you guys don't know? You are better informed than most worlds."

Bart smiled. "That's the point. Keep Tierra safe. Jan and Amy started that over a century ago. Can't trust aliens. Not you, of course, or Nadja," he hastily amended.

Lena laughed, "That's a generality if I ever heard one. Better say can't trust some aliens who have ulterior motives. I wonder what's happened to Konrad? Can we check up on him somehow?"

Anita answered, "I've been looking for clues. I mean, when I heard that Queen Altha was looking for Neva's heirs, I thought of Konrad right away. It seems he's disappeared — vanished without a trace. Curious, isn't it?"

Lena bit her lip, deep in thought. "You know, I know for a fact the Imperium was using him as a spy, ferreting out traitors on planets we still controlled. I have a bad feeling about this. Look, if the Legates thought Neva was such a huge security threat, Konrad might also be looked upon that way. Both came from Tierra with telepathy. I have an idea. I need formally to resign my post. Can you make a connection to the Hub Sector 1's ID Minister from here?"

"Sure, if I have the codes, but gosh, the time delay will be huge, probably an hour or more," Bart replied.

"Can I watch, dad?" Lilly asked. She'd been listening in to the two.

He grinned and Lena gave him the data. "Okay, you best do the talking. You're up."

"Hello. This is Sector ID Minister Lena Squire." She rattled off her security codes. "I am on Ashford-5 at the moment. I wish to speak to the current Hub Sector 1 ID Minister. I need to resign my post and also want to make one small suggestion, if I may. Over and standing by."

"Now we wait. This could take quite a while, if they even deign to reply," Bart advised.

"Oh they'll reply. My codes guarantee that one. I could

use a cup of tea about now. How about you? Crap, I can't carry anything," Lena suddenly realized her limitations once more.

Lilly spoke up, "I'll get it. You know, Lena, I saw something that might help you out — carrying things that is. Back in a bit." She returned with some tea and some nut bread. Already everyone knew how much Lena loved their make-do bread. While the others preferred the "real wheat" bread, Lena didn't, much to the surprise of everyone else around the Underground. Most were glad to let her eat all she wanted of the obviously inferior bread. She poured Lena a cup and sat it on the floor where she could reach it.

"I have a boyfriend in Brom who's a miller's apprentice. He has this yoke contraption that rests on his shoulders with baskets on each side. This way, he can carry twice as much flour. I'm going to see him and see if he could adapt something like that for you to use," Lilly explained. She added, "We do have a lot of inventors in Brom; they seem to flock here. Can't see why, winters are atrocious."

"I've yet to experience your winters," Lena chuckled. Lilly smiled. They waited patiently for the return call. It came about two hours later.

"Acting Hub Sector 1 ID Minister Hans Henkle here. Greetings Lena. We've all heard of your tragic misfortune. Under the circumstances, resigning is best for everyone. I'm sure your retirement funds will be sufficient to pay for your nursing home care. I've filled out your resignation and retirement forms for you, since you are unable to do them yourselves. Quite tragic. Your crew wants me to express their sympathies for them. Since there is no base on Ashford-5 at this time, your funds will be held, waiting the reopening of the spaceport there. I assure you at that time, you'll be able to withdraw funds as needed. If what I have done is agreeable to you, please so state formally for the record. Over."

Lena smiled. "Perfect. Congratulations on your new appointment Hans. Yes, your arrangements are perfect. Obviously, I can't fill out the forms or sign them. Life is quite challenging for me now. I have one final suggestion to make as one former ID Minister to another. It concerns the disappearance of Governor Konrad. If you will search my files, you will see that during the war, he and Neva were being used as Class V telepaths on the outer rim worlds, searching out spies and traitors. I've heard he has vanished without a trace. This is not expected behavior for the most famous Imperium governor this century. My suggestion is to search the records and find out what planet he was last assigned to. Then, search the various morgues there looking at all unidentified bodies. I suspect he too was assassinated by Legates Daag and/or Herman, who also saw him as a threat to the Imperium high command. That's all. Best of luck, Hans. Over and out."

"Who is Hans?" Bart asked.

Lena chuckled. "He was one of my junior officers, who always tried to brown-nose me. Not the most competent ID agent or the brightest. Of course, I always ignored him, but apparently, he now has my old job. I wouldn't give a hoodie's ass for the president and Senate's security now," she replied.

"What's a hoodie?" Lilly asked.

Lena flushed. "Best you didn't hear that one. Okay, it is something like a really foul-smelling mammal found on some hub planet worlds and now has been hunted to extinction, thankfully. Leave it at that." Lilly grinned.

Later, Lilly and her friend, Thomas visited Lena. He took some measurements of Lena's height and promised he would have just the invention for her. The next day, he returned with a modified yoke. A light weight board rested on her shoulders. It was curved nicely in its center so that it went halfway around her neck, leaving the remainder of the board resting squarely on her shoulders. Attacked to each end of the board were two three-foot tall sets of legs, which rested on the floor when she squatted down. A pair of wicker baskets dangled from each end.

"See, you put things into the baskets and step beneath it and lift it up on your shoulders. You ought to be able to carry most anything as long as you keep the baskets properly balanced. Come on; let's try it out," Thomas suggested.

Lena squatted down and moved beneath the yoke and lifted it up. "Hey, it's light."

"Of course. Now let's put stuff in it." Lilly accommodated him and shortly Lena was carrying some folded sheets around the room.

"Thanks, Thomas. This works well. Now, I am not so darn helpless. Thanks." Lena was rather surprised at his inventiveness.

"Excellent. I'll make you a few more so you can keep them in different rooms. All I ask is you let the katalyein see them. I expect they might like some of them too," Thomas replied, rather proud of his achievement.

For the next few days, Lena got introduced to where everything was located. Bart fully briefed her on his extensive electronics operations, while Anita went over their complicated tower communications monitoring network. She had a lot to learn, but Lena was very well versed on the electronics equipment. "My god, you can hook into their geo-sat systems! Is there nothing you guys can't get into?" she teased Bart.

"Compliments of Empress Jan. She set all this up and got most of the equipment as well," Bart replied. "I wish I could take credit for it, but not even my dad, Tim, was able to do that. I only know how to operate the machines. I could sure use your talents on maintaining them. I don't know much about that area at all. Dad used too. I suppose if anything major goes wrong, we could have Jan work on it, but she's supposed to go off with Amy, who is going to be trained by Queen Altha soon. It's right after the Fall High Council meeting. Which reminds me, I am supposed to tell you that you and Bernardo are to teleport to Isabella's place tonight. She wants you in attendance this time. The council meeting starts tomorrow morning. Sorry, I forgot to tell you sooner. I was too excited about the long distance communications and all."

"Best find Bernardo and get packed," Lena replied and headed off to find him. On her way, she felt Queen Isabella in her mind. *Oh! This is so cool. I hear you, Queen Isabella.*

Hope I am not disturbing you. I just heard Bart forgot to tell you that I need you here tonight. I want you to observe the High Council meeting. I have to leave right after its done. You'll need to dress up, I'm afraid. This is always a formal affair. If you want, drop by Elegant Fashions Inc and see

Inez. She can fix you up with proper gowns, if you need some. Oops. Have to run. See you tonight.

She found Bernardo working on a project with Ken. "Yes, just heard. Bart is forgetful sometimes. We best get packing. Mom said I should take us both over to see Inez. I have to dress formally this time. So much for being an adult; now I have to look the part. Don't worry; you will too, but I'll be at your side all the time to help out. Come on; we best get going."

An hour later, they walked into Elegant Fashions Inc and unsurprisingly found Inez was expecting them. "Mom?" he asked with a grin.

"Never doubt her. She wants you both to make a very good impression on the many lords and ladies. Now then, I've a perfect gown for Lena. I know how you like yellow, but I am afraid that reds are in for this fall. You'll stick out like a plum in the pudding, if you wear your yellow gown," Inez pointed out.

"Okay as long as I don't have to get those monstrous lip plate things," Lena said. "By the way, how do I pay for them? I have an Imperium account if you can tap into that."

"Yes, I can do that, though it's harder now that the spaceport is closed. If you want, I can also withdraw more and give the balance to you in local coins and gems," Inez volunteered.

"Incredibly perfect. Yes, I don't have any local funds, and I owe Amy a little too. Let's get this done," Lena replied.

Inez fixed her up with a tight-fitting gown that prominently displayed her assets. While full length, the cherry red satin gown did have a walking slit, a small one. Still some of her seamed nylons would show. Lena grimaced at the matching six inch heels of the oxford style shoes. She asked, "Why haven't some of the many other style heels been adopted here, only the oxfords?"

Inez smiled. "Who knows about fashions? I think around this world, they believe shoes need to have ties or they aren't proper shoes. You do look smashing. But you probably ought to get a pair of the long, dangling earrings. You will look out of place without them. All the women are wearing them now."

A bit later Lena complained, "My god, Inez. They are going to pull my ears off!"

Inez laughed. "Everyone says so, but in all these years, none has yet to have that happen to them. Now, you sit quietly, and let me deal with Bernardo here. Your mom wants you to look like a proper lord too."

"Hey, none of those huge lip plates, Inez," he protested.

Lena realized he'd played right into Inez's pocket. Having him protest that and getting his way, he readily accepted the fancy suit she had intended outfitting him with. Inez was clever, she realized. "I feel like a stuffed bear," he grumbled.

"That may be, but you make a handsome bear, right Lena?" Inez replied, standing back admiring his new look in his suede suit.

Lena winked at him. "Yes, indeed. I won't be able to keep my hands off of him."

He grimaced and then broke into a roaring laugh, joined by the two women. "That's a good one, Lena! You got me and that's saying something! Now you are going to have to watch out for me. I am an active member of the Gang of Eight, you know. Hey, we're going to have to make it the Gang of Nine now." All three laughed some more.

As they prepared to leave, Bernardo tied Lena's new money pouch to his waist. "I ought to make you walk home by yourself," he teased.

"Don't you dare! I can barely walk at all in these heels. You men should try that sometime," she replied.

"Don't worry. I won't," he leaned over and stole a quick kiss. She smiled. His arm was securely around her during the short walk back to the castle. They arrived in time for supper. When they walked into the dining room, they saw Amy and Jan were also dolled up in their finest gowns as well.

Jan looked miserable though. "Hi all. Now I'm screwed. Look at my feet, will you. And I can't breathe in this pipe corset." Both did. "See, I've had to get them modified like Amy's so I can be a proper assistant for her in Queen Altha's court."

"Yes, but this time you get to keep your voice, and you don't have to lose your arms either," Amy countered. "I'm the one who has been screwed this time, as always." Jan briefly smiled at that. She added, "Besides, mom is right. You need to get used to them before we go."

Queen Isabella broke in, "Lena, you look lovely, my dear. Red looks good on you, and your earrings will be perfect. You'll see." Lena smiled, but decided not to say anything about them.

She added, "Bernardo, remember, you are the hands of Lena now."

"I know mom, I know," he grumbled. Lena knew even if she could somehow remove her heels and nylons so she could use her feet and toes, the tight gown would prevent her from being able to reach anywhere near her mouth. No, it was like Drina pointed out, dolled up, she had given up her independence, and depended now on Bernardo.

Lena said, "Queen Isabella, I want to thank you for handling Neva's affairs. That was thoughtful and kind of you. I just heard about that from Queen Altha."

"Thanks. It had to be done, though I doubt that we'll ever find any of her relatives. No one knows where she came from. She just appeared on the Lord's doorstep."

Drina spoke up, "I know I've been away from mom and dad for years, but I think something is up with them. They were talking privately and shut up whenever I entered the room. I wonder if it has anything to do with the council meeting?"

"I am a little worried about this one myself," Isabella replied. "You see, this fall, most of the new rey and reina terms are about to expire. New ones must be elected per the various laws that are supposed to limit them to two terms of office. I guess we'll see how smoothly this goes. At least the various Senates are working out, as well as their local Justice Courts."

The next day, Queen Isabella sat on her throne accompanied by Hernando, awaiting the arrival of the many leaders and advisors. Lena, Bernardo, and the others in the Gang of Nine stood at the back of the room alongside of Inez, Lilly, and Peter. As always, she and Lilly had their clipboards with them, ready to take notes pertaining to fashion requests. One by one the many began arriving.

"Welcome to Tierra, Lena," Reina Edda of Turda, Alba, said slowly, making sure she was understandable. She wore a tight fitting gown, toe shoes, and the huge lip plates that draped down onto her chest. Her earrings, Lena noticed, were quite similar to hers. "I am so glad to meet you at last. I am Reina Edda Turda." She began chatting with Lena and Bernardo, introducing her Sisterhood Ministers as well. Before long, others moved in, wanting to both see and greet this dark skinned alien, who had taken up residence in Queen Isabella's court.

Bernardo whispered to her, "Looks like everyone knows about you. Small world. Telepathy, you see."

She grinned. "Just don't you let go of me!"

Before long, the room was filled. Lena saw Inez was right. Nearly everyone present was very well dressed and most all wore the large lip plates. About half also wore toe shoes or boots. Nearly all the women sported pipe corsets, which Lena had thus far avoided, as had most of the Gang of Nine. Well, except that Jan had now joined Amy in the shoes and corset department.

Queen Isabella rose and spoke both clearly and slowly so that she could be understood well. "Welcome one and all to the Fall High Council. I have music and entertainment scheduled for this evening. Lunch will be at noon and supper at six. I hereby formally turn the meeting over to Rey Wye." She sat down and Rey Wye rose and moved to the front, stepping up on the raised platform and stood in front of Queen Isabella. Constrained as she was, she could not move to see beyond him, a perfect snub.

He spoke both loudly and slowly so there would be no misunderstandings due to his lip plates. "After consultations with all the 'so-called' elected leaders of the various kingdoms, we all detest these new terms, rey and reina. Henceforth with, we shall be known once more as king and queen. Let the Imperial Court records so indicate."

Queen Isabella was a little annoyed they would unilaterally choose to return to their old titles. She had wanted them to make clean break from history. Well, she thought, if this is all they want, I can live with this change.

King Wye continued. "Again, I and many other kings have thoroughly discussed our present situations among ourselves. We and our extended families own much land in and around our various kingdoms. Many of our friends, the noblemen and women, own even more — perhaps as much as half of the lands within our respective kingdoms. Thus, we believe we ought to have the greater say in the ruling our lands. At the moment, this enforced new form of government foisted off upon us by Queen Isabella here, is dictating we rulers can no longer rule our own kingdoms." A loud round of support echoed in the Great Hall. Queen Isabella did not like the sound of where this was heading, though.

"Each of us has reached the enforced term limits. Supposedly, we must stand aside and allow our peasants to elect an unknown man to rule in our place. While none of us discounts Queen Isabella's new policies have put an end to the rebellions in our kingdoms, we, those who own so much land within our kingdoms, are being pushed out of our lifelong positions, positions some of us inherited by our forefathers and they from theirs, going back centuries, in my case. There has always been a Wye ruling our lands. We need continuity in our kingdoms, not total change every few years. Look at all the good work that Queen Edda Turda has done to rebuild Turda. Now you want them to toss her out on the street? Some thank you that is." Many here-here's echoed around the room, and he paused to allow them to express it. Isabella began to think this was a well-orchestrated plot thought out ahead of time.

"After lengthy consultations with our nobles and with other kings and queens, I stand before you to proclaim our ultimatum to this Imperial Supreme Court. You have two choices. One, you can force our various Senates to alter the length of office for we kings and queens to the lifetime of the person. Or two, we will divide our kingdoms into halves; part will belong to the peasants and their laws and their own 'elected' leaders," he added snidely, "and we kings and nobles will form our own kingdom from that part of our lands that we own, subject to our own laws and such. We would continue to use this Supreme Court to settle matters between our new kingdoms and the old ones, though."

A loud round of applause drowned out the cheering that many added. At least with the lip plates, they couldn't whistle, Lena thought. She picked up on Isabella's distress though. King Wye continued, "Now I would like to call upon our newest alien who is living among us, Lena Squire. She can tell us how other quote primitive societies unquote deal with rulership issues. She's seen them all. Lena, front and center," he ordered, shocking Lena considerably.

You don't have to obey him if you don't want to, Isabella sent her. Many of the tower members were just as shocked by this surprise move as Queen Isabella was. As Lena looked around, she saw many of them with that familiar blank stare indicating that they were communicating telepathically with others in the room, most likely.

Isabella! This is the first I've heard of such a thing, Venerada Maricela hastily sent. By the time Lena made her careful way to the front, standing beside King Wye, Queen Isabella had heard from most of the venerados and veneradas. All were taken by surprise. She concluded these men and women had worked all this out without using the normal tower personnel. That alone meant they were dead serious about this.

Lena knew she was on the spot. Had someone found out that she liked to dabble in anthropology in her spare time? That she'd studied many cultures? Well, at least studied the various published reports on them. She swallowed and stood erect. *If he wants me to cow-tow to him, he can forget it.* "Hello everyone. I am Lena Squire, ex-Hub Sector 1 ID Minister for the Imperium. Yes, I have read many anthropological studies on more primitive cultures. By primitive, let me be perfectly clear. I mean those cultures that have yet to invent or use space travel."

"The evolution of human beings, people with our distinctive bodies and minds, has always followed similar developmental stages, no matter on what planet they're found. True, there have been some divergences based on the individual planet and its resources. Tierra is one such example; there are almost no heavier elements on this world. Iron is extremely valuable here and in short supply. That said, the earliest inhabitants often make and use stone tools — made from flint and easily worked stone. They make their living by hunting, fishing, and gathering what bounty the land provides them. Naturally, these people are basically nomadic, moving from place to place as they exhaust the local game and produce, moving on into fresh areas. Socially, they consist mostly of extended families, small groups. We classify such civilizations as Old Stone Age. Obviously, Tierra is not in the Old Stone Age," she glared at King Wye.

"What usually happens next in their evolution, is brighter men and women domesticate local plants and animals, often by settling down close to wild patches of wheat and harvesting it year after year. Suddenly, these people have finally a surplus of food and usually develop or invent fire-baked pottery in which to store their grain. They salt or dry their meat for long term storage as well. We classify these civilizations as being in the New Stone Age. For your information, the Imperium always classifies any world in the Old Stone Age or the New Stone Age as automatically being a Closed World, until they develop further. Again, that does not apply to Tierra. What we see here with agriculture and animal domestication is a settling down of the people and a local population explosion, since they can support more people per unit of land."

"What usually happens next is they continue to invent and work out how to make tools from copper and often work out how to make bronze, a tin and copper mixture. These are easier to work and melt metals. From copper or bronze, they make and use all manner of tools. Cups, bowls, silverware, pots, knives, swords, spear tips — all manner of things. That is, the people have moved into being metal workers now. This stage of development is called the Bronze Age, even if they use only copper. Their societies often tend to begin to form towns housing several thousand people. With so much extra food being produced on a single farm, via taxation, they are able to support the artisans, the craftsmen, and a ruling elite class. Some go so far as to have official classes. We often see elaborate gold and gem stone settings being made for the wealthy, who are getting *fat* on the labors of the farmers or the lower classes." She put that notion in for Lord Wye's benefit, adding a little disgust to what he saw as his right to rule. "Usually each of the towns has its own rulers. There is no central unifying government, just widely scattered city-states. With planets that have developed to the Bronze Age, the Imperium gives them the opportunity to be either an Open or Closed World. Again, though you make and use bronze and copper, this does not apply to Tierra."

"The next step is the discovery and use of iron, which requires far hotter fires and skill. The forging of steel into plow hoes, swords, you name it, brings a civilization far closer to the modern worlds. We call such civilizations as being in the Iron Age, and they are given the choice to be closed or open worlds. Here, one begins to see what we would really call cities with populations in the tens of thousands. Often, they have centralized governments, such as kingdoms, who often war with each other, trying to gain more land, people, and valuable resources, such as gold and iron mines. Here is where Tierra would seem to fit in the Imperium classification."

Many 'alrights!' and 'here-here's echoed for a minute. It was clear to Lena many kings were about to use this as further justification for their totalitarian rule. She went on, "Next, there are worlds that have moved into the so called Manufacturing Age. These worlds are usually opened and welcome the incredible technological advances the Imperium can offer them. Great cities of hundred of thousands to millions of inhabitants are found. They develop steam power and/or electrical power, and use them to build all manner of great machines. They build roads connecting their cities and rural villages. They build various types of wheeled transportation vehicles, unlike the horse-drawn wagons found here."

"Finally, there are the rarely found worlds whose civilization has progressed into the Space Age. Admittedly, with these the Imperium usually invades and conquers, adding them to their collection of planets, that is, if they don't accept the Imperium's initial offers."

"King Wye, none of this addresses rulership issues. There can be clan leaders, usually the strongest or best fighter or hunter. There can be kings or monarchs, such as you have had here for centuries, as I understand from what little I know of your history. Queen Isabella has probably already told you there can be benevolent monarchs that do right by their subjects and horrid tyrants who abuse their people. I can tell you this, no monarch ever considers himself a tyrant, not even the sociopaths. While destroying his country, the sociopath still believes he is doing what is best for his land. No, the real problem with monarchies is two-fold."

"One, the citizens have no choice of who will lead them, and two, almost never is a benevolent monarch replaced with one of equal caliber. I guess there is a three. Sometimes, the monarch divides up his kingdom giving a portion to each of his sons or daughters, thereby weakening it, and these smaller kingdoms are then swallowed up by their neighbors. The truly stable countries have some form of —." She was abruptly cut off by King Wye.

"That will be all, Lena. Thank you. As she has just shown us, Tierra is in the Iron Age and as such, kingdoms are the norm, as are we ruling kings. So we rest our case, Queen Isabella. You have your choice. Force our various Senates to alter the length of office for us kings and queens to the lifetime of the person. Or we will divide our kingdoms into halves, the part that we own and the part that will belong to the peasants and their laws and their own 'elected' leaders."

Finally, he stepped away from in front of Queen Isabella. She rose, "You cut Lena off. Would you mind finishing your last idea, please."

Lena smiled. "The truly *stable* countries have some form of elected government. Those that do not are *never* very long lasting. However, I must also say that elected governments also have their problems too. Any group of people can be manipulated into believing a totally wrong course of action is the right action, leading to their downfall and destruction. There is no perfect government, but an elected one has the *best* chance of long term survival." She nodded and carefully made her way across the room to

Bernardo's side.

You did good, dear, he sent her.

Queen Isabella now rose. "King Wye. What will happen to the standing armies of the existing kingdoms? What will happen to the Royal Guards who are to protect the Senators as well as the kings? What about the towers in your cities?"

He turned and answered. "The soldiers will be given their choice to remain with us, swearing oaths of loyalty or they can depart to wherever they wish to go. Same with the Royal Guards. The tower members will have to swear loyalty oaths as well or leave the towers. Simple. There are plenty of new *mentales* gifted who can replace those that leave. You don't have any say in this matter, except which path we follow, one or two."

"Interesting that you dump this on my plate just as I am about to leave to visit Queen Altha in the Ataro System. If I didn't know any better, I might think you planned it this way." She detected a rise in his emotions and knew that she'd hit the mark.

"I wish to confer with the venerados and veneradas and you current kings and queens — privately. I hereby cancel this session for the time being. Kings, queens, go take an early lunch. Venerados, veneradas, stick around. I'll call on the individual rulers to come before me after while. Go now." She barked her orders.

At this point in time, there were around three dozen separate *Círculo de la Torres*. Each had its own leader, the venerado or venerada. These leaders remained behind, along with Isabella's personnel and the Gang of Nine.

"Isabella, I had no idea this was being planned," Venerada Maricela began, as soon as they were alone. One by one, the others agreed with her. "They've been very clever about this one. What are we going to do now?"

Queen Isabella said, "I cannot accept their first choice. If they go against the will of their people, that will undermine them and eventually destroy all that they've worked so hard to bring about. No, it has to be their second choice. But I am worried about you and your tower personnel."

Maricela pointed out, "But those men and the nobles

own and control the choicest parts of their kingdoms.

Venerado Pino Valen spoke up. "Hey, you are overlooking a very significant detail, Queen Isabella. All of us are. Not all the rulers are desirous of this change. With the exception of our own so called king, most all the rest of the City-States want to continue down the current path. So is Brom, I think, and Malaca too. Only about half of them are behind this plot to subvert your new form of government."

Venerada Maricela spoke up again, "I think you are playing right into their hands with this one. They want you to allow them to divide up their lands. They become richer still, and the rest of the kingdom becomes even poorer. We need to think this through more clearly."

Another added, "She's got a point. If you allow them to disband their kingdoms, we are going to have massive new problems. We can all see why they are so desirous of this, though. They have history on their side. There has always been a Wye running that city. Reina Edda Turda has worked very hard to restore Turda after the barbarian invasion nearly wiped the city out. Now her terms are up, and we all know she is a very popular ruler there. So is Reina Sofia in the Arad. So is Lord Bolivar in Brom. Many kingdoms currently have benevolent monarchs right now, all of whom are about to be thrown out of office. They are fighting to hold onto their positions at all costs, it seems."

Queen Isabella calmed down. "You are right. I was reacting and angry at having been so blind-sided by this sudden change. I see what you mean; dividing up the kingdoms is a really bad idea just now. What about making a proposal to each kingdom's Senate that they are allowed to re-elect their current rulers as many times as they desire. Have a vote of retention or not. If the people do not want to keep that ruler in power, then new elections must be held."

"That might fly," Venerada Maricela suggested. "Of course, who is going to force the ruler who has been rejected out of office? There is no Tierra-wide organization or army to dispose of those who are unwilling to abandon their position when the voters vote them out of office."

The small group discussed this for a while longer. They

all agreed with Queen Isabella's proposal. They also agreed that some type of Tierra-wide organization had to be created to help enforce rulings that went against other rulers. Isabella realized this was the fatal flaw in her grand plan. She then recalled everyone back into the Great Hall.

She rose and made her formal declaration. "I have decided to send out a petition to each kingdom's Senate asking them to relax the two term limit on the kings and queens, substituting instead a mandatory vote to retain or get rid of the current king or queen. Said votes will take place each six years. As long as the current ruler continues to win confirmation, he or she will be allowed to continue to rule. When their people vote not to retain him or her, he or she must leave office, and the people shall elect a new king or queen. That is my final verdict in this matter. I'll have the petitions drawn up and sent to each Senate President before I leave tomorrow. By the time I return, the results will be back, and I'll go from there."

"Lord Wye, I turn your High Council meeting back to you." She sat down and he resumed the meeting, but now only more mundane matters were discussed. One aspect that caught Isabella's notice was many rulers were inclined to want to send official ambassadors to other kingdoms. Reputedly, they would be working on trading arrangements and such. Just now, she decided not to intervene in this matter. She had far bigger worries. What if the Wye Senate rejected her proposal? Or the Valen Senate? How could she get those kings removed from office? She had no means short of assassination, which she would never use.

Part II The Return

Chapter 12 Decisions and Actions

The deep space transport lifted off from Plateau Grado, carrying Hernando, Queen Isabella, Amy, and Jan. Queen Altha's ship had arrived and been refueled, though it was Lena who taught Bart a new trick: how to read out the current quantity of fuel in the base's underground tanks. In the past, the Underground had no need for such information. It was useless data. Now Queen Altha's advisors needed to know if there was still enough fuel to refuel their ship upon arrival. The trip from Winno-3 to Ashford-5 consumed nearly a full tank, making a complete refueling necessary. Otherwise, a tanker would have to be sent along as well. The alien evacuation was completed so quickly there had not been time to bring in tankers to also take the fuel reserves.

Jan was miserable. She was now wearing the highly restrictive pipe corset. She'd almost forgotten how confining they were. "Well, I've had fourteen years of freedom. I suppose that'll have to do for a while," she grumbled. "Why do they really have to make it almost impossible for you to live just to wield power? It seems to me they ought to pick their leaders better or to install some better checks and balances like your mom has," she added.

"I agree, Jan, but I can't do anything about it," Amy replied. "Obviously. We have to make the best of it. I promise you I'll work as hard as I can so we can get finished and go back home as fast as possible. I still remember most of what we learned way back then. At least I hope so." That appeased Jan somewhat.

Queen Isabella was deep in thought. The shocking surprise dumped upon her yesterday had really upset her. She broke in on her teen's chatter. "It is my fault really. I failed to give that aspect the weight I should have."

"What's that mom?" Amy asked, realizing she was talking. She had been silent since liftoff.

"That the current leaders worked so hard to restore order and prosperity and that they hated being replaced for no

210

other reason than a silly notion of mine that their terms of office should be so limited. That was my mistake. I hope it doesn't cost me everything I've worked on for the last fourteen years. I must discuss this with Queen Altha. I'll keep my visit short, a week perhaps. Then, I really must return and follow this through. Travel is going to add nearly another week to the total time that I'm away. Surely by then, the various Senates will have voted one way or the other."

"It will work out, mom. It always does," Amy tried to sound optimistic, but privately, she wasn't.

The ship traveled at top speed consuming more fuel than normal. Two full days later, the ship descended onto Winno-3 near the capital city of Winiana. Soon, they could see the wasp shaped buildings of Queen Altha's palace complex. Jan assisted Amy, while Hernando helped Isabella get safely out of the ship and onto the tarmac, where Queen Altha herself was waiting to greet them.

As Isabella walked slowly and carefully towards the smiling queen, she had the strangest sense that someone was watching her. With her immobile neck, she dare not try to glance over her shoulder. That would mean physically stopping and turning her body around. She quickly forgot about it during the warm welcome from Queen Altha. Soon, they were being whisked from the port to her palace, chatting all the while.

At least this time our necks aren't fused, Jan sent Amy. *If we can remember it all from fourteen years ago, maybe we can get this done quickly.*

That's my plan, Amy sent back. *Wonder if we'll have the same suite as before?*

They did, in fact. The two queens met, while the same servants the teens had before took them to their suite, helped them get unpacked, and settled into their new daily routines. The first few days seemed like one party or celebration after the other. Many wanted to honor Queen Isabella for what she'd been able to do on Ashford-5 to help spread their methods of ruling. Indeed, the two queens spent quite a lot of time discussing the situation that Queen Isabella was facing. Further, Queen Altha insisted Isabella cut the trip short, and return after only spending three days on Winno-3.

Thus, Amy's official training began on the fourth day after they arrived. However, they all took Queen Isabella to the spaceport and saw her liftoff, along with their farewells.

Neva had lost track of the days she'd been patiently waiting for a ship that brought Queen Isabella to Winno-3. Suddenly, her patience was rewarded. She saw Queen Isabella disembarking from a deep space transport. Her physical appearance was wholly unique and unmistakable! *It won't be long now!* Neva found it hard to remain calm. Soon, she would hitch a ride back to Tierra. She spotted Queen Isabella making her way back to the same transport ship. Neva made darn sure the queen got onboard this ship, before she moved inside as well. Neva took up a position near the ceiling of the main passenger compartment and waited.

Again, Queen Isabella had the uneasy feeling that she was being watched, but try as she might, with her severely limited mobility, she could not see anyone. She forgot about it and settled back for the two day return trip, allowing Hernando to care for her needs, as he always had.

Late September 1290, Neva floated out over Plateau Grado, ignoring the aliens who were arranging transport over to the Imperial Castle for Queen Isabella and Hernando, and refueling the ship. *Home! Where do I go now? Westerlings. No way do I want to go to the Midlands or do I? I have to find a new baby body. Crap, I have to wait so darn long that way. Can I steal a body? Is that even possible? Where? Valen is close. Go there. Follow the road.* Neva sailed off following the twisting road that led from the plateau down into the high foothills and eventually to the mighty city of Valen some two hundred miles away.

It's big. Watch and learn. She floated over the castle and perched on one of the barbicans at the top of the tall tower. From here, she had a good view of the bustling activities below, primarily in the giant courtyards. *There's nothing to keep me from getting one of the ruler's new babies. Then, I would for sure have some power here. Money too. Influence.* She watched and waited, learning who was who.

Giant snowflakes fell. Days passed, and the world turned white. Towards the end of October, Neva noticed a number of worried looking tower members hastening over and into the castle. Curious, she floated along after them.

King Alano Valen, now forty-four, paced the hall just outside his family suite. "Ah, good. It's Zarita. Concepcion thinks it's the Verge Sickness. Get her cured, that's an order," he threatened the tower healers.

"We'll do our best," one woman replied. "Let us do our job, My Lord." She whisked past him and entered the plush central common area. The smell of many herbs and incense overwhelmed her sense of smell, as it did with her two companions.

"In here," Concepcion called out. The three headed into the child's bedroom, where Concepcion and three of her servants were wiping the sweat off her thirteen year old daughter. "High fever. You must save her. Be quick about it," she barked, as if these tower women were subservient to her. Neva liked Concepcion's attitude and watched more closely.

The healer bent over and opened one of the teen's eyes, then laid her hand on her head, quickly withdrawing it. She checked on her pulse and observed her shallow breathing. "How long has she been sick?" she asked.

"About four days. We thought it was an early winter cold. Is it Verge or not?" Concepcion asked, clearly worried.

"I am afraid that it's Verge Sickness. Well advanced case."

"Well, don't just stand there. Cure her!" Concepcion barked. Neva noticed the healer was a bit cowed by this woman.

Neva liked that. *A powerful woman. Good. Now how do I steal this body?*

"We'll do what we can. Brew some *bacal* tea at once. Have you considered taking her to Brom Tower and letting one of their katalyein work on her?" the healer asked.

Concepcion grimaced. *That's the last damn thing that we want to do. Alano will never hear of it with Zarita. Now, if it was our son, you bet he would. Damn men anyway.* "Not a viable option. You *must* save her," she barked.

Neva tried to push her way into the teen's head but found Zarita there. She was encased in a mound of black mental mass of some kind. Neva tried pushing her out but lacked the force. *I need my crystal. Shit. Don't have it. Can't use the healer's, it's attuned to her. Crap. Where can I find one that I can use? Think, Neva. Think. Now is your golden opportunity. Think.* She did just that. *Oh, maybe I can find one like the one I did on Gamelon.* She focused and began pervading first the castle and then the tower, followed by the lands around Valen. She was amazed. *Look at all of them!* She found one inside the tower, but it was already attuned to something or someone else, she couldn't be sure which. Those outside and beneath the ground were raw crystals. She latched onto a large one and felt its power surge through herself.

The healer was forcing the foul tasting tea into the teen's mouth. *Damn, she might recover!* She focused and placed a thought into the middle of the black mass. *Your body has died. Time to go.* She gave both the teen and the mass a bit of a push.

To her amazement, Zarita thought, *I am dead. Got to find a new body.* She watched as Zarita floated out of the body, abandoning it. Neva dove back into its head and commanded it to heal, forcing it to gasp for breath.

"Look! It's working! It's working!" exclaimed Concepcion, hovering over her youngest daughter.

"Too soon to tell. *Bacal* takes some time to work, but she is responding, My Lady," the healer replied. A bit later, the healer added, "This is amazing. I've never seen *bacal* work this rapidly! Her fever has broken; her pulse is back to normal. Look, she's stirring. Amazing."

All four women hovered over Neva or rather Zarita. Neva opened her eyes. This body felt so strange, so funny to her. She tried to sit up. Quickly, the healer helped her, propping a pillow behind her. Neva realized she was in a pickle. She didn't know any of these people. For an instant, she panicked. "Who are you?" she mumbled.

"I'm Yesenai, the tower healer. Don't you remember me? You've had a close call, Zarita. We very nearly lost you. How do you feel?"

214

"Strange," Neva answered honestly. Then, she got a bright idea. "I can't remember things. Your faces seem sort of familiar, but I don't know you. Where am I? Who am I? I'm so confused. What's happened to me?"

"You are in your bedroom, Zarita. It'll be all right now," Concepcion said both relieved and worried. She looked at Yesenia and whispered, "Has she lost her mind or something?"

"Sometimes such a high fever causes mental problems, like amnesia. She's strong and responding well. Her life is spared. Give her time to recover her memory, My Lady. Perhaps, you should explain who and where she is. Alleviate her fears of the unknown."

"You are my youngest daughter, Zarita. I'm your mother, Concepcion Valen. Your father is King Alano Valen. He's just outside. You are in your bedroom here at Valen Castle," she said softly. "Do you remember any of this?"

"Valen. That sounds familiar. Things are familiar, and yet not. It is so confusing. Will I be okay? Will I get my memory back?" Neva went along with their diagnosis. This is perfect, she thought.

"Yes, give it time. You've had a close brush with death, dear. Now, you'll be well soon. I must let your father know. He's been worried sick," she added. Neva picked up her after-thought. *Not enough to get her the proper care from a Brom katalyein.*

Shortly, a middle aged man entered. "So the healer has worked her magic on you, Zarita. Good. See, Concepcion, I told you that our healers are just as powerful as those idiots in Brom Tower. Now you rest up, Zarita. You've got a lot of tower training to do real soon." He turned and left, somewhat relieved.

Something began to bother Neva. King Alano seemed somehow familiar to her, but she knew she'd never met him. Well, that was not entirely true. She recalled seeing him at the High Council of Lords when she went with Governor Konrad. She'd been so preoccupied with being a great lady that she'd barely paid him any attention. The nurses left them and Neva ventured, "Such pretty quilts. All this beautiful needlework. Mom, who made these?"

Conception flushed. "Well, you did, Zarita. No one has ever done such fine work as you, dear."

"How very strange, mom. I don't remember doing them. Worse, I don't remember a thing about how to make quits or use a needle! Have I lost my mind? I'm scared, mom," Neva began playing her mother.

"Oh dear. Please don't worry about such mundane things. Give yourself time. I'm sure it'll come back to you. Besides, now you have your *mentales* gifts turned on full. Those are vastly more important, dear. As soon as you are well, you'll get your tower training and your own crystal. I know how much you've always wanted that."

"Oh. My own crystal. Yes, I remember wanting that very badly. I feel better already."

"You just rest a while. I'll go see they make you some healthy broth for lunch." Concepcion left.

Neva relaxed and began thinking about King Alano. *I know him somehow, but how? Where? It wasn't the High Council. He seems so intimate to me.* She pondered this for some time. In a flash, it came to her. *Mario! He's Mario, the man who set me up and made me into a great lady. Oh god! He's Mario! Now, I truly must be very careful around him. Maybe he'll have totally forgotten me. Shit, I must avoid him as much as possible. No telepathy with him, not ever!*

Left alone, she began to move around her room, getting used to the feeling of her new body and exploring her possessions or rather Zarita's things. She had good taste, she thought, expensive too. Slowly, she became familiar with Zarita's possessions and dresses.

Later that afternoon, her older brother and sister came to visit her, bringing their wife and husband with them. Again, Neva was lost and played her new role well, rapidly learning to put faces with names. She could tell her older siblings were concerned about her well-being, but with little true affection. That suited Neva just fine; besides her older sister was almost double her own age. They had little in common, thankfully.

Several confusing days later, Zarita was led over to Valen Tower and introduced to its members, particularly Venerado Arturo Valen and Capa Alicia Valen. It was Capa

Alicia, who would give her Zarita her tower training. Nothing but the best for another Valen was the motto around Valen Castle and Tower. Of course, Zarita was pleased.

"Good god! Zarita is amazing," Capa Alicia exclaimed. She was meeting with her husband, Venerado Arturo. "She's picking up these attack and defense modes like a pro, and she's incredibly powerful. Just phenomenal."

"That's hard to believe. Two weeks ago, she was doing needlepoint, and we'd written her off. Now, you are telling me we have a hot one here? How is this possible?" he replied, growing more interested.

"Indeed. I don't understand it either. I thought she was only good for marrying off to someone of Alano's choosing. Now this is an entirely different matter. I'd appreciate it if you would check on my work with her. Perhaps test her yourself," Alicia suggested.

"I'd better. Take me to her now," he requested.

"Zarita, Venerado Arturo here is going to test you to make sure I've been training you well enough," Capa Alicia explained to Zarita, who was waiting patiently in her office.

Something is up or she wouldn't be bringing in the big gun. Best be careful, Neva thought.

"Capa Alicia tells me you have already mastered the attack and defense modes. Is this true?" he asked, studying the thirteen year old teen, who he'd long ago written off as not tower material. A weak telepath at best.

"If she says so, then I must be," Neva replied, playing her role.

"Okay then, let me test your defenses. Prepare yourself," he ordered.

She did so. Suddenly, she felt herself being attacked with powerful feelings of utter worthlessness. She was not worthy of even being a telepath. Neva reacted. *No man can do this to me, not ever!* She reached out to one of the buried raw crystals out on the green pasturelands beyond Valen. Pulling in its raw power, she sent it all back at Venerado Arturo, blasting his own mind in like kind. *You worthless piece of horse-shit!* She sent back, having purged her mind completely of his intrusive thoughts.

Venerado Arturo was momentarily stunned. It was all he could do to break the connection. He slumped over for a moment, causing a sudden wave of fear to sweep over Alicia. She touched his mind, sending him soothing thoughts. He pushed her away, regaining his composure. "Well done," he finally found his voice. "I agree. You've mastered them, Zarita. Let's move on to work out the direction your powerful gifts have sent you."

Later, when he and his wife were alone, he commented, "My god! Zarita is a powerhouse. She very nearly did me in when I tried to attack her. Look at the forms her *mentales* has taken. Total control of others by all mental means. Crap, she could dominate you or me, if she has a mind to do that! We must warn Alano and Concepcion about her. What have we got on our hands with Zarita anyway?"

"I don't know, but she must be the most powerful gifted we've had in a century, Arturo. You are right; we must let the others know never to cross her or to antagonize her. My god, the repercussions could be severe. We need to get this one into our tower circles, don't you think?" Alicia suggested.

"Yes and no. Yes, if she desires it. No, if she doesn't. If anyone tries to force her to do something she doesn't want to do, my god, there'll be hell to pay!" he replied. "We best get a hold of the others right away. Summon the pentagram members, please."

A half hour later, the five met in secret. Venerado Arturo explained what was going on with Zarita in detail. "Yes, she damned near fried my own mind, and she didn't even have her germanium crystal yet! If she had one in her possession, I can't think what would have happened! My Lord, for heaven's sake, treat Zarita with kid-gloves."

"You're kidding me? Right? It's Zarita we are talking about, not Pino?" King Alano questioned in disbelief.

Arturo gave him a very nasty look. "Look, once she has her crystal, which we must give to her soon, she'll be able to dominate even you and probably with the *greatest* of ease. Treat her with kid-gloves or there'll be hell to pay, Alano. I swear to you; we aren't lying about this one. She's a powerhouse."

"Can't you get her into the tower and out of our way?" he asked.

"Only if she wants to become a tower technician," Venerado Arturo answered. "If anyone tried to force her to do something she doesn't want to do, heaven help them."

King Alano sighed and then smiled. "Ah, so we have another valuable object we can add to our arsenal. Okay, we'll take it easy with her for now. Do try to get her to join the tower for a while. We can't have her interfering with this current kingdom business, now can we? I promise you we'll use her in the best way we can, but all in good time. Incredible. Zarita. Who the hell would've thought she had this buried inside her all these years?"

"I think she inherited some of it from me," Concepcion pointed out. "It's like she has my skill set, only magnified considerably." Alano gave her a rather dirty look, but said nothing.

"Perhaps, it would help tone her down if she got fancy body modifications done. Corset, lip plates, toe shoes?" Concepcion pointed out. "These do limit my physical activities considerably. If you remember, before she got sick, she was always begging us to get them done. We kept telling her she had to wait until she was of age, fourteen."

"I like that idea, dear. Temper her down somewhat," King Alano agreed with her. "How soon will she be fourteen?" he asked.

Concepcion gave him a rotten look. *Just like a man not even to know his own daughter's birthday. Sure knows his son's though.* "May 6th. I'll talk to her about it. Perhaps if she still wants them, you can convince Elegant Fashions Inc to perform them a bit sooner than May, My Lord." She nudged him in the right direction, and he agreed.

"You or I?" he asked.

"I'll do it tonight at supper," Concepcion replied.

"I have to be fourteen to get all that done mom," Zarita replied. She was sipping her after-dinner tea. Concepcion had just told her it would soon be time for her to get all those modifications done that she'd been begging to have for the last two years or more. Neva thought hard and quickly. *I need to get my hands on a bunch of those big crystals as soon as I get out of the tower training. I best get to finding them even in the snow.*

"That's true, dear," King Alano replied, seemingly backing her up. Then he added, "I might be able to pull some strings and get them to do yours a bit earlier. After all, you are nearly fourteen now."

Neva panicked a little. She had no idea when her birthday was. She needed time. "I want to do some horse riding this winter. Maybe we can do it in the spring, if that's all right, dad?" Zarita suggested.

She sensed he was becoming curious. Why would she want to go riding in the winter? That seemed wholly incongruous with his daughter, the one that he'd known for thirteen years. Still, she'd changed after that awful bout of Verge Sickness; that must be the cause, he concluded. He remained curious, though, but he took Arturo's advice seriously, and didn't prohibit her from doing what she desired to do. "Sure dear. Just let me know when, and I'll make the arrangements. After all, you do want to look like the royal princess you are." He decided to play this angle. It always worked before with the women he knew.

Zarita knew she would have major problems riding out of Valen Castle on her own. As the king's daughter, she'd have security guards riding with her wherever she went. For a time, she toyed with the idea of perhaps trying to Mind Wipe them, after they saw her digging up one of the crystals. Then, she vetoed that one. Surely the tower folk would discover her tampering, and she'd have a price to pay. If it were only springtime, then she could find a way to sneak out of the castle late at night and find them. As she looked out of her bedroom window at the raging blizzard, she decided she had to wait for spring.

Of course, now she had to deal with becoming an adult in the royal court. She knew darn well as a princess, she had to look the part. That meant getting her body modified, so she could wear the fashionable gowns that her mother and the other noblewomen, who visited the king's court, wore. Once she turned fourteen, she would be of age. After that, everyone would fully expect her to look the part of the king's available daughter. She even fretted about the possibility that King Alano would arrange a marriage for her as well. *If he tries that, I'll have to use my powers on him. No way am I going to let that get in my way!*

She then spent hours thinking about whether or not, if she were modified, could she still ride and retrieve the precious crystals? Concepcion never did that; she always traveled about in the royal carriage. If Neva did that too, she'd have an even harder time trying to retrieve the crystals. *No, I have to find out if a modified person can still ride a horse. That's the key. Now how do I do that?* Then, she realized only the toe shoes would impair her ability to ride, perhaps. Once on the horse, she shouldn't have any problems at all.

In mid-November, she sensed both parents were really getting worried about her. Sensing her mother's thoughts while Concepcion was sleeping, she realized, if she got modified, that would greatly ease both their fears. *I can't believe they're both scared of me! Well, they ought to be.*

The next morning at breakfast, she made her parents extremely pleased. "Dad, I think I ought to get properly modified soon, so I can dress like your princess. But I still want to go riding in the springtime."

He looked rather surprised, but recovered quickly. "Sure, that would make me quite proud, Zarita. I'll see about it today. Pull some strings and all that."

Considering she and her mother were escorted into the city later that afternoon, Zarita knew he wasn't going to take the slightest chance that she would change her mind by tomorrow! "No, I want the kind of toe shoes that Queen Isabella wears," Zarita insisted. She knew how awful the other toe shoes had been, the kind that fused her feet into an en pointe position. She probably could not ride if she had those. Her mother graciously allowed her to get that style. "I want red gowns. With my black hair, that would look best on me," she added.

The manager then brought out a mahogany box. "King Alano wanted you to have these incredible earrings, Princess Zarita. Just look at them!" She did and was appalled. They were huge, heavy, and so long that they rested on her chest. Zarita didn't know why Alano wanted her to have these. Yes, they were worth a fortune, but why such huge earrings? Was he trying to constrain her further or show her off to men? She sighed. She had no choice in the matter. Well, she could have, if she wanted to use her *mentales* gifts on them all. Not for such a trivial matter, she decided.

A couple of hours later, she was roused, fully modified and dressed in the latest high fashions of Tierra noblewomen. Her waist had been reduced to the fourteen inch standard; her feet now were permanently modified so only her toes rested flat on the floor. Her lips ached from being stretched over the giant foot in diameter lip plates. Her design displayed a giant crystal. She couldn't breathe properly, and her ears felt like they were about to be pulled off. She could not help but remember these same feelings and pains when, as Neva, she had been properly modified down in Arabella. Again, she played her role well, allowing her mother to dote over her, to help her walk, and to get into their carriage. "Give it time. All we women have to get used to these changes. In no time, you'll be very comfortable with everything. We'll practice your walking after supper. I promise."

At dinner, she could barely eat anything, but both of her parents were very pleased with her new appearance. King Alano seemed to be greatly relieved, Neva thought. *Well, if they are appeased, perhaps they'll forget about me for a while. Spring, please hurry up!*

During the long winter, Zarita began making her preparations for spring. She accumulated a number of pod silk bags in which to store the crystals. She discovered she already owned a horse. In spite of the difficulty she had walking, especially over the snow-covered courtyard, she managed to visit the stables several times, casing the place out. She'd have to make her moves late at night. She befriended the stable lad who was caring for her mare. He was a simple lad, whose mind she could easily control when the time came.

The giant, steel reinforced castle gates proved too great a barrier. She cleverly learned they were shut at night. Only the captain of the guards was allowed to open them, not the usual old gatekeeper who was on duty during the daytime. He too had the *mentales* gifts, and she dared not interfere with his mind. That was sure to rouse suspicions. In December, she finally realized she needed to be somehow staying overnight in Valen proper, outside the castle. As a princess, this proved more difficult.

At last, she got another bright idea. She befriended the manager of Elegant Fashions Inc. Valencia was thirty-three and had run this office since she was twenty-one. Zarita learned that frequently out of town guests stayed in her store's guest rooms. Now, she had her way out of the castle. In January, she began asking if she could spend the night with Valencia, supposedly studying all the fashions and helping Valencia with her store.

"Look dad, I want to always be up on the very latest fashions. You want me to look my best don't you?" she played King Alano well. He consented, and she began to spend one night a week sleeping with Valencia. She did learn quite a lot about all the various fashions and was able to acquire a well-made leather riding outfit — pants and top that fit her well. She also purchased toe boots and a small shovel. Now all she had to do was wait for spring to come. Both of her parents were pleased she was taking such an interest in fashions and not using her immense powers for other mischief. Valencia was also very happy with the arrangement, since she could boast she was hosting the king's daughter from time to time.

As spring finally came, Zarita found it a simple matter to hire a stable hand to saddle her horse for her. "I want to go on some midnight rides," she explained to the rather dim-witted lad, who didn't question her further. At last, on the fifteenth of April 1291, Zarita made her first midnight foray out on the rolling grasslands west of Valen. She had long ago pervaded the area and knew precisely where six such crystals lay beneath the surface. Mounting the horse had not been a problem. Rather moving around on foot and trying to dig them up proved terribly challenging in her toe boots. More than once, she cursed herself for having gotten her feet so drastically modified. Nevertheless, Zarita was able to recover six giant germanium crystals and stored them safely in her pod silk bags. Unfortunately, the whole game changed drastically by the last of April.

The family was having breakfast when a guard came running in, "Your Majesty, we are being attacked!"

"Well, get the damned gates closed! Coming," he barked. The guard raced off to make sure that was done. King Alano sent telepathic messages, and then headed off to see what was going on. Zarita headed to the castle's balcony as fast as she could, pitifully slowly. Her tight gown and impossible toe shoes only allowed her to take tiny, measured steps. Panting from the tight corset, she finally reached the balcony. From here, she could see a band of armed men marching up the long paved causeway that was raised over the western marshes at the outer edge of the city. The stone road led straight to the castle's gates. No mistaking the men's intentions. The castle was their goal. Zarita sensed that they were very determined. Then, she also sensed raw crystal power! One of these men also had a giant crystal.

She saw the tower Circles had been roused and two full circles had taken up defensive positions on their observation deck at the top of the tall tower. Venerado Arturo was leading them. Below, King Alano was mustering the Royal Guards, some hundred strong, positioning them before the gates. Then it happened.

Zarita, along with all the various *mentales* gifted, sensed a huge flow of psi energies. A deadening thunder echoed through the castle and tower, as the mammoth gates were ripped asunder. Steel hinges were shattered; the gates lay askew. The invaders came rushing forward. Now giant balls of fire appeared over the hundred Royal Guards, who dove this way and that to avoid being incinerated. Zarita felt another surge of energies coming from the giant crystal and looked over at Venerado Arturo. He fell back holding his head and then collapsed out of sight. She knew he was the most powerful of the tower folk. She heard some of the tower women screaming.

Looking down on the conflagration, she sensed some guards were dying from the flames, but King Alano dashed back into the castle. Coward, she thought, and prepared to meet this invader herself, calling upon her own secret crystals. Just as she was about to unleash her own counter-attack, King Alano reappeared holding a strange alien stick. Boom! He fired. To her amazement, she saw the man who was holding the giant crystal collapse onto the ground. Bang! King Alano fired again, dropping the leading man who was closest to breeching the gates. She heard her father yell, "Go get them! Kill every last man!" About half of the Royal Guards were able to respond to his command.

At this point, the tower came to their aid, dropping small balls of fire on the rear of the invaders. Within a few short minutes, the attempted coup was over. Others now rushed out to aid the fallen, burning guards. Zarita gambled she had time to make her pathetically slow way down to the scene of the attack. Hoping that she wouldn't miss any action, she left her balcony post and headed down stairs and eventually out into the courtyard. Capa Alicia led her Circle out of the tower; her face was terribly grim.

As Zarita met up with the ten, she asked, "How's Venerado Arturo? I saw him go down. How did dad kill those men?"

"Bad, I'm afraid we may have lost him. Healers are doing their best. Alien guns. Come on; we have to find out how that man was able to destroy the gates. Immense power, beyond anything I've ever seen!"

Stepping over and around the fallen, smoldering bodies, Zarita didn't fall behind the ten. They were just as slow as she, picking their way through the carnage. All eleven glanced at the shattered gates as they passed through them. Now they had to pick their way around the dead invaders and finally reached King Alano. He was standing over the *mentales* gifted he'd shot. He still held his rifle in one hand, using it to roll the giant crystal around, sizing it up.

"Ah, good. You are here. What do you make of this? Is this thing what gave him such powers?" King Alano asked Capa Alicia.

"Yes, it is a giant germanium crystal. Those things have been extinct for centuries. If I am right, those were outlawed back in the early days of the emperor and empress. Arturo might not make it. He took a mind blast head on," she added grimly. "Don't touch it with your flesh. It could kill you. Hernando, go fetch a pod silk bag for this monster." One of her Circle members dashed off to get one.

"Where the devil did he get it?" King Alano asked, just as grim faced as she.

Capa Alicia bit her lip. "I think this might be related to what we've been hearing from other towers. Remember, others have been reporting some giant stones have been uncovered in the Midlands and elsewhere. I suspect this man somehow found one and decided to use it." She spat on the corpse, as if that would somehow get revenge for her husband.

"Good god! We are going to have to find some of these ourselves. If it hadn't been for my alien hunting rifle here, we'd all be dead! This is the most serious threat we've ever experienced! Get all the tower members together. Zarita, you grab your mother too. We need everyone present. Somehow, we must find some of these or the next time, the rebels may well kill us all while we sleep. Good god, if they'd done this at night, we all would be!"

"Yes, My Lord. On it now. Come on, Zarita; let's head back, and get everyone assembled. Hernando can bring us this stone in a bit," Capa Alicia ordered and Zarita followed her.

An hour later, every tower member was present, save one healer who was tending Venerado Arturo. They were meeting in the Great Hall, and Hernando had gently placed the seemingly harmless germanium crystal on the table before everyone's eyes. It was about a foot in diameter, about the size of each of Zarita's six crystals, which she had already managed to attune to her own frequency.

For a time, they discussed the crystal and what it meant. Everyone was both shocked and terrified of the consequences, should another one of these find itself in the hands of rebels. "Look, it is obvious we must acquire a number of these or we are doomed," King Alano declared. "So how do we find them? We can't go digging up every square inch of the kingdom."

"I have no idea, My Lord," Capa Alicia replied timidly. "I've never seen such a giant crystal before. How do we detect them?" She looked from tower member to member; all had blank stares.

Zarita sighed. She had to make another decision. After all, she was living here too. Her father's words, that they could be killed in their sleep, truly upset her. At last, she ventured, "Dad, I can find them. There are a number of them out there in the grasslands to the west of the city. They are buried about a foot or so beneath the surface."

King Alano gave her a very queer look. She sensed he was putting two and two together. At least, he had the good sense not to openly discuss his suspicions before everyone here. Instead, he replied, "Okay Zarita. I am counting on you to help us find lots more of these. Tomorrow, Capa Alicia, you are to take your Circle out onto the grasslands, and let Zarita show you where to dig. I will send along fifty guards for your protection. Find us a bunch of these. Then, figure out how the devil we can safely use them. Meantime, we had all better combine our powers to get the gates repaired. Take that hideous thing away, Hernando." The meeting broke up.

"Stay daughter," he commanded, as Zarita was about to leave with the tower members. He also dismissed his wife and everyone else. When they were alone, his eyes drilled into Zarita's. "So how did you know these stones were out there? How long have you known? Are they the reason you wanted to go riding out there? Speak daughter." He thought better of ordering her; she sensed he was still somewhat fearful of her.

"I can sense them, dad. Since last winter. I didn't know they could be used to blow up our gates or I would have said something," she replied feigning meekness.

"I see. Well, none of us knew that either. I was just as surprised as everyone else was to see those massive gates so easily destroyed. Okay then, make damned sure you find us a bunch tomorrow. Okay?"

"Yes, of course, dad. How many do you think we need?" she continued to play meek.

"Hell, I don't know. A dozen maybe," he replied. Zarita relaxed, she knew she could easily find that many without much trouble. "Come on, dear. We had best check on Arturo. I don't know what I'll do if he dies on me." He rose, and she followed him, noticing he slowed down and put his arm around her, helping her with her precarious balance. Until now, he'd never done that, she noted. Was she gaining his respect, she wondered?

The next day, dressed in her leathers, Zarita made her slow way to the stables. Already, the fifty guards were mounted and impatiently waiting. Capa Alicia was still issuing orders to her Circle, and Zarita quietly mounted her mare. "All right, Zarita, you lead. We'll be right behind you. Guards, some of you flank her. Let's get this recovery mission started." Zarita had no doubt about Capa Alicia's ability to lead; she was a take charge type woman, impressing Zarita.

As they rode along, Zarita noticed the nine Circle members were watching and studying her very carefully. Obviously, they were looking for clues about how to find more of these crystals themselves. She sensed several were very annoyed at having to have the simpleton daughter of the king leading them on this mission.

That changed when she led them to the first one. She stopped and pointed. "Down there is one. No, a little to the left." She remained mounted, knowing how awkward it had been for her to even stand, let alone walk, on this rough terrain. Several Circle members began digging, while the guards sat around looking bored. A clanking noise brought smiles to everyone's faces. Shortly, the first large crystal appeared. Hernando carefully rolled it into a waiting pod silk bag.

They rode hard that day, covering nearly forty-five miles, recovering seven crystals before returning to Valen. For her part, Zarita did receive praise from King Alano. After she left his throne room, he asked Capa Alicia how it went and if she had figured out how his daughter was able to locate them.

"Aye, yes and no. Yes in that wherever there lies a buried crystal, there is a small hollow in the ground with a rise around it. I liken it to what you see if you drop a raisin or nut into a bowel of pudding. Now, we know just where to dig, once we spot that feature. No, in that we don't know where these holes are located. Honestly, Zarita has an uncanny knack for locating them. She just rides straight from site to site, though they be many miles apart. We must have covered fifty miles today," a tired Capa Alicia replied.

"I see. So you're telling me you still need Zarita to locate them easily?" he asked, pulling on his chin. *Why does it have to be her and not Pino, who has this strange, but valuable gift?*

She shrugged her shoulders. "We could take fifty men and fan them out and sweep across the land, systematically searching for the typical craters. I don't know if that would be any quicker. I doubt it. Let's face it; she is a force to be reckoned with, My Lord."

"Aye. That she is, but she's my problem. Best go see how your husband is doing." She left him deep in thought.

For three more days, they continued their search for more large, buried crystals, recovering another ten. However, now they had to go many miles from Valen to find one. With seventeen of these, King Alano was satisfied for the moment, and then challenged the Circles to figure out how safely to use them. He visited the still unconscious Venerado Arturo, wishing he would recover soon. Now more than ever, he needed the skills of his tower leader.

A week after the attack, Arturo finally awoke. "My head feels like it has been turned into mush," he whispered to Alicia, who hovered over him, mopping his brow. "What happened?"

She explained how the attack had gone, telling him about the giant crystal the man had used to destroy the gates. She related the amazing four days with Zarita and the recovery of seventeen of the stones. He whispered, "From the holes, they must have hit the ground from above. Perhaps, they were part of the meteor storm that struck when the moon exploded."

"Wherever they came from, they litter the lands, but only in certain spots. We rode over some rocky lands, and I saw many blue shards, as if some landed there, but shattered upon impact with the stony ground. All the ones we found landed on the soft grasslands," she explained. "Here comes the healer with some soup. Eat well; we need you back on your feet soon. He's charged us with figuring out how to use these stones. I believe they'll give us immense powers, perhaps as much as in ancient times." He smiled.

With the hunt over for now, Zarita pondered her situation. Intuitively, she knew eventually, they would discover her own personal small stash of the crystals. While she could easily best anyone here, one on one, she knew she could not take on a whole Circle, should they demand she hand hers over too. *Once they figure out how much power is in these stones, men will want all they can get. Mine will not be safe. He'll swear it is for the good of the kingdom, but he means to keep them for himself. If I were Pino, he'd probably let me keep them, but not me. He doesn't respect women much at all; that I can tell. I have to get away from here while the getting is good. How? Where will I go?*

Her mother actually gave her the idea. Over breakfast, she mentioned, "You know, it's been a couple of weeks since you spent the night with Valencia at Elegant Fashions Inc. By now, she must have more fashions coming in for the spring, getting ready for the May High Council meeting in Exchange City. Or aren't you interested in that anymore?"

"Sure am, mom. Dad's been keeping me busy. If he doesn't need me today, can I go spend time there? Be back tomorrow around supper." That brought a smile to Concepcion's face. She readily agreed. "Can I buy some more outfits, please?" she added.

"Hi Zarita. Yes, the new spring styles are here. Come look. I say, some women are going to be far more daring that I am. These are strapless no less!" Valencia readily admitted to Zarita. Together, they sorted out the large crate of gowns before tackling the second crate of heels and accessories. Of course, both women then just "had" to try on one of these new styles. Valencia had no problem with the gown, save for her sense of modesty. Her fully developed bust, so typical here on Tierra, made sure it could not be pulled down by accident. Not so with Zarita, and that gave her a point of entry she desired.

"I want to wear these too, but I'm not developed enough am I?"

Valencia smiled, "To be honest, Zarita, give it time. In a few years you'll wish you were still small."

"But dad wants me to look my best. Look how easily it

can slip off me. Can't you use your machine to make mine as large as yours are?" she asked, knowing full well Valencia only knew how to do a few very specific body modifications with the medical machine.

"Alas, no. However, Inez in Exchange City certainly can do that, if you really want them larger."

"Well then, that's settled. I'll have to go visit Elegant Fashions Inc in Exchange City, won't I?" she giggled and Valencia smiled.

The next evening, she presented her case to her parents over dinner. "Look, the new styles are fabulous, but strapless. I just have to get mine bigger before the High Council meeting, dad. You don't want my gown to slip down and embarrass both of us, do you?" she pleaded like a small child might.

"Okay, I agree. The High Council is going to be the tenth of May. I'll have the tower teleport you to Elegant Fashions Inc tomorrow, if Inez will agree to put you up there for a while. I expect to see you at the council looking stunning. Okay?" She readily agreed. As she left the room, she sensed both of her parents were rather relieved at her departure. She smiled smugly and headed to her room to begin packing. *I might not ever be coming back here!*

Lilly, not Inez, met her when she arrived. First, she was teleported to the Imperial Tower. From there, while some servants carried her many bags, she walked carefully over to the store next to the Imperial complex and took the elevator to the top floor. "Hello. You must be Zarita Valen. Mom's indisposed right now. I'm Lilly. Come on in; I have a room waiting for you down on the fourth floor. I'll see your things are taken there. King Alano Valen said you want to be able to safely wear the latest spring strapless gowns?"

"Oh yes. Yes. I've spent days helping Valencia there in our Valen store. We tried them on, but with me, a slip could be disastrous. Dad said you could help. I'm fourteen, but I need them large, like the other adults. I can help out around here too, if anything needs to be done. Hang gowns on racks, store shoes." She tried to sound helpful, but this store was huge and wholly unfamiliar.

"Well, let's see just how big they need to be, shall we?"

231

Lilly replied. An hour later, Zarita sported a greatly enlarged bosom, nearly as large as the fully developed women of Tierra. Of course, none of her current clothes now fit her. Some, Lilly sent downstairs to be altered. Some, she took in as trades. Both women enjoyed re-outfitting Zarita. "You have excellent tastes, Zarita," Lilly complimented her.

That done, Zarita insisted on wearing one of her new strapless gowns for the rest of the day. "Have to get accustomed to wearing it. It is so elegant and risque, isn't it?"

Lilly chuckled, "That it is. The young men will be staring at you for sure."

A bit later, Nita came back from the Imperial Castle to work her shift. She was pleased to meet Zarita, who was just a little younger than she was, but looked much older now with her full bosom. The two hit it off, and Zarita was able to gather the information she wanted from Nita, a fountain of knowledge about Exchange City.

The next day, after Nita dashed off to visit with the Gang of Nine, Zarita took one of her special crystals and headed out onto the streets of Exchange City. She found navigating the undulating streets more than a challenge in her toe shoes, and once more cursed herself for having gotten them so drastically altered. At last, she found the establishment she was looking for: Adrian's Jewelry. She took as deep a breath as her restrictive corset allowed her and entered.

A middle aged man looked up, and suddenly paid close attention to her. He was head blind, and she knew he sensed she was a "Great Lady." "How may I help you, My Lady?" he said politely.

"I have found a wonderful gemstone that I want to have cut down and made into some fine jewelry for myself. I wonder if you can do such a thing?"

"But of course, My Lady. I am Adrian, and there is no finer jeweler in all Exchange City. May I see your prize, and then we can discuss just what you would like for me to design for one so pretty as yourself." He poured it on a bit thick, she thought, but soon realized he really wanted to make this sale, figuring she was someone important. *Well one day I will be that again,* she thought and brought out one of her "stones."

"I know that it isn't jade or ruby, but I just love its pure blue colors. Can it be cut and made into jewelry?" she asked her key question. So much hinged on his reply.

"Why yes it most definitely can. I am sure it will polish up very nicely. But it is so large. Oh, you have such magnificent earrings already."

"Yes, I would like two rings with a inch stone in them. I would like a tiara with a dozen inch stones in them. I would like a butterfly hair clasp with two inch stones in them. Then, use the rest to make me another pair of earrings similar to the ones I am wearing. Will this be large enough for all that?"

He grinned. "Indeed, My Lady and then some. Please. This way. Let us pick out your designs and measure your sizes." An hour later, she returned to Elegant Fashions Inc a very pleased young woman. In a week and in time for the High Council, she would have her new "jewelry" to wear. However, that evening while in bed, she worried she was losing one of her seven crystals. She focused her attention and began pervading the local green lands to the east of the city. She smiled. More were here for the taking. All that remained was the how.

Two days later, Nita invited her to join the Gang of Nine, as they went out riding. "Of course, two of us are off-world now, so we're only really seven now. Please come; it'll be fun," Nita pleaded with her. Of course, she agreed, and an hour later met the Gang of Nine, which now included Lena; Amy and Jan were still on Winno-3. She had an enjoyable outing with the teens and purposely made friends with them all. She sensed they were somehow important teens. At least she learned they had schooling from Nadja, who was also an alien like Lena. This Zarita duly noted.

The next day, armed with more pod silk bags, she went off riding by herself. When she returned, she had recovered another three more crystals, making ten large ones now in her possession, not counting the one that was about to become her jewelry. *I'll never again be caught without my crystals. These people here only have the one they wear around their necks. If anything happens to that, they are cooked, just like I was on Gamelon. That's not going to happen ever again if I can help it!*

While helping out around the store, she began to practice the one new skill she'd developed during her tower training. She was able to make small things appear invisible. Zarita had it all worked out. Just as soon as she got her jewelry, she would put on her two rings and make them invisible. Those would be her ultimate, last ditch protections. She could not hide her hair clasp nor her earrings. Then, she got the idea of having some more stones fabricated into a gown belt and began to think of other possibilities.

Finally the great day came. She made her slow, careful way to Adrian's shop, once more cursing her feet, which made walking up and down the hilly streets almost unbearable. Out of breath, she slipped into his shop. "Ah, My Lady Zarita. I have your new items ready. I do hope they meet with your approval. There was quite a bit extra, so I took the liberty of adding another pair of strands to your earrings. They can be removed if they are too heavy for you. Come, let me show you some of my finest work."

Zarita was very pleased with his work. The rings fit well, sporting a brilliantly polished germanium crystal as large as the one she was given to wear around her neck. The tiara was quite elegant in design, gold, and the ten blue stones were blended perfectly. Not ostentatious, the circlet was perfect. Her earrings now had five strands of varying lengths, the longest two rested on her now quite pronounced bosom. Exquisite, she thought. More importantly, each earring held oblong crystals, fifteen on each side. The gold settings were quite similar to those on her current pair. She was quite pleased, and Adrian was also, as he debited King Alano's account.

"I may return to have more made, if I can find another one of these incredibly beautiful blue gemstones."

"I am here to serve you, My Lady Valen. Any time."

In the privacy of her bedroom, Zarita began to work on her new jewelry, beginning with her rings. After attuning them to herself, they would be useless to another *mentales* gifted. Next, she focused and shortly, the two rings vanished from sight. Zarita was most pleased. Next, one by one, she attuned the other stones to her. She fastened her hair with the new clasp, which held two crystals. She could hardly make those invisible, nor could she, her tiara. Still, an hour later, she had them all attuned and on her body. She sensed the power she could now tap, at least fifty times that of the usual *mentales* gifted on Tierra! Zarita grinned, but decided more would be even better. She looked at her appearance in the mirror. No one would recognize her crystals, at least not readily. All were highly polished and looked like true gems, not the rough, irregular shaped one that she wore around her neck. Perfect!

Chapter 13 Reactions

While Queen Isabella was off-world, Ken had accepted the burden of keeping track of the various Senate results. According to her, she expected to be gone three weeks, cutting her trip back significantly. For the most part, Bart would have the dirty work of monitoring communications and promised to keep him informed, as soon as he heard anything being sent about Senate results. Of course, his worry was how to respond to the results. He could see why many of the current rulers would want to continue at their post.

Queen Edda Turda, for example, had already done an exemplary job of restoring the sacked city-state of Turda, Alba, Easterlings. She'd more than earned their faith and trust. From the chatter at the new tower there, Ken suspected the citizens of Turda wanted her to continue bringing them prosperity. A similar case could be made for Queen Sofia of Tecuci, Arad. Other cases were not so exemplary. King Alano Valen was still making a mess of his much reduced kingdom of Valen. Chatter there indicated that many wanted a change in kings, but he wasn't about to leave his post.

Confounding the mess was the simple fact that these current rulers, kings or queens, owned outright a good deal of land and businesses within their kingdoms. All had been inherited, of course, handed down from father to first-born son, in many cases. They had a legitimate claim. Combine that with the additional lands and enterprises owned by these ruler's extended families and closely related nobles, often the heart of the kingdom was under the king's direct control, leaving rather impoverished areas available. No matter how the cookie was cut, these current rulers would have powerful influences on what went on in their kingdoms. Even if others were elected to run the kingdom, these men and women would literally tie the hands of the new rulers. Economic ropes would make the new kings all but mere puppets. Of course, that totally defeated the intent behind the new system of rule Isabella had established fourteen years ago.

Ken also realized back then, Isabella, Crystal, and he hadn't looked this far ahead, focusing on just trying to get the basics implemented throughout the many kingdoms of Tierra. Now he realized he had been shortsighted. Once more, he wished Benjamina was still around. He could use his mother's advice and wisdom. At best, Ken hoped the Senates would agree to this one-time term limits extension Isabella had proposed. If not, he was certain some rulers would indeed further divide their kingdoms, retaining what they owned outright as their kingdom. What would be given to the others would be the less populated lands, leaving many impoverished kingdoms with little hope of ever gaining prosperity. That would also likely lead to wars as well.

If all this wasn't enough, he was also worrying about the startling discovery the Gang of Nine had made this past summer: giant germanium crystals. Obviously, they were fragments from the destruction of their blue moon that had rained down on them in the meteor shower of the century. At that time, no one realized such significant fragments had actually landed. The only saving grace Ken saw was the fact that they plunged into the earth and now lay buried at least a foot below the surface. Of course, some could well be found, as had happened with the unfortunate man up north.

What worried Ken the most was such giant crystals falling into the hands of the towers. From verbal history handed down in the Underground from the days of Emperor Amy, he knew giant crystals such as these had been adapted into massively powerful weapons. Worse, they were used to destroy other towers. Old Portillo Tower and Duero Tower came to mind. Now they were just ancient ruins. If these crystals were discovered and if tower personnel figured out how to use them, Ken feared Tierra would be right back where they were centuries ago — once more on the brink of destruction. It would be on his watch. Perhaps that was what bothered him the most in all this. He felt powerless to do anything about it.

A week after Isabella left, Senate results began coming in. They were being reported to the Imperial Tower, but intercepted by Bart. "Ken, the Turda Senate has okayed the term extensions. So has the Tecuci Senate. Valen Senate failed to pass it. Brom Senate has also okayed the extension, so King Bolivar is safe for now."

"Thanks. Keep me posted," Ken replied, marking them on his chart of kingdoms. By the time that Queen Isabella returned, all the Senates had taken their votes. The kingdoms of Valen, Rusden, Wye, Northend, Matruk, Malaca, and Domei had all rejected her proposal, but for different reasons. All others accepted her proposal for temporary term extensions. In Malaca, for example, Rey Gervasi Quito Malaca and his mermaid wife Rosita had turned sixty and wanted to retire from public service. Hence, Malaca rejected the proposal and scheduled an election for a new king and queen. In Domei, their current king had failed to bring back prosperity and was being tossed out on his ears. In the other five though, bitter hatreds caused so much friction that their Senates wanted a total change in kings, no matter what the cost.

Lilly and Tom, Bart's teens, summoned Ken to the Comm Center. These two were now in charge of monitoring tower communications. As he joined them, he was frustrated with the way the Senate results had gone. At least five had to be handled at once, but he hoped Queen Isabella would arrive before the kingdoms took their own actions. "You have good news for me, I hope, kids," he said a little exasperated.

"Hardly boss," Lilly replied. "We've finally figured out what some of these messages are about. They've been using quite a lot of code words lately. Big stones, large rocks, small boulders, blue stones, big rocks, big ones. We've finally figured out they are referring to those giant germanium crystals, like the one that nearly killed that Hilliard Heights man this summer. Nearly all the towers have found some now."

Tom added, "And now they've figured out just what they are! Bedwurth Tower in Wye has gotten one attuned to their tower's main Circle. They are reporting a giant leap forward in their Circle's available psi energies. I think the word is spreading to all the other towers now. That's not good, is it?"

"No. It is more of a disaster. We could be looking at the beginning of the end of Tierra as we know it. Why is this happening on my watch? Mom! You should have stuck around," Ken lamented. He'd reached the limits of what he could handle at one time.

"Why so doom and gloom? If the towers can harness these giant crystals, they'll have more energy available to build more stone buildings far more quickly," Lilly pointed out.

"Right, the towers can do far more than ever before. It's a godsend for us all, don't you think?" Tom added.

Rather sarcastically, Ken replied, "Oh sure. At the beginning, some will have altruistic motives, but soon, they'll begin using them for other purposes, probably under the banner of being better able to defend our kingdoms. They'll make weapons out of them, just as they did way back in our Dark Ages, the Age of Chaos. As mom would have said, their use of technology has vastly exceeded their development of their humanity."

"Oh surely they won't do that!" Lilly declared flatly. She put her hands on her hips in a defiant gesture.

Sometimes, Ken thought life was just an orchestrated game that someone was playing. This was one of those times. Right then, he received a message from Venerada Maricela. *Ken, Maricela here. I need to see you right away. Brom Tower now has a dozen of these strange crystals. They are turning up in farmers' fields right and left. We know they can be attuned to our Circles and maybe even networked together for even greater potential like your battery things. Need to see you now.* He replied he was on his way, but he grabbed Crystal, briefing her on the latest terrifying developments.

A half hour later, Ken and Crystal entered her office. There on her desk sat four of the crystals, each between nine and twelve inches across, irregular in shape, raw germanium crystals. Maricela looked a bit grim. "Have a seat. For some time, these things have been being discovered, mostly by farmers plowing up their fields or during their first tills of new acreage. Most were found having been added to farmer's rock fences around their fields, if you can believe that. Obviously to the head blind, these are just another pesky rock in their fields."

She continued, "So as our Circle members have been going about their visits to outlying villages and such, I told

239

them to keep an eye out for more crystals like Nadja's group encountered this summer. We've found a dozen of them so far, all by accident. My capos have been studying them, and they're really germanium crystals, giant versions of those we all wear around our necks. Already, one Circle had networked six together to quintuple their power reserve, allowing them to quarry three times the amount of stone. Now all the capos are demanding that we launch a massive search for more of these stones. I am concerned, frankly."

Maricela finished up, "I've been in touch with other towers. Nearly all towers either have been finding them or are getting started looking for them. Why am I worried, Ken, Crystal? I can't put my finger on it, probably because I don't have any fingers." She jested a little, trying to lighten her own mood.

Since Ken didn't say anything, Maricela outlined what else she'd researched. "I've been searching our ancient records, but someone has purged most all references to those giant crystals of power that our ancient ancestors used back in the Age of Chaos, the Dark Ages. At least, just how to put them to good uses has not entirely been wiped clean. Probably that's a good thing. Still, it's clear to many of us that these stones can be put to very good uses. Obviously, tripling our production of cut and finished stone will aid Brom. Already, the new Leeds Tower has found a new use for them, initial plowing of new acreage for spring crop planting. Now several other new towers are following in their footsteps."

Finally, Maricela voiced what had her deeply worried, "What has me so concerned is the recent report from Valen Tower. It seems a rebel *mentales* gifted has used one of these crystals to destroy Valen Castle's massive gates in an attempt to overthrow King Alano Valen. The message indicated there was a significant loss of life via subsequent massive balls of fire. Further, King Alano won the battle by using an alien hunting rifle. I've no idea what that is, except it must be an alien weapon. How the devil he got his hands on that, I've no clue, but I intend to bring that up at the next High Council meeting. So already, these crystals are being perverted into weapons of war. That is what has me so worried, Ken, Crystal."

Ken slumped in his chair. "Already? I had hoped using them for war would not be thought of for perhaps years. Maricela, this is really bad news. You know that?"

Maricela sighed, "Of course. But my hands are tied. I must think of the welfare and long term survival of our kingdoms, Ken. I have no real choice but to send out search parties to locate as many of these crystals as possible. For one thing, we cannot let them fall into non-tower *mentales* gifted hands. We don't need a repeat of what Nadja encountered this past summer. We don't want bandits getting their hands on them either or they could well attack Brom Castle like they did Valen Castle. Any time now, I expect to hear from King Bolivar about just how I will be protecting the castle from similar attacks, as has just happened to Valen Castle. Plus, my own tower members are begging to be allowed to acquire many stones and to work out new ways to utilize the tremendous potential they represent. I am going to have to make a full scale project out of this, I'm afraid. I have no real choice."

She explained, "If I do nothing and let this pass, then I am putting all Brom at a terrible risk. We could be easily conquered, for one thing. Others will be making good use of the stones for plowing and construction, leaving us in the dust as they thrive and expand. No, I have no choice but to send out search parties now, while allowing the capos to experiment with the stones we now have."

Trying to sound a little optimistic, Crystal suggested, "Well, the snows are coming soon. That ought to put a halt on everything until spring, except their researches. That'll give us a little time, Maricela. By then, Amy and Jan will be back, I hope so anyway. Those two are the only ones around who can remember that terrible era of history. Maybe they'll have some better ideas of how to proceed. Besides, maybe the towers will find ways to put these to very good uses this time and not make war with them."

She added, "So many in Brom had have their Basic Therapy now, Maricela. I can't imagine they would so crave a destructive war."

Maricela agreed, but countered, "Yes, Crystal, that's true, but only for Brom. Benjamina's therapy is still pretty much isolated here. It's a shame there has been no way to get it into more widespread use in all the kingdoms."

Ken muttered, "Maybe they'll be slow in learning how to use the stones. From our monitoring of the other towers, it's taken them this long to figure out what the blue stones actually are. So maybe they'll take years to figure out how to use them effectively."

"I hope that you're right, Ken. If only that man had not used one to attack Valen Castle. Every tower on Tierra now knows about that and the role the crystal played in it. You can bet they are all working on putting some of their stones to similar uses, either to offensive or defensive ways. Anyway, I thought you both needed to know why I am sending out searching parties. Let's stay on top of this if we can." Ken and Crystal agreed and returned to their Underground quarters, far more solemn than before.

Later, they summoned all the Underground members for a big meeting to discuss the discovery of these giant crystals and what they represented. Ken outlined what was known to date. "So you see, all the towers now have some of these large crystals, and at least one outlaw has used it to attack Valen Castle. You can bet all the towers are going to be looking for ways to make use of these for their own protection and for their own attacks should they be assaulted. And yes, several towers are also developing constructive uses for the crystals as well. Good and bad."

Ken finished up, "We must continue to actively monitor all the towers and keep track of their developments with these crystals, somehow. I expect much will become secret information before long. Plus, we must try to find some way to counter them, if there is such a way."

Lena chuckled. "Ah the age old who has the bigger stick."

Ken didn't appreciate her comment. "Care to elaborate, Lena?"

She smiled. "Don't think our world here is any different than any of the other hundreds of worlds in the vast Imperium. It isn't. Not from what I've seen of it. You just have different big sticks, that's all."

Seeing a captive audience, Lena went on, "You see, on any world, whenever one country or state has a technological breakthrough, invariably it somehow gets militarized in some way shape or form. As soon as the other countries or states see that other one as having an 'ultimate weapon,' they go all out to acquire it as well. The original country believes that, if they have a superior, master weapon, then no other country will dare attack them. This is almost a universal law. Have a superior weapon and that'll be a total deterrent; no others will dare attack you."

She saw several nodding their heads in agreement with this notion. She ended that quickly. "It's utterly wrong! In time, either the other countries develop that weapon or one similar to it or some fool uses it, wiping out civilizations or setting them back centuries. It's utter folly to believe, if right now you have a massively destructive weapon that no one else has, then that alone will guarantee you peace and prosperity. While it might seem so and be so for a short time, in the long run, it never works out as planned. There are some uninhabitable worlds out there in the Imperium, where they believed in such nonsense, and they have managed to wipe out their entire worlds. Not even plants have survived on those worlds."

"All throughout the Imperium, the rush is on to find a bigger stick than your neighboring planets. That is one benefit of a world becoming a part of the Imperium. The Imperium puts a complete stop on developing bigger sticks," she explained.

Ken asked, "So how does the Imperium deal with rogue worlds that do go ahead and develop a bigger stick?"

"Simple. That's what is lacking on Tierra. The Imperium central command and Senate oversees all worlds that have joined the Imperium. If a member world tries to develop a bigger stick or actually does, the vast resources of the Imperium are so much greater than one single world, that they can easily step in and confiscate it or destroy the bigger stick. No single world within the empire can stand up to the combined resources of all the other worlds. So the Imperium has the ultimate big stick," she explained.

Crystal added, "And then the Imperium ran into another empire, the Federation of Planets, who also had the ultimate big stick. Then, it was big stick against big stick, only on a vastly larger scale."

Lena grinned, "You're absolutely right, Crystal. You've got the idea down pat." Several chuckled, and Crystal smiled, pleased.

Ken spoke up. "So Queen Isabella is partially right, when she told us what is lacking is the means by which she can enforce her rulings over the other kingdoms. She has no Tierra-wide army, for example."

Lena mused, "Right, Ken. She is on the right track with what she is trying to establish on Tierra, at least in my opinion. However, she doesn't have the infrastructure to back her up. From what little I can tell of the ancient emperor and empress, they also didn't really have the infrastructure to support their works either. In time, what they established was circumvented. I wish someone would have written detailed history books or journals of what went on. We could learn from their past mistakes."

Ken replied, "What she needs is some kind of United Kingdom of Kingdoms here. I'll talk to her about that when she gets back. What are we going to do about the explosion of these giant crystals? Every tower has them. In a few years' time, everyone is going to have the big sticks." No one had any real answer for him, but then he didn't really think they would have. It seemed an unsolvable problem to him. All roads led to doomsday in his mind. While others didn't care to admit it, they too felt the same way.

Lena spoke up, "Ken, may I ask a question out of my own ignorance?" He nodded. "Most of the current kings and queens or reys and reinas do not have the *mentales* gifts. Why is that? I would have thought the leaders would all have the gift. With just telepathy alone, they could rule far better."

Rafaela looked at Andres, and he decided to answer her. He explained, "Long story, Lena. Some of our records are quite sketchy. Centuries ago, the head blind as we call them, were the rulers. That was before the first appearance of the *mentales* gifted on Tierra. In time, the *mentales* gifted formed the first *Círculo de la Torres*. Later on, these very towers took over and, for some time, ruled all the kingdoms. That failed completely; massive, destructive wars between the towers nearly destroyed all Tierra. After that, the towers were outlawed from governing kingdoms. Still, everyone saw how beneficial it was to have a ruler with the *mentales* gifts, and most all kings were *mentales* gifted. But they too failed miserably, aided by the treachery of Lord Valen and his virus hoax that cost those kings their hands and feet. Turned into very nearly helpless men and women, the kingdoms decided that *mentales* gifted should only be their advisors and run the towers. So the head blind took over as the kings."

Andres continued, "All of the head blind kings and queens have now heard about the attack on Valen Castle. Even King Bolivar has asked me about it. He even asked me what I thought he ought to do to help protect Brom from such attacks. I think history is about to change once more. I'm sixty-six now, well twenty-one really, but I would bet anything before this body dies, we'll see another huge change."

Taking a deep breath, Andres said, "Let me explain why I sense change is coming yet again. Within a short time, all the many towers will have put these giant crystals to use. You can bet some will be developing Lena's big sticks out of them. A head blind king stands no chance in either understanding these new weapons or how to counter them. In short, the citizens will demand their new kings be either *mentales* gifted or be the towers themselves. I can see our next ruler as Venerada Queen Maricela, by popular vote."

"You're kidding, right?" Crystal asked in disbelief.

"Not at all. In time, she alone will be commanding the biggest stick in the Brom Kingdom. So it will be with all the other kingdoms. Their tower's venerado or venerada will be the single person with the biggest stick in their possession. The throne goes to the person with the biggest stick. Citizens vote out of fear as well as wisdom," Andres answered, sobering everyone.

Crystal asked timidly, "Does she know this?"

"I've spoken to her about it, but she is refusing to believe it would ever come to that," Andres answered.

Ken declared, "Then, we all need to get going on making Lena's United Kingdom of Kingdoms! I will speak to Queen Isabella about this when she returns." That ended his meeting.

As the meeting broke up, Bart caught Lena's attention. "Lena, we've received some requests for your advice. One from Hilliard Heights and one from Brom. It's about agriculture. They want to meet with you. What should I say?"

"I don't know anything about agriculture," Lena protested slightly.

"I told them that, but they keep on insisting. Since you were an Imperium Sector ID Minister, they think you know everything," Bart teased.

"Okay, I should at least meet with them. Set it up and let me know," Lena replied. "I don't mind looking like a nincompoop — not now. I used to, but not any longer."

Two days later, Lena and Bernardo, along with Bart, entered one of King Bolivar's studies. There a dozen key farmers from Brom were assembled, teleported here by Brom Tower. "Welcome, Lena. We are very pleased you agreed to meet with us. We are influential and experimental farmers. I am Henry Fielding from Brom, Tomas Hilliard from the Heights." He rattled off the other names, but they became a blur to Lena.

Henry then explained, "We want your vast Imperium experience to help us solve a most serious agricultural problem that not only we but every farmer on Tierra is facing. Let me explain. Long ago, farming exploded. Wheat, barley, oats, various other cereal grains are grown, along with all kinds of beans and vegetables. Each season, we have been planting the same crops in our fields. However, we have also been keeping accurate records of our harvests, handed down by our parents and grandparents. Over these many years, we've seen the productivity of our crop lands diminish to alarmingly low levels. Plants are simply not doing well at all. Weeds are sometimes taking over the fields, in spite of our best efforts. We have made some improvements, largely up in Hilliard Heights. There, they discovered that spreading horse and reindeer manure over the fields before planting improves the harvest and plant growth. Here in Brom, I have been trying to develop a strain of wheat that'll grow in our harsh, short seasons. Tomas' people have been experimenting with nut trees, and their work is now showing promise. What we all need to know is this. Are there other ways of farming that'll make our harvests more productive? Are there better ways of growing crops? Can you help us?"

Lena thought better of just saying she knew nothing about farming. Instead, she replied, "I can try. While I know very little about agriculture, I have heard there is something called crop rotation. Can I have some time to see what I can find out for you?" *Bart, can your Comm Network tie me into the Imperium Internet?*

Of course. We do that all the time.

"Okay, gentlemen, give me a few hours, and I will have some answers for you. Okay?" Lena asked.

Tomas and Henry smiled. Henry said, "Amazing. Yes, by all means. See, I told you Lena would know and be able to help us." The dozen nodded and smiled broadly towards Lena. She, Bernardo, and Bart rose and headed back into the Underground.

A few minutes later, Bart had her all setup using a voice-activated computer. Lena began by doing a search on crop rotations. Without her asking, Bernardo began making notes for her. She looked up and said, "Thanks, Bernardo. I can't write anymore."

His reply startled her. "Of course, dear. You haven't had time to learn to write with your feet yet."

"What? That's impossible!" Lena declared.

"Drina does it all the time. Okay, I got that written down. What's next?"

An hour later, Lena was back in the study with the dozen eager faces listening intently to what she had to say. "To grow, plants absorb nutrients from the soil. When you grow the same crop year after year in the same plot, slowly those plants absorb or leech all the nutrients out of the soil. Insect infestations grow, as do weeds. This corresponds to the steadily decreasing yields your records clearly show. The remedy for this is called crop rotation."

"What you must do is alternate crops on one plot.

Specifically, different crops need different nutrients from the soil and leech them out. However, each crop also replenishes the soil with other nutrients. By a judicious choice of alternating crops, each one can replace what the other takes out, balancing the soil. Further, crop rotation will help eliminate pests and weeds too. So you want to alternate your legumes with your cereal type crops. Alternate wheat with pinto beans, sugar beets, potatoes, barley, and corn, for example. Growing a season of alfalfa or clover will put back what the previous crop of wheat used up. Various beans, peas, and lentils will do almost as well to replace what the wheat has used from your soils."

She went on, "For your vegetables, a four year rotation is wisest. Plant potatoes one year, then plant squash, corn or pumpkins the next. Then plant peas and various beans. Then plant cabbage, lettuce, and broccoli. Then back to potatoes. You'll get the best yields this way without any deterioration of your soils. In short, always rotate your legumes with your wheat and cereal grains."

Lena watched as the men made notes to keep track of all she'd said. "Brilliant, positively brilliant! Thank you, Lena, thank you. See," Henry exclaimed, "I told you she was a smart one and could help us!"

Tomas spoke up, "Lena, I'll name my next new variety of domesticated nut tree in your honor! Soon, Hilliard Heights will be sending Brom goodly supplies of Lena Nuts." She laughed; it sounded rather strange to her. Indeed, within two years, Lena Nuts became widely available in Hilliard Heights; as well as Brom. Lena thought they tasted a bit like peanuts.

On their way home, Lena commented to Bernardo, "It seems I really can make contributions to the people of Tierra."

"You are one of us too," he added.

She grinned. "Yes, I am that, aren't I?" He grinned back and gave her a quick kiss.

Queen Isabella and Hernando arrived in two weeks, not her planned three weeks. Now she had to deal with the results of the Senates. One by one, she summoned each of the kingdoms to her court. It took all her abilities to negotiate to settle the division of the kingdoms. Valen was the easiest. The northern part joined with the newly formed Kingdom of Portillo. The western portion merged with Central Trujillo, the southern portion merged with Almendia. The Kingdom of Valen now consisted of a circle about four hundred miles in diameter.

The Kingdom of Rusden split into four pieces. Both the Kingdom of Leedsburough and Woodhill were small and occupied the eastern third of the old kingdom. The Kingdom of Oakham was restored, occupying its ancestral lands, the foothills of the Goza Mountains. Similarly, the Kingdom of Wye was divided into three parts. Haverhills regained its identity in the foothills, like Oakham. The Kingdom of Wycombe in the central zone was formed, leaving Wye controlling the eastern half. On it went, as the five kingdoms divided up, allowing the five kings and their extended families and nobles to retain control of their lands, going against all the other kingdoms, who were still trying hard to make Queen Isabella's new system work.

Once that mess was settled, at least for the winter, Ken met with her to go over the terrifying news of the giant crystals and the attack on Valen Castle. After Ken's lengthy briefing, she replied, "Yes, I can see we simply must come up with some kind of United Tierra-wide group to oversee the kingdoms and keep them from warring with others. Ideas?"

Ken had none at the moment. He commented, "What's lacking are your system of checks and balances on the *mentales* gifted and the tower personnel. They can pretty well do whatever they want to do. Like Lena says, they'll soon be building themselves bigger and bigger sticks. What's going to happen when the tower's power so vastly exceeds that of the common man, the common citizen? They'll live in fear and terror of the towers and what they can do. So much for the freedom of the common man. He who has the biggest stick wins the day."

Queen Isabella grimaced. "Well, I can't go around cutting off the arms of all the *mentales* gifted and hobbling their feet like mine. That would certainly do it, though."

Ken laughed. "One thing is for sure. The towers are

going to start keeping secrets from each other, as they develop their new big sticks."

She added, "And there goes trust down the drain." Never had a winter looked so gloomy for Isabella, Ken, and Crystal.

Chapter 14 Demands

"Relax dear. It will work out," Diego attempted to calm Isabella down. It was the night before the May 1291 High Council of the Lords. She was nervous and fearful of what the morrow would bring.

"I wish Amy were here," she lamented. "I feel so constrained it's not funny, Diego. I can barely move."

"I know, you have done miracles already. I am sure things will work out," Diego replied, holding her in his arms.

The following morning found her no less uptight, but Diego dressed her in her finest new gown, one of the new strapless spring styles. Hers was a pale blue with matching heels.

In other rooms, the Gang of Nine was also dressing for the big meeting. Isabella asked them to attend. Somehow, she was growing more dependent on the young teens than she cared to admit, especially so since Amy and Jan were off-world.

Bernardo dressed Lena in her new strapless red, pod silk gown, stealing a kiss in the process. "Dear, the dress is so tight that I can't walk in it," she complained.

"I won't let go of you, I promise," he teased her, and she knew it. "Besides, you look fabulous. Your hair sure has grown some. I like it this long." She smiled. Never in her long life had she ever had it this long, down to the small of her back. Yet, as she looked at her image in their full-length mirror, she did look good. For once, she admitted it to herself.

Lilly helped Zarita get dressed, as well as Nita, who then returned the favor, helping her into her new gown as well. All three were wearing Lilly's new style strapless gowns that fell to about six inches from their ankles, but had only a tiny walking slit, forcing them to take small steps. In her toe shoes, Zarita could only manage those anyway and wasn't as bothered as Nita was. She placed her new tiara on her head and secured it. Then, she fastened her new butterfly hair clasp with its two polished crystals in it, securing the back of her hair. Brushed out, it now draped across her back down to her lower back. Still, her bosom was nearly that of a full grown adult, and she knew Nita envied her and was worried about having a gown "mishap" because hers were still rather small.

"Make sure it is really secured," Nita fretted, as Zarita double-checked her clasp.

"Okay, everyone ready?" Lilly finally asked. "We best get going." She, Nita, and Zarita headed over to the Imperial Castle, where Henry had already gone, so he could escort Adrianna. They arrived on time, and Nita and Zarita joined the others in the Gang of Nine. The women began chatting about their new risque gowns, but soon, Zarita's unusual new jewelry drew their praise and comments.

Drina asked, "Aren't those gems germanium crystals like we wear?"

Zarita had no choice but to answer truthfully, not if she wanted to keep these teens as her friends. "Why yes. I had some made into my tiara and earrings. Don't they look just super?"

"Yes indeed. Say, have you attuned them to you? Are they working stones too?" Drina followed up.

Zarita smiled. *Drina is incredibly observant.* "Why yes they are. Now, I cannot easily be taken by surprise. I don't have all my eggs in one basket, as they say. I was worried. What if some evil man takes my working crystal from my neck? I'd be very nearly helpless and at their mercy. This way, I have a better chance."

"Way cool, Zarita. But do you think that's likely to happen? I mean someone stealing your crystal?" Drina asked innocently.

"The way things are going, they might. I saw that man disintegrating the massive gates of Valen Castle and then burning up all those guards. I don't trust men at all. Do you?"

"Oh, I trust Ben here," she gave him a playful bump with her hips. "And the others in our gang. So you are an official princess?" She decided to change the topic.

"Yes, but I am not advertising that. I don't fit in with mom and dad at all. That's why I am staying here with Inez, Lilly, and Nita. They made me help them find more of those giant crystals."

"They did?" Bernardo inquired, growing curious. "So you can somehow find them?"

"Well, yes, that's relatively easy. Look for raisin splashes in puddings. They must have fallen from the sky, you know. When they hit the ground, they made little holes with raised sides like a raisin does when it falls on some pudding. They are easy to find," she explained, but didn't reveal she could sense where they were located.

Adrianna, bored with such talk, asked her, "So has your dad planned a marriage for you? Or do you have a boyfriend back in Valen?" Such was more interesting to her, holding onto Henry's hand for support.

Zarita laughed. "No to both. I won't stand for any arranged marriage. Dad knows that. I think he is afraid of me. I've no desire to be held back by boys. I have big plans, if only the aliens will return to Tierra. I want to go see the universe out there, one day." She didn't add and wipe out the other men who had blown up her transport ship, killing her Neva body and ending her great game of ensnaring President Snarry.

Their chat was cut short. The many kings, queens, advisors, and tower folks began entering, rapidly filling up Queen Isabella's throne room, her Great Hall. Shortly, with Hernando's help, she rose and stood erect before the packed room. "Welcome to the Spring High Council meeting. I have one small announcement. After the meeting, I would like to meet personally with all the venerados and veneradas for a while. As always, Diego and the Imperial Court Musicians will be playing for our dance this evening. I officially turn the meeting over to King Rusden." She carefully returned to her seat, where Hernando adjusted her long hair and helped her to sit down gracefully.

King Rusden began by explaining the division of his former kingdom, pointing out that his new, smaller kingdom was following the "old ways" of rulership. He then announced similar changes to Valen and the other three kingdoms that chose to divide up rather than to go along with their Senate's desires to oust them as their kings.

After that, they launched into the heart of the meeting,

dealing mostly with new trade agreements. Brom also brought up the new ideas about crop rotation, claiming Lena had assisted them in working out a solution for their dramatically reduced harvests. That brought some rather intense discussions and promises to give those ideas a try, especially the breadbasket kingdoms.

After the lunch break, King Alano Valen was called to address the assembly, outlining the rebel attack on his castle. Many drilled him on just how his massive gates had been so easily destroyed. That a giant crystal had been used was now confirmed, which is what the many rulers desired. However, many complained he ought not have those alien hunting rifles. That, he promptly ignored.

The rest of the meeting was quite boring, discussions of future trades for the coming season's crops dominated the late afternoon. Interestingly enough, Valen began offering swords for sale. "It's our new marketable commodity," King Alano explained.

As they broke up for supper, King Alano joined his daughter at the back of the room. "You look well, Zarita. Are you planning to return home with us when the conference is over?"

"Nope. I like it here. I'll be staying in Exchange City at Elegant Fashions Inc," she replied a bit tartly. The Gang of Nine watched his reactions closely. For the briefest of instants, his face showed signs of relief. How strange, Drina thought.

Later, the dance began. Nita, who like Zarita, had no current boyfriend, danced with her. Both chose not to accept several younger men's offers for a dance. Zarita was not interested in them in the slightest, and just now, Nita was more interested in learning dress design and store operations than boys. Both teens saw men as detracting them from their current goals.

The next day, as the meeting broke up, Queen Isabella asked the Gang of Nine to stick around for the meeting with the tower leaders. They in turn asked Zarita to stay with them. Curious about what this was about, Zarita agreed. This time, chairs were provided, much to the pleasure of the women.

Queen Isabella began her plea for sanity. "As you all

know, giant germanium crystals are being uncovered all over Tierra. We are all experimenting with them, trying to find good uses for the incredible powers they give us. Please do not forget our ancient history, when crystals much as these very nearly destroyed our whole world. Let's use them for peaceful works. Use them to help the citizens of your kingdoms, which you are pledged to support. I trust each and every one of you will do just that."

"The attack on Valen Castle is quite alarming. I am proposing today that the towers make a concerted effort to find other such crystals, which may be in other rebel hands, and confiscate them. We don't want brigands, thieves, and rebels having that kind of raw power in their hands. That should be obvious to us all. Upon us has been placed the sacred trust of our people to use our given gifts for the benefit of all humanity. I trust you will share among yourselves any bright uses to which these crystals can be put. Enough said on that topic."

"The other reason I wanted to talk to you all today is this: what is currently lacking here is some form of worldwide ruling body whose tasks would include enforcing the peace. No longer can we afford one kingdom to go to war with another. Too many alliances will force other kingdoms into such conflagrations. That barbarian very nearly wiped us all out. I know you know that I believe ultimate power must have ultimate restrictions upon those who wield it. Tierra is not Ataro, though my daughter and I have had to agree to their physical limitations being placed upon their queens in order to be well educated in their ruling technologies. I don't intend to ever place the physical limitations I endure on any other human being."

"Rather, I am trying to install a system of checks and balances on those who wield great powers. The Senate, the king, the courts, for example. Thus far, it appears to be working well. However, there is a glaring hole in the system of checks and balances. The towers. You all wield great powers, soon to be perhaps enormous powers. I want you to all think about what kind of checks and balances you could impose upon all the towers, so no tower could abuse theirs. I am not a tower technician. Initially, I am leaving this up to you to attempt to work out."

"By this fall, I would appreciate hearing back from all of you on just what kinds of checks and balances we could implement to prevent any one tower from grossly abusing the sacred trust we all have placed in it. Comments?"

The room was silent. At last, Venerada Maricela spoke up, "We're all just now realizing how much power we really do wield, Queen Isabella. While I can see the need for checks and balances, with us towers, I don't see what could possibly be done. Just as in the Age of Chaos, any one of us could abuse our powers. Yet, what could effectively be done to inhibit such abuses? I surely don't know."

She went on, "Physical restraints are pointless. You and your late two wives are proof of that. Senator Carlos did all this to you and to your wives, and yet you still were able to undo him and escape, returning home. Like you, I have no arms, but I assure you I am quite deadly, if I have to be. Our powers do not come from our bodies; physical restraints simply won't work. I surely don't know what would, to be bluntly honest. However, I think that I speak for everyone else here. We will consider your request and see if we can come up with some ideas by the fall meeting."

Queen Isabella replied, "Thank you. That is all I can ask of you. Thank you for making the attempt." That ended the short meeting.

However, she asked her Imperial Tower's venerado to remain. "I know you are also desperate to obtain a goodly supply of these giant crystals. I am assigning my Gang of Nine and Zarita, if she'll participate, to help you search this area for such crystals. We need to make sure rebels don't get their hands on them as well. I'll leave you all to work our how you can do this. Thanks."

Zarita was quite pleased to become a part of the gang. Secretly, she hoped to be able to acquire a few more of the crystals for herself. Besides, she realized being somehow close to Queen Isabella's court was important. She seemed to be the person most in charge of everything. The meeting didn't last long at all. Ben suggested the Gang search the countryside for more buried crystals, while the tower folks dealt with any in Exchange City who may have found some.

The next morning, Zarita dressed in her leathers, as did Nita and Henry. He then got their horses saddled and ready for them, helping Zarita mount. "Got to be hard on you in those toe boots," he said sympathetically.

"These lip plates are more annoying," she replied, "thanks for the lift up." She watched as Henry also helped his twin sister mount as well. Considerate of him, she thought. The three headed over to the Imperial Castle, where Ben and Bernardo were helping the others mount up. Zarita could not imagine how either Lena or Drina could possibly ride and watched them curiously. Lena mounted easily, biting down on the wooden block that Bernardo handed her. Likewise, Ben got Drina up and ready, much to Zarita's amazement.

"I didn't see how it was possible for you two to actually ride a horse. Terrific," she praised the two teens. After Henry helped his girlfriend Adrianna up, the three men got on their horses. The group headed out of the castle into the rather crowded streets of Exchange City. Everyone wanted to be outside; their long bout of cabin fever was at an end for a while.

As they reached the southeastern edge of the city, the vast rolling green pasturelands between the impassible rocky ridges shown in spring splendor. A heavy dew covered the new growth, adding a bit of a sparkle in the early morning orange-red sun. Rain was likely by afternoon, but they all knew that, even Lena suspected such.

"Okay Master Finder Zarita," Ben called out, "which way do we go?"

She grinned and focused. While she saw two relatively close, she decided to leave those for herself. She pointed, "That way about two miles, I think."

"Lead on, Master Finder," Ben teased her. She felt pleased by his jovial attitude. Further, he was respecting her opinion, she noted. Unlike her father's group who ordered her about, the Gang treated her as one of them. She liked that feeling and led the way.

About a half hour later, she slowed down and began

looking at the ground. "There is one," she exclaimed, reining in. She knew better than to try to dismount. In her toe boots, she had a devil of a time negotiating the rough ground. A glance at Lena and Drina and she knew she was wise. Neither of them dismounted either. Adrianna retrieved a shovel, handing it to Henry.

Everyone watched, and Adrianna declared, "She's right. See the little ridge around this central dimple. Like a raisin landing in pudding." Within a few minutes, Henry scooped out a large, irregularly shaped crystal, which Ben carefully stowed into a pod silk bag. Adrianna tied it to her saddle. After covering the hole, they mounted up, and asked Zarita to guide them to the next one.

Unerringly, she led them to another ten that day, covering some twenty-five miles. "Aren't we heading back now? It'll be dark soon," Zarita asked, as Ben bagged the tenth.

"Nah. We'll camp out. Ever camped out, Zarita? You'll love it," Henry suggested.

Zarita had never camped out. Further, she simply could not envision either Drina or Lena being able to manage such a thing. "It's really hard for me in these boots," she replied as Henry lifted her gently to the ground.

"We know," Bernardo replied. "Amy wears them too. Jan always has to help her. But now, Jan's feet have been altered like yours and Amy's, so one of us is going to have to help them whenever they get back. No problem. You and Nita can bunk together in one tent. Lena and I will have one, so will Drina and Ben. Henry and Adrianna get the forth tent. We'll have to get one more when Amy and Jan get back."

"I hope they come back soon; I miss them," Drina replied. Turning to Zarita, she added, "Obviously, Lena and I don't do a whole lot of camp setup. Maybe you'll be able to help us cook."

"I'll do what I can," Zarita answered. In fact, the three had very little to contribute until they had the fire going.

"I'm pretty useless," Lena added. "But we can use our feet to stir the pots once Adrianna gets them on the charcoal."

As the evening progressed, Zarita began to see that neither Drina nor Lena was entirely as helpless as she had thought they would have been, based on her life as Neva. As they ate on warmed stew and nut bread, Zarita decided she really liked camping out of doors. The air was fresh. It had rained earlier that afternoon; the land smelled good to her. She realized for a very long time, she'd smelled only the concrete-steel-oil of the so called "civilized worlds" she'd once called home. Even at her fancy estate, she still smelled that sterile odor, though it was masked a good deal by the large flower gardens at the center of the U-shaped plaza just beyond the swimming pool.

The next day, they roamed even farther afield, but once again, Zarita proved invaluable, leading them directly to another dozen stones. Out of supplies and with all their bags filled, they headed back to Exchange City the following morning. Once back and the crystals handed over to the venerado, they met with him and Queen Isabella.

"She's got the knack for finding them," Ben reported. "She can sense them somehow. Uncanny."

Queen Isabella thought for a moment and then asked, "Zarita, when you are looking for these stones, can you see just the next one or do you see several of them at once and just head for the nearest?"

"The nearest of course. I can see a great many of them, like a field of them. It's kind of like how I sensed that giant one on Gamelon and used it to reach out to Emperor Kino. It took that powerful a crystal to reach across so much space," she explained. No sense in pretending otherwise, she thought. Zarita felt a kinship with these people she'd never felt before. They treated her with respect.

"I see. What I need to know is how many more are out there across Tierra? But that's probably impossible to tell. Are they in clumps or spread out uniformly?" she asked, still thinking this through.

"Clumps. Some areas have several within a few miles of each other. Then, there are big gaps where there aren't any at all. I've been going to the clumpier areas, if you follow me. Is this important?"

"Yes, that might make sense. If these came down during the Great Meteor Shower, I suspect clumping might result. If they were spread out uniformly, I might think they had some other origin than the breakup of our moon," Isabella replied. "I suspect all the other towers are also out scouring the countryside around their kingdoms for fields of these giant crystals. Of course, there are hundreds of *mentales* gifted out there, who do not belong to a tower. At least one of them not only found one, but also figured out how to use it and attacked Valen Castle."

She went on, "That is what I fear the most at the moment — having one or more of these fall into non-tower hands. While I have to believe most of us gifted would only use the power for good, obviously some will not. I'd like you all to pack up a lot of supplies and sweep far more of the valleys around here, acquiring all that you can. Meantime, I think I should spread the word far and wide. I will pay handsomely for such crystals. Hopefully, those who find them, even the head blind, will consider turning them in for the reward rather than keeping them for themselves. What do you think of that idea?"

"Where will you get the funds to pay them?" Ben asked.

"I've been using my own personal funds to operate the Imperial Castle and Tower already. I'll use them to pay finder's fees. Do you think offering a hundred gold per crystal will be sufficient to convince someone who finds one to turn it in?" Queen Isabella asked.

Drina answered first. "That is a fortune for most people. I'm sure the head blind would jump at such a chance."

Bernardo pointed out, "The other towers might get annoyed with your finder's fee and offer even more so they could acquire more of them too."

"Even so," Henry added, "other *mentales* gifted would likely be inclined to help hunt for them too. If they found ten of them, they could make a thousand gold. That's a lot of incentive."

Lena decided to speak up too. "It would be wise to first let the other venerados know what you are planning so they are not blind-sided by it. With a lot of folks out there hunting for them, quite a lot could be found this summer."

Zarita asked, "Can I have one more of the crystals that I

find? I want to make a matching belt to go with my earrings and tiara?"

Queen Isabella smiled, though it was invisible. "Sure dear. Consider it payment for your help. Kids, if you want to keep one and have it cut up for jewelry, that's fine too. I owe you all big-time for your help. I'll see you are all remunerated for your work. I think you will be working at this all summer." Everyone laughed. Tierra was huge. They could be spending the rest of their lives on this project!

The next day, Ben led a string of four packhorses, laden with food and water supplies, along with a large quantity of bags. Queen Isabella had worked out a scheme, whereby when they had recovered a number of stones, Ben would contact the Imperial Tower. They would teleport the stones back to the tower, and teleport more food supplies in return. This would enable them to cover far more ground without the necessity of frequently returning to the castle to resupply.

That day, Zarita led them to the two she'd passed by while they were on their way further down the long valley system of these eastern foothills. During their first week out, they uncovered another two dozen stones. According to Zarita, that was the last of those within some twenty-five miles of Exchange City in this upper part of the valley. From here, they headed further down the valley, passing over an area that had no crystals, and still, they encountered almost no signs of civilization, only one lonely ranch with its flock of sheep.

Some forty miles east of Exchange City, they came to another field, as Zarita began calling these patches. "There's another twenty scattered around here," she explained. Drina made a Mind Link to her, and Zarita shared what she was "seeing" with her new friends.

"Way cool, Zarita!" Drina exclaimed, as she now saw the bright glows that Zarita saw. Her enthusiasm was shared by the others, including Lena. Zarita felt rather proud of herself and quite pleased. This far down the valley, small groves of resinous pines dotted the ridge lines to the north and south, sometimes creeping out closer to the grasslands of the center.

On the tenth day out, without warning, a band of six well-armed men rushed them, while they were dismounted and digging up another crystal. "Bandits!" yelled Ben. Hastily, he, Bernardo, and Henry formed a line in front of the women, but two to one odds were not good. These were rough looking men, well used to fighting. Nita and Adrianna quickly gathered up the reins of the horses, knowing that, if they lost them, they would be in serious trouble. Lena, however, moved out in front too, surprising everyone, especially Zarita, who could just barely walk and stay on her feet in her toe boots. She'd backed up to cover Drina.

The six men charged into them, yelling loudly, hoping their noise would help scare these young teens into fleeing. They saw them as easy prey. Swords met swords in resounding clashes, breaking the peace of the grasslands. Lena acted swiftly. As her man threatened her, she saw her opening, and landed a powerful circle kick on his neck, breaking it. The man dropped to the ground. Seeing this, another moved to take his place, no longer faking an attack on this armless woman, whose skin was so black. He swung three times before Lena was able to land a kick squarely on his neck, dropping him.

Meanwhile, Bernardo managed to wound his man, who dropped back, allowing the last unwounded bandit to take his place. Zarita's many crystals began glowing, just as one of the bandits managed to knock Henry's sword from his hand. Lena knew she couldn't get to him in time and feared the worst. Suddenly, all four remaining men dropped their swords, throwing their hands up to their heads, as if trying to keep them from exploding. All four dropped to their knees, screaming in pain. Then, they slumped lifelessly to the ground.

Zarita's crystals dimmed. "God damn men anyway!" She spat towards them. While Henry retrieved his sword and called out a blanket thanks, not knowing who had stopped them, Bernardo and Ben quickly knocked the swords further away from the fallen men, and then checked them. "Dead." "This one too." "Dead." The men's panting voices called out. All six were dead.

"I can't believe you dropped two of them, Lena! They came at you with real swords!" exclaimed Zarita. "How could you do that? I was scared."

Lena looked back. "Had to keep you all safe. I'm not as

helpless as I look and sometimes feel. Who the hell were these men? Bandits?"

"Think so," Ben replied. "Come on; let's search them. I suppose we now have to bury them though."

"But who got these other four and saved my butt?" Henry asked, looking back at the women.

Zarita smiled. "I did it. I had to do something, so I lashed out at them. I think I turned their brains into mush or something. Please don't cut them open to see. I don't want to see."

"Well, thank you, Zarita!" Henry replied.

"Thanks for saving my Henry," Adrianna added her praise to Zarita as well. "Oh yuck! Look!" A bit of smoke or steam or vapors were oozing out from the four dead men's eyes and ears. "Bury them fast!" she ordered.

The three men enlarged the hole that they had dug to retrieve the crystal and then buried the men. That took them several hours though, so the women made lunch while they were waiting. All were glad to leave this place behind them, as the afternoon rains descended as usual.

"Camping is more fun among the pines," Zarita commented, sitting around their campfire that evening. They had settled just inside a patch of resinous pines, whose tendrils had crept down from the ridge line several miles north of them.

"Yes, the ground is softer," Drina added her point of view to the conversation. "The needle bed is nice, but I can see it is also a fire trap too. One lightning strike and all this could burst into flames."

"That's why there are all the Fire Patrols," Ben pointed out, "though down here, I don't know if they have as good a ones as we do in Brom — what with the gliders and all." Zarita had no idea what a glider was. Ben was only too eager to explain about them in detail, rather boring the others. She decided she needed to see them herself and maybe con someone into giving her a ride in one of them.

Later as they lay back in their pup tents in pairs, Zarita felt at peace; the first true peace she'd had for a very long time. She listened to the easy breathing of Nita beside her. I feel at home among these, my new friends, she mused. For a time, she began sensing for all the other buried crystals that lay out there in the vast grasslands. Suddenly, she got a full picture of Tierra and its germanium content. She saw that there was a huge up-thrust ridge of pure germanium just under the mesas of the Buku Hills and realized most of the small personal crystals that the *mentales* gifted were given came from there. However, further down in the core molten, layers more resided, waiting for a chance to pour upwards. She saw other deposits scattered all through the Goza Mountains, but these were harder for humans to reach, save by mining. Seeing the vast amount of it, she knew that Tierra would never "run dry" of these precious stones. That also comforted her.

The next day, they encountered a small ranch and an extended family, the Worthhammer clan. Foot tall stone fences outlined several crop fields, which tended to keep the herd of sheep from invading the gardens. A rickety split rail fence kept a herd of a dozen cattle corralled and six horses milled around the crude barn. A chicken coup lay long one side of the barn. An orchard of nut trees grew on the north side of the ranch, while an apple orchard lined the south. As they rode up, men, women, and children were going about their late morning chores.

As soon as they were spotted, the clan sounded a gong. Children raced into the sprawling ranch house. Teens, women, and the men darted about, grabbing whatever they had for weapons. A tall, thin greyish young man had a sword, and he took the point before the others, while an older man came running in from the south apple orchard. He too had a sword and moved in front of the strange greyish man, awaiting the arrival of the eight riders.

When they were a few hundred feet away, Zarita could see them all relaxing. She sensed them spotting Drina and Lena, in particular, though they also noticed more briefly Nita, Adrianna, and herself. The two men sheathed their swords, and the older man waved. "Hail strangers. What brings you to the Worthhammer lands?"

One younger girl looking out from the doorway exclaimed, "Look mom, those two don't have any arms!" Her mother told her to be quiet.

Ben took charge, "Hello. We are from Exchange City, the Imperial Castle, and Queen Isabella Valen Gervasi to be more accurate. Fine place you have here."

"Welcome then. Been some bandits harrying us of late. Can't be too careful these days. Name's Amos Worthhammer. My clan. This here's my hired hand Ackner," he motioned to the tall greyish young man, who looked to be in his early twenties. He was obviously a half-breed, part Rigel-3, Ben assumed, probably a cross between one of the spaceport workers and a local woman.

Ben replied, "Say, were those bandits six rather grubby looking men? If so, you don't ever have to worry about them again. They attacked us, and we've buried all of them a ways back."

"Yah, that 'em. Been trying to steal our womenfolk all spring. Come on, Martha, get some tea on for these young'ens here." Amos took charge. "Come on; we'll show you around. Don't get many visitors out here. You must be tower folks."

They dismounted. All eyes watched Drina and Lena mostly, but soon some also watched Zarita because of her strange looking toe boots and her difficulty in walking on the uneven ground. Ben answered his question, "No, we're not tower folk, but we are working for Queen Isabella and the Imperial Tower. Bernardo here is her son." He proceeded to introduce his group, and Amos followed suit. Soon, he was ushering everyone inside, where the women were bustling about preparing hot tea and nut biscuits.

The dining room was large but the table, while long, was rather crude, made of roughhewn planks set on stumps. Still, the place had a warmth about it that was so often lacking back home, Zarita noticed. Amos asked, "So what brings yea out this far from the city? Must be important business."

"Aye, we are on a mission to gather up all the blue stones that fell from the sky during the Great Meteor Storm," Ben answered. Seeing the blank looks, he excused himself and retrieved one from their bags. "They look like this," he slipped the large, irregular crystal out of its protective pod silk bag.

Instant recognition. "Ah, pesky fellows. Yah, we found

'em in our fields. Useless stones. Not good for anything, so we just put them into the fences. Got to keep the sheep out of the gardens, you see," Amos explained.

"Well Amos, this is your lucky day!" Ben replied. "Queen Isabella is paying a hundred gold for each one of these stones that you have or can find."

"Whoopee! Did'ja hear that pa?" a twelve year old boy exclaimed. "Pa, we got lots of 'em!"

Amos' eyes lit up. "A hundred gold? You must be kidding. Worthless stones, not good for anything. Well, as soon as we have our tea, my boys'll fetch them. Got plenty of them, that's for sure. A hundred gold?"

"Yes, a hundred gold. She wants them badly for tower use," Ben reiterated.

"My goodness. We can finally afford a new wagon and some of those steel-bladed plows," Amos declared.

"And some new material for clothes," his wife reminded him of her needs too.

Ben smiled. "Yes, you should be able to go on a goodly shopping spree."

"Pa, ask them what kind of a bad accident those two had and how she got all burned up? Her face is really black," a six year old girl asked. She wasn't interested in gold, but the two strange looking women.

Drina answered, "I was born this way. I have special powers I use to help others when they get sick. Lena's skin is black because she came here from another world, one out there among the stars. A bad man cut her arms off."

"Did it hurt?" she asked.

Lena grinned, "Not too bad. It hurt worse trying to learn to live without them. But I'm doing well enough now. I killed two of those bandits myself. Kicked them with my feet."

"Wow!" the little girl's eyes lit up, very much impressed with Lena.

Sensing her next question, Drina added, "So now she and I use our feet like you use your hands. Say, is that an apple?" She changed the topic.

Amos beamed with sudden pride. "Why yes. I am trying to develop my own strain of hardy apples that will not only grow this far north in the cold but also taste good. Try one. Mind you, it's last year's, so it isn't as fresh." Ben hastily took one and cut her a slice with his knife.

"Hey, you all ought to try this. It's really sweet," Drina replied. The others tasted it as well. Drina then suggested, "Hey, come fall harvest, you ought to bring a load of these up to Queen Isabella in the Imperial Castle. I am sure she would purchase all the apples you want to sell. Name your price. These are really good."

Bernardo added, "She's right. I'll tell mom to expect you this fall. How about it, Amos?"

"Sure thing. Sure thing," he exclaimed rather surprised at his newfound luck.

After tea and watching Lena devour more than her share of the nut biscuits, much to the farm women's pleasure, they headed outside to round up the crystals. Soon, they handed over fifteen of them. With this many at one time, Bernardo arranged for the tower to teleport them right now and asked for fifteen hundred gold too. The whole clan watched in awe, as the fifteen bags simply vanished from the ground. A minute later, a large, heavy bag appeared with the gold, well silver coins worth to be more precise.

"We're rich!" exclaimed several of the teens.

As the gang rode off further east, they left behind a celebrating clan. Zarita also verified there were no other stones in this area. She then asked about the tall, thin, greyish man. Ben explained his theory. She replied, "Isn't that just like a man! Get a woman pregnant and then abandon them both! Men are pigs, present company excluded though." Everyone laughed.

A few days later and several more ranches or farmsteads later, they were approaching the lands claimed by Haverhills to the south and Wycombe to the east. Off to the south, from a rise they could see fields dotting the landscape, the beginnings of the breadbasket lands of the south central part of the continent. More importantly, they began to run into patrols of soldiers, who were also scouring the countryside for the stones on the orders of their respective kings. Wisely, Ben decided that they should not press their luck and head back.

No sense in getting into arguments over whose stone was whose. Already they had amassed several hundred for Queen Isabella and the Imperial Tower.

Over twelve hundred miles to the north of them, Josh and his Pentagram of Power wives faced an altogether difference menace. Beginning in late May just after the High Council meeting, Josh began once more to see troubling future paths. Perhaps, it was triggered by Maricela's return from the meeting. She held a lengthy meeting of all the tower members, outlining their massive push to acquire as many of the giant crystals as possible. That the queen was offering a steep reward to anyone who turned one in also added emphasis.

Have I saved us from one catastrophe only to encounter another? Josh was worried. Partly, it was the "soon to arrive" aliens on Plateau Grado, but more than that, these crystals presented a grim future, massively bleak. In spite of their Closed World status, Ashford-5 had now come to the attention of many others in the vast Imperium — others who were not ethical or respected their status. Somehow, this and the crystals were rapidly becoming linked together.

This dominant future was horrid to see. He could see enterprising individuals from Tierra, who were armed with the incredible, ultimate power of these crystals, swarming outward onto the planets of the Imperium, conquering one planet and civilization after another. No one could stand against the mental dominance of those whose very thoughts could kill. The Imperium would soon have a new taskmaster, one that would lead the vast Imperium into an enormous Dark Age. One did as the taskmaster asked or one died by the taskmaster's mere thought. One could not even justify all this as revenge for what Imperium personnel had done to Tierra over the centuries.

Somehow, Josh had to help bring about another future path, this time not only for Tierra's sake. Confluence. That was the catalyst. The return of the aliens to Tierra's base, their new demands that would follow, the widespread availability of the giant crystals of power, the weak rulers of the many kingdoms — all these were rapidly joining the same time stream. It seemed inevitable that they would merge into the nightmare Josh was glimpsing. He knew he had to do something.

Somehow, someway, Josh just had to keep these four events from merging into the same time stream. Isolated as events, each might well be handleable, but not together. Down that path lay the destruction of this arm of the spiral galaxy and perhaps even the other arm, where somewhere out there was his own home world, though he knew not where it was located.

Lack of sleep began to take its toll on Josh and his four wives, as they spent far too many hours each day in their unique pentagram rapport searching for a path that led elsewhere. It was a sleepy Domenica, who inadvertently led to the path. Jokingly, she muttered, "At least, you do not have to worry about potatoes again." All five chuckled.

But the mention of potatoes got Josh thinking about them again. His memories of running away from home to avoid being forced to become a potato farmer like his father filled his mind. As he shoved them away once more, he saw a potato field on Winno-3, one of the planets in the Ataro Empire. His attention went to Amy and Jan, who were there and about done with Queen Altha's training. Soon, they would be sent home, and Amy would be taking Queen Isabella's place. Already he knew this was wise. Isabella's life would be cut short because of complications arising from the fusing of her neck vertebrae many years ago.

Now, he saw Amy and Jan's immediate future as well. Once more, he didn't like what he saw. A fifth event was rapidly joining the other four! He began to wonder what if this one was altered? Would it help in any way? Could the inevitable be somehow avoided here? What if he made a tiny adjustment? He looked down that dim future path. Here was a way out! But in doing so, he was condemning two whom he greatly respected. Two versus countless billions. Josh sighed, the demands —the weight upon his shoulders was enormous. He acted, a very tiny tweak, minuscule, and yet it massively altered the future of the entire Imperium including Ashford-5.

Camping out within the resinous pines, Bernardo

received a telepathic message from a frantic Queen Isabella. *Bernardo! Amy and Jan have been kidnaped! Please come back here immediately. I've arranged for Bart to bring you and the horses back, as soon as you all get packed up. Hurry!*

Chapter 15 Treachery Among the Wasps

It was middle May 1291 back on Tierra, but mid-summer on Winno-3. Flowers were everywhere within Queen Altha's palace. Amy had just passed her final test that afternoon. "I just can't believe it, Amy!" Queen Altha gushed. "No one has ever taken such a short time to master everything! You have been a stellar student. It gives me the greatest of pleasure to announce to the world that you have also become Queen Amy of Ataro, just like your mother. You are only the second person from worlds beyond our system to have become one of our queens! Tomorrow, the emperor will be here personally to congratulate you and present your emerald of office. Of course, there will be a great feast in your honor and a dance too."

"But I don't know how to dance to your music," Amy protested.

Queen Altha laughed. "So like your mother. She said the very same thing. Come, this afternoon, I will teach you, just as I taught Queen Isabella. The honor you have shown us will go down in our history books."

Amy grinned. She was very glad the training was over, very eager to return home. "So will you, Queen Altha. You've trained both of us. You'll be in your history books as well." The queen grinned broadly, allowing herself a small bit of vanity.

Exhausted from the long afternoon practice session, the two settled down for the evening early. Amy fell asleep at once. Jan however did not. She felt restless, uneasy. At last, she dozed off but had a horrid nightmare, waking only to find one of the women in her nightmare rousing her, her servant woman. For an instant, Jan panicked and then got a grip on reality.

"Bad dream, dear?" Amy asked.

"Yeh, really bad dream!" Jan looked around the room and then at the two servant women, who had just brought in fresh flowers. *My god!* She thought, *these are the same ones as in my dream! Is it really happening or going to happen? I should alert Queen Altha about this!*

As Jan allowed her servant to properly dress her and brush out her long hair, preparing her for breakfast, she thought about how best to bring this up as they dined. Suddenly out of nowhere, she had the thought: *Don't be silly. That was just your imagination at work. Winno-3 is a totally safe world in the Empire of the Wasps.* She then thought, *Yes, I am being silly. There is no place safer than here. It was just a bad dream. Best keep my mouth shut. We'll be going home tomorrow. Just get through one more day of this.*

Back on Proxima Prime, President Snarry Knoschy faced serious problems. Two of the six Legates had mysteriously died. Worse, both were now connected to the assassination of Neva Burkhardt, the hero of the recent war. His many plans for galaxy-wide celebrations in her honor were gone. True, her death came as an extreme blessing for him. He was terrified of her mental abilities, just as the two Legates had warned him about. He was very pleased with the news of her untimely death, confident nothing could possibly connect her assassination and the treason of the Legates directly to him. Of that, he was certain. The only evidence was a brief sentence from one of the Legates telling him the Neva problem was being handled. That could mean absolutely anything.

No, President Snarry was not worried about being caught in the web of deceit of the two Legates. Rather, he now faced obtaining proper replacements for the men. Plus, he saw the extreme need to have a telepath in his pay as well. Neva's aid during the war convinced him of that. Yet, telepaths, true telepaths were rare. Except on this Ashford-5.

Hence, one of his appointments, or promotions actually, was that of Sector ID Minister Emeryk Donat, originally from Rigel-3, but who had been the acting governor of Ashford-5 for many years, until the outbreak of the war with the Federation of Planets. The tall, thin man, dressed in his official Imperium uniform knocked and entered the President's office. He was a long way from his post out on the rim of this arm of the spiral galaxy.

President Snarry sat behind his huge desk, motioning

for the minister to have a seat before the desk. He'd chosen this desk with great malice a forethought. Behind it, he seemed massively impressive, while those who met with him seemed so small. He looked Emeryk over. He'd recently undergone a bit of rejuvenation and looked twenty-five once more, as befitting his role in gaining victory during the war. Indeed, he was something of a war hero out there in the rim for having protected so many worlds. That he also lost some battles went unnoticed.

"Emeryk. Is it okay if I call you that?" President Snarry began. Emeryk nodded, and he proceeded. "Good of you to come all this way. I've been looking over your record of service to the Imperium. As you know, recently there have been some untimely deaths, and I have to nominate replacements. What would you say if I offered you the position of Legate, filling the late Legate Daag Taal's position?"

Emeryk was obviously not expecting this. Rather, he had assumed the President wanted personally to give him a medal for his gallant defense of the rim worlds. Everyone else was doing that. He looked quite surprised. "Mr. President. I don't know what to say. I am shocked and surprised. Yes, I would love to be the next Legate."

"Excellent, excellent, Legate Emeryk. I'll put the papers through today. Considering your impressive record, the Senate confirmation will be automatic. Congratulations."

"I don't know what to say. How can I ever possibly thank you? I look forward to working closely with you, securing and rebuilding our explorations on the outer rim," Emeryk replied. Then he added, "I'm not currently married. Will that be a problem?"

President Snarry smiled, "Of course not. Well, maybe for you. I suspect you'll find many courtesans fawning all over you at the formal affairs." Both men grinned.

"There may be a way that you can repay me, Legate Emeryk. You've spent a lot of time on Ashford-5. You know those people well. Let me explain this unfortunate mess that Legates Daag and Herman have left us. It concerns former residents of Ashford-5, these uncanny telepaths. It began when we had to abandon our fuel refinery there. Governor

Konrad and his wife Neva were evacuated from that world along with everyone else. The Sector ID Minister discovered they were both telepaths. Considering how badly the war was going at that time, he wisely put them to use on other rim worlds, ferreting out spies and traitors. That worked out well, as you probably know."

"Yes, both were effective, according to the official reports. I've kept up on them, Mr. President."

"Snarry, just Snarry when we are alone. Yes, well, they did come to the attention of those two Legates, particularly Neva." He began to outline what all he knew about Neva's contributions and the Legates' terror of the potential damage Neva could do to everyone. He talked for over an hour, briefing Emeryk fully.

Then he asked, "From your experience, do these Ashford-5 people possess such powers? Can they kill someone just by thinking it so?" He was testing the man, seeing just how much Emeryk actually knew about Ashford-5.

"Absolutely Snarry. That is only one of the many possible avenues their *mentales* gifts, as they call them, can take. Thank god very few of them have that potential — to kill with a mere thought. As you say, if Neva was one such person, then it's perhaps wise she met with that 'accident,'" he suggested.

"Quite right, quite right. As you know, I have been cleared of having had anything to do with her assassination. Still, no one's more pleased than I am. She was clearly about to return and make my life utter hell. She was going to force me to divorce my wife and marry her. She would then be in complete control of the Presidency of the Imperium! You can understand my position." Emeryk nodded.

"However, there's no denying while Neva was here, her services were utterly invaluable, priceless, if I say so myself. I've come to realize we do need an official telepath here on Proxima Prime to service both the Legates and the Presidency when needed."

Legate Emeryk replied, "Yes, there is no denying that a telepath would be extremely valuable, but also quite dangerous and prohibitively expensive. Legates Daag and

Herman were well aware of those dangers and gave you good council about them."

"Indeed. Of course, we don't dare go to Ashford-5 and kidnap one of their telepaths to use. While the psych man's magic worked and kept Neva in line most of the time, what with this current scandal, we dare not be so overt about such things. They were right about one thing — limit her physically. I wonder something, is it really possible Neva could have killed the two Legates? She was half a galaxy away from them at the time."

Emeryk smiled, "Now there I can help you. Their skills are limited in range. No Ashford-5 telepath can reach off-world. While they can communicate to anyone on Tierra, they lose contact the moment the person takes off in a spaceship. So no, Neva, despite her many talents, simply was far, far out of range to use her deadly gifts on the two Legates, Snarry."

"We think alike, Emeryk. We do indeed. That was my tentative conclusion too. So it does appear physical limitations combined with psych behavior modifications can bend one of their telepaths safely to our will," President Snarry concluded.

"Not so sure about safely. Telepaths are always dangerous people. But yes, I see what you mean. Neva could barely function, and she had to have a constant personal assistant with her. Yet, there's more to all this, isn't there?" His intelligence service training kicked in.

President Snarry smiled, "Again, we think alike. If Neva was incapable of killing both Legates, then the only conclusion I can reach is that we have yet another one of them somehow hiding or lurking in the background and who actually did kill the two men. Autopsies state clearly they did not die from natural causes."

"Precisely, Snarry. Precisely. There's likely a traitor somewhere close at hand, close enough to get to the two Legates, whose security is top of the line. I verified that myself when I learned of their deaths," Emeryk replied. "You were with them. Your own life was at risk."

"Excellent, a man after my own heart. Yet, how to ferret out the culprit remains a serious problem. What else are these telepaths compromising? I've asked myself that many times since their deaths. Frankly, I don't see how we can do business any longer without having our own telepaths close at hand, verifying what is said or not said."

"I would agree, Snarry. Having our own private telepaths would be a very wise course to follow. Yet, how can you afford one now? The cost of the war has been enormous. I suspect the treasury has been pretty well drained," Emeryk hinted.

"Right again. We have no funds with which to compete with the wealthy businessmen over the very few telepaths out there. Yet, we desperately need some."

"As your new Legate, let me explore some avenues that may prove fruitful. I now have access to far more information than I did as a Sector ID Minister. Perhaps, I might find a way," Emeryk suggested.

"Excellent, Emeryk, excellent. Just make sure nothing can be traced back to the Presidency."

"Of course, that goes without saying. I'll get on it as soon as I get my new clearance codes."

"Come, let's get that handled right now," President Snarry suggested eagerly. "I'll have the Senate approve your appointment tomorrow morning."

The next day, Emeryk moved into his new office on the ninetieth floor of the giant skyscraper, Legate Daag's former office. All the previous tenant's things were still there, and Emeryk spent the day sorting out and tossing much. The second day, he was at last able to get to work. As promised, the Senate had approved him, and he now had access codes only one short of those of President Snarry himself. He just could not believe his incredible good luck with this promotion!

After a few days of searching records, he came across an interesting detail. Queen Isabella's daughter, Amy, and her friend Jan were on Winno-3 receiving training in the Ataro System of government. He brought up some news accounts of them, skipping over the text, hunting for photographs. He smiled. Amy was already partly restrained, as any leader in that system had to be. Crazy people, he mused snidely, discounting the role the emperor had played in ending the war.

Still, thinking of the emperor and his wild tale of the events on Gamelon, Emeryk studied those reports carefully. The Imperium was helping Gamelon dismantle and recover from their extremely nasty situation. Over half of their women, who were on the milking machines, were brain dead, their bodies kept alive only by the machines. Of the remainder, all those of childbearing age had now been impregnated in a last ditch attempt to bring forth a new generation of women, preventing them from becoming an extinct race.

He read further that the Imperium was confiscating the equipment in the factories, as they slowly came off line. Already some two hundred machines in the alien women's factory had been dismantled. An idea began to form. Dutifully, he began to explore its possibilities. No way could the Imperium hazard kidnaping anyone from Ashford-5, not in the current political climate. Emeryk felt nothing but disdain for this upstart Emperor Kino of the Ataro System having ended the war. He had wanted to win it, not call a truce.

Emeryk knew also he had to be extremely careful that nothing could ever be traced back to him, much less to the Presidency. His many years of service in the ID ministry were put to work. He had many, many contacts, some were quite nefarious to say the very least. Slowly, his plan evolved. Find the right men for the right jobs. That took him several weeks to work out. He was in a position to know intimately all the ways crooks abused the system. He'd caught many over the last century. Thus, it was a simple matter for him to use these same methods. Money, or credits rather, was a powerful motivator among those he selected for the many individual tasks at hand. Further, they were men who would not be missed in the slightest. Some would say good riddance.

At last, he had everything in place, but almost no time left with which to carry out the plan! The latest news told of Emperor Kino's planned celebration. The next day, a transport was scheduled to depart, returning the pair to Ashford-5. Emeryk had to act now or lose this golden opportunity to kill many birds with one stone.

His cover persona, aptly called "The Shadow," issued the many orders. Funds exchanged hands, as well as certain items. Now Emeryk sat back. Everything was in motion. With any luck at all, his and President Snarry's needs would be nicely met. Nothing could possibly lead anyone to connect this deed to either man. It was a perfectly designed mission. Nothing was left to chance. Nothing could go wrong.

Amy with Jan's arm around her walked carefully into the throne room, where Queen Altha sat on her smaller throne. Her face shown with pride. At her side on the larger throne, Emperor Kino sat watching the pair make their entrance. To either side of them, their own assistants stood watching. He wore a light green tweed suit with a white satin shirt. His toe shoes were highly polished and black, reflecting the sunlight that illuminated the room. He also had a nicely trimmed moustache that matched his black hair. She wore an emerald satin gown with matching heels.

As instructed, Isabella walked up to the emperor and stood before him, accompanied by a musical fanfare. She tried to flow as gracefully as Queen Altha had demonstrated to her many times and hoped that she did. Behind her, the throne room was utterly packed with guests. Later, she got to look at them. All wore elegant gowns and suits. Many had tiny waists and toe shoes as well, but not all did. Only a few were missing their arms like herself.

When she stood before him, the emperor rose and a hush fell on the room. "Today, we are gathered here to welcome the graduation of a new queen. But she is not an Ataro Empire of the Twelve Sacred Planets of the Wasp queen! No, we are incredibly honored to present the second queen of Ashford-5! This is an historic day for the Ataro Empire, for at long last, another world beyond our system now has their second fully trained queen. She'll be helping out Queen Isabella Valen. Some of you know that we emperors, empresses, and queens have been trying for over two millennia and then some to get other worlds out there in the vast galaxy to emulate and duplicate the fantastic success we have had here. Today, Queen Altha has made this a reality for only the second time in our history! To commemorate your stellar achievement, I wish to present you with this emerald necklace engraved with your name and your achievement."

Queen Altha rose, while Evon placed the small engraved emerald on a gold chain around her neck. She received a loud round of applause. He then spoke again, moving closer to Amy. "Be it known throughout the empire that as of this day, I hereby proclaim from this point in time forward that this woman you see before me shall be known as Queen Amy Valen Gervasi, deserving of all the rights and respect of any queen of the Ataro Empire. Yes, I have examined her training and do hereby certify she is as capable as any of our queens! Indeed, she has been perhaps pushed even harder than we push our future queens in training. That is because she is not from the Ataro Empire, and we wished to make very sure she is more than capable. Ladies, gentlemen, it is with immense pride that I present to you Queen Amy Valen Gervasi." Jan slipped the small emerald on a gold necklace around her neck, adjusting her very long black tresses. Again, the room erupted into a loud round of applause. As instructed, Queen Amy then took her seat beside Queen Altha. Jan dutifully moved to her side, emulating Evon.

While the musicians played background music, many of the guests moved up to greet the emperor, empress, and Queen Altha. More importantly, they all greatly desired to introduce themselves to Queen Amy. Quickly, she lost complete track of who was who, but she did realize these men and women were some of the most important and powerful people in the entire Ataro Empire of the Twelve Sacred Planets of the Wasp, just as her mother had done some fifteen years before her.

Finally, they took their lunch break or rather indulged in the Royal Feast, but only about half of those here actually ate any significant amounts. Naturally, those with the pipe corsets could only eat relatively small amounts. Around one, they again headed back to the throne room for the Royal Dance. As anticipated, the emperor requested the first dance with Queen Amy. She nervously took her place before him. How strange, she thought, we are facing each other, but neither of us can actually touch or hold the other. That was the same thought her mother had when she first danced with

Emperor Kino.

Then the music began, and Amy focused all her attention on duplicating the dance steps, trying hard to follow his lead on the turning. At least he was forced to be as careful as she to avoid taking a tumble. She sensed he was as nervous about doing this dance as she was and that gave her some comfort. Shared misery.

Fortunately, the dance was not very long, just a couple of minutes, out of respect for the extreme difficulty the two had in dancing. He then took another turn with the empress and then one more with Queen Altha. However, Queen Amy didn't get to sit down. Just as had happened with Isabella, many other men came up to her asking her to dance with them as well! She dare not turn them down, though she desperately wanted to do just that. After the two additional short dances on the emperor's behalf, the musicians then played longer sets for the benefit of the guests.

Poor Amy, man after man requested to dance with her, dance after dance. Before long, she was gasping for breath, but she persevered in spite of her growing discomfort. In a way, she felt elated by being almost swung around by the men, her hair flying out behind her. Finally, Queen Altha intervened, allowing her to finally sit down and catch her breath. By the time the dance ended, Amy was exhausted.

Later, Jan helped her to their room. "Last time we come in here, Amy. Tomorrow, it's homeward bound!"

"I can't wait!" Amy replied. Shortly, their two assistants came and quickly got Amy undressed and into bed. She fell into a deep sleep at once; she was quite pooped.

Jan, however, felt quite uneasy. All the actions the two servants were doing seemed identical to her nightmare. After getting her tucked in, the two left. Jan held her breath. Would they return as they had in her nightmare? Shortly, both women returned carrying a pair of vases with some unusual flowers in them. Jan began to panic, but one servant held up a paper for her to read. "Accept these flowers from your emperor." Jan knew she dare not reject them, but if her nightmare was to be believed, she dare not accept them! The two servants carried one over to Amy's bed, placing them beside her, while the other did the same, setting them down beside Jan. *Don't breathe! Don't breathe!* Jan told herself. This was all happening, as she had dreamed it would. At last she had to gasp. In came the most unusual fragrance she'd ever smelled. Sickly sweet, yet intoxicating. She told herself not to breathe again and tried to get up out of the bed. Her servant pushed her back down again, and she had another whiff of their incredible odor. Her mind felt light headed. She had to take another sniff and then another. Valiantly, she tried not to breathe to no avail. Then, the world went dark. She didn't see the two servant women collapsing on the floor beside the two beds.

Earlier that evening, a deep space transport from Beta-9 arrived to pick up some cargo. When it was dark, six men dressed in black, carrying blasters and wearing masks, stepped surreptitiously out of the cargo bay. Two carried collapsed boxes. Another carried a pair of electro-magnetic carts, which when activated, could carry heavy loads, while moving utterly silently. One merely activated them and then pushed them along to wherever their cargo was needed. It eliminated the need for heavier equipment to move large and heavy cargo rapidly.

The men rented a shuttle, paying cash for it, but swiping forged ID cards to rent it. A bit later, they arrived outside the Royal Palace. Two armed guards stood on duty, protecting the entrance. Two d-guns fired. Both fell before they could even challenge the six. The guns fired again, knocking out the surveillance cameras just outside the palace. They entered the palace and fired again, eliminating two additional guards just inside. They fired once more, destroying the interior cameras. One pulled out a map and then led the way to the elevator.

As they stepped off, two fired again, eliminating the upper story guards. Silently, they entered the bedroom. Again, they fired, putting clean holes in the two servant's heads. While they could not speak, they could write. Another pair of men pulled out syringes and injected something into the necks of the two unconscious women. Then, they opened the collapsible crates and stuffed the two unconscious women inside, reforming the crates. Two pairs of men lifted the crates onto the electro-magnetic carts and activated them. While two pushed them, two others took point and two fell back watching their rear. Within minutes, they were back outside the palace. Two minutes later, they had the crates aboard and headed back to the spaceport.

A half hour later, the transport rose unexpectedly into the air. Naturally, the control tower challenged them. The pilot replied, "Emergency lift off. Got orders to report back to Beta-9 at once." He received clearance and engaged hyper-drive. His destination coordinates were automatically sent back to the control tower. Once they had been sent, the pilot, now quite some distance from Winno-3, dropped out of hyperspace and entered a different set of coordinates, reactivating the hyper-drive.

Two days later, they landed on a small moon base of Dillard-3. Here, they unloaded their cargo. A pair of men handed them their pile of credits and the transport lifted off. One of the men, who had handed them their pay, pushed a button. Both men looked up into the sky and watched the ship explode into a thousand pieces. Both smiled. "Waste of credits. Well, we have work to do. Let's get started. We are making a fortune on this one." Both chuckled.

"Okay doc, you do your thing first. I'll lend you a hand with these women. Don't know why the boss wants them so screwed up, but with what we are being paid, I could care less. Looks like one is halfway there already." Both men chuckled wickedly.

Together, they lifted Amy first and, after cutting away all her clothes, put her into a medical machine. Then the doctor began activating the complex menus. Fifteen minutes later, he pressed the Execute Program button. Amy's feet were removed with her lower legs now nicely conical, ready for prosthesis. Her breasts were now giant sized. Although neither man nor Amy knew it, they were the same size as the women who were being milked on Gamelon-3. Her voice was also silenced. When the process finished an hour later, the two men lifted her out and sat her unconscious body on a chair, then placed Jan's body in the machine.

Now the second specialist set to work. He placed earphones over Amy's head. He'd already adjusted the volume. Pressing the playback button on the attached computer, he sat back and finished another beer, allowing his behavior modification program to run its course.

Over and over, in Amy's head the soft, commanding voice repeated the message. "You have forgotten your name and your past. Your name is Yarri of Belgese-3. You have been rescued and given a new job that you dearly love. You love your new job as an Imperial Telepath. You lack for nothing. You love being sexually stimulated many times each day and look forward to your milking with the greatest of pleasure. Your body is hypersensitive to sexual stimulus, and you need and crave this relief many times each day. You could not be happier with your most valuable service to the Imperium as a telepath. Your telepathy is vital to the survival of the Imperium, and you want always to do your best. You love your job and your life."

In his own defense, the renegade psych man did not know what the message, which was playing repeatedly into Amy's head, actually said. He was given the file and told not to listen to it on pain of death. He wasn't even curious, not with the amount of credits he was being paid for this "job." An hour later, he helped lift the lighter weight Jan out of the machine and onto a second chair. Now he took the headphones off Amy and put them on Jan's head. Again, he set the timer for an hour. The speech was identical except her name was Zarri of Belgese-3.

Meanwhile, he helped the doctor pack up, and then the two sat down for a beer. Finally, the timer went off. "Nearly done. Check if the transport is coming," the psych man ordered, while turning off the computer. The doctor checked, reported that it was on approach, and would be landing in about a half hour, bringing them their pile of credits. Hastily, the two wrapped both women in blankets and put them back into their crates, and waited anxiously for their payment. "I can get off this hell-hole of a world now," the psych commented.

The doctor chuckled. "Same here. Ah, I hear their

engines now. Credits, beautiful credits here we come."

Presently, four men entered. While two men lifted the crates onto electro-magnetic carts, the other two counted out the substantial pile of credits into the eager hands of the pair. "Satisfied?" a bass voice asked.

"You bet. A job well done. Let us know if we can be of any use on future jobs," the doctor replied. The man nodded, and the four left, pushing the crates on the carts out to their waiting transport ship. Once onboard, the man with the bass voice pushed the button on a handheld device. Then, he headed for the pilot's seat. Another commented, "Shame to lose all 'em credits."

The bass voice replied, "Well, you can go get them if you like."

The other laughed. "No thanks. That gas'll kill me before I get two feet inside. Those two are quite dead by now. It'll take a week for the gas to dissipate. When this is over, why not come back for the credits? They ain't any use to them now."

Both chuckled. "Deal," the bass voice replied. He punched in coordinates for Abeliard-6, another remote planet somewhat closer to the hub of the galaxy.

Two days later, the ship landed after dark, according to the orders. They handed over the two crates to another pair of men and received their hefty payment. Shortly, their ship lifted off. It also exploded just outside the atmosphere of the planet.

Meanwhile the two men began their work. Both were renegades from Gamelon-3. With the credits they were making on this deal, both could afford new identities and get back in the mainstream once more, instead of hiding out here in the slums of the galaxy. After un-crating the women, they first laced up special boots. The footwear came from a remote planet on the rim of the galaxy where the women there had some strange genetic defect and were born without feet. These ballet style, knee high boots came from that world, though these two didn't know that. Then, they put Amy's body onto the metal frame with dolly wheels that leaned back slightly, placing each foot some distance from the other as far as the base of the dolly would allow them. Then, they began adjusting the many components of what had been a former milking machine. It required very careful adjustment. Once they were satisfied everything was hooked up and aligned properly, they tested its operation. Neither could afford the slightest mistake here. Finally, both men checked the other's work.

Satisfied, they then surrounded each framework and body with a cylindrical encasement. Again verifying all was still properly aligned, they attached hoses to the valves at the top of the cylinders. A chemical similar to industrial insulation foam rapidly filled the cylinders, entirely encasing the women, the apparatus, and the metal framework. The framework was more like a dolly cart with wheels allowing them to be easily moved around by two handles on the back.

Now, they set about making all the necessary "plumbing" connections. Two removable bags would collect their bodily excrements. Another would collect their milk. Next, they attached the mouthpieces securing them tightly around their heads. They inserted two small oxygen tubes through their nostrils and attached them to oxygen tanks stored behind the dolly framework. At last, they attached a liquid food cylinder back there, connecting its hose to the mouthpieces. They then opened both valves and adjusted them for optimum operations. Finally, they activated the timing mechanism that would control the milking operation and the pleasure giving devices.

Both men sat back and looked at their handiwork. "Incredible. Still don't know why anyone would want portable milking cows, but with what we are being paid to do this, I ain't ask'en no questions." They helped themselves to a pair of beers, while awaiting the arrival of another transport ship.

It landed an hour later. Four men came into their building. While two checked on the two women, the other two counted out the credits to the two Gamelon renegades. After both parties were satisfied, the four left. As their transport lifted off, one pressed a button that released a toxic gas. The two Gamelon men never knew what hit them.

A day later, the boss said, "Okay doc. According to these here orders, you are up. We are about a day from our destination. You know what to do?"

"Yes, I have been monitoring them and giving them their injections. They ought to be fully primed. Let me know when we are arriving."

"Aye, aye, doc. Piece 'o cake. Say, they ain't going ta make a whole lot of noise are they?"

"Not a sound. They don't have voices. Silent screams perhaps. We'll see." He headed back to where the women on their dollies were strapped to the side of the cargo bay. He checked on the exterior equipment and then emptied their bags. Finally, he opened a small vial and held it to their noses, hoping a little would seep in around the two clear plastic tubes. It did and both women finally roused. They had been unconscious for over a week now.

Chapter 16 Terror

Amy came too. She couldn't move. A mouthpiece was in her mouth. She could see some tubes leading to her nose and breathed in some oxygen. The other tube came up to the mouthpiece. She was groggy. Some voice was talking to her inside her head. She sensed her breasts were far too heavy. Now she felt an alternating suction on them and felt what had to be her milk being sucked out of her. Then, the pleasure giving devices activated. She tried to scream or talk, but no sounds came out. All she could physically do was turn her head. She saw Jan beside her encased in some kind of orange cylinder, hoses going to her head and out of her bottom. A strange man was just now moving back into a position so that both could see him.

"Hello. Yarri and Zarri. Sorry, I don't know which is which, but it doesn't matter. I hear the motors running. First, I don't know what terrible disaster befell you both, but it must have been horrible. However, other doctors have saved your lives. Don't try to talk, your voices were removed, and the disaster cost you your arms and your feet. You are wearing some kind of special knee high toe boots from some strange planet where their women have no feet. At least you are able to stand with this special support system. Anyway, your breasts have been greatly enlarged, though neither you nor I can see them. I've been told that they are whoppers. Right now, they are being nicely milked so that you can survive. You should be experiencing the sexual pleasures that I'm told you both crave and simply must have. They are on timers set up by the doctors, who were able to save your lives, though I can't imagine how they were able to work this miracle. As far as I can tell from the equipment here, the milking operation occurs twice a day, but the pleasuring occurs seven times. Anyway, don't worry about having to go to the bathroom. It is being collected in a pair of bags down by your spread feet. When you are hungry, suck in and the special liquid food will come in through the tube in your mouth piece."

"As you have requested, we are delivering you to your new jobs as Imperial Telepaths. We should be arriving at your new homes later today. Like I said, I am not sure how you were rescued or what horrible virus you both must have gotten. It is a miracle that you are still alive and on this amazing amount of life support. I guess that is because of your incredibly valuable skills. I am a mere doctor charged with making sure you are comfortable and well cared for during this trip. I see everything is operating properly, so I'll leave you to relax and enjoy your pleasures. Don't forget to suck in your food when you get hungry. I am told there are some painkillers are in it."

He rose and left the cargo bay. Jan looked at Amy. Terror radiated from both their eyes, tempered by the massive dose of pleasure coming from below. *My nightmare has come true! Help! I can't take this!* Jan sent to Amy. She inhaled oxygen until she felt faint and lightheaded. Terror and pleasure mixed throughout her entire body or rather what was left of it.

I can't move. I can't take this. Help me, Jan, Amy sent, wild with panic and terror, also heavily mixed with sexual sensations. After this initial exchange, neither could focus enough to use their gifts. After what seemed an eternity, the suction ceased. Her breasts felt better; that initial aching had subsided. Amy felt starved. *When have I last eaten? Suck. That's what he said.* She did so, nearly choking on the first batch of liquid food that entered her mouth. Again, she panicked unable to move or do anything about it. More cautiously, she began sucking in food. She ate until she felt satisfied. Her leg stumps ached but she couldn't move any part of her body except her head. She turned and saw food going up the tube into Jan's mouth and relaxed a little. *At least she is able to eat too.*

Finally calmed down a little, the voice began reciting words in her mind again. Beside her, Jan was hearing the same thing except for her new name. "You have forgotten your name and your past. Your name is Yarri of Belgese-3. You have been rescued and given a new job that you dearly love. You love your new job as an Imperial Telepath. You lack for nothing. You love being sexually stimulated many times each day, and look forward to your milking with the greatest of pleasure. Your body is hypersensitive to sexual stimulus, and you need and crave this relief many times each day. You could not be happier with your most valuable service to the Imperium as a telepath. Your telepathy is vital to the survival of the Imperium, and you want always to do your best. You love your job and your life."

Try as they might, neither could get the voice to stop. Over and over, it kept talking. They didn't yet realize they were listening to that speech being repeated for nearly an hour. When it finally stopped, both women were confused. Amy tried desperately to make sense of everything, as did Jan. *Have I gotten sick somehow? Did I nearly died? Rescued? Maybe barely. What kind of disaster would cause me to lose my voice, arms, feet? Monster boobs that had to be milked? Think, think. Remember. Can't remember what happened. Must remember. Can't remember. This is hell. No, I love my life. But I do love life. I can't live like this, but I love it. Got to have pleasure. Why? Someone please help me. Oh god no, not again. Oh yes, yes!* The pleasuring machines began working again. The timer was utterly merciless.

A half hour later, the machine stopped much to the relief of both teens. Both felt hunger pangs and hastily ate again. Satisfied. Both were able to think again, barely. Thinking yielded only more terror and panic, and they desperately wanted the machine to turn on again, if only to suppress their growing fright, which fought with their strange feelings that they loved this new life.

The doctor fellow appeared again. "I'm told we are about to land on Proxima Prime. I must check to see that all is well with you." He began examining the visible parts of their equipment. Apparently satisfied, he added, "It won't be long now until you get to your new home. I'm told you'll just love it. Now, I have to buckle myself in for the landing." He took a seat just out of their view, but they could hear buckles clicking. They felt the ship vibrating a little, as it began its descent.

Legate Emeryk and President Snarry looked over the

dispatch that had mysteriously arrived, addressed to the President. His advisors had gone over it and pronounced it valid. It read:

> A band of rebels has kidnaped a pair of young telepaths from Belgese-3. Having crippled them physically, they are trying to sneak them onto Proxima Prime, where they are going to try to use them to obtain Imperium secrets. They are on Transport 32487. Agent Gashgold.

President Snarry had already checked with Agent Gashgold. He had sent the message, adding, "This is the scuttle butt I've heard here on Belgese-3. I cannot verify its authenticity, but I knew it might be vital information, so I relayed it to my Sector ID Minister."

Legate Emeryk had their Hub Sector 1 ID Minister verify there was indeed a transport ship with that ID number. They'd discovered it existed and had filed a flight plan. It was due to arrive around noon today. Unwilling to risk the security of Proxima Prime, the Hub Sector 1 ID Minister took the threat seriously, ordering an entire squad of heavily armed Security Guards to meet the ship when it landed. Their orders: shoot to kill. Both President Snarry and Legate Emeryk stood on the tarmac behind a large, transparent blast shield that would protect them from d-gun blasts during the expected firefight with these rebels. Shortly, they spotted the transport descending from the sky towards the concrete and steel surface of the spaceport. Of course, the entire surface of Proxima Prime was covered in concrete and steel, the real surface of the planet was miles below this artificial one.

On the transport, the captain and pilot barked his orders to the crew over their private comm system. "Okay, remember your jobs. When we land, expect to be in a firefight with Security Guards. Remember to play dead once you are shot by their fake weapons. Make it look good, boys. An hour from now, we are all going to be wealthy men. You too, doc. Okay, touch down in one minute. Make it look good, fellows. Out." The doctor heard the words from his head set and smiled. Such luck landing this high paying job. He'd had to do almost nothing to earn ten thousand credits!

After the ship touched down, the four crewmen joined the doctor in the cargo bay, followed by the captain, who nodded to the doctor. Then, he used his fingers to count down from three and opened the bay doors. The six had their d-guns drawn and at the ready. As the doors opened wide, there stood two dozen Security Guards, just as their orders had suggested. At once, they acted surprised and opened fire. A brief firefight erupted. For some strange reason, the rebel's d-guns apparently did little or no damage to the Security Guards. However, the Security Guards' d-guns quickly killed the six men, much to their total surprise. Of course, dead, they could hardly protest or complain they'd been tricked.

Amy and Jan saw the firefight erupt and grew even more frightened. What was happening? They were completely physically helpless and could do absolutely nothing except pray they were not hit by the rapid fire! Security Guards raced on board the ship, calling out "Clear!" as they searched the various quarters. At last, President Snarry and Legate Emeryk came out from behind their blast shield.

President Snarry exclaimed, "My god. This warning was real. Look, there are two women, just like the report suggested. Come on, Legate Emeryk; we must help them. Ladies, I am President Snarry Knoschy. We've just gotten word you were kidnaped from Belgese-3 and crippled. My god, what have they done to you both? You are safe now. Men, get them carefully out of here. Take them to my office, while we sort all this out!" He looked terribly concerned and worried, Amy thought. Strong arms took hold of her dolly and began pushing her down and out of the ship. All this only added to her total confusion. *Rescued? What is happening to me, to us?*

The trip to the top floor of a hundred-story skyscraper was a total blur. Strange air shuttles seemed to fill the skies, like silver butterflies. Everywhere she looked, tall steel and glass skyscrapers rose upwards, like some crystals gone mad. Mad? She felt as if she already had gone mad!

At last, their dollies were parked before a huge mahogany desk in some very plush office. From the many windows, they could see out onto the unending city with the silver butterflies darting about everywhere. Their world had gone mad! Just then, President Snarry and Legate Emeryk entered. The President sat down across from them, behind his dominating desk. He sighed.

"Okay. I received this field agent report that said that you are both telepaths. Apparently, you were kidnaped from Belgese-3 and were being brought to Proxima Prime to spy on the Imperium for the rebels. That transport was searched, and we've found many liquid food canisters for you. Also, we found some written instructions about how to care for your needs. Don't worry; we believe we have enough information to ensure you can continue to survive well. Apparently, you will both die horribly if removed from your specially sealed containers. I'll have some of our doctors check on your health shortly. But I must ask you, are you really telepaths? If so, I would love to hire you and give you well-paying jobs as Imperial Telepaths, working for the good of our beloved Imperium. Now, I must ask you is this so? Are you really telepaths? Can you communicate to me? If not, then perhaps it would be best to allow your crippled bodies to pass away."

I am a telepath! I'm Yassi. I'm terrified! What has happened to us? I want to be an Imperial Telepath. I can't be any happier than to be an Imperial Telepath! It is the most valuable service I can give to the Imperium — being an Imperium telepath. Telepathy is vital to the survival of the Imperium. I must always do my best. You love doing this. I love my life like this. Please help me. Please help us! Amy sent. Jan did also, telling him that her name was Zassi.

President Snarry visibly relaxed. "I hear you both! Incredible. It looks like we stopped the largest security breech in history! Legate Emeryk, issue a promotion to that field agent who uncovered this diabolical plot. Yassi, Zassi, you are safe now. I hereby appoint you both to the posts of Imperial Telepaths. You'll want for nothing, I assure you. I'll have our best doctors make sure you are all right. Since you have to live in those cases, I'm going to have you live up here in my office. This is perhaps the most secure location in the Imperium! No one will ever harm you again. I give you my word on that."

He went on, "I do have need of your services. Legate Emeryk and I do fear there is a renegade telepath somewhere around here. He or she has already murdered two of our Legates. We need your help in locating this traitor. But enough of work. Let the doctors examine you and get you settled in." He pressed his intercom button, and shortly two guards entered and wheeled the two into an adjoining office. Several doctors examined them, well their heads only. The rest of their bodies were encased within the orange cylinder. Soon, they reassured the two women that they were perfectly healthy and doing well. They then left them alone.

Once the doors shut, before either could think of anything else, the pleasuring machines began again, running for another half hour before stopping as suddenly as they had begun. Both women were panting through their noses. Hunger then swept over both, and they sucked in their liquid food. Finally satiated, both began to relax some and began thinking once more.

I am Yassi. I am so scared. I can't do anything, but I seem to love my life. How about you?

I am Zassi and I am terrified. I can't even wiggle! Somehow, though, I love and crave this. What's happened to us? None of this makes any sense. It is a nightmare without end!

I can't live like this! But I love it too. How can this be? Amy replied. *I have to be an Imperium Telepath. I want to be one. I love it. I don't want this, but I love this. I am so frightened and scared, but I love this, I must somehow.*

Me too. So confusing. A nightmare. Jan replied.

Amy began thinking more clearly. *Something is not right here. He said that the disaster caused me to lose my voice, arms, feet. But I never had any arms as long as I can remember. Plus I feel I have monster-sized boobs that have to be milked. I've heard something like that before, if only I can remember it. Think, think.*

Jan felt that something Amy had just thought was vitally important. *A nightmare. What is it about a nightmare? I know that I must be having one now. This can't be real, but is it so very real. Think. Nightmare. Yes, I am in bed dreaming. Where is that place? Oh, it is Queen Altha's guest bedroom. Now I remember! I'm Jan, she's Amy. My god, my nightmare has come true! I should have said something to Queen Altha, and we would not have been captured! Those flowers — they put us to sleep somehow! Can't remember anything after that though.*

Amy pondered her two discrepancies. *They must be important. I've never had arms so how could I lose them? Wait, milking. Someone is telling me about just that. Remember, I have to remember!* She strained to recall. Suddenly, her memories of Queen Altha describing her horrible period of captivity on Gamelon-3 returned to her, along with her memory.

Jan! You are Jan! I am Amy! I remember now, she sent.

Me too. I remember too. Our servants — they brought in those strange flowers that put us to sleep. Well, you were already asleep, pooped from all that dancing you did. We got kidnaped, just like we did in my nightmare. It's my fault. I should have warned Queen Altha. She has traitors in her midst!

Amy sent, *Jan, you don't by chance have another spaceship around here do you?*

Hardly. I can't believe that I got taken by surprise like this! God, we can't do anything now. We're more helpless than helpless.

Is that even possible? Oh god, it's starting again. This is too much of a good thing, but somehow I am craving it. Oh god. She lost her focus again. Jan already had.

An hour later and once more stuff with their liquid food, they could finally focus enough again. Amy sent, *Jan. We best play along with these men for now. Somehow, we have to figure a way to get out of this incredible mess.*

Right. I thought about just killing them all, but then we'd soon die ourselves, just as soon as the food tank runs out or the batteries need recharging. Play along. I'll think of something somehow, Amy. She didn't add that she thought their situation was probably quite hopeless this time. The only motion they could make was turning their heads a little, hardly enough to allow her to do much of anything to help them escape. She added, *For now, don't let on that we have regained our memories. Play along with this game of theirs.*

That was easy to do. A bit later, they were wheeled back into President Snarry's office. "Hello Yassi, Zassi. The doctor's report gives you both a clean bill of health. They assure me they can care for your equipment and needs, so that's a relief. Now then, beginning tomorrow, I'd like your help ferreting out the telepathic spy or spies in the administration. I think the best way to do this is to bring each of them by to my office here for a chat. Will you be able to tell just from that?"

Amy sent, *Sure. We can sense other telepaths easily.*

"Oh that is perfect! I can't wait to discover the spies! The traitors! They might have cost us the war, you know. I can't ever repay you enough for your help. I'll have a dividers brought in and have you positioned behind it so no one can see you are here. Let me know the second you detect one of the spies, okay?"

Sure. We love to help you, Amy sent.

"Excellent, excellent, ladies. Well, it's suppertime. I'll leave you here in my office so you can at least look out on the best city in the Imperium. Actually, Proxima Prime is really one giant city covering the entire planet. I'm told that the planet's surface is somewhere below us, but I've never seen it. Enjoy the view. Until the morning then," President Snarry explained and left them alone.

I didn't sense he knows anything about us or what happened to us, Amy sent.

Ditto. That whole mess was so very strange. I awoke on that transport and everyone got shot when we landed. Everything else is blank. Can you see his calendar? What date is it? Oh god, the milking suction thing is beginning again! She lost her focus. Amy did too.

Much later, Amy was finally able to let Jan know the date. Jan worked out they had lost about two entire weeks. *My god, Amy. We've been unconscious for at least two weeks before we woke up on that transport!* That was sobering to both women.

Beginning the next day, the two were wheeled behind a divider, and long processions of Imperium workers began filing in, meeting with President Snarry. Mostly, he just thanked them for their years of service and unfailing help during the long war years. The process consumed an entire month!

At last, President Snarry began to relax. "Well, Yassi, Zassi, we are in luck. It seems that the traitors, whoever they are, are not part of the Presidential bureaucracy. What a huge relief that is! I feel like a tremendous weight has been lifted from my shoulders! Now, I can get back to official business. I will use your talents on various business meetings. Let me know when someone is lying to me or if they are a telepath too. Thank you both for your immense contribution."

Both women thought he seemed sincere. However, that did little to lessen their continuous nightmare. One thing President Snarry did do for them was to install a music system. At night, they listened to music for several hours before the lights were turned off. That helped them preserve their sanity if only somewhat briefly.

Mid-June their time, Jan finally gave up. *Amy, I've failed us. I can't think of any way we can escape this. Perhaps, we should just call it quits with these bodies and try to find Tierra from here. Start over again.*

You haven't failed us, dear. Someone did this to us. We still haven't got a clue who. The why seems pretty clear to me. Someone wanted Snarry to have us telepaths working for him. I agree, there's not much point in sticking around here. I think we ought to go on the offensive first and learn all that we can about these people and what goes on here. Time to probe Snarry and some of these others in this building who we can reach.

Hey, I like that! Let's drain their minds of anything useful!

A few days later, the two pulled out of President Snarry's mind details on a secret project, one that interested them. For some years, highly classified work was being done on cloning. Centuries ago, cloning was outlawed throughout the Imperium, after an episode in which the then president tried to remain eternally in office by periodically substituting clones of himself. When that was discovered, public outcry was so strong that the incoming new president was left with no choice but to order the destruction of all cloning research and methods. Considering that was all in computer records, the wiping of knowledge was as simple as pushing the Delete key. The Senate made cloning totally illegal and punishable by execution. Development had taken a different direction: the use of stem cells by medical machines to repair and heal existing bodies, as well as improving the rejuvenation machines.

What the two discovered from President Snarry was he had initiated some top secret research into cloning. It had begun as a war effort, sold to him as a way to make an unlimited army of top soldiers. They had picked three of their very best soldiers, who had impeccable records, and had begun to reinvent the cloning process. By the war's end a few months ago, they had been quite successful. Five clones of each of the men had been made and were being field tested — in different parts of the vast Imperium, naturally.

The two focused more on issues that might deal more directly with their own world, Tierra or Ashford-5 as the Imperium called it. Whether President Snarry wanted to or not, he kept finding his mind going over issues involving Ashford-5. Not unexpected, they learned within a few months, the Imperium was planning to return to Ashford-5 and rebuild the fuel refinery on the blue moon, Palidez. They were waiting on the Senate's choice of a new governor. Already, the Senate and the President had agreed that upon their resumption of activities on their base at Plateau Grado, they were going to make several new demands. First, Ashford-5 would have to begin to provide telepaths for Imperium work. Second, they would have to appoint a new senator. Third, they would have to accept a change in the world's status to that of an Open World and thus begin accepting Imperium technology. According to the Senate legislation, these three were not negotiable.

Amy and Jan knew they had to find a way to get this information back to the Underground and to Queen Isabella at the very least! If only Jan could somehow find a way to "see" President Snarry's computer. From their usual positions behind the screen, they couldn't see much at all during the day. At night, they were positioned behind the desk, looking out of his windows. Neither could turn her head enough to see behind them.

Their mind probes had not gone unnoticed. Ever since the arrival of the transport ship that brought the two here to Proxima Prime, Legate Emeryk had wisely avoided being anywhere near President Snarry's office, preferring to meet with him in a private room on the bottom floor, commandeering one of the normally pubic rooms. Here, President Snarry frequently met with him. It was now July by the women's calendar.

"I don't like it, Legate Emeryk. I think they are probing my mind."

Legate Emeryk frowned and scratched his face. After a pause, he asked, "What leads you to believe you are being probed?" He had long ago considered this possibility, which is why he was exercising extreme caution and not making his presence known to the two telepaths. If they were actually able to probe another's mind, they could easily learn his part in their abduction. He was certain he'd left no physical trail that could be followed by anyone, not even the cleverest ID agent, but a telepath, now that was an entirely different matter.

"Look, I've been thinking about the cloning project. I've tried to put that one out of my mind since the war's ended. All real work on it has been temporarily halted, except the field trials. Yet, I seem to be reviewing all of it! Then, only last week, I seemed to be recalling all the recent rulings, plans, and agreements with the Senate on our return to Ashford-5. You can't call that a coincidence, can you?" President Snarry challenged him.

Legate Emeryk sighed, rubbing his face in thought. "No, no I can't. Telepaths can be a double-edged sword. That's become clear to me. Of course, they are helpless and cannot do anything with whatever they are discovering, now can they? Have you ever seen anyone more helpless than those two? Relax." They chatted further, and the President left none too happy about how this whole telepath project was going. Somehow, it was not doing what he had hoped it would do for him.

Chapter 17 On the Trail

Queen Altha was shocked, almost beyond belief. Security Guards executed with blaster holes in their heads — two of her servant women similarly executed — her newly made Queen Amy and her assistant Jan kidnaped — such an event had not happened anywhere within the thirty-six worlds of the Ataro Empire in recorded history! At once, she summoned Emperor Kino, who launched a full-scale investigation. "How could this have happened?" she wailed, for once wishing that she had arms with which to punctuate her extreme distress.

Emperor Kino personally took charge of the investigation. To say that he was upset by this would be a gross understatement! A crime against a queen, empress, or emperor was the most serious within the Empire of the Wasps, punishable by execution. He had not only acknowledged Amy as one of their queens, but he had personally given her the sacred emerald of office. This crime simply had to be solved, and the guilty, executed. His own position was being threatened!

Word of the kidnaping of one of their queens had already traveled all thorough the system. Many were demanding swift and just action. Others were questioning palace security measures. Others were asking how could this have happened? Emperor Kino had to resolve this one and fast!

His agents quickly found out the two servant women had been coerced into taking the deadly flowers into the women's room that fateful night. That they too had been executed prevented them from being questioned. A back trace on the flowers yielded that they had been purchased by an off-world man on the day of the kidnaping. He was seen giving them to the two servant women, just outside the palace just before suppertime, while the big dance was still going on. Further backtracking yielded the hotel where the man was staying. His executed body was found there, along with several thousand credits lying scattered around his room — a dead end.

The deep space transport that had arrived and departed with the women proved untraceable. Originally, it had been stolen from Beta-9 only a few days before it had landed on Winno-3 that fateful night. It certainly had not been returned nor had it been found. Another dead end. Regrettably, Emperor Kino had no choice but to make the call that he dreaded making, letting Queen Isabella Valen Gervasi know the awful news.

Just as he was about to make that call in June, one of his investigators made a discovery. "Emperor Kino, the officials on Beta-9 have provided us with the transponder codes for that transport ship. I impressed upon them the gravity of the matter and called in a favor on your behalf. With these codes, it is possible we can trace that transport and discover its current location."

"Make it happen! Well done! Best news yet!" Emperor Kino commented him, finally relaxing a little. Based on this news, he decided to withhold making that dreaded call just yet. They might be able to recover the transport and the women unharmed.

"We will need to send out a search ship. I've taken the liberty of scanning our empire for the ship. No trace. Figures they would leave the Ataro System, emperor."

"Okay, I am coming with you. Let's get this going as fast as possible. The sooner we find them, the better their chances for survival," Emperor Kino declared.

A day later, the heavily armed cruiser lifted off from Winno-3 with the emperor and Queen Altha on board. She, too, had insisted on coming along. It had happened on her watch. She also felt responsible. The cruiser began making an outward spiral centered on the sprawling Ataro System. Each spiral was just within the detection range of their transponder detection. Mid-June Ashford time, they finally picked up the transponder's signal! A day later, the cruiser dropped out of hyperspace and found the remains of the ship! They were in a low orbit above the moon base called Dillard-3.

"Search the remains. What happened here? Is our queen dead? Perhaps they landed on the moon. We need facts now!" Emperor Kino barked. He need not have been so dictatorial, for the cruiser's major knew just how important this mission was.

"On it Emperor Kino. We will have results soon; I promise you!" He was right. Within hours, his many scout ships began filling in details. They'd recovered several dead bodies. Facial recognition software identified these as the men who had kidnaped and murdered the men and women at Queen Altha's palace. The bodies of the women were not found, though. "Emperor, we've found some disturbing evidence on the deserted moon base. I think that you ought to come see them for yourself."

A half hour later, the Emperor personally examined what they had found. Besides the dead men and all the credits, they found Amy's emerald of office and their two germanium crystals. More disturbing, they found medical machines and grim remains: four feet and a pair of arms! "We are reverse engineering the medical machine as we speak," the major explained. "Soon, we will know the last operations that were done with it. Doesn't look good. There are some nightgowns over there too."

"Okay, I now have no choice but to make that call to Queen Isabella," Emperor Kino sighed. "This is the worst day of my life. See if the credits can be traced. I am seeing a pattern here. Hire thugs by offering substantial credits. After giving them their payments, eliminate them. Any idea how these two died?"

"Yes, gas. Lethal. Died within a few seconds. This also means that another deep space transport must have been here and picked up the women and gassed these two dopes," the major replied.

"Sir, we've found something else. You need to listen to this!" one of the technicians hollered, holding the earphones that were still connected to the computer.

"Put it on speaker-phone," the major ordered. Shortly, the voice of some psych man was heard by all: "You have forgotten your name and your past. Your name is Zarri of Belgese-3. You have been rescued, and given a new job that you dearly love. You love your new job as an Imperial

Telepath. You lack for nothing. You love being sexually stimulated many times each day, and look forward to your milking with the greatest of pleasure. Your body is hypersensitive to sexual stimulus, and you need and crave this relief many times each day. You could not be happier with your most valuable service to the Imperium as a telepath. Your telepathy is vital to the survival of the Imperium, and you want always to do your best. You love your job and your life."

"My god!" Queen Altha gushed. "That sounds an awful lot like what Neva, Lena, and I had done to us on Gamelon-3!"

"Emperor, we'll follow up on these leads," the major barked. "Now, we're getting somewhere. Best make your call, sir."

A half hour later, Emperor Kino sadly placed his call to Queen Isabella, going through the Underground first, though he didn't know that detail. A half hour after that initial contact, Queen Isabella appeared on the monitor. "Queen Isabella here. I'm told you have some bad news for me? Over."

Sadly, Emperor Kino relayed all the terrible news, adding in the latest details they'd just uncovered on this abandoned moon base. "If you or some of your people would like to come and assist with our investigation, I can send a fast transport to pick them up and bring them to my cruiser. Over."

"Thank you! This it horrid! I will get some ready to go at once. Pick up on Plateau Grado? When? Over."

After a brief consultation, he answered, "Be there in two days. Have them wait at the perimeter fence. The base security fence is still armed against intruders. I'll keep you fully abreast of further developments. I'm more confident now that we'll get to them. We have many clues to follow. Over and out." He sat back.

"She took that better than I would have if it was my daughter," Queen Altha commented.

"Yes, she is a very impressive queen. Okay, let's get back to the cruiser and see what our people can find out about these credits. Follow the money trail," he suggested.

Bart, Lilly, and Anita operated the teleport controls as rapidly as they could, bringing back the Gang of Ten, less Amy and Jan, along with their gear and horses. The horses were startled and spooked suddenly to find themselves no longer on the grasslands but inside the Imperial Castle's courtyard. For a few minutes, they caused a bit of confusion. At last, the stable hands got them under control, while the eight rushed over to where Queen Isabella, Hernando, and Gabriella were standing, waiting for them.

Bernardo knew something was horribly wrong. His mother's face was white as a sheet. Hernando's face was grim-set; his sister's eyes were red from crying. "Okay, what's up mom? What's happened to Amy and Jan?" he asked, as the other seven crowded around.

"Kidnaped and worse," Hernando spoke for her, while she tried to regain her composure. Then, she told them all Emperor Kino had just told her before her Imperial Circle had teleported the three of them back here.

"Their feet? Their arms?" Bernardo exclaimed.

"Milking machines?" Lena exclaimed too. "Oh my god, not that! Who? Why? I'll kill them myself!"

"We don't know who or why. Please, he is sending a cruiser to pick some of us up to go help find them. I don't dare go and leave Tierra in the mess that it's in right now. I'm damned near useless anyway. Bernardo, will you go?"

"Mom, a team of horses couldn't keep me from going. When?" Bernardo replied immediately.

Without any hesitation, the other seven added, "Me too." Lena said, "Where you go, so go I. You need me along. I still have my mind."

Zarita thought fast. "Count me in too. Although I haven't met them, I want to help too. Please."

"Kids, I suppose you should ask your parents first. This could be very dangerous," Queen Isabella countered.

"Who gives a crap about King Alano? Not me. If they go, so do I," Zarita replied, putting her hands defiantly on her hips.

"We are all adults now. So we really don't need our parent's permissions," Drina pointed out. "But we'll let them know the situation. I'm sure they'll back us. But even if they don't, I'm with Zarita. We go. It's Amy and Jan that we are talking about!"

"Thank you all. Get cleaned up and packed. You have until the morning to get ready. You're supposed to be at the fence. It's armed or something. They'll meet you there," Queen Isabella replied. She looked a little better, Bernardo thought. Hastily, they headed off in different directions to get ready; Nita and Zarita headed next door to Elegant Fashions Inc.

"What should we wear?" asked Zarita. She and Nita had taken baths, but only after Nita explained what had happened to Amy and Jan and that they were going off-world to help search for them. Inez backed Nita all the way, much to her surprise. She'd figured her mom would raise the devil with her going off-world with total strangers.

"Let's wear a simple gown but take our leathers in case we need to get into action," Nita suggested. They each packed a small bag with a change of clothes and a few personal items. Zarita added one of her large crystals as well. After eating breakfast the following morning, the two headed off to the Imperial Castle next door. Nita kindly kept her arm around Zarita, helping her move as rapidly as she dared in her toe shoes.

The others were just finishing getting themselves ready. Both Lena and Drina wore small backpacks, while the others were donning theirs. Bernardo gave his mother a quick kiss and a hug to his dad and sister. Lena promised, "We won't come back without them, I promise."

They walked the short distance to the southeastern corner of Plateau Grado where they waited beside the barrier fence. Before long, they watched as a very large cruiser slowly descended to the surface. They were all very impressed with its sheer size. Now, they waited. Soon, several electric cars came zipping silently up to them. A man got out, entered a code, and waved for them to enter, motioning for them to get into the cars. "We can understand Imperium Standard," Bernardo spoke up.

The Security Man relaxed. "Ah, that's a pleasant surprise. I was going to have to get these ULAT boxes on you somehow. Good. Ship is being refueled now. Let's get you aboard."

To say that these eight were impressed with the

spaciousness and size of the ship's interior was also an understatement, except for Lena, who had been on many of these light cruisers in her long life. She took charge, explaining about the ship, as they were escorted to their suite of cabins. "Ah, we are being given the fanciest quarters on the ship, save that of the major and his officers. We must rate," she suggested. The others simply continued to look about in awe.

"Come on; we can watch the liftoff from the port-side viewports. This way," Lena suggested. Before long, they felt a slight vibration, and then the spaceport began moving below them.

"How come the spaceport is moving while we aren't?" asked Adrianna, a little confused.

Lena laughed. "Illusion. We are moving. Tierra isn't."

"Oh! Now I see it. Isn't that interesting? I can make it seem either way. Terrific!" Adrianna gushed excitedly. "This is really neat, isn't it?"

Lena smiled, recalling her first trip in a cruiser almost a hundred years ago. She sat back and allowed her friends to enjoy the experience. Once they entered hyper-drive, there was nothing to see except blackness, and they returned to their suites, while Lena checked with the major to see if there had been any further news. There had not been, but he told her they would be rendezvousing with the emperor's cruiser in one day. Lena now knew that they were going at top speed! Impressive, she thought, and wise. The more time that elapsed in a kidnaping, the less chance the victims had.

Other than Lena, none was bored. She had to answer many "What's this?" questions from the others, obviously much impressed with the cruiser and its accommodations.

Right on schedule, they met up with the emperor's cruiser still in orbit above the moon base on Dillard-3. They took a small shuttle to the other cruiser and were met personally by the grim-faced emperor and pale Queen Altha. "Come, let's get you settled into your quarters, and then we can go over what we've discovered so far," he suggested.

A half hour later, they all met in the major's conference room. After Emperor Kino outlined what they had thus far pieced together, he then described their current avenues being investigated. "We are tracking back on the destroyed transport ship, but we don't expect to learn much more from that. Sensors have verified that another ship, probably a deep space transport, did come here around the same time as the destroyed one. We presume those people picked up the women and gassed the doctors. Yes, we've identified them both. Disreputable men."

"We know this is the emerald of office I gave Amy the day before the abductions. Can you identify these crystals that were found? We believe those were the stones the two always wore around their necks," he asked.

Bernardo focused and gently slipped into rapport with the stones. He looked up, "Yes, that one is Amy's, and the other is Jan's definitely. So they have had their feet cut off? Grim. They must be completely helpless now, at their mercy."

"Unfortunately, we agree. We still have three avenues that we are exploring. We are trying to trace the origin of the credits we've found on Queen Altha's servants, those recovered from the exploded transport and those on the base with the doctors. Perhaps we'll get lucky on that line. We are searching for other reported stolen transport ships or missing ones. Meanwhile, we are studying the importance of the brainwashing behavior modification speech, if that's what it is. Let's go over it again. I'll play it back for you," he nodded to his silent assistant who did so. The eight listened.

"You have forgotten your name and your past. Your name is Zarri of Belgese-3."

Emperor Kino nodded and his assistant paused it here. He then explained, "We checked, and there is no record of them on that world; they know nothing about all this. Zarri and Yarri are quite common first names on that world. Dead end there. Continue, please."

"You have been rescued and given a new job that you dearly love. You love your new job as an Imperial Telepath. You lack for nothing." Again, he signaled a pause.

"Here, we believe they are trying to confuse the women, by making it seem like whoever they are now with have in fact somehow rescued them from their kidnapers. After the mutilations of their bodies, they may well believe this part. The big clue is in the second sentence and Imperial Telepaths. I checked. There are no such things. I think this may be a very fruitful avenue to explore, though. I believe it may give us a clue as to their current location or employment. Continue. I warn you, this next part is quite disturbing."

"You love being sexually stimulated many times each day, and look forward to your milking with the greatest of pleasure. Your body is hypersensitive to sexual stimulus, and you need and crave this relief many times each day." Lena cringed, as did Queen Altha; none saw Zarita also react as well.

"Based on this, we believe they are being treated much as Lena, Neva, and Queen Altha were back on Gamelon-3. We are checking on that avenue. Thus far, we know the Imperium is helping them dismantle those machines, and that the Imperium is confiscating them, supposedly recycling them. Our major is looking into that angle right now. Continue, please," he ordered.

"You could not be happier with your most valuable service to the Imperium as a telepath. Your telepathy is vital to the survival of the Imperium, and you want always to do your best. You love your job and your life." The recording ended.

"Again, Imperium telepaths is mentioned. You see why I think this may be a clue worth following when all else fails?" he asked. They agreed.

They spent some time discussing these ideas further. Zarita wished she had met either teen. Then, she might be useful in locating them. Instead, she decided to experiment a little. She focused and her many crystals activated, but no one noticed her. She gently slipped into rapport with one of the crystals. She noticed the second one seemed to be at very nearly the same frequency, an indication the two teens were very close indeed. Now that she at least could sense their unique frequency, she tried to sense their spatial location compared to hers.

At last, she spoke up. "Gang, they are that way from here. I can sense it." If I had more power, I think I could locate them. Perhaps, if we get closer to them, I can find them."

"Terrific Zarita!" Bernardo exclaimed. "Emperor, what's that way from here?"

"Only the center of the galaxy — an enormous number of worlds to search."

Just then, the major entered. "Got some news that's perhaps worth tracking down. Just intercepted a message that some wreckage has been located in orbit around the world of Abeliard-6. It is quite a remote planet somewhat closer to the hub of the galaxy. Permission to check this one out," he deferred to the emperor.

"Let's. It is in the direction that Zarita is suggesting too. Make haste, major. Well done, sir," Emperor Kino replied. He saluted and left. Shortly, they all felt the cruiser shift into hyper-drive once more.

Two days later, the cruiser dropped out of hyperspace and near the small debris field. Several Imperial ships were there, collecting remains and using magnets to clean up the mess, attracting metal bits that could rupture hulls of unsuspecting ships. Naturally, the major visited them and personally examined what they had found. He returned with a big smile. "Coincidence? The salvage crews recovered another large amount of credits along with a couple of bodies, tentatively identified as down on their luck merchants, to be nice about them. More like space pirates. The presence of the credits is highly suspicious. I'm going to keep doing some more investigating on my own."

Lena felt rather helpless and useless. If she were whole, she knew precisely what she would do now. At last, she spoke up, "Major, check on the scrapping of those Gamelon-3 milking machines. Look for any discrepancies. I have a hunch, if our two were put into those kind of machines, then their kidnapers would have stolen a couple somehow, rather than to try to invent machines like those. I'll bet you that you'll find two or more have somehow vanished."

He smiled, "You sound like one of those Sector ID Ministers."

"I was before I lost my arms," she barked. He gave her a funny look and headed off to do as she asked.

A day later, he reported back. "Uncanny, Miss Lena. You were spot on. Indeed, three of the milking machines have gotten lost in transit to the recycling center. Not sure how we can track them from there though."

Lena advised, "Easy. Check the shipping records for any packages to be delivered here to Abeliard-6. If you find some, check on the size of the crates, just where they were to arrive, and then who picked them up."

"On it," he saluted her and left. She smiled. This was more like the responses she'd always received as the ID Minister.

She explained further. "All shipping is logged into computers somewhere. The automated cargo system requires such, so they can move the cargo to the proper ship for transport without human intervention. While they could easily disguise what the cargo is, they cannot hide the location to which the machines take it for loading. We might get something from that. We'll see. Patience rewards."

Two hours later, the major reported back. "Miss Lena was right again! Three crates were shipped here to Abeliard-6! We've traced who picked them up, and I've sent a boarding party down to check out that old warehouse." He left them with this optimistic note.

An hour later, the group landed at the warehouse. The major insisted they come see what was found for themselves. Already the two corpses were covered with a plastic sheet, awaiting the arrival of the local authorities. The major pointed out one of the disassembled milking machines, causing both Lena and Queen Altha to flinch at the nasty memories it brought back to them. Again, no one noticed Zarita's reactions. She was standing at the rear of the group, wisely.

"There are signs three crates were brought here. Again, there is the pile of credits, just as before. While we haven't found any direct signs that the teens were actually here, it is most probably, Emperor Kino," the major reported with some satisfaction.

"Indeed, I believe so. What are those cylinders?" Two security men were examining them. The conclusion was that they contained some form of liquid.

Lena bent over and took a sniff. "Damn! I hoped I'd never again smell that! It's the same liquid food we had, Queen Altha. But what are those giant cylinder things?"

The group fanned out and began examining all the piles of things in this abandoned warehouse. Nosing around, Drina made the next discovery. "Look at this, gang. It's a dummy encased in this orange stuff." They crowded around and looked at the strange object Drina had found in one corner.

A dummy's head protruded out of the top of the orange cylinder that encased the body of the dummy or so they presumed without cutting it open, and a dolly lift whose back had been altered. A new leg support had been welded to its back so that it sloped slightly backwards. "My god! Are they encased in something like this?" Bernardo exclaimed, crushed. "That's inhuman!"

"I'll kill whoever ordered this!" Lena swore with a vengeance.

Emperor Kino swallowed and took charge. "Let's remain calm and observe. We need to find more clues to know where they were taken from here. Major, continue looking for more missing transports and/or findings of destroyed ships, please. Are we getting anywhere on the money trail?" The major shook his head no.

Lena then suggested, "You could have your Sector ID Minister search all private communications looking for relevant key words. Surely, whoever orchestrated all this had to have sent numerous orders to all these men who are now dead. You might find out something that way. However, if this man is really clever, he would never have done that. If I were planning something like this, I would only deliver orders face to face, leaving no trail whatsoever. He's obviously done something like that with all these credits. Pig in a poke, but you could scan all bank records looking for a withdrawal for the amount of credits we've recovered so far, plus a little more."

"Since they were obviously transported from here, add another couple ten g's to the total," she added. He nodded and issued more orders, while the others searched further.

Lena thought some more, "You know, sooner or later, whoever has them are going to have to make or purchase more of that liquid food. Perhaps that can be tracked or traced. I think sooner or later we'll find them, gang."

"But how can they live — if they are like this?" Drina asked worriedly.

Lena shrugged her shoulders. She didn't want to say she thought it would be nearly impossible for them to live much of a life now. It was too depressing.

They hung around this world for several more days, hoping to gather more clues. However, nothing more turned up. When asked, Zarita continued to point to the direction where she felt the women now were located. Always, Emperor Kino noted it was towards the heart of the Imperium in the galaxy's central hub area.

With no further clues, Emperor Kino decided to head towards the hub. At last, he finally made up his mind to report all this to President Snarry Knoschy. If there were telepaths on the loose somewhere in the heart of the Imperium, he had to be alerted. He asked his assistant to make the connection for him, as he took his seat in front of the video camera of the comm center on the cruiser.

"Emperor Kino Sango of the Ataro Empire calling for President Snarry Knoschy. Urgent, top secret matter. Security code 10, please." Now he waited. He felt certain the president would take his call. After all, the Ataro System carried an awful lot of weight within the Imperium.

After a ten minute delay, the monitor activated. He saw the well-dressed president sitting behind his enormous desk. "Welcome Emperor Kino. To what do I owe the pleasure of speaking with you again? It has been quite some time since I presented you with your award for ending the war with the Federation. Code 10? Has something happened? Have they broken the treaty already? Over."

"Hello Mr. President. No, this has nothing to do with the Federation, I don't believe. Rather, it is a very serious matter that has happened to one of my queens." He outlined in detail what had happened, and what he had uncovered thus far. He talked for nearly a half hour before finally saying, "So if some of our enemies have done this and are making use of these women as telepathic spies, even your own office could be endangered. Over."

President Snarry listened to the tale; his face grew

redder and redder. He was very thankful for the long communications delay. Kino wouldn't be able to see his very visible reactions! That he had their two missing women was plainly obvious. Now, he suspected Legate Emeryk had somehow cleverly orchestrated all this! Damage control. Avoid collateral damage, he thought.

"I am so glad you chose to bring this to my attention. I have wonderful news for you. I have the missing telepaths here with me. Yes, in my office. Long story. We received a report from one of our field agents that some spies were trying to being in a pair of telepaths to Proxima Prime, just as you were warning me about a moment ago. We were able to track down their transport ship and met them when they landed. Yes, they put up quite a fight using d-guns. All were killed, I am happy to report. We rescued the women, but considering the condition they were in, I brought them here to my office. They insisted they were supposed to be Imperium Telepaths and begged me to let them help me. You know we still haven't tracked down who was responsible for killing the two Legates a while back. So I asked them to help me ferret out any spies within the presidential chain of command. Alas, they didn't find any telepaths in my employ nor the guilty party or parties. Yes, I have had my staff take very good care of the women, but they are — well, how can I put this, there's barely anything left of them. I'll have my staff meet you at the spaceport and bring you directly here to see your queen and her assistant. I must caution you, their condition is something beyond description. I'll make the full support of the Imperium available to help track down those who were behind this. Over."

A bit later, an elated Emperor Kino reported what he'd just heard to the Gang of Ten and relayed the message to Queen Isabella as well. "We've found them at last! Zarita, you are amazing; they were where you were pointing. Well done everyone. Of course, now comes the terrible part. They must be in absolutely horrific condition. Their minds might even have been irreparably damaged — what with the illegal psych behavior modifications. They might not even remember who they are. Brace yourselves for the very worst," he said very solemnly.

When Zarita retired for the night, she got her large crystal out and focused, activating all her many crystals. She focused on the frequency of Amy's crystal and reached out across the void, searching for that unique mind. *Hello. I am Zarita. Are you Amy?*

Yes, but wait a bit. I can't focus. Milking. Amy tried with all her might to send those brief thoughts over the overwhelming sensations flowing through her body. She lost it and could not even think. Later after nearly frantically sucking in some food for her starved body, she finally relaxed and began wondering who this Zarita telepath was. Would she try again?

Hello again. Has the machine stopped?

Yes, I am reading you clearly now. Are you on Proxima Prime? Who are you? I — we need help badly!

I am with the whole gang. Bernardo, Drina, Lena. All of them. We are with Emperor Kino and Queen Alta on his fancy cruiser. We are on our way to rescue you now. We've been tracking your kidnappers. We know what they've done to your bodies. It's worse than what was done to Lena and Queen Altha. But are you okay mentally that is? Kino was suggesting your minds would be destroyed too.

We are okay mentally. We broke through the psych man's behavior modifications. Please come help up. I don't know how we can live anymore. Not like this. Thank you and tell everyone that we're okay mentally that is.

Will do. See you in person soon. Bye.

After the intimate connection broke, Amy remembered what she wanted to ask. How could Zarita have made contact from so far off-world? She focused and tried to see if Zarita was somewhere on Proxima Prime. Nothing. Now, she had something to think about as she relayed what had happened to Jan.

How can she reach us off-world? Jan sent. This gave the two something to ponder, besides the immense relief that their rescue was close at hand.

"How can you reach her? She's way off-world from us?" Bernardo asked Zarita early the next morning. She'd just relayed her brief chat with Amy.

313

"You can do a whole lot more if you have enough crystals," she replied. "She's anxious to be rescued, but I don't see how she can even live the way they've been treated." She deftly changed the subject. They all began making suggestions.

Around noon, the cruiser began its descent onto Proxima Prime. The Gang of Ten watched out of the window in awe. Lena, however, felt pangs of homesickness. For years, she'd watched over this world, its guardian and security protector. Perhaps President Snarry would not recognize her. She dreaded the embarrassment if he should.

"Where's the planet? I only see monster buildings and flying things," Drina asked.

Lena replied, "The entire surface of the planet is below the concrete and steel surface that you are seeing. Miles below. The whole planet is nothing but one monster-sized city of hundreds of billions of people. That tallest building there is our destination, the Presidential Office. That oval one is the Senate, where Queen Isabella was at. Those flying things are called personal shuttles. People park them on their balconies outside their condos. To get anywhere on this world, you have to take one of them. They are all computer controlled so that there are no accidents, well rarely anyway." She pointed out a few more features, before they were too close to the giant spaceport.

"Plateau Grado is minuscule compared to this one!" Adrianna noted, very much impressed. "But how can they live without crop lands and herds and nut trees?"

"All of their food is either imported or grown in hydroponic tanks below the visible surface," Lena explained. "We are about to land. Can you buckle my belt, please?"

A few minutes later, the gang joined Emperor Kino, Queen Altha, their assistants, and the major with his small security detachment. Zarita watched how the two managed to descend the ramp onto the tarmac by taking very careful steps. She emulated their moves, but Nita was right beside her and slipped her arm around her, whispering, "Got you."

President Snarry and a group of his own security men stepped out of the giant building personally to greet the party. "Emperor Kino. So good to see you in person. Regrettably, I wish the circumstances were far better. If only you had called sooner," he began, returning the emperor's bow and then that of the queen's.

"Couldn't be helped. We only finally figured it all out just before I called you. Such a tragedy. Any further news on who might have been responsible? Any chance of tracing who those men were working for or to whom they were planning to deliver the two telepaths?" he asked, as they made their slow way inside the building.

"Not yet. I am not holding out much hope. We've been trying to discover that since we had the shoot-out with those men. Mind you, there's not been a shoot-out on Proxima Prime in recent memory. Rather wild, if I say so myself. Of course, I was safely behind a blast shield." He chatted away, while leading them to a large shuttle.

A few minutes later, they entered the hundred-story office building. Again, all save Lena, were very much impressed, especially with the "moving small room," as Adrianna called the elevator. They got off on the top floor, and he led them into a side room where he kept the two telepaths when they were not needed.

"Oh my god, Amy?" Bernardo gushed as he ran over to his sister. Only her head protruded from the orange cylinder. Tubes came out her nostrils and a big plug was in her mouth, a feeding tube dropped down to the pressurized canister of liquid food. Tears trickled down Amy's face. The gang swarmed around the two.

Get us out of this if you can somehow, please, Amy begged him.

He turned and relayed her request, as the emperor and Queen Altha nodded to both women. President Snarry spoke up, "I've had my doctors working on this. There are some complications to be solved. None of us are sure what we'll find when we somehow cut them out of this mess. I wanted to wait until you were all here before trying anything, just in case, well you know." He didn't have to finish his thought. They all knew what he meant. Once removed from this contraption, the two might not even be able to live.

He added, "If you are ready, we can take them down to

the medical lab and begin to see what can be done for them."
Bernardo wheeled Amy, while Ben wheeled Jan, following the
president and the others. Soon they entered a spacious, white,
sterile medical laboratory, fully equipped to handle any
emergency that might befall the president of the Imperium.

They allowed the doctors and technicians to work on
the two women, while they discussed all the events and
findings with President Snarry, and he in turn told them about
the firefight. He even played a video that had been taken of
their "rescue." "Oh my, you weren't exaggerating about the
fight!" Emperor Kino commented.

With three men working on each woman, it took nearly
an hour to get their bodies finally cut out of the dried foam
encasement, revealing their naked bodies with various things
protruding from their bottoms. As they then disconnected the
rest, both women needed to be physically supported. Their
legs gave out on them. Further, the damage was significant.
Their bodies were covered with a nasty looking rash and
worse. Both were carried over to the waiting medical
machines, and their strange boots removed, revealing their leg
stumps. Bernardo gagged, fighting to control his own reaction.

"Dear god!" whispered Queen Altha.

"I'll kill whomever did this to them!" Lena swore.

"Lena? Is that you, Lena Squire?" President Snarry
asked. "I didn't recognize you with your long hair." He politely
didn't comment on her empty shoulders.

"Yes, it's me, president. No arms, thanks to the men on
Gamelon-3. I swear I'll find whoever ordered this mutilation
and kill them!"

"You might have to wait your turn on executing them. I
want first dibs," President Snarry countered.

"Can they be cured?" asked Drina. "That's what's
important right now."

One of the doctors looked up, glanced at the president,
and then answered, "Recovering their voices now. The rash is
the worst we've ever seen, but give the machine time. I believe
they will make a full recovery in an hour or so. The group
waited patiently, chatting quietly among themselves, until the
machines finished their work. Meanwhile, two wheel chairs

arrived. Once the machines finished their work, both women were lifted out, covered in hospital gowns, and placed in the wheel chairs. During this, everyone could see that their rash and other injuries were healed. Pinkish skin now covered their bodies.

Next, trays of a light lunch arrived, and Bernardo and Ben fed them the first semisolid food that they had in months. That done, President Snarry took them all back up to his office, sitting himself behind his mammoth desk. Aides had brought in chairs for the rest of the party.

"Okay, I guess the question is now what do we do for the two telepaths of yours, Emperor Kino. In the weeks that they've been here, they've worked hard for me. I can now rest assured we don't have any telepath spies within my administration. I was terrified I had one or more. I'm able to sleep nights now. I must insist they have fair compensation for their work for me."

Jan looked at Lena and took a gamble. *Lena. Ask him about the top secret cloning project. Maybe he can clone us each a new body. That ought to be a fair recompense. Without it, Amy and I can't go on like this.*

I thought that project was declared illegal years ago. Is it still going?

We probed him. It was disbanded but resurrected during the war. They are trying to make a bunch of identical super-fighters or something.

Lena spoke up, "President Snarry. You can do more than that. We all know they can't live like this. Who wants to be a helpless cripple for the rest of their long lives? Besides, Ashford-5 is a primitive world and cannot possibly support them with the kind of care they'll need. Might I suggest you clone them a pair of new bodies?"

His face flushed. "That was declared illegal years ago."

"Yes, but the powers you were given during the war supersede that, and we both know it. You've had some good success with it so far. It's only right you and the Imperium give these poor women a chance at a better life," Lena demanded.

"How did you know about that?" he asked, his face flushing. "Well, this is top secret, but you are right. The

Imperium ought to do what is right for the Ataro System's queen and her assistant." President Snarry was flustered. He knew that he was facing one of the most powerful men in the Imperium, but one who almost never interfered in Imperium politics of affairs, save ending the recent war. With the secret project out of the bag now, he needed desperately to appease the emperor. If Kino went to the full Senate and told them about this whole nasty affair, the political repercussions could well spell the end of his career. If he went public, matters would be far worse than that. He also knew he was following the advice of Legate Emeryk. They had held some serious discussions several weeks before.

Legate Emeryk had pointed out that though the telepaths were performing as desired, their physical upkeep was a bit much. They were also severely restricted on how they could actually use the women. Field work, for example, was an impossibility. Already, President Snarry had taken a lot of flak by having everyone in his administration report to his office to be secretly checked out. "Let's clone them, and see if the clones will work for us freely," Legate Emeryk had suggested, adding, "if they won't or cause problems, we kill the clones."

Already that project had born fruit. Duplicate bodies of Amy and Jan were nearly complete, as he spoke. Well, they had gallons of the women's DNA, and more could be made. He had to save face and extricate himself from all culpability. President Snarry smiled, "It would be my honor to do just that. Already, I'd been thinking along those lines of somehow being able to give them a new life. After all, emperor, if it's within our powers to do this, we owe it to them. However, now that the war is over, this must remain a secret between us. If others find out about this, both you and I will be ousted and brought up on criminal charges."

"This can be done for them?" Emperor Kino asked very much surprised.

"I believe so. If we do this, I must swear each and every one of you to absolute secrecy in this matter." Everyone hastily swore, and President Snarry made sure their oaths were captured on his surveillance camera, as an added insurance policy. He then said, "Why don't you take them to one of my guest suites below, until their clone bodies are ready for them? It shouldn't be more than a few days at most."

A while later, Bernardo and Ben wheeled the two women into the fancy guest suites. Adrianna hastily put each woman's crystal around their necks, bringing a smile to their faces. Then, she and Nita took off to find them something better to wear than the hospital gowns.

Jan focused and began a thorough search for spy devices. She found five and disabled them by frying their circuits. "There, we can talk. No more eavesdropping."

"How did you find out about the cloning?" Lena wanted to know.

Jan explained, adding, "We probed him for all kinds of data on their plans for Ashford-5. In case we don't survive this, you guys have to know this! Of course, they are planning to return to Ashford-5 and rebuild the fuel refinery on our moon, Palidez. They are waiting on the Senate's choice of a new governor. What's bad is that, when they get back to Tierra, they are going to demand we begin to provide telepaths for Imperium work. They'll insist we appoint a new senator. What's really bad is that they're going to try to make us accept a change in status to that of an Open World and accept all kinds of Imperium technology. You've got to warn everyone back home if we don't make it!"

"I promise we will, Jan," Bernardo swore. Hastily the others did as well. Jan finally relaxed.

"I can't believe how helpless we are like this. We can't even stand up now," Amy complained.

Emperor Kino then asked, "Queen Amy, Jan, what can you remember about your abduction? We still want to find the person or persons who orchestrated this kidnaping and mutilation of you two."

Amy sighed. "Emperor, not much. We were unconscious until we woke up on the transport ship with the men, who shot it out with the president's security men when we landed."

Jan added, "Our servants brought in some strange flowers that knocked us out. Amy was already asleep. That's all I can add. We've thoroughly scanned President Snarry. He's not the most ethical person, somewhat devious, but then aren't all politicians of the Imperium like that? Anyway, he really doesn't know any more than he's been saying about it. Some field agent sent him a warning about it. They investigated and found it might be true and sent the security men to meet our transport, just in case the warning was correct. He's been as kind as possible to us, under the circumstances."

A curious Emperor Kino inquired, "Queen Amy, what's going to happen with you once this clone body is ready? Will we need to retrain that new Amy? If so, I'll make darn sure that something like this never happens again!"

Amy smiled. "If the bodies really are clones of us, then Jan and I can slip out of these and into those. We'll remember everything. It's us, after all. We are not these bodies, as pathetic as they've become now."

He looked confused. "What will happen to your bodies now?"

"We'll see that they die right away. We're all really immortal spiritual beings. We're not our bodies, like your wise sages tell you," Amy began explaining it in terms the emperor could grasp, based upon their own cultural beliefs.

"Then, you have a way for a person to know their true natures?" he asked. "As you know, our wisest men have been searching for that answer for millennia."

"Yes, we do. We call it therapy. I know, Emperor Kino, I will try to have someone from Tierra come to Winno-3 and show you all what we mean. If you like, that is," she added hastily.

"Yes, yes, that would be amazing beyond belief!" he replied. They chatted about the spiritual nature of man for some time. Eventually, the men stopped to feed them their supper. All ate there in their suite, not daring to leave either woman alone. Safety in numbers, Lena suggested. She still didn't trust the president or others around here.

During the long two-day wait, everyone lent a hand with the two women. Unable to stand, they had to be wheel around and carefully lifted onto the stool or into bed or onto the couches. Neither Amy nor Jan wanted to use their telekinetic skills around the emperor or queen. After these two days, both of the rulers saw just how hopeless the teen's lives would be if this clone business failed.

At last, President Snarry had them all come to the ninety-third floor. Everyone gasped. There on two cots lay two completely whole duplicates of Amy and Jan, being artificially kept alive by some equipment. "As promised. Of course, I've no idea if they'll retain their memories or such when they're aroused. How do you wish to proceed? Wake them up?" he asked. Clearly, such matters were beyond his knowledge. All he knew about this project were the results on the super-soldiers.

"Wake the bodies," Amy replied from her wheel chair. The medical doctors did as she asked. The two bodies coughed for a minute. Amy and Jan slipped out of theirs and into these new ones, forcing them to gasp for air, just to make sure that they had a secure grip on them. Even though both bodies were quite naked, both Amy and Jan began to flex their arms and legs, getting used to the new but same bodies. Jan stood up but found her legs were a little wobbly. Amy discovered hers were too. Satisfied, she sent, *Okay, Jan. Let's fry the other one's brains.*

While everyone was watching them stretch, their mutilated bodies passed away quietly in their chairs. "Okay, you can all stop staring at my naked body now," Amy said rather tartly, causing embarrassed laughs from all quarters. *No jokes either, brother,* she sent Bernardo.

"Oh, these are dead," Emperor Kino exclaimed, noticing the mutilated bodies. Quickly, the medical attendants removed the corpses. After that, Bernardo and Ben lifted the two and put them back into the wheel chairs, covering them with a couple of hospital gowns.

"So are you still my Queen Amy?" Emperor Kino asked.

"Yes still me."

"Pardon me, but I must ask you a number of questions to verify you've not forgotten all of your queen's training," he said humbly.

"Time enough for that. I'm hungry," Amy replied, while Adrianna carefully placed her crystal around her neck, having retrieved it from the corpse. Nita did the same for Jan.

"Excuse me, but Queen Amy, might I inquire if you still have your telepathy?" President Snarry asked her.

Sure do, she sent, bringing a smile to his face.

"Yes, she does," he explained to the emperor. He seemed greatly relieved in telling the ruler this, though.

"Excellent. President Snarry, the Ataro Empire will not forget what you have done for these women and our queen. We have taken up too much of your precious time already. With your permission, we'll return to my cruiser and head for home."

"Yes, of course. I'm only glad that this has worked out so very well for all of us. I'll see their payments for their telepathic services are sent to you, and you can see that they are forwarded to them," President Snarry answered.

An hour later, they were safely back on the cruiser. After liftoff, both Emperor Kino and Queen Altha quizzed Amy for several hours. "Yes, again, I officially proclaim you Queen Amy Valen Gervasi," Emperor Kino finally said. "Forgive me, but I had to make sure that you retained all your knowledge."

"I understand. What is bothering me right now is am I going to have to have my arms removed right away and my feet altered? I've undergone quite a lot recently," Queen Amy asked.

Emperor Kino smiled. "Queen Amy, no one should ever have to undergo what you and your assistant have endured and suffered. I can see you are still recovering and your legs are not yet working properly. I cannot find it in my heart to make you endure more just now. I give you my permission to retain them for now. I hope in the future, once you have fully recovered from your hideous ordeal, you'll once again honor our fundamental principle of tempering great power with physical restraints."

"Thank you, Emperor Kino. I appreciate it. Right now, my legs are still too shaky to trust standing by myself."

He smiled. "And now, I must go and relay this good news to your mother, Queen Isabella. You've held your head up high through all this, like a true queen of the Ataro Empire. You've made Queen Altha and me very proud of you." He bowed and left them with their friends.

Jan said, "Whew. That's a good break. I can't walk right yet either. I can't wait to get home. Say, what's all this about giant germanium crystals?"

Nita laughed and began filling them in on what all they had been doing in their absence. Both Amy and Jan appreciated hearing about "normal" things once more.

Later, they learned the emperor had ordered his cruiser to use top speed to get them safely home in barely three days. Queen Isabella, Hernando, and Gabriella were there at the fence waiting them with their carriage. She had tears in her eyes as she met them and pressed her body into the emperors, whispering, "Thank you for saving my daughter and Jan."

Chapter 18 Other Plans

From a side door and with great relief, Legate Emeryk watched Emperor Kino's cruiser lift off Proxima Prime. He had followed President Snarry and now joined him in his shuttle. "Well, this has worked out far better than either of us could have anticipated," he said quietly to the president.

"How so? It's been mostly a disaster," President Snarry commented snidely, still smarting from all he'd been forced to do over this telepath mess.

"First, you've gotten certainty the telepath assassins are not among any of your people. Second, we learned some very valuable lessons about these incredibly powerful telepaths. They can be physically constrained and forced to work for us, though the cost to us for their upkeep is rather prohibitive. Third, we know the cloning process works on them, as well as our soldiers. Fourth, you have Emperor Kino owing you a very big favor. Fifth, he has no choice but to keep your cloning experiments a secret now. He'll never dare divulge that. Doing so would also condemn himself to execution."

"Well, I do like the first and last bits, but I'm not sure all this was worth it."

"Have faith, Snarry. We have lots of those women's DNA now. Gallons of it. Already, Amy-2 and Jan-2 are being prepared. This time, we'll have a pair of telepaths who belong exclusively to us. With some behavior modification, we'll guarantee their total loyalty to you. Now, we can manufacture all the Class V telepaths you could possibly desire, Mr. President. So I would call this mission a total success, perhaps beyond our wildest dreams. Besides, nothing can ever be traced back to you. You were, as you have said, completely blameless. Despite all their sleuthing, nothing has been or will ever be traced back to me. We're completely safe. We should be able to check out our handiwork next week."

"Well, that's saying something. All that we could desire? I can desire a lot of telepaths, Legate Emeryk. Think of all the intelligence they could gather. Place one on each of the key worlds. Incredible. Yes, let me know when they are ready," President Snarry said with a smile, thinking that perhaps it wasn't such a disaster after all.

Two weeks later, he stood in the medical lab, as the doctors awoke Amy-2 and Jan-2. Legate Emeryk stood proudly at his side, watching the two women awaken. Both looked terribly confused. After the doctors got them oriented, President Snarry spoke up. "Well, Amy, Jan, I'm pleased to meet you. I'm your president. You are the first two women of our Imperial Telepath Division."

"Hello President Snarry. Thanks. What's a telepath?" Amy-2 asked.

A week later, the doctors injected a poison into both women. The great experiment had failed. Well not exactly. They had successfully cloned another pair of Amy and Jan's, but that's what they had: two identical human bodies. Neither had any idea what telepathy was. Neither had any education; worse, both were effectively morons. After disposing of the corpses, the carefully stored DNA samples were also destroyed. Perhaps, sticking to powerful fighters was a better plan after all, the president thought.

"Don't worry. The Senate will be demanding Ashford-5 send some telepaths to work for the Imperium, Legate Emeryk. So one way or the other, we will have our volunteers," President Snarry explained. "By the way, I'd like your opinion of my choice for the next Ashford-5 governor, Miss Rae Mc Greggor. Here's her dossier." He handed Legate Emeryk a red folder, marked top secret.

He read over the report of her career thus far and glanced at her ID photo. "Looks promising. We should interview her first."

"Excellent. I've asked her to be here around one this afternoon. I'll certainly value your opinion; after all, you had a long stint as their acting governor while you were that sector's ID Minister." Emeryk smiled, recalling those often-ambivalent times.

Rae Mc Greggor was an unmarried fifty year old woman, who looked twenty-five. She was short, barely five feet. Unattractive, she always dressed in men's suits; her tiny bosom was barely visible. Bossy, hard-nosed, blunt, no nonsense, something of a bully, Rae always got her way with others. That's why she had risen among the ranks. She'd started her career as an ID Field Agent. She was well-muscled and a master of several forms of martial arts. Few ever dared to challenge her. The last man, who had sparred with her, left with his arm broken in three places. Her skin was a light yellow. Her hair and eyes, a light brown. Her hair was cut shorter than many men's. She'd left the ID sector primarily because a woman of her appearance seldom fit into any society, even that of her own world Abelard-2. She was just too abrasive.

She'd then entered the diplomatic corps, but that had not worked out either. It was her way or not at all, the wrong attitude for a "diplomat." Rae finally found her niche as a governor. Already, she'd been very successful on two other postings, forcing the locals to bend to her will. That the president of the entire Imperium wanted to interview her for another position impressed her. It was obvious to her that finally those in power had noticed her incredible skills and natural talent. She looked at her image in the mirror, adjusting her tie slightly. Her brown tweed suit was perfectly pressed. Her men's shoes, nicely polished. She'd seen to that the night before. The only piece of jewelry she ever wore was one small jade broach that had belonged to her long dead grandmother, whom she had adored as a child.

Satisfied, she left her condo and stepped into her shuttle. A short while later, she stepped out before the towering Presidential Office, where an attendant took her shuttle for her. As she walked briskly and confidently into the building, an aide spotted her. "Miss Rae Mc Greggor. This way to the elevators. President Snarry Knoschy and Legate Emeryk Donat are expecting you." She nodded, not deigning to speak to such a lowly aide, as this man must be, a door greeter, following him into the elevator.

She stepped out onto the hundredth floor and followed the man into the president's main office, noticing the aide quickly stepped back outside, closing the door behind her. Her sharp eyes took in the scene rapidly. She marched briskly up to the overly large desk, knowing President Snarry must feel insecure to have to have such a larger than life sized desk. She extended her hand, ignoring Legate Emeryk for the moment. "Governor Rae Mc Greggor, sir," she barked, almost as if she was a soldier, extending her hand.

She shook his firmly, until he just barely flinched, and sat down, while nodding to the lesser man, this Legate. "You sent for me sir?" she said calmly.

"Yes, indeed we have. Legate Emeryk Donat. We have an important governor post to fill and are considering you for this one. Have you read of the proposed assignment on Ashford-5?" President Snarry asked politely.

"Yes, Mr. President, what little of it that was not marked classified. A Closed World. Prime producer of our valuable fuel. Something of a telepathic society or some such nonsense. Out on the rim. Primitive culture over all. Strange manner of dress and even stranger ornaments. Not much of an assignment, sir."

"I see. Yes, much about it is classified. If you are chosen, I assure you that you'll have full access to all information we have on that world. So tell me, you are not intimidated by these native telepaths prying on your secret thoughts?" he asked curiously.

"Hardly. Look into my mind, and you'll see precisely what I'm saying. Period. End of story. Besides, it's all mumbo jumbo, by and large," she replied tartly.

His eyebrows rose. "Oh, I assure you their telepathy is quite real. Now then, have you read the rather verbose and extensive reports on Ashford-5 filed by its previous Governor Konrad Burkhardt?"

"I have sir," she answered briskly and unemotionally.

"I see. So what do you think of his theories about going native to get the natives to agree with demands? He won the Top Governor of the Century award for his works. He's racked up an impressive list of conquests of primitive worlds."

Is he attempting to needle me, she thought? "Bunch of poppy cock! Signs of a weak man. Having to stoop to pretending to look like aborigines so they will listen to you — a wimp, sir," she barked. Rae always said precisely what she was thinking — what her honest opinion was. She was not about to cease now, just because he was the President of the Imperium.

"So you don't intend to go native on us?" he half-teased her.

"Hardly sir," she said quite sternly and forcefully.

"I see you are something of a martial arts expert," he changed the topic.

"Black belts in five disciplines, sir," she answered dryly.

"Good. So if you are attacked by a man with a sword — that would not bother you? D-guns are outlawed on this world at the moment," he asked.

"Hardly sir. Must be a coward to have to hide behind a sword, sir," she said with an audible trace of contempt in her voice.

"Very good. How would you describe your style of governorship?" Legate Emeryk asked, anticipating her answer.

"No nonsense. Straight to the point. Not open to discussion. What I say goes. They do it. Period," she barked straightforwardly, finally turning her steely eyes upon this second in command, but only briefly.

Legate Emeryk wasn't finished, though. He drilled his next question into her, "How do you intend to handle the telepaths with their powers trying to force you to change your mind?"

"Strong, fit bodies are immovable, just as with a rock-solid mind. Bring them on, sir," she decided at least to acknowledge his presence. Of course, his question was pure balderdash. No one could force another to change their mind, not when they were as solid and determined as she always was. Silly question, she thought.

Brash, determined, and very foolish, Legate Emeryk thought. He smiled disarmingly and then said, "Governor Konrad Burkhardt published his set of guidelines, which suggested to gain the understanding and cooperation of others, especially primitives, first you need to build some degree of liking, of affinity, between them and yourself. He went on to say that was best achieved by dressing in native apparel and adopting native customs. According to Konrad, that then built some reality between the natives and you. From there, given a halfway decent ULAT script, real communications can then proceed to an understanding between you and the natives. What is your opinion of his theories, and how do you intend to achieve the objectives of your assignment there, given that as yet those have not been spelled out by President Snarry?"

"Silly poppycock, sir. Wishy-washy methods. Who the hell cares whether the primitives like you or not? That's completely irrelevant. You must be strong," she pounded a fist into her other hand, "forceful, even domineering if needed. Simply press your agenda forward. My will is stronger than mere primitives. They do what I tell them to do. Simple. No back talk. No discussion. Just do it, and we'll get along. Force. You simply show the primitives that you mean business. They'll fall in line. Who cares whether they like you or not? Irrelevant. Get in, get the job done, get out. Quick, expedient, highly efficient. Let the mousy Konrads of the Imperium come in and play their games with the primitives later on, if they so desire." She'd just said far more than she was accustomed to saying, a woman of action, and of few words. Well, he provoked me, she justified and shut up.

"Very well, Miss Rae Mc Greggor. Will you please wait outside in the hall while we make our decision? I assure you that we'll be swift."

"Of course, Mr. President," she nodded to him, rose, and again shook his hand a bit too firmly for his liking. Standing perfectly erect, she fairly marched out of his office.

"Well, what do you think?" President Snarry asked. "She's certainly a handful, despite her size. Determination and will are not lacking. But how will she hold up against the telepaths?"

Legate Emeryk rubbed both hands over his face. "Personally, I would be hard pressed to force her to change her mind. I can only hope the telepaths will have as much difficulty doing that as I would. Certainly, she ought to be able to achieve one of the three objectives easily, forcing them to send a new senator to the Senate. A steel-will might be what's needed to obtain the other two objectives. I am only slightly hesitant. There is no denying that Governor Konrad, despite

329

his faults, was highly effective in achieving his objectives in short order, more so than any other governor in centuries. Still, we both know the solid wall she'll encounter from the telepaths on the other two objectives. Perhaps with her attitude and determination, she can succeed. We don't have anyone better at this time, do we?"

"Afraid not. There are some up and coming young trainees, but good lord, I don't want to put them into this nasty pickle barrel," President Snarry replied. "Okay then, I'll make the appointment now." He buzzed his intercom and his aide opened the door. Miss Rae Mc Greggor marched back in and took her seat.

"After due consideration, Miss Rae Mc Greggor, I am officially appointing you as the next governor of Ashford-5. Presently, you'll have total access to all the records of that world. Now then, as you know, we'll be reopening our extremely valuable fuel refinery on one of their moons. When the fleet returns to that world, the many missed yearly lease payments will go with you. That ought to smooth the way for your acceptance."

"Thank you, sir. You can count on me to get the job done. What precisely are the objectives that must be accomplished and the time frame for achieving them?" she barked.

"There are three. First, they must send a new senator off to the Senate by October at the very latest. You should be there by July, Ashford-5 time. Second, they are to send along ten of their telepaths to serve as Imperium Telepaths here on Proxima Prime. Men, women, we don't care. Again, the due date for their departure is October. Third, they must accept a change in their world's status from that of a Closed World to an Open World, followed by a rapid importing of our valuable Imperium technology. I'll give you until next spring to make that happen, considering how downright nasty their winters are on that miserable world."

"Is that all? Seems easy enough. Count on me. Have them for you on time, Mr. President," she barked in her usual manner. She didn't add she was quite relieved at these very simple demands. She had been a little concerned that the orders would have been far more difficult to achieve. It was wholly inconceivable to her that any world would not jump at the chance to have the magnificent Imperium technologies for their worlds. The need for a senator was plainly obvious. If they did indeed have these telepaths, they would jump at the chance to come to the most advanced planet in the galaxy to work and make a small fortune in no time. This was entirely too easy. What was the catch, she wondered.

"Yes, that is all. Your contact will be one Queen Isabella Valen Gervasi, who is located at the Imperial Castle, built on the very southeastern corner of the spaceport. She conducts or hosts the frequent meetings of the various leaders of Ashford-5's kingdoms. She was their senator before the abandonment of the rim planets during the war. As far as your team goes, you may pick them. Most of those who used to work on Ashford-5 have long ago been reassigned. However, if you should desire one or more of them, perhaps I can pull some strings," President Snarry replied.

He rose, and she did likewise. "Good luck. Your ship leaves in four days." He again shook her hand, grimacing a little from her vice-grip. She marched erect out of his office, heading for her own temporary quarters.

Once there, she tried out her new pass codes and discovered she now had access to volumes of reports! "Well, I certainly need a computer whiz with all this. A geologist would be ideal. I might be able to open up some new mineral deposits and make something useful out of this backwards planet after all. Gosh that much snow? Okay, a meteorologist is a must. Hum, they mostly had Rigel-3 personnel there for the past three centuries. It is time for a change. I hate looking up at those skinny, tall, grey folks! Probably ought to have a good doctor on hand. Lord knows what primitive viruses I'll encounter. Hate getting sick. Interferes with work.

She stopped looking over the voluminous reports and opened up the available personnel files looking for a computer technician, a doctor, a meteorologist, and a competent geologist. She found the latter three relatively quickly. All three had outstanding backgrounds working on primitive worlds. She fired off emails to the three outlining her request to have them report to her for an interview. The computer technician position was more difficult to fill. It seems that as of this time, what with the war and all, they were in great demand everywhere, repairing damaged systems. She did fine one promising candidate and emailed her as well.

Within an hour, she had acceptances from the first three, but the computer technician posed a problem. She would consider the assignment but only if her mate, an archaeologist, would also be assigned along with her. *What the hell do I need an old bones digger for?* She very nearly deleted the email and continued to search for another one, when she thought, *oh what the heck. On this primitive world, anything to make her happy. I need her skills.* She fired back a return email agreeing to her terms. Within minutes, the computer technician also agreed to meet with her.

Around one two days later, Miss Rae Mc Greggor marched into a temporary meeting room, where the five candidates had already arrived and been seated. As she entered, they all rose, sitting when she did. *Good, respect. We're getting off on the right foot.* "Welcome. I am Governor Rae Mc Greggor. The primitive world that I mentioned is called Ashford-5. First, introduce yourselves please, and we'll get started."

"Carla Childa, my mate, Elfe Heilwig. Computer technician, archaeologist." The two women were from Garsh-4. Both were twenty-eight. Carla was blonde with blue eyes; Elfe had black hair and black eyes, reminiscent of those from Rigel-3. Rae suspected Elfe might have some of their blood in her ancestry. Both women looked fit, which pleased her.

"Doctor Becktold Hardt of Grund-3. I look forward to this assignment. I just received a prize for the discovery and cure of a new, virulent strain of the cocophylus virus on Bela-9." Bit cocky, Rae thought of the twenty-five year old doctor with brownish skin, black hair, and moustache. "I look forward to handling all your medical needs. Quite competent." Rae smiled; she liked his attitude.

"Henkel Smith, meteorologist." He was thirty-five and from Ganemon-4. His skin was quite black, as were his hair and eyes.

Rae asked, "Ganemon-4 is a hot world. Ashford-5 is a frigid one, if I read the reports right. Will you be all right with this?"

"Aye. Bundle up," he replied tartly. She smiled and looked at the remaining member.

"Jaques de Marie, Ettine-3. Geologist. They use horses for traveling. I'm a good rider and should be able to adapt to their environment well." He was thirty-nine, tall and fit, she noted, a rugged type person.

Satisfied with her selections, she began to outline their new assignment. "I know this is terribly short notice and all that, but can't be helped. Leave tomorrow at six p.m. Have your things at station 35942 by then. I've cleared your access codes. Of course, you'll be restricted to the reports that are relevant to your positions. Questions? Good. Let's get packing." She dismissed them. "Oh, word with you, Miss Carla," she barked.

"Yes, governor?" the blonde woman asked politely.

"The reports are voluminous. I need a program soon. I enter a few key words. Program spits out relevant sections from the mountains of reports. Need it shortly after landing. Problem?"

"No, I'll work on it while we're en route."

"Excellent." Seeing that Rae had nothing further to say, she turned and joined Elfe.

"This is going to be an interesting assignment," Elfe whispered. "No one has done any kind of archaeology on Ashford-5, not in the three centuries of occupation."

Her mate grinned, flashing her white teeth. "Go for it. Perhaps I can find some clues about where to start in all those records."

"Good god! This is daytime!" exclaimed Rae, looking out of the window of the deep space transport, as they began their descent onto Plateau Grado. All were gazing at the dull planet with its even duller red-orange sun, high in the afternoon sky. It was the third of July 1291 on Ashford-5. The aliens had returned to Tierra at long last.

Chapter 19 The Return of the Aliens

"Well, this is a sight that's hard to miss!" Queen Isabella declared. She, the Gang of Ten, and nearly everyone else at the Imperial Castle and Tower were standing outside looking up at the enormous fleet of silver colored ships descending from the skies onto Plateau Grado. Many were still circling the planet, waiting their turn to land. Without a control tower in operation, they had to land manually, careful to avoid setting down too close to other ships.

Within minutes, every tower on Tierra knew of their arrival, though many others witnessed the flotilla of spaceships flying overhead. Even the Underground stepped out onto the streets of Brom to get a glimpse of the huge fleet circling the skies. Impressive," Bart commented, "but big trouble." All the Underground knew just what new demands were soon going to be made of Tierra. So did nearly all the other towers and kingdom leaders. Jan had been quite thorough in relaying just what the Imperium was going to demand of them when they returned. She didn't want everyone taken by complete surprise. She'd given them a couple of weeks advance notice. Now trouble had definitely arrived.

Amy commented to Jan, "I sure am glad Luisa and Jamie gave us our therapy as soon as we got back. Here comes real trouble."

"Hey, I am just thankful Emperor Kino didn't make you lose your arms again," Jan replied.

"Well, he did suggest I lose them before I take office when mom retires," Amy pointed out. "I get a respite it seems. Mom is taking it in stride."

"I know; you compromised." Jan meant that Amy had gone ahead and gotten her body modified to wear the requisite pipe corset and toe shoes like her mother wore. Zarita had been quick to let everyone in the Gang know that she was pleased to have someone else who was as hobbled as she was. She didn't feel quite so left out now, since she and Amy both wore the restrictive corsets and toe shoes. Of course, she sported the huge lip plates, the only one of the Gang who currently did, but they all knew Zarita held out hopes the others would one day join her in looking their best as befitting nobility.

Jan asked somewhat rhetorically, "Wonder how soon your mom will get a visit from the new governor, whoever that is?"

"Soon, I would expect. They want some major concessions that they are not likely to get. At least I hope so, or our world will be destroyed," Amy replied. "Of course, with all these giant crystals around now, we may well destroy ourselves before then."

"Well, mom will be pleased," Nita commented. "Now she can get in more bolts of cloth and more stem cell reloads for all the medical machines of Elegant Fashions Inc." Amy smiled, wondering where Tierra would be without those machines. She was quite cynical after her recent ordeal.

"Hey, let's take a pool on how many days it takes for this new governor to contact mom," Bernardo suggested. "Dibs on three days."

"You are on, buddy, I'll take two," Lena added, "but what's the bet going to be, buster?"

"Whoever wins doesn't have to do any camp chores on the next trip that mom assigns us," he replied.

"Okay, I'm in. I'll take one day," Drina giggled. Soon the others joined in choosing the remaining days. Adrianna ended up with ten days. Drina added, "But today doesn't count. He comes tomorrow, I win." Everyone laughed.

"Kids! This is incredibly serious," Queen Isabella scolded them.

"Lighten up mom," Bernardo countered.

Lena won the bet. Around ten on the second full day after their arrival, the new governor came calling, accompanied by her new handpicked staff and a dozen security guards, who all were Rigel-3 men, the tall, thin, grey aliens.

Governor Rae Mc Greggor marched up to the huge wooden gates and knocked loudly. "Governor Rae Mc Greggor to see Queen Isabella Valen Gervasi right now!" she barked to the gate man, who opened the gates, motioning for her party to enter. His crystal emitted a brief soft glow, while he led them across the stone courtyard and into the castle section, depositing them in her throne room or Great Hall. The Gang of Ten dashed to form a line behind the throne, while Hernando led Isabella to her throne and adjusted her hair for her. Gabriella stood beside her mother, in case she needed anything.

Governor Rae marched straight into the throne room, glancing first at the line of teens and then the obvious queen. She did flinch slightly as she saw the pathetic shape the queen was in. She marched right up to her and barked, "Governor Rae Mc Greggor. My staff, Carla Childa, computer technician, Jaques de Marie, geologist, Henkel Smith, meteorologist, Doctor Becktold Hardt, physician, Elfe Heilwig, archaeologist."

Sensing the woman was finished, Queen Isabella introduced herself, her younger daughter Gabriella, Hernando, and then her twins. "Queen Amy and Bernardo, my twins." She went on down the line, introducing the others.

"So these are your staff?"

"My kids and their friends. On behalf of all Tierra, I would like to welcome you to our world," she said graciously.

"Accepted. Now then, to business. Back lease payments have arrived. How soon can your people take delivery of them?" Governor Rae barked tersely.

"Well, it takes time for them to bring their wagons here to pick up the loads."

"Primitive transportation. Well, that'll soon change. Okay, two weeks. Exchange City. Have the wagons here, or we will dump the ores onto the streets. Now then, changes. You need to elect a replacement senator for the Imperium Senate. They have to depart no later than the first of October."

"That's going to be a problem," Isabella countered, sizing up this new governor.

"Hardly. Elect someone pronto," Governor Rae barked.

"Look at me. This is what they did to our previous senator. Cut off my arms, fused my neck, encased my neck like this, gave me these lip plates, cut up my vocal cords, and much more. They also did it to my two late wives. No one here wants to go anywhere near your damnable Senate!"

Governor Rae glared at Queen Isabella. "Unfortunate. Nevertheless, you *will* have a new senator ready to depart by the first of October! If you can't pick someone, then I'll pick someone. Now then, the Imperium demands that Ashford-5 sends ten telepaths to Proxima Prime to become official Imperium Telepaths. They are scheduled to depart on the first of October as well. Chose them or I will. Starting now, Ashford-5 is going to be an Open World. I'll bring the marvelous Imperium technology to this backward dump of a planet soon. Now then, in keeping with this new policy, some of my people will begin surveying the planet. My geologist, in particular, will be traveling all over your world."

"I am sorry, but I do not have the authority to do any of these things that you are asking of me."

"Who does?" Governor Rae barked, displaying extreme displeasure in her contorted face.

"The High Council of Lords. They'll be meeting in late September here at the Imperial Castle. You can address them about making such changes then."

"Hardly! You get them all here in say a week. No time to lose. You pathetic people. You need roads, better housing. The list is endless. One week. Not a day more. You hear me? Meantime, Jaques will begin his survey of Ashford-5."

"Tierra," Queen Isabella corrected her, just to provoke her.

"Much to be done. Oh, Lena Squire. You are alien to this world. The Imperium wants you to depart on the next shuttle back to civilization, where you can be properly assisted so that you can at least live a better life. That is all," she turned around and marched out of the throne room.

"What the hell was that?" Bernardo exclaimed after the governor had left.

"Major trouble," Queen Isabella replied. "Jan, did all that get sent to the towers and rulers?"

Jan grinned. "You bet. That'll give them all something to think about!" She had rigged up a video camera system in the throne room. It had captured the entire brief meeting, broadcasting it back to the Underground, who had then cleverly inserted the sound portion into the tower comm network, as well as sending a few still images of the governor and her small group. In turn, the towers relayed it to their leaders. "I wonder how soon messages start flying about! Poor Bart, Anita, and Lilly."

Amy teased her. "You ought to be there helping your folks out."

"Nah, I hooked it all up here," she grinned back.

"Kids, this is extremely serious business," Queen Isabella scolded them. "We've very little time to deal with this crisis. I need you all working on it."

"You aren't going to let them take Lena away, are you?" Drina asked.

"Not if I can help it," Queen Isabella answered, clearly frustrated.

Lena offered, "You know, dual citizenship might be the answer. She can't deport Nadja because she has dual citizenship."

"That's right. We need to get you to have Tierra citizenship right away," Queen Isabella replied.

Lena looked at Bernardo. She grinned and asked, "Bernardo, will you marry me? Like right now, right away?"

He laughed, "Thought that you'd never ask!" The Gang roared with laughter. "Seriously, sure, love to. Mom, we should do it right away before that short pig tries to take Lena away."

"Son, are you sure? Lena, don't you want a fancy wedding and all that? It's supposed to be your very special day," Queen Isabella asked, worried both for her son and for Lena as well.

"No, not really. Keep it simple and fast. I can't wait to see Rae's expression when she finds out she can't make me leave," Lena replied.

While Queen Isabella had misgivings about this rushed marriage, she consented. "As the head of the Supreme Court of Tierra, I have the power to marry a couple. Gang, you'll be the witnesses then. I hope you two know what you are doing."

"It's going to be strange calling you mom, though," Lena

338

teased her. Bernardo roared and the others joined in. Isabella smiled too, but it was invisible.

A half hour later, the simple ceremony was finished. Hernando drew up the official document, signing for his wife. He then made a copy of it and drafted an official letter to Governor Rae Mc Greggor stating the Lena Squire Valen Gervasi was now an official citizen of Tierra or Ashford-5 and was refusing to leave. After everyone inspected it, he sent it to her via a castle courier. Lena commented, "I sure wish I could see her face when she receives it! I'd give anything to see that one."

Coyly, Jan asked, "Lena, you won the betting pot. Are you willing to give your prize of not having to do any camp duties on the next assignment that Isabella gives us to me in return for seeing that?"

"Sure. It's just camp duties. How?" Lena asked.

"Come on; we're going to the Underground for a bit," Jan replied. A few minutes later, Bart teleported the two to his pad.

"What's all the rush?" he asked.

Jan said hastily, "Move over. Have to make some connections fast." Her fingers flew over the keyboard for several minutes. Then, she sat back and waited. "Patience. Patience. There!" She had hacked into one of the many surveillance cameras. On their big monitor, they could see the short woman sitting at her desk, scrolling through computer records. "Wait for it, wait for it," Jan whispered.

Bart was pulled away for a moment, because the others in the Gang demanded he teleport them here too. Soon, they all gathered around the monitor. Then, a Rigel-3 courier walked in and handed her the official document. "Wait for it," Jan whispered. Presently, the whole room erupted into a hearty roar of laughter.

Hardly able to stop laughing, Lena called out, "Jan, that's worth the camp duties!"

Bernardo added, "Now, I don't have to sneak kisses anymore, Lena." She grinned and pressed her body into his, then kissed him.

"Hey, I am swamped with work here. You all going to

stay and help us out?" Bart pleaded.

"Hardly. Mom has lots for us to do," Amy cleverly got them out of the busy work. Bart groaned and teleported the lot back to the castle.

They had just returned, when Queen Isabella sent Amy and Jan off to Brom Tower, because Venerada Maricela had begged her to meet with her. She could not be in a dozen places at once. Next, she sent Bernardo and Lena off to meet with the City-States Alliance and their tower folks. Adrianna and Henry headed off to meet with the Kingdom of Rusden, while Drina and Ben headed for Bedwurth Tower in Wye. Nita and Zarita were sent to Adelmira Tower in the Easterlings, after which they would drop in on Queen Edda of Turda.

After the Gang had left, Queen Isabella sank into her chair. "Hernando, what are we going to do to stop this? If she does make Tierra an Open World, everything will be gone in a generation."

"At least you've gotten everyone's agreement to meet here on the fifteenth. That's a start," he replied softly.

King Emilio Bolivar and Venerada Maricela Wait's response was rather typical. Ken, Crystal, Amy, and Jan met with the two in his office. Considering the urgency, none wore the customary fancy clothing, which suited Maricela just fine. "We simply cannot allow this to happen. Making Tierra an Open World and bringing in all that Imperium technology will wipe us all out in likely one generation!" she exclaimed angrily.

"I agree fully," Ken backed her up.

"Well, we could accept some schools and medical centers," King Emilio pointed out. "We all did agree to allow those before they abandoned that project. Nadja's school is starting to get significant attention from the other kingdoms. But I sure as hell don't want their monster machines carving up the Goza around here!"

"Yes, but what can we possibly do to alter their plans?" asked Crystal. "Amy, Jan, ideas? You have more experience dealing with these people than we do."

"I surely don't know. This new governor is a very pigheaded woman," Amy replied.

Jan was not so kind. "She looks like a man without any

common sense at all. A my way or else kind of person. I say either fry her brains or modify her mind. This is as good an excuse that we need for such meddling. Look what they did to Amy and me? That was hell!"

"No, we should not use our powers on her mind," Venerada Maricela countered. "We must not stoop to their level. We'd be no better than she is." Jan flushed, knowing she was right.

"Well, we can certainly present a united front and protest her unilateral decisions," King Emilio suggested. "Perhaps, if she sees we are all a hundred percent against these decisions of hers, then she might back down. Worth a try, don't you think?"

Jan didn't comment. Short of tinkering with the woman's mind, she knew Rae wouldn't change her opinion. She considered the people of Ashford-5 not even to be real human beings, rather more like some kind of animals.

Near the end of the day, all the Gang of Ten members finally returned home. Each had pretty much the same things to report. This event had the rulers and the towers in agreement with each other. Somehow, they had to prevent the change in status and prevent the arrival of planet-wrecking technology. Further, after learning of the horrific treatment of Amy and Jan, all refused to send another telepath off-world.

However, one ruler took a different approach. King Alano Valen and his Pentagram of Power watched and listened in amazement at the brisk meeting of the new governor and Queen Isabella. When the transmission ended, he suggested, "Well, it is about time! Open World. Terrific. Now, we can get the alien technology that's long been denied us. I should pay this new governor a visit soon, before the others begin their harping and bickering to her."

"Dress nicely, dear," Conception suggested. "Make a good first impression on her, though she looks a bit stern to me. Still, we must take advantage of this golden opportunity."

"Hey, see if you can get us more of the ammunition for the hunting sporting rifles. We're nearly out now," Venerado Arturo suggested. They chatted a bit, and he headed into his bedroom to change. He put on his finest suit, a brown camel hair jacket, and pants. His pipe corseted figure looked quite pronounced, as he adjusted his tie before his mirror. He wore his highly polished toe boots and strapped his sword to his waist.

"How do I look dear?" he asked Conception.

"Handsome as always. Here, let me fix that tie a bit better. There. Size her up. Find her weakness. We must make use of this new governor, dear," she suggested.

A half hour later at around four that same afternoon, one of Valen Tower's Circles teleported him to the courier station at the southeastern corner of Plateau Grado. "King Alano Valen to see Governor Rae Mc Greggor, please," he announced politely to the Rigel-3 guard. He spoke into a handheld device. Shortly, an electric car came speeding up to the post.

He walked carefully up to it, noticing the still settling dust cloud, marking its passage. Inside, the guard demanded he relinquish his sword. Although that had never been requested before by Governor Konrad, he complied. After all, his sword was merely for show. His weapon was his *mentales* gifts. Shortly, he arrived at the twenty-story Admin building with which he was quite familiar. Changes and yet no changes, he noted as he was escorted to the top floor. Here was a new group of aliens, but there seemed to be little changes from their predecessors.

"Ah, one of the local kings, eh?" Governor Rae looked up from her computer monitor. "Well, don't just stand there, sit. Speak. I haven't got all day."

"I am King Alano Valen of the Kingdom of Valen."

"Ah, the lands that abut to the west," she replied tartly.

"Yes, we Valens have always had good relations with the various governors of Tierra. We have been staunch supporters of making this an Open World. We welcome the introduction of Imperium technology."

"Who wouldn't? Point being?" Governor Rae replied.

"I wanted to meet our new governor personally, and let you know you can count on Valen's backing at the coming High Council of Lords," he replied politely, though growing a little annoyed with her brusque attitude.

"That's fine. Don't really need your support. Anything else?" she replied.

"I take it you are not much of a conversationalist," he countered, growing very annoyed with her. He was trying his best to be polite.

"Have you anything significant to say? I thought not. That will be all," she motioned to a Rigel-3 man, who opened the door for him. He rose and tweaked her mind, giving it a nip.

After he'd left, she barked, "Bring me an aspirin. I've developed a nasty headache. These primitives give me a headache! Honestly, he looks like some freak! Send Jaques to me," she barked.

"Ah, Jaques. Have you prepared for your first geological survey?"

"Yes, these mountains offer the best chance to study their more readily available minerals. I'm taking horses. They will fare better in these rugged mountains. Be gone several weeks."

"Take six of the security men. Rigel-3 men. Expect daily reports. That will be all," she barked. He turned and left.

He met Elfe in the hall. "Good, caught you in time. Take me with you, please. This is the first chance any archaeologist has ever had to prospect for ruins on this world," she pleaded her case.

"Sure, but we're taking horses. Henkel says the wind currents are too treacherous for a shuttle up in these Goza Mountains. Can you ride?" he asked, suspecting that she couldn't.

"No, but I can learn. I'll pack my gear. How long are we to be gone?" she asked.

"Two to three weeks on this first excursion. Cleared it with the boss yet?" he responded.

"That old bag? No need. I have the authority now to go as I please. When are we leaving?" she asked.

"Around nine. I've arranged for horses and gear in Exchange City. You sure can get most anything in that place, but it's the same way at most such cities on more primitive worlds," he declared.

"And civilized ones too," she added with a grin.

That night, Carla held Elfe close to her. "I will miss you terribly."

"I know. And I, you. Hold me close. I'll call in every evening. Good luck with the old bag," Elfe whispered back. Carla did as asked, adding a passionate embrace as well. Soon, their passions ignited one last time before Elfe was to depart for three weeks. In the morning, Elfe suggested, "If she gets to you too much, bury yourself in all these computers."

Carla laughed, tossing back her curly blonde hair. "There sure are enough of them to get back online again. You be careful out there." They exchanged a farewell kiss.

Lugging her heavy pack, she headed down to the main doors, where Jaques was already waiting for her. He had four packs with him, but was able to get some of his Rigel-3 guards to carry them for him. They took one of the larger electric cars and headed off to Exchange City. As they left, he commented, "An adventure of a lifetime. No one has ever done a ground survey of this world. Wonder what all we'll find out there?"

She laughed, tossing back her black hair, "Ruins, I hope." He smiled. Those were not what he had in mind.

Chapter 20 Confrontations

Queen Isabella made her last minute preparations for hosting this emergency High Council of the Lords. She verified her staff had been able to lay in sufficient provisions and were prepared to house so many guests for several days. At such times, she had to take on extra servants from Exchange City to handle the close to five hundred who would be arriving shortly. The Gang of Ten kindly did most of the arduous details for her; such was far too difficult for her, as physically limited as she was. "I'm getting too old for all this, Hernando," she lamented.

"But you are only thirty my love," he teased her. She grinned, and he sensed it. They were very close now and could read each other very well, in spite of the giant lip plates, which they wore and which tended to mask normal facial expressions.

He escorted her to her throne, got her seated, and her hair arranged. Then, he took up his pad, ready to jot down ideas for her. The Gang of Ten wandered in, all dressed up nicely, she thought. Bernardo and Lena's wedding had inspired the others. Henry had asked Adrianna for her hand in marriage. Jan had likewise asked Amy. On the other hand, Ben had asked Drina for her foot in marriage, bringing a hearty round of laughter from the Gang of Ten. Well, Queen Isabella thought, the kids deserve an outlet. This is going to be a very nasty business.

Soon, the Great Hall began filling up. This time, she had her staff provide chairs for the attendees, and she watched the Gang of Ten, chatting gaily, eventually taking seats behind her. Amy was watching her back, or so she claimed. Now the many kings, queens, advisors, and tower folk began arriving, chatting among themselves. Purposely, she'd arranged for them all to meet an hour before Governor Rae was scheduled to make her appearance. At last she rose and called the meeting to order.

"Welcome everyone. I'll be blunt and to the point.

You've all heard the new Governor Rae's ultimatum to me. In an hour, she'll be here and meet with us. You can perhaps get more out of her than I could. Surely, we do not want to send more of our telepaths off-world."

"Hell no!" yelled King Rusden. "Look what happened to you, to Amy, to Jan. They are uncivilized butchers out there. No way!" The room erupted in a loud round of voiced agreement with him.

"I concur. The Open World status is sure to come up. For one, I see this as being the ruin of our world." She went on to elaborate her ideas about what it would mean to have Tierra declared an open world. For once, she was surprised to find universal agreement, save for King Alano Valen.

He spoke up, "We could use 'proper' alien technology. Medical centers, central heating, electrical lights — surely some of these things would be welcomed by one and all, unless you love to be chilled within your stone castles in the wintertime."

"Yes, but are they likely to stop at that? What benefits will they get out of giving us those things?" King Rusden pointed out. "Nada. Zero. Mark my words, they'll want to mine Tierra of all our minerals. Probably take many of our *mentales* gifted off-world to serve higher powers."

King Alano found himself standing alone on this issue. "I concede you are probably right, King Rusden." That appeased the large group.

"But what can we do to stop them?" asked King Wye.

Ideas flew hot and heavy, but no consensus was reached. At last a trumpet fanfare silenced them. A bass voice announced, "Governor Rae Mc Greggor and party." All heads turned to watch the man-dressed, short woman march to the front of the Great Hall. At least her bodyguards had the common sense to remain at the back of the room. Carla, Henkel, and Doctor Becktold followed her.

Governor Rae stood on Queen Isabella's raised platform, looking out on the assemblage. *Stupid idiots,* she thought. *Look at all the freaks with their giant lip plates. Men wearing corsets. Toe shoes and boots? Disgusting primitives. Well, this should be easier than I thought.*

She cleared her throat and used a megaphone to ensure she was clearly heard or rather that her ULAT box was heard. She spoke in her own language of Abelard-2. In her man's suit, many thought at first she was a man, but her voice gave her away. It did look strange, seeing her holding the megaphone down by her waist where the ULAT box was located.

"Hello. I am Ashford-5's new governor, Miss Rae Mc Greggor. My Computer Minister, Carla Childa. My Meteorologist, Henkel Smith. My doctor, Becktold Hardt. I will be brief. To the point. The Imperium has returned. We've brought the backlog of iron ore and gold lease payments. We bring other changes. First, you're to send ten telepaths off to become Imperial Telepaths. Second, you're to elect a new senator. You've until the first of October to get both of these to me or I'll pick them for you. Third, Ashford-5 is now going to be an Open World. Soon, I'll be bringing Imperium technology here. It's time you move out of the Dark Ages. Time you pulled your own weight in the Imperium. That is all. Good day." She started to leave.

Nadja spoke up, "Excuse me Governor Mc Greggor. Linguist Nadja here. This isn't right. Tierra has a bronze-iron age culture and, as such, is guaranteed under Imperium Law to be given the protection of Closed World status, so they can develop naturally on their own."

"Not any longer. Wars cost money. Time for this world to step up. Be counted. Enough said." She glared at Nadja, as if she could shut this woman up with her eyes.

King Rusden yelled out, "You can't do this. We'll not give you more of our telepaths so you can cut their arms and feet off them. You Imperium people are nothing but savages. We'll not stand for your interference in our affairs!"

"You going to stop me?" She felt another migraine coming on. "You forget who has the d-guns. Who has the technology. You get me those ten telepaths and senator by October, or I'll get them myself! Good day!" She began marching out, amid may curses and cat calls. Her Rigel-3 bodyguards all drew their d-guns to protect her.

Queen Isabella sensed very serious trouble was about to happen. There was no time to go searching for whoever was actively fomenting all this trouble between the Imperium and Tierra. She focused and made contact with the giant crystal beneath her throne. She was not in time. An aide to King Rusden drew his sword in an obvious reaction to the Rigel-3 men drawing their d-guns. Before she could act, one of the Rigels fired, putting a nice round hole in the aide's head. His sword clanked resoundingly on the stone floor. King Rusden's Venerado responded, liquefying the Rigel's brains. He dropped to the floor quite dead. Queen Isabella was finally able to act. All the many d-guns in the room were ripped out of hands or from their holsters, rather shocking Governor Rae, who felt the sudden jerk and saw her own gun floating over her head.

"Stop it this instant!" Queen Isabella shouted, her voice of command enormously aided by the giant, unseen crystal. "That will be enough. Your d-guns will follow you out of here. Take your dead man with you. He shot first. Your people provoked this by needlessly drawing your weapons. My decision is final!" A hush came over the assemblage. Her head throbbing, Governor Rae marched on out of the room, as if nothing at all had just happened. Outside, she grabbed her gun, holstering it. The weird woman was right; the Rigel-3's had provoked them and drawn first blood. She swore it would not be the last blood, though, if only her headache would cease.

Carla stood where she had been, up front, horrified, watching her boss defiantly march out. She finally swallowed. "Queen Isabella, please excuse us. We're not all like her."

Queen Isabella smiled, though she knew Carla could not see it. "I know. Tempers get the best of many. You best leave or Rae might think we're holding you prisoner or something."

"Thanks. Nadja is right, you know. What's she's doing here is illegal, at least it was when I went to school," Carla whispered back and headed for the doors.

Once the aliens had left, the room erupted. Everyone had something to say, none remotely complimentary. It was all Queen Isabella could do to maintain some slight semblance of order and was thankful to turn the meeting over to King Wye, whose turn it was to conduct the High Council.

Emotions ran high. Queen Isabella was powerless to do

much of anything, except to use her powers to send out calming waves across the room. Against such powerful emotions, she had very little effect. At least the Gang of Ten continued to assist her with this, as well as keep a watchful look out for more treachery on the part of the aliens. At last, Amy sent her, *The aliens are back on their own land now, mom.*

Drained, Queen Isabella was never so thankful to hear the dinner gong sounding. The many kings and tower folks adjourned for supper, carrying their heated discussions with them. She collapsed on her throne. Hernando carried her out, accompanied by a worried Gang of Ten. "Oh I'll be all right. I'm starving, but I can't face joining them. Hernando, could you bring something to my room for me please?"

"I'll get it mom," Gabriella volunteered and headed off as fast as she could in her tall heels.

An hour later and somewhat restored by the high protein meal, Queen Isabella discussed what was happening with Queen Amy. "Look, obviously there is a hidden person behind all this. Pigheaded Rae is just a mouthpiece. There is no reasoning with her. If we do nothing," she began to say, but Amy interrupted her.

"Mom, the towers will be declaring war on all the aliens. That's what is going to happen. With all these giant crystals in everyone's hands, it's going to be one hell of a blood bath! We need to find a way out of this."

"I know, I know. But for once, I don't see how."

"Why don't you call Emperor Kino and tell him what's going on? Ask him for advice on how we can defuse this, before it becomes an all-out war?" Queen Amy suggested.

"Good idea. Hernando, can you carry me to the teleport pad?"

"Hold on mom. I'll get Bart to take you and dad," Amy insisted.

An hour later, Queen Isabella finally finished outlining the disastrous situation on Tierra. "Please, I am at my wits end with this one. The third party is obviously not on this world. There is no time for me to go off-world in search of who is behind this."

"I understand fully, Queen Isabella. You are correct; someone has incited this action against your world. Let me see what I can find out. In the meantime, try to keep the two sides from further aggression," Emperor Kino responded. "Over and out."

"Well, I hope he can work another miracle," Queen Isabella stated flatly. "Cause without one, Bart, war with the aliens is just around the corner."

"But we can win it, can't we?" he asked.

"Of course not! They can bring in one of their battle cruisers and disintegrate us from space."

"Yes, but those giant power crystals will extend our reach, won't they?" he countered.

She didn't reply. This was precisely the thinking that the many tower folks were propagating.

The next day, she again lost all control of the meeting. Worse, they decided to work on the problem elsewhere. Venerada Maricela explained, "Look, the towers have been charged with working up a defense against the aliens, as well as perhaps an offense. The many kings and queens have given them carte blanche to do whatever is necessary. I have to go along with them, but I'll try to keep you appraised. Have to run. Sorry." She headed off with her husband to prepare for teleportation back to Brom Tower.

In the ensuing days, a quiet ensued, more or less. Hundreds of wagons and people flocked into Exchange City, swelling its numbers enormously. All wanted their share of the iron ore and gold. Queen Isabella asked the Gang of Ten to spend the daytime hours outside watching for trouble and defusing it if possible.

Quickly, Zarita and Amy joined forces, since both had difficulty walking in their toe shoes. Hence, it made sense they would stick together helping each other. Jan paired up with Nita. The five groups migrated around the sprawling city, keeping an eye on things. However, it was Amy who first spotted the tower members that had also arrived and were quietly watching as well. *Mom, I think nearly every tower has one person here monitoring the situation.*

Well, as long as they watch, that's okay. We can't keep

them away, she sent disgustedly. *Just keep an eye on them too.*

By mid-August, nothing more happened. The last of the many wagons had finally been loaded with the many tons of iron ore and gold and were on their way to their homelands. The chaos in the streets began to subside. Queen Isabella had heard nothing from Governor Rae and hoped she would back down on her threats, for everyone's sake.

"She needs to be informed of just what can happen if she continues to provoke us, mom," Amy advised her. "Look, why don't I go visit her and try to get her to see reason. At least, let her know what could well happen if she provokes more trouble."

"Dear, you've already been tortured enough. I don't trust that woman in the slightest. She could have you shot or imprisoned," Queen Isabella said worriedly.

"I can work out a way to protect her," Jan offered.

"From a d-gun?" she asked, not believing Jan had that much power.

"I think so. Hope I'm not tested though. It's worth a try. She's new to this governor's job. She hasn't had time really to learn what the *mentales* gifts are all about. If Amy can get through to her, perhaps some good will come of it," Jan replied.

"Yes, point well taken, Jan. She certainly doesn't know much, if anything, about the gifts and the forms they take. Okay, guard Amy with your life, Jan," Queen Isabella relented.

"Of course, I'll guard my mate with my life. Don't I always? Oops, well I wasn't able to that last time," Jan admitted.

She then headed to the Underground, shoving Bart out of the way. "Let a pro in here. Amy's life is in my hands." After making a number of adjustments, she sent, *Okay, Amy. I'm ready when you are. Have at it.*

Teleport me to their gates. A moment later, a startled guard looked up at Amy, who suddenly appeared before him. She wore a yellow satin gown and carried no weapons, preferring to appear as a defenseless young teen. "Queen Amy to see Governor Rae please."

A half hour later, she made her careful way into the governor's office on the top floor, blinking from the bright yellow lights, so vastly different from Tierra's red-orange light. Governor Rae looked up at the nicely dressed young teen and motioned for her to have a seat. "Queen Amy, is it?" she asked.

"Yes. I've come to have a chat with you, governor. I wanted to explain about the *mentales* gifts that many of us on Tierra have."

"What's the point? No one cares about your mind games. Get me the ten telepaths soon and that senator. Then, we can talk further. Good day." Governor Rae attempted to dismiss Queen Amy.

"Are you always this rude to queens? I came here to explain to you what you probably do not know. There are some of us who can do some amazing things," Queen Amy tried once more to get through to this woman.

"Yes, I am sure they make nice parlor tricks. Good day, Queen Amy!"

"But," Amy tried to persist.

Governor Rae put down her pen and looked up at Amy, drilling her with her eyes. "Look, I came here to do a job. A job I will do. They want ten telepaths. I will give them ten. They want a senator. A senator they shall have. Period. End of discussion. Now good day or I'll have my man escort you out of here." She motioned for her guard.

Amy's crystal activated. The door slammed shut in his face. No matter how hard he tried to open it, the door would not budge. "Now look here, governor. You have to understand what you are getting yourself and your people into here with us," Queen Amy tried once more.

"Nice parlor trick. Now get out or I will shoot!" Governor Rae had quick-drawn her d-gun, pointing it at Amy. Jan acted. Amy vanished from the chair. The guard burst in through the door, losing his balance from the sudden loss of Amy's counter-force, landing in a heap on the floor. "Well, that is interesting. Where'd she go? She can't have vanished. Some trickery. She must know martial arts. Sound the intruder alarm. I want this complex thoroughly searched!" she barked loudly.

"Of all the single-minded, obstinate people!" Amy declared as she materialized on the Underground's platform. "Honestly. She is so pigheaded!"

Jan grinned. "That didn't go so well." Amy had her hands on her hips, defiantly. "Hey, been a long time since I saw that pose, my love. You look adorable."

Amy relaxed and smiled. "It has been at that. Well, back to the drawing boards. We need a new plan."

The Gang of Ten continued to monitor the situation around Exchange City during the following days. Bart and Anita continued to monitor the geo-sat images over Plateau Grado, looking for a mass of security men heading for Exchange City, figuring that would be the prelude to some action the governor was about to execute. He was right. On the first of September, Anita spotted a large bunch of men moving towards a group of electric cars. She alerted Jan, who alerted the others in her gang, *Something is up. Stay alert. Anita says a whole bunch of men are heading here. For heaven's sake, stay in the alleyways out of the lines of fire.*

A dozen cars descended on the main streets of Exchange City. Security men piled out, mostly all Rigel-3 aliens in their unisex plastic uniforms. All carried d-guns. The streets were rather filled with folks going about their daily activities. For a time, the men merely marched along with the locals. Then, they stopped a well-dressed man. "You there. You are one of those telepaths, aren't you?" They were close enough to Jan for her to hear.

"Well, yes, but really, I am just a tailor for Elegant Fashions Inc. Could I interest you in a fine looking suit instead of that thin, plastic garment that you are wearing?" he replied politely.

"You are coming with us. You are hereby appointed to be one of the ten new Imperial Telepaths." Several strong arms grabbed him and threw him into an electric car, intent upon taking him back to the spaceport.

At that moment, all hell broke out! Jan watched carefully from her hiding place in the alleyway. The tailor had the most surprised look on his face, as he suddenly vanished from the car. Jan instinctively knew one of the towers had just teleported him to safety. Two of the men who had tried to abduct him suddenly found themselves in the center of an enormous ball of fire! Their plastic uniforms melted and then burst into flames, as they ran shrieking down the street, a pair of flaming meteors.

The other eighteen men drew their d-guns and began blasting away at anyone on the street, killing a small boy, two women, and one teamster, who was driving a load of wheat into town. Without warning, they dropped their d-guns and grabbed their heads before collapsing on the ground, quite lifeless.

Inside her office, Governor Rae heard a booming voice call out. "Your men just killed innocent men, women, and children. Here is our answer." Her head was forcibly turned to her window. A transport ship was just beginning its descent to the tarmac. Suddenly, it began to accelerate and then crashed into the concrete and stone, bursting into a ball of flames. The voice said, "From now on, we'll destroy one ship for every person you aliens abduct or harm."

She paused a second. Hearing nothing further, she then began barking orders. "Put out that fire. Get me the flight log. Why did those fools accelerate during landing? Are pilots now idiots? You there, go find out what's going on with the retrieval of ten telepaths! I won't stand for this!"

As Amy watched from her alley, townsfolk ran chaotically in all directions. Soon what seemed to her as mass pandemonium became people heading to their homes. Now she relaxed some. They are smart enough to get cover, she thought, which we best do too. She sent a message to her gang, and they headed to the roof of the Imperial Castle. "We should be safer up here," she explained, as the others joined her.

"I was going to retrieve their baster guns," Jan pointed out, "but someone or someones beat me to it. Amy, our people now have at least a dozen alien d-guns!"

"Oh crap! That's not good at all. Have you told mom?" Amy asked.

Jan shook her head no, adding, "I was hoping to see if I could figure out who took them. Best let her know. She focused and sent Queen Isabella this disturbing news.

354

Below, the dead Rigel-3 bodies and their electric cars were clearly visible from their high vantage point. By now, the streets of Exchange City were deserted, unheard of at this time of day! Smoke curls dotted the tops of many buildings, where cooking fires were left unattended at the multitude of small eateries around the city. About an hour after the attack, Bart notified them that an even larger force was on its way there in more of their electric cars. Plus two flying shuttles were just now taking off as well. Jan relayed the news. "Get ready to dash indoors, if they start shooting down at us. We are sitting ducks up here."

"We aren't the only ones still watching," Amy pointed to several windows.

Zarita added, "See four more over there too, Amy."

Bernardo added, "I think some are from the towers, keeping an eye on things. I hope these new aliens just come to pick up their dead and retrieve their car things."

Shortly, the two shuttles hovered over the carnage scene, joined within minutes by what seemed a squadron of the vehicles. Two dozen heavily armed men poured out of the vehicles and surrounded the dead. As the Gang of Ten and hidden others watched, some formed a circle around the fallen, facing outwards, guns drawn. Others tended to the fallen, carrying them into the abandoned vehicles. Soon the original cars were driven back towards the space station. Now the watchers paid close attention. "Don't do anything more, please," whispered Amy.

"Why not? They are pigs that deserve to be slaughtered," Zarita whispered back.

"Because this will only escalate big time. Think what's going to happen if they bring in a battle cruiser and use it to fire down on our towns from miles up there," Amy pointed out.

"Point taken," Zarita replied, but began to wonder if she had enough power to pull a battle cruiser down, if she combined all her crystals together.

Although she didn't know it, parallel thinking was taking place among the venerados and veneradas at many towers. Many of the giant crystals had been found by every tower, and experimentations with them had already begun in earnest. Some of these crystals were already being used to boost Circle's overall power, as witnessed by the downed transport.

As they watched, the aliens began using hand signals, pointing to houses. Now some eighteen headed down the street. Twelve formed up a protection line before a block of houses, while six broke into pairs, each pair heading towards doors. Overhead, the shuttles moved to either end of that block, providing air cover for the ground troops. "This is not good," Amy whispered.

Most doors in Exchange City were intended to keep the snow and rain out of living areas. Unlike doors on Imperium buildings, these had no locks and were relatively flimsy, designed to serve the purpose at hand. The three pairs kicked in the doors and charged inside. Amy held her breath; the conflict was escalating before her eyes. Kicking and screaming, one woman was being carried out of one of the homes. Shortly, a young child perhaps twelve years old was carried out, tucked under the tall alien's arm, while his partner fired his blaster towards his protesting parents. Amy couldn't see if they were shot or not. At least the third pair came out empty handed.

Just then, the two men carrying their captured woman and child dropped dead in the street. As they fell, they released their grip on both, who immediately vanished from sight. Amy and her friends recognized a pair of teleport spells had activated and knew the two abductees had been rescued. However, now the alien soldiers began firing wildly at all the buildings. Round holes appeared in doors and walls, even through some of the stone buildings.

One open air diner that Bernardo often visited was stuck. One of the roof's supporting timbers shattered. As he watched, the roof took on a dimpled shape, and then collapsed downward at its center. The owner of the diner, Lisabeta, came diving out of the crumbling building, only to be hit by three blaster strikes. In horror, Bernardo watched as the innocent woman dropped dead onto the ground just as the central portion of the roof crashed onto the floor, sending a small cloud of dust and debris shooting out what had been the front of her small business.

Before he could even react, three of the soldiers, who had just fired on Lisabeta, dropped their weapons, throwing their hands up to their heads, before slumping dead onto the ground. That only escalated matters. Others began firing wildly, but wisely, none of the locals was actually visible.

Overhead, the shuttles spotted the ten on the castle roof and opened fire on them. From eight hundred miles north, Bart had already hacked into the live streaming video being sent back to the spaceport from the attackers. Figuring they would not be safe, he'd preset his teleport controls. As they opened fire on the Gang of Ten, he activated the teleport, depositing the ten in Queen Isabella's throne room.

"What?" exclaimed Amy rather startled. She lost her balance and fell down. Likewise, Zarita was taken by the surprise move and fell as well. However, she was mad and didn't get up. She focused, calming her racing mind. One by one, she joined with her many giant crystals and then acted. Above ground, without the slightest warning, the two shuttles were shot far out into space! The sudden acceleration greatly exceeded the capacity of the four men's bodies to withstand g-forces. Two were manning the guns, and two, piloting. Their crushed bodies slumped to the floor of the shuttles. The sides of the shuttles caved in and shortly exploded. Both ships then floated aimlessly a very great distance from the planet.

Zarita, now quite calm, broke her connection. She looked up. Nita was trying to help her get back onto her feet. She allowed her friend to lift her up. "Thanks. That's the end of those two shuttles!" Zarita declared.

"What did you do?" Amy asked, having recovered her poise. "I saw all your small crystals glowing."

"I tossed them into outer space or whatever you call it out there. They won't be back, that's for sure. Damn men anyway! What's going on now?"

"Thanks," Amy replied. But just then a massive explosion shook the very floor. "What the hell was that?" she cried out.

Alarmed, Bernardo, Henry, and Ben made a dash out to the courtyard in time to see a huge column of black smoke arising from miles away at the spaceport. "Glad that's over there and not here," Bernardo exclaimed. "Best get back under cover," he added. The three turned and raced back inside to tell the anxious others what they'd seen. "Something exploded at the spaceport! Huge column of black smoke," he gushed.

Jan said, "Isabella wants us all in the basement now. Zarita and Amy have already headed down there. Come on fellows. This isn't the time to stick your heads out there!" They concurred and followed the other women.

"You're safe! I was so worried," Queen Isabella exclaimed, as she saw the last of the Gang of Ten joining her and everyone else in the cellar among the many stores of food. "Are they bombing us or something?"

"This castle ought to withstand that," Hernando tried to calm everyone down a bit.

"Spaceport. Something exploded over there. Huge smoke column. Can't see much, mom," Bernardo explained, slightly out of breath. Everyone began talking at once. Speculations ran wild.

About a half hour later, Bart sent Jan, *The soldiers have left Exchange City and are heading back to their base now. A tanker that was just lifting off came crashing down and exploded. Can't tell how much damage it has caused, but it must be substantial. Fire crews are swarming the area now. You all safe?*

After replying, Jan filled the others in on Bart's report. Queen Isabella sighed, "Okay, I need to get to Bart now. I must tell Emperor Kino what's going on before this gets totally out of hand."

"Mom, it already is out of hand," Bernardo countered. "I'll get Bart to teleport you. Hang on a second."

An hour later, Queen Isabella finished outlining what she knew had happened. "Emperor, it's gotten out of hand. Governor Rae's soldiers are trying to kidnap our people and simply murdering innocent women and children. This has to stop or I think our people will explode and totally destroy the entire spaceport! They'll send battle cruisers next. God help them if they do that! Help us please. I beg you. Over," she pleaded desperately.

"Relax, Queen Isabella. Calm down. I believe I have concocted a solution, but I'll need your approval and possibly your citizens. Over."

"Please, this can't be allowed to continue. What solution? Over," she replied, gasping so hard she nearly fainted. She wished she wasn't wearing the damned corset right now.

"Since you and Amy are official Ataro Empire queens, I am prepared to accept Ashford-5 into the Ataro Empire. As such, you will be under our control, not the Imperium's. That means that I can put a stop to the attacks on your planet. I can force the Imperium to keep Ashford-5 a Closed World, halt the import of Imperium technology, and the kidnaping of your telepaths. Over."

"Do it. I'll take the responsibility on my head for this. If the leaders of the kingdoms later reject this alliance, I'll resign and let Queen Amy take over. Over," she replied.

"Agreed. I'll make the calls now. Welcome to the Ataro Empire of the Twelve Sacred Planets of the Wasp, though the number of worlds will now be thirty-seven. Over and out."

Queen Isabella sat back, stunned at what she'd just done. "Have I sold us out? Hernando, I feel faint." She did pass out, but he was there to catch her. Bart quickly teleported them back to her castle, where Hernando carried her to their bed and gently laid her down.

A short while later, the Gang of Ten and Gabriella gathered around her bed. "Well, kids, I surely did it this time!" Queen Isabella said softly.

"Mom! What have you done?" Amy asked, startled.

"Tierra is now part of the Ataro Empire of the Twelve Sacred Planets of the Wasp. We will remain a Closed World, and the kidnaping of telepaths will end."

Chapter 21 Politics

"Yes, that's right, President Snarry. I'm invoking Senate Ruling 1042. Quote. Any planet that has a fully trained queen, emperor, or empress of Ataro Empire of the Twelve Sacred Planets of the Wasp shall be considered a part of the Ataro System, subject solely to their ruling authority. Unquote. Ashford-5 has two trained and both legally and formally declared queens — Queen Isabella Valen Gervasi and Queen Amy Gervasi Bellweather. Thus, at this time, Ashford-5 is now officially the thirty-seventh planet in the Ataro Empire, subject to our rules, not directly the Imperium's rules. I demand your forces there cease their attempted kidnaping of telepaths, the slaughter of innocent men, women, and children, and the destruction of private property and buildings. I request the withdrawal of Governor Rae Mc Greggor immediately. I'll have to agree on your choice of a new governor for Ashford-5. Do I make myself perfectly clear, President Snarry? Over."

"You — you can't do this! Ashford-5 is nowhere near your empire of planets. The Senate ruling didn't imply you could commandeer worlds half the galaxy away from Ataro! We both know that! Over!" President Snarry grasped at straws. What the hell was happening out there on the rim? This was supposed to be an open and shut operation! How could Governor Rae have so botched this assignment that Emperor Kino was intervening?

"The Senate Ruling 1042 makes no mention of distances, Mr. President. You're perfectly within your rights to bring this matter before the Senate for a hearing, Mr. President. If you do so, then I'll have no choice but to present video evidence of your soldiers kidnaping women and children, and video evidence of your soldiers firing d-guns at primitives, destroying homes and murdering an innocent woman cook. Video evidence of two armed shuttle craft firing upon ten unarmed teenagers standing on a rooftop. Do I make myself clear? Over."

Video evidence? How can that be? Did that fool Rae

make a video of all that? Damn her! "Legate Emeryk, what the hell do I do now?" His companion was standing beside him and had heard the interchange between the two men.

"Devilishly tricky. If he has such video, Snarry, that'll be severely damaging to you. We must take steps to minimize the collateral damage. Even if Ashford-5 becomes a part of the Ataro Empire, there are still ways to achieve your goals. You must do as he asks. Survive to fight another day. That man has built up far too much influence in the Senate just now. Hell, he's the Imperium's biggest war hero right now. The senators will obviously back him all the way. It's a fight you cannot hope to win. I assure you that in time, we can find other ways and means. Think of this as a temporary setback, nothing we can't handle."

As he talked, President Snarry began to calm down, which was Legate Emeryk's intention. *How can such a buffoon have become President? He needs to be replaced as well! Time enough for that.*

President Snarry sighed. Pressing the talk button, he replied, "Okay. I agree to your proposal. Ashford-5 is now the thirty-seventh planet in the Ataro Empire of the Twelve Sacred Planets of the Wasp. I concede the issue. I'll recall Governor Rae Mc Greggor today and order a halt to all operations she has ongoing there. But they must have an official senator. You know the rules. Over."

"Excellent President Snarry. Ashford-5 will remain a Closed World. I'll see that a senator is appointed and will be sent off by your October deadline. Of course, their senator will still not have a vote because of their Closed World status. Their senator will sit with those from Ataro and be under their protection. We don't want a repeat of what happened to Senator Isabella and her two wives, now do we? Over," Emperor Kino sat back with a smile on his face. He'd won yet again. Now, he had to conduct an investigation to lay bare whoever was behind these latest atrocities. Time enough for that later. He had to get the bloodshed ended before it escalated any further. Good god. Somehow, these primitive peoples had destroyed two shuttles, a transport ship, and a large tanker. How they could have done that was beyond his imagination, but in a way, he felt rather proud that they had.

"Accepted. See that their senator is on their way by October. Over and out," President Snarry replied, sitting back. "What a damnable fiasco this has turned out to be. Okay, let's get Governor Rae on the line."

An hour later, a frazzled Governor Rae replied to the video conference request. "Governor Rae here. Rather busy at the moment. Make it quick. Rebel uprising in progress. Downed tanker. Lost two shuttles. Guards dead. Bunch of incompetent pilots are flying here. Over."

"Governor Rae, you are hereby relieved of your post effective immediately. You are to take the next transport off Ashford-5 and report to my office post haste. Cancel any and all your orders regarding Ashford-5. Issue orders to bring spaceport security up to Level 5 immediately. That is all. Over and out." He sat back. "There, that's done. The fool doesn't even realize what's going on. Pilots don't crash their ships!"

"That's obvious. The rebels must have infiltrated the spaceport and planted homemade bombs of some kind," Legate Emeryk speculated. He didn't want to reveal that he had other suspicions based on his knowledge of the ancient document called Marisol's List of *Mentales* Gifts. He also knew in ancient times, other spaceships had been brought down under equally mysterious circumstances. He didn't want President Snarry to know any of this. He was too incompetent to handle such potential power.

"Yes, that's as plain as the nose on my face! So what's next? I suppose we have to find a new governor," President Snarry replied.

"Yes, we should get on that immediately. Whoever it is, the person must meet Emperor Kino's approval. We need to pick someone who will be *particularly ineffective*. Come, bring up that list of possibilities you had before," Legate Emeryk suggested.

The two poured over the relatively short list. One caught Legate Emeryk's eyes. "Hey, how about this one, Katrina Lutgard."

The president protested, "She's just graduating from the Academy, barely twenty-one. She's never had an assignment."

"Yes, but look at her comments. She is praising Governor Konrad's approach: going native and all that," Legate Emeryk pointed out.

"True, but look, she's an avowed lesbian," the president added.

"We don't want to seem discriminatory on sexual grounds. We can't pick anyone with *worse* credentials! She's perfect," Legate Emeryk declared.

"Oh, I see. Yes, we couldn't put a *weaker* person in as governor, could we? I'll send word to her right now. Bet old Kino won't be expecting us to react this swiftly!" President Snarry smirked. "My god, she'll make a *complete* mess of things in no time at all! Emeryk, sometimes I think you're a genius!"

After the Legate departed, President Snarry made arrangements to interview Katrina the next day, forcing her to take an immediate transport flight from the Academy in order to make the meeting. "Give her a bit of a hassle," he smirked. Then, he entered some codes and fired them off to the computer technician on Ashford-5. When Carla received those direct orders from the Imperium President, she grimaced. Nevertheless, she obeyed, entering the new codes that blocked Governor Rae out of everything except her own apartment.

At one the next day, a harried Katrina stopped briefly in the women's restroom on the first floor of the Presidential Office building. She touched up her makeup, brushed her curly blonde hair, and then arranged her dress. She wore a white silk blouse, a dark grey business suit jacket and matching skirt, revealing the black nylons that she so loved. Her pumps were black patent, low heeled, but very expensive. As the oldest daughter of one of Grund-3's senators, she could afford such luxuries. She detested the odor and look of the Imperium Standard unisex cat suits that nearly everyone else wore. Satisfied she looked as good as she could muster on such short notice, she turned and walked out, heading for the elevators. There a guard met her and escorted her to the top floor, opening the door to the President's Office for her.

Her eyes took in the spacious, luxurious office, and the

two men there. President Snarry sat behind his monstrous desk, but she already knew about his desk from her father. She didn't recognize the other man. "Katrina Lutgard reporting as ordered, Mr. President," she said politely. She had no idea why the Imperium President had summoned her from her classes at the Academy. But whatever it was, she felt certain it had to be important.

"Welcome, Miss Lutgard. May I call you Katrina?" President Snarry said.

"Yes of course." She took the only seat before the giant desk, determined not to make a fool of herself. She demurely crossed her legs, ready for whatever was about to come.

"This is Legate Emeryk. I've asked you here today to interview you for a very important position. I am sorry we had to pull you out of your classes, Katrina. A governor's position has just opened up yesterday, a very critical, vital one at that. It must be filled immediately. We've been going over your qualifications and believe that you are the one for this position. However, as you know, we must verify this for ourselves, this being such a critical assignment."

Katrina could scarcely believe what she was hearing. A governor's assignment! Most of her fellow graduates had to wait sometimes years to get their first posting! "Yes, of course. Ask away." She swallowed hard, trying to calm her sudden adrenaline rush.

"Of course, we only have limited information about you. It says here that you are a firm believer in the ground-breaking path that Governor Konrad Burkhardt has broken in the field of governorships. Is that true?"

"Oh yes, very much so. His work very clearly demonstrates how rapidly and effectively to gain the trust and most importantly the understanding of more primitive peoples. First, one simply must generate some degree of liking, affinity if you please, between them and yourself. He has shown repeatedly that this can be done very rapidly by adopting the local apparel and customs right from the start, assuming of course that the initial language studies have been done. In doing so, at once, you have built some degree of reality between yourself and the local inhabitants. That then allows a free and open dialog to begin. Understanding between yourself and the locals is then easily achieved. He has shown this to be highly effective and quite rapid. So yes, I am a firm advocate of his ground-breaking methods." She hoped she had not talked too much. Obviously, the president must already know all about this method. She felt a little silly for having said so much.

Legate Emeryk asked, "So you don't have a problem adapting to local dress and perhaps even requisite body modifications?"

"No of course not. Most all can be easily undone once the assignment is finished. Governor Konrad also pointed this out." She decided to keep her answer shorter this time.

"Excellent," he replied. "One final question, Miss Katrina. I do hope that you won't take offense to this, but we have to ask. Do you believe your professed sexual orientation will interfere with your job as governor?"

She flushed slightly. She had always known this would present potential problems. How best to defuse this one? She replied, "I'll do my utmost to keep my private life completely separate from my professional life. Yes, I'm fully prepared to endure sexual activities with primitive cultures, where it is customary for the local leaders to swap marital partners with the governor to cement and bond their association. Governor Konrad has pointed out that can often become the make-break point in establishing relations with some primitive cultures. I'll do my best always, sir." *God, I hope I answered that one well enough!*

President Snarry glanced at Emeryk, who made a very slight nod. "Congratulations Governor Katrina Lutgard." He smiled broadly.

"What?" She was taken by total surprise.

"Yes, you are the Imperium's newest governor. Your assignment is a most critical one at that. I regret we have to throw you into the fire pit almost immediately. Your predecessor has apparently made a complete *mess* of things. You are to be the new governor of Ashford-5, located on the rim. As you might not know, they have the largest deposits of the critical fuel that the Imperium must have to continue our extensive operations on the rim of the galaxy. This posting is a particularly critical one. I do hope you will be up to the challenge."

She swallowed hard. "I'll do my very best, sir!"

"I'm certain that you will. The position must be filled almost immediately. I'll arrange for you to receive your diploma from the Academy immediately upon your return there tomorrow. I need you to leave for the rim within two days. I know this gives you very little time, but there is a most serious situation there. One small detail not for public release just yet, I have to make the formal announcement to the Senate tomorrow, but Ashford-5 has become the thirty-seventh planet in the Ataro Empire. Hence, on your way there, you'll have to stop and meet with Emperor Kino, who has the final say in your appointment. My advice to you is to be as forthright as you have been with us, and he'll not object to your posting there. I'll release activation codes to you tomorrow. You can study up on Ashford-5 during your flight there. Again, congratulations, Governor Katrina Lutgard." He rose and she did too, shaking hands.

She left, hoping the men didn't see her legs wobbling or that she might collapse on the way out. Katrina kept it together until she reached the first floor, where she immediately headed to the women's restroom. Inside, she exploded, punching her fist into the air and gushing, "Yes! Yes!" Then, she did her best to calm down. After returning to her transport and getting airborne again, she began to make plans. Everything was so rushed! First, she made a connection to her father, Senator Helmut Lutgard. "Dad! You'll never guess what's happened to me! I'm now Governor Katrina Lutgard! Over."

"Incredible! But you haven't even graduated yet. Where? What world? Over," the pleased senator replied.

"Ashford-5, dad. Over."

"Ashford-5! Now that is incredible news." The two chatted a while before they ended the call. Such calls from hyperspace were prohibitively expensive, but she just had to share the news with her father. She took heart in that he seemed extremely pleased and proud of her amazing accomplishment. *Now what to take with me?*

After Katrina left the two men, President Snarry commented, "She can't help but make a complete mess of things for Emperor Kino! We couldn't have found a worse candidate." Both men laughed heartily.

"We'll be arriving in the Ataro System in twenty-four hours," the captain of her deep space transport told Katrina as she boarded. She'd only been able to bring one crate of her clothes and possessions with her. There wasn't time for more.

"What? Ataro is halfway down the spiral arm, isn't it?" Katrina asked, rather shocked at the short amount of time. As they lifted off, the captain had just made his announcement. She'd hoped to have a week to get more familiar with the volumes of data in the official records that her new access codes had allowed her to open and begin reviewing.

"Critical mission. We are flying at top speed, using an amazing amount of fuel. You must be on a *very* important mission," he replied.

She began reviewing the reports. *Telepaths? A telepathic society? How unusual. No wonder this is so critical.* She continued thumbing through the voluminous reports from nearly three centuries of occupation. At last, she found entries made by Governor Konrad and she squealed. "He was here. I'm following in his footsteps! My god!" Now she brought up images of the locals and also images of Konrad and his wife Nadja. "Oh!" she exclaimed as she saw the images. She dug deeper into his reports, discovering he'd divorced Nadja and married a local woman. Then, she put it together. "Neva! That Neva, the woman who helped Emperor Kino end the war! My god! This is incredible. I hope I can handle this assignment! I'm following the path of giants!"

Late the next day, she faced Emperor Kino himself. Although she had known how these rulers of the Ataro System looked, it was quite another thing to see them in the flesh. She was more than a little shocked at his appearance. She still wore the same outfit, as she had with her presidential interview, fresh blouse though.

"So you are the new governor. It says here you are a

firm believer in the methods developed by Governor Konrad Burkhardt. Is that so?"

This time she decided to keep her replies short. "Yes, absolutely. It's a must, if you're to gain the trust and respect of the local people in short order, emperor."

"Excellent. That'll be your most important task upon arrival there. Well, I certainly do approve of President Snarry's choice. You've my full support, Governor Katrina. Bit young, but you have a bright mind and future ahead of you."

"Thank you emperor," she replied. "I'll do my very best."

"You'll have to. I'm afraid the Imperium has really made a complete mess of relations on Ashford-5. So bad that I had to intervene and make Ashford-5 part of the Ataro Empire! You've inherited an extremely explosive situation. Let me explain what has been happening there these past few weeks." He outlined in detail what Queen Isabella and Bart had both told him and sent him, namely the streaming videos Bart had captured.

Katrina turned white as a sheet. "My god! Did they just gun down that helpless woman trying to escape the collapse of that building?"

"Afraid so. She took three d-gun shots to her chest and head. There's more." He continued his presentation. "I'm afraid you are inheriting this horrible mess. Somehow, you must regain their trust and confidence. My Queen Isabella Valen Gervasi and her daughter Queen Amy Valen Bellweather will be your close contacts there. Follow their advice implicitly, and you stand the best chance of avoiding further bloodshed and strife. Of course, since Ashford-5 is now part of our empire, you can call me at any time for my advice or opinion. The only immediate request I have of you is somehow they need to elect a new senator and have him or her on their way to the Senate on Proxima Prime by the first of October, their time. Queen Isabella will be able to help you achieve that objective. By the way, Ashford-5 will remain a Closed World indefinitely. Questions?"

Katrina had many, but knew she could find the answers in the voluminous records. "Are there any staff still there? No one has told me about what kind of support staff I'm inheriting."

"Yes, there is a competent computer technician and her mate who is an archaeologist. Not sure why there is an archaeologist there though. There is a good geologist, meteorologist, and an excellent medical doctor. None of those have been involved in this fiasco, I might add."

They chatted a bit more before she left. When she returned to the spaceport, the captain announced, "Okay, governor. We are fully refueled. Time to liftoff. Be there in another twenty-four hours."

"Amazing. Top speed again?"

He grinned. "You must really, really rate, ma'am!" Now, she knew why the incredible rush.

Queen Isabella had to act. She issued an official summons, demanding all rulers and their tower leaders to come to the Imperial Castle the day after she received Emperor Kino's proclamation declaring Tierra was now a member of the Ataro Empire. She insisted she had vital, critical information for all of them. As before, her gang of teens stood behind her throne, while Gabriella and Hernando were at her side. In pairs, the rulers and tower folks arrived. This time, that was all who came: kings, queens, venerados, and veneradas. She immediately sensed why. The others were involved in protecting activities and monitoring the aliens. All anticipated another even more deadly round.

"We are at war with these aliens!" declared Lord Wye, as soon as most everyone had arrived. "We will not stand for such blatant treachery. We'll fight to the death, and you can't stop us, Queen Isabella!" Many others echoed his sentiments.

As soon as Amy let her know that the last had arrived, she rose. "I've handled this mess for us all. As of today, Tierra is now the thirty-seventh planet in the Ataro Empire of the Twelve Sacred Planets of the Wasp."

"What the hell is going on, Isabella?" yelled King Wye, outraged.

"As such, Emperor Kino has declared Tierra will remain a Closed World, and the attempted kidnaping of our telepaths by the Imperium must cease immediately. Further, the Imperium has recalled Governor Mc Greggor to Proxima Prime, where she will stand trial for her crimes here on Tierra. In short, any further dealings that the Imperium has with us will *first* have to go through Emperor Kino. In short, we are secure once more. While there will soon be a new governor, Emperor Kino will have to first find the person acceptable. He will be a buffer between us and the Imperium, as well as our protector, safeguarding our rights."

"And what has this cost us?" King Wye asked derisively.

"We will be paying a small tithe to the empire, based upon what we produce. Since we're still classified as a primitive world, such will be fairly minimal. We will also need to continue to have one of their trained queens here in my position as head of the Supreme Court. Amy has already had that training and is officially a queen of the Ataro System. She is my heir when I step down. So there is no need to worry about this aspect for quite some time. As I understand it, I'll now have a deep space transport ship docked here on Plateau Grado so we can travel to and from the Ataro System. That is also a first for us."

"They won't be interfering with us?" asked King Rusden.

"Not unless some situation arises that either I or Queen Amy cannot handle. But we will have to send another senator off to the Senate. However, this time, he or she will be seated with the Ataro System senators and be under their protection. Hopefully, nothing will happen to them like it did to me. Now then, I would like your suggestions for who will become our next senator by the middle of September. Next, I must insist any and all alien d-guns that some of you might have confiscated the other day be returned to me so I can hand them over to the new governor. We don't need that kind of deadly force being used against us by our own people. Also, I've been asked to determine if we wish to have all the Rigel-3 aliens removed from the spaceport or not. There is obviously a great deal of hostility between our two races at this point. They wantonly murdered us, though I must say we retaliated in kind."

"Hold on a second," King Wycombe spoke up. "If they remove the Rigels, their replacements might look more like ourselves. They could then more easily infiltrate our courts, senates, and lands, spying on us. If we keep the Rigels, they stand out like a sore thumb. I say keep them here for that very reason."

After a good deal of discussion, King Wycombe's suggestion to keep the Rigels passed nearly unanimously and for that very reason. It was at this point that Venerada Maricela asked, "So how did those two shuttle ships that were firing on your castle disappear? We all saw it happen."

Queen Isabella had no idea. Carefully, she used her feet to turn her body so she could see the teens. Zarita spoke up, "My doing. I got rid of them by throwing them way up into the sky somewhere. I think I killed them, though. Sorry."

"Well don't be. They would have destroyed the Imperial Castle if you hadn't acted," Venerada Maricela replied. "When we saw that happening, several of our towers began to make preparations to teleport everyone here to safety. So who pulled down that big one that exploded on Plateau Grado?"

"Our doing," Venerado Arturo answered, "us and Venerado Valen of the City-States Alliance. We gave them something to think about. These new crystals are proving their worth, are they not?" Queen Isabella grimaced. This is exactly what she didn't want — having the towers finding them exceedingly valuable. Somehow, this threat to Tierra also had to be handled, but not now. Others soon began sharing the roles they had played in the two assaults, proud of their counterattacks. The idea that "we taught them a lesson they won't soon forget" was the commonly held view among all the tower folks, echoed more reservedly by the kings and queens. Isabella already saw the rulers had begun to fear their own tower members and for good reason, she thought.

She dismissed them, adding, "Please get the d-guns teleported here, as soon as possible please."

"Well, that went better than I thought it would," Amy conceded. "I wonder who will be the new governor? Can't be any worse than Rae."

Three days later, via Bart, Queen Isabella told everyone,

"Our new governor is a young woman, twenty-one and unmarried. Emperor Kino says she is a believer in the pioneering methods that Governor Konrad has developed. I think she may be a vast improvement. We should know tomorrow. She's scheduled to land then, but I don't know how soon she'll pay us a visit though. I'd hate to inherit the mess that Governor Mc Greggor left her."

Governor Katrina's transport slowly began its descent onto Plateau Grado, providing her with her first glimpse of Ashford-5. "Tierra," she kept reminding herself to use the local name as much as possible. "So dim. Such a queer light. Red-orange." She double-checked her short list of immediate actions to take. After the briefing by Emperor Kino, she hastily jotted down what had to be done as her first actions, beginning shortly after she landed.

As the ship drew very close, she could see the blackened remains of the tanker, which had crash landed, and those of the two smaller transports that had crashed earlier. She sighed, wondering if sabotage was at play here. She discounted pilot error that her predecessor was claiming. Pilots were not that dumb. Crash landings were extremely rare. The automated guidance systems made such far safer than being struck by lightning. She took a deep breath. No time to even freshen up her makeup or change her clothes.

As the doors opened, she got her first smells of this new world, though clouds of dust floated around her. The plateau still had not yet been cleaned. Acrid stench from the fire still dominated, but she also sensed many unusual smells. Was that pine, she wondered? A woman and two men were standing outside the Admin Building waiting for her as she set foot on Tierra for the first time. The woman waved to her, and she smiled back, making for them, trusting the ground crew to bring along her solitary crate.

"Hello, I am Governor Katrina Lutgard," she said politely. "Sorry that I look a mess. Been rather a hectic two days. Can you believe that? All the way from Proxima Prime in just two days? Incredible."

"They must have burned up an enormous amount of

fuel! Hi, I am your computer specialist, Carla Childa. My mate, Elfe Heilwig, is out in the field along with Jaques de Marie, your geologist. He's doing the first ever ground survey for minerals. This is Henkel Smith, your meteorologist and Doctor Becktold Hardt. Welcome to Ashford-5."

"Tierra. We should start calling it by the local name. Very pleased to meet all of you. I wish the circumstances were far better. I have made this list of immediate actions to take. I guess you had better show me to my office," she suggested.

As they walked, Carla asked, "So we're in the dark here. Got orders to lock Rae out of everything, and they shipped her off days ago. I've issued President Snarry Knoschy's other orders too. The base is under very tight security, but so far, nothing has happened. The Rigels are demanding that something be done. Many died."

"Yes, strangely," Doctor Becktold added. "I've done autopsies on all of them. Never seen anything like this."

Governor Katrina asked, "How so? Sword wounds? I understand those are the allowed weapons on this world."

"Negative. Their brains were, how shall I put this, mostly liquefied. Never seen anything like it!"

"How can that be? I've never heard of anything like that, though my medical knowledge is scanty," she asked. "A virus perhaps?"

"That was my first idea. No virus. I can find no cause whatsoever. Tried every medical machine on them too. Nada. Highly unusual. I'll be studying this for some time. I will find the answer, I assure you," he pronounced.

"Here's your office. Your things will be taken to your apartment down on the tenth floor," Carla announced. "Guys, you can leave us for a while. I have to get her new ID card made and make sure she has proper access codes." Both men nodded and went their separate ways.

Governor Katrina found Carla was very efficient. Shortly, she had her new card and clipped it to her jacket pocket. Carla entered her codes, the ones that President Snarry gave her. "Now you enter whatever password you desire. That will lock me back out. I was sort of acting governor for a few days. Very glad that I don't have your job!"

She waited patiently while Katrina entered her choice. Then, she watched to make sure that there were no glitches.

Satisfied that she'd handled the brief transition of power, she spoke up. "I took a look at your bio on file at the Academy. Very glad that you are here. Elfe and I both are. Company. If you need some support, you have us."

"Oh," Katrina flushed. "Well, yes. I so hoped that being so open about it would not cause any problems. Guess it hasn't, though the President did ask me about it. I'm so glad that you and Elfe are here too." She grinned. Carla knew what she meant. "Well, to business. I need a clear channel so I can speak to everyone on the base."

"Coming up boss," Clara grinned.

"May I have everyone's attention for a few minutes? Thank you. I am Governor Katrina Lutgard. Tierra or Ashford-5 is now the thirty-seventh planet in the Ataro Empire of the Twelve Sacred Planets of the Wasp. Yes, they have become a member of that system. As such, Emperor Kino Sango must approve everything that we do here. Further, the status of this world remains that of a Closed World, as it legally ought to be, since they are in the Bronze-Iron Age and must be given the opportunity to evolve naturally. There will be no further attempts at kidnaping their telepaths. I will deal quite harshly with those who try it. D-guns will no longer be permitted to be carried when anyone leaves the spaceport. No exceptions; this is a Closed World."

She continued, "We will have a funeral for those who lost their lives in the recent conflict just as soon as the doctor releases their bodies for burial services. For those who were involved in that conflict, I will not be issuing any reprimands. I know that you were just following ex-Governor Mc Greggor's orders. Soon I hope to meet with the locals and attempt to smooth things over so that we can return to more friendly relations here. Finally, before I lower the security level to normal, I want to meet with the Security Captains to make sure we do not have infiltrators on the base. We don't want any more ships crash landing. Thank you for your patience, while I get a handle on my new job. That is all."

She looked up at Carla, "Well, what do you think? Off to

a good start?"

"I'll say. Many of us were quite upset with the way that the old bag handled things. Very few of us agreed with her orders to kidnap the telepaths, let alone kill all those local people. We thought that was downright criminal of her, but to be honest, Governor Katrina, we were powerless to do anything about it, except keep clear of her and that whole mess. We all did, the five of us, that is. So what's next?"

"I need to review all the security logs to make darn sure there are no saboteurs on this base. Perhaps, you could handle that one. I must meet with the Security Captains right away. And please, just Katrina, when we are alone."

"You got it, Katrina," Carla grinned, and set to work on the logs. Meanwhile, Governor Katrina summoned the ten Security Captains and had a lengthy chat with them. She learned as far as they could tell, there had been no security breaches whatsoever.

"Then, how do you account for the loss of the transports and the tanker? Have the two shuttles that somehow disappeared been located yet?" she asked.

"Rae claimed pilot error, but we've gone over and over their readouts. Checked the automated guidance systems from top to bottom, governor. Frankly, we are all mystified."

"Explain in language I can understand. Sorry, such things I know very little about," Katrina admitted, being honest with them.

"According to the readouts, everything was precisely correct. Then suddenly, the ships were simply pulled down hard and fast to the ground. All three pilots reacted per protocols, firing their thrusters. The tanker had its thrusters going full throttle upwards at the moment of impact. It is as if some unknown force was pulling them down from the sky. We've no explanation how."

"I see. A real mystery then."

"Precisely, boss. We've had a few scouts out looking for the two shuttles. No word back yet. I can tell you this much, neither is within ten light years of the planet, and they are out of hailing range or their comm equipment is damaged. We will find them eventually," he promised.

"Okay. In your opinion, is this base secure enough that we can lower security back to normal?" she asked. All the captains agreed that it was. She dismissed them, thanking them for their efforts. She then turned to Carla and asked, "Anything from the logs?"

"Nada. No intruders whatsoever. If sabotage was involved, like a bomb, it had to have been planted on the ships while they were on other worlds. We should request the ID division to look into that possibility," Carla suggested.

"Excellent, Carla. Go ahead and send off the request, along with what details we have. And while you are at it, lower the security levels back to normal. Everyone will appreciate that move. Now what's next on my list? Ah, I need to review the more recent history of Tierra. Guess I have a lot of computer work to do."

Carla smiled and explained, "I wrote a Finder program. That icon there. Click it and then enter the series of keywords. It'll then bring up all references that match. The sheer volume of reports from three centuries of occupation is staggering."

"Thanks dear. Beautiful work," Katrina praised Carla and set to work. First, she typed in "telepath" but the returned listing contained thousands of entries. Then, she recalled something she'd read while on the transport. She typed in "*mentales* gift." This time, there were only a handful of entries. Many were fairly recent references to Governor Konrad's documents. She brought up one and began reading. Soon, she found a reference to Marisol's List. She opened a new window, brought the Finder program up and searched on that. Up came that original listing of skills.

Fascinated, she began reading the very long list of special skills that such people could have. "My god. Balls of fire! They can think a person to death?" Curious now, she opened yet another instance of the Finder program and entered "mysterious space craft crashes." She discovered well over a century ago, there had been similar crashes noted. Further, someone named Lech had reported some of the *mentales* were pulling shuttle craft down from the skies, crashing them into the ground.

Katrina sat back. *No wonder half of the galaxy is*

interested in this world. My god, if President Snarry knows about this, it's no wonder why he wanted to get his hands on some of these people, who can do these kinds of things! This is all so unreal, and yet it must be true. This is anything but a primitive world that I've inherited! I must find out far more and fast!

An hour later, she realized the magnitude of what she needed to read in order to have a better understanding of this world. Hence, she moved on to the other items on her list of immediate things to handle. "Carla, I need to meet with this Queen Isabella Valen Gervasi. How does one arrange such a thing? They don't have a comm system do they?"

Carla laughed. "Not that I know about. No, you simply have to go knocking on her door. She lives in that big Imperial Castle on our plateau. They have a sublease for it from our main lease. Take an electric car and head to the extreme southeast corner. There is a guard station there, where they sometimes come to request a visit with us. You can't miss the castle. Just go out on the road and turn left at the first corner. Their front gates are right there. Want me to come with you or should I arrange a security attachment?"

"No security guards! Not at this point. We don't want to provoke any more confrontations with these people. If you are willing to risk your neck, I'd appreciate the company," Katrina suggested.

"Love to. We three need to stick together. Lousy timing for Elfe to be out wandering around the planet. She's lucky she missed all the battles. Come on; let's get going."

"Hold a second. I ought to change. I've been wearing this same outfit for three days now. Do you have anything to wear other than that awful unisex cat suit?" Katrina asked.

"Not really. Real clothes are beyond our budgets," Carla answered truthfully.

"Come on; maybe some of mine will fit you. We must make a reasonable first impression with this queen. Tomorrow, I am going to have to visit this Elegant Fashions Inc place and get myself outfitted more like the women of power on Tierra. Say, why don't I also get you and Elfe fixed up as well?" Katrina suggested.

"But we can't afford such nice dresses — real dresses I mean. They cost a fortune, especially real heels like yours. Real leather, right?" Carla countered.

"Yes, real leather. There is nothing finer. Hey, it's on me. I've a healthy discretionary budget. As you said, we three ought to look out for each other. Lord knows, men certainly won't." Both laughed at that remark.

An hour later, both were dressed in clean white silk blouses, a grey jacket with matching skirt. "These feel so wonderful on my legs. I've never worn nylons before, let alone real leather shoes," Carla exclaimed. "I so wish Elfe could see me now. Of course, if she did, why you'd be delayed some!" Both women chuckled.

"Okay, Katrina, you can do this," she took a deep breath. "Bit nervous. Well, let's get going. I do hope this goes well enough."

"You look very good, Katrina. Come on. I'll drive you," Carla offered.

"Is it always this chilly?" Katrina asked, as they got out of the electric car and walked to the huge, imposing castle gates.

Carla chuckled, "This is actually rather warm, as far as I know. Henkel has told us that winters here will be really cold with a lot of snow. Many feet according to him. Winters last a long time on this world, at least at this latitude and elevation. Here comes someone now."

The gate man opened one door. "Hello, I am Governor Katrina Lutgard to see Queen Isabella Valen Gervasi." She noticed that her ULAT box spoke in a strange language, that of the Midlands. The man paused momentarily. For a second, Katrina thought he would deny her entrance.

Then, he opened the door wide. "The queen will see you in her throne room. I'll lead you." He beckoned them inside.

As they followed behind him, Katrina whispered, "Remind me to start using the computer language disks tonight. I have to learn their language fast. If this wasn't such an emergency, I would have delayed this visit until I could at least speak her language some. This place is huge." She began noticing the tall ceilings of the narrow hallway. Just before they turned to their left, she saw that the hallway seemed to go on forever with many side rooms.

They entered a giant room, the combination Great Hall or Throne Room, depending on the situation. Just now, it was her throne room. Hernando was just helping her to get seated as they walked into the room. A bunch of teenagers was also filing in, taking up a position behind the throne. Katrina and Carla gasped at the sight of Queen Isabella's physical condition. While she had seen the armless emperor, she looked similar but very different. Metal golden rings held her head motionless. Her bosom was extremely large, accented sharply by the pipe corset she wore. Her feet looked terribly small, but her toe shoes were extremely well made, leather, Katrina noticed immediately. She walked up and stood before her.

"Hello, I am Governor Katrina Lutgard, my computer technician, Carla Childa. I must apologize for being wholly unable to speak your language. I have only just arrived on Tierra. I do hope that our dress will not offend you."

"Welcome to Tierra, Governor Katrina, Carla. I am Queen Isabella, my doting husband, Hernando, youngest daughter Gabriella. Behind me are my twins, Queen Amy and Bernardo. He's recently married Lena Squire, a former ID minister. Amy's betrothed, Jan." She continued introducing the others.

Katrina looked from Isabella to Lena to Drina. As if reading her thoughts, Queen Isabella explained, "This is part of what was done to me when I was our senator. I'm afraid my neck has been fused. I can't move my head at all. Lena lost her arms when she, Queen Altha, and Neva were mutilated, while they and Emperor Kino were trying to negotiate an end to the recent war with the Federation of Planets. Drina was born without them; she is what we call a katalyein telepath. Her gift is to remove mental blocks that prevent someone's *mentales* gift from activating, thereby saving their life. Anyway, how can I help you this late afternoon?"

"Thank you. I am beginning to understand a bit better, though I have a very long way to go. Emperor Kino ordered me to visit you immediately upon arrival. I want you to know that the former governor has been arrested and taken back to Proxima Prime. I presume she will have to stand trial. I have ordered everyone on the base to desist from any further kidnaping of any kind. I have issued strict orders that none of us is to carry a d-gun beyond Plateau Grado, and especially not into Exchange City here. I want to reiterate that Tierra will be remaining a Closed World. It's my sincere hope we can prevent any further conflict between our peoples, and indeed open a new page in understanding and cooperation. I'll do my very best to make this happen, but I need time to learn your ways."

"You've made an excellent beginning, Governor Katrina. I know some of our people stole some d-guns from the fallen soldiers. I've issued orders they are to be returned to me. As soon as I have them in my possession, I'll return them to you. D-guns are not needed on Tierra. For my part, I hope and pray that I have calmed the many rulers down, and that they'll not cause any further troubles either. We both realize that you and I have much to discuss, but it would be inhospitable of me not to give you time to get up to speed in your new position. We're both about to undergo many changes, for the better I do hope and pray. As it's very hard for me to get around much, please do come and see me, as often as you desire. When I need to see you, I'll send one of the teens here to your gate man by the fence. Will that be acceptable?"

"Certainly. Yes, I understand. I can't imagine how awful your life must be. I do need some time. There's so much to learn, and I do want to be as good a governor as Governor Konrad Burkhardt was. I've studied his ways and will do my best to follow in his footsteps. I plan on visiting this Elegant Fashions Inc store tomorrow and get myself more presentable to your people. I do hope you will not hold my current dress against us."

"Of course not. Nita here is the youngest daughter of the owner, Inez. I'm sure that they can get you properly attired. Let me give you some hints though. The rulers of this world are rather fashion conscious." Nita giggled. "Okay, fashion crazy, as Nita is hinting. Most all women of nobility insist on wearing these restrictive pipe corsets. Right now, these toes shoes of mine are in vogue, but almost equally in style are an alternative type of toe shoe in which one walks on the tips of one's toes. Both styles require a permanent foot alteration. I urge you exercise caution in such decisions. Also, these monster lip plates that Hernando, Zarita, and I are wearing are the latest fashion for both men and women of power. I rather wish they were not, but they are. Nadja has already altered those language boxes of yours so they can translate our modified speech, since we cannot make certain sounds any longer. Again, I urge you use some caution here as well. However, I'll have to admit that Governor Konrad found the rulers of Tierra accepted him very readily, when he and his wife wore these things. I too have to wear them for much the same reasons."

She continued, "One final caution, since you are a woman and a pretty one at that. Here on Tierra, if you are accepted by the rulers and nobles, as Konrad, Nadja, and Neva were, you'll find that you'll instantly become a fashion setter. The many women will quickly adopt the fashions that you wear. I know; it's rather silly of them, but that's life on Tierra. Oh yes, one other detail that you both probably don't know yet. On Tierra, all women's bosoms become melons like mine. The teens behind me are already beyond your sizes. What you'll soon discover in your records is any alien woman, pardon the expression, who lives for about six months on Tierra also ends up with their bosoms growing to match ours. We don't know why this is. Some suspect it is a fertility thing, providing more milk for our young is the theory. So be advised, by spring both of you will be sporting melons like mine. By the time the teens behind me reach eighteen, they too will have monsters like the rest of we Tierra women. Inez can help you with that aspect."

Katrina swallowed hard. "Goodness. Thanks for the head's up alert! I'll look for that in our records. Like I said, I've so very much to learn about your interesting world."

Just then a gong sounded. Queen Isabella explained, "That's the supper gong. Would you both care to stay for supper with us? You're under no obligation to do so. This is your first day on our world, and you haven't even had a chance to get settled in, I expect."

"Why, I'd be delighted to dine with you. I do have so

many questions. I hope everyone doesn't mind my insatiable curiosity," Governor Katrina replied.

"Not at all. Come, dinner waits." Hernando carefully helped her rise. Katrina and Carla saw, as constrained as she was, even rising from a seat was a challenging proposition. Both also saw how Jan put her arm around Amy, assisting her to walk more easily. Likewise, Nita assisted Zarita.

The spacious dining hall dwarfed the small group. As everyone got seated, Amy explained "We host all the rulers and their aides here at the many High Councils of the Lords. Sometimes, five hundred men and women dine here at the same time. Quite crowded."

Jan pointed out, "That's roast chicken; that's roast pork. Cheese and Lena's favorite, nut bread, but I'd recommend that one, wheat bread." Katrina smiled, and watched as the serving trays began to circulate around the table. She felt quite comfortable, so different from eating in the sterile cafeterias of the Admin building and those in the Academy.

Quickly, she noted that Hernando had to feed Queen Isabella and that she really could not chat at the moment. However, they did see both Isabella and Zarita's lip plates now seemed locked in a horizontal position instead of drooping down to their chests, facilitating eating.

Both Carla and Katrina noticed just how close Amy and Jan were. "So you two are getting married?" Katrina made pleasant conversation.

"You bet we are, in a month," Jan replied.

"Sooner, if we can get mom to agree," Amy added.

"So I take it that female-female marriages are not taboo on Tierra?" Katrina asked curiously.

Amy grinned. "Nope. Little weird, but accepted." Amy and Jan looked over at Katrina, and Amy simply smiled and added, "Understood."

Carla said, "I'm glad of that. Elfe and I have been more or less keeping a very low profile. I guess while we are here, we need not."

"Not around here," Amy declared. "Bernardo and Lena just got hitched. Governor Rae was trying to order Lena off-world. Now that they are married, she can't order Lena any longer."

Katrina looked over at Lena, rather surprised to see she was using her feet and toes in place of her hands. Drina too. She asked, "So I take it, Lena, you have your new dual citizenship ID card? Bernardo too?"

"Yes, we both do. I made that pig Rae give them to us," Lena replied, not even trying to mask her hatred of the former governor.

"So Amy, Jan, you will be entitled to triple citizenship when you marry: Tierra, Imperium, and Ataro. Let us know, and we'll get you your new ID cards too."

"We certainly will," Jan agreed.

Lena was curious about one aspect of the new governor. She asked, "Katrina, you must have only recently graduated from the Academy?"

Katrina flushed. "Well, yes. I was a month from finishing up, but President Snarry wanted me here now and pushed my graduation through. I know I lack experience, Queen Isabella, but I'll do my very best. You'll see, but this arrangement will take a bit of getting used to. You see, as a member of the Ataro Empire, I have to get Queen Isabella's okay on any major decisions, but I'm allowed to reach out to Emperor Kino, if I think it's necessary. I have to clear any Imperium orders, which have a significant impact on Tierra, with Queen Isabella first. It's kind of like having three bosses. At least, the Imperium is at the bottom. I hope the many rulers here will take that into consideration, when they form their opinions of me."

Lena smiled, "If you explain that to them, I'm sure many will do just that."

"Oh I do hope so, Lena. Might I ask you a personal question?"

"Only if you try that nut bread first," Lena teased her. "It is simply amazing, but the locals think normal wheat bread is superior. Not me."

"Say, what an unusual flavor. It is delicious. I don't see the nuts," Katrina replied. Carla also sampled it and agreed with her boss, asking if they could take some back with them for breakfast.

"You see, the original aliens had a refinery on Plateau Grado. It somehow exploded and knocked this world off-kilter somehow. The climate shift nearly wiped us all out. That was a couple of centuries ago now. What used to be the breadbasket lands could no longer grow wheat and other cereal crops. However, various nut trees were domesticated. Their nuts are harvested and ground into a flour from which the bread is made. Nut bread is found mostly here in the northern lands. Down south, wheat is now grown, but it has to be imported up here," Lena explained.

"Incredible. Well, I love it. Say, do you have history books? I'd love to read about your history," Katrina asked.

Everyone laughed. "Sorry," Amy spoke up, "no one has ever bothered to write such things. Only now are Nadja and Diego writing the first books for use in their school. It's mostly an oral history and that's quite spotty. We here have just graduated from Nadja's school. Eight years of study. Ugh. Some of us don't want to see another book for a long time."

Katrina grinned. "Now I see what was so funny. Yes, I am rather tired of all that book learning myself. I'm so eager actually to do some useful work. Oh, I remember, I was going to ask you, Lena, how come you decided to stay on Tierra instead of returning to your home world?"

Lena expected such a question. "Simple really. On any other world but this one, I would be doomed to a life of a helpless cripple. Here, Drina and Bernardo have been teaching me how to be mostly independent and self-sufficient for the most part. Then, they also have developed this incredible therapy, which actually erases all the trauma that a person has suffered. I could go on and on about that, but I won't right now. I've never felt so alive. Then again, I got the *mentales* gifts too, which is helping me a whole lot. Plus, I have fallen in love with Bernardo, this world, and its people. All the spaceships in the Imperium can't drag me away from here now."

"Wow. I see. Powerful motives indeed. So you got this telepath thing while you were here?" Katrina asked. "I know so very little about it yet. I read that they all have yellowish eyes. Everyone here has them. Does that mean that you are all telepaths?" she asked.

"Yes, we all are. Yellow eyes with brown speckles are a dead giveaway that the person has the gift, Governor Katrina," Queen Isabella spoke up, making it official that she knew this detail.

Carla flushed, "So you can all read our minds, our thoughts?"

Queen Isabella answered this one. "Yes we can, but we don't. It is highly impolite to do that without the other's permission first. Actually, it is a high crime to do that to an unwilling participant, equivalent to mental rape. Of course, there are always some unethical people who do such things, until they get caught doing it. So don't worry, no one is going to pry into your private thoughts without asking you first, governor."

"Well, that's good to hear," she replied, just as much relieved to hear that as Carla was. "It could be very embarrassing."

"Precisely so, that's why it is illegal and a crime," Queen Isabella restated it for emphasis.

"I can see I have so much to learn. I do hope I can learn it fast enough," Katrina volunteered.

"Give yourself time, governor. We're here to help you as you need it," she added. "I'll try to arrange a meeting between you and the rulers around say the fifteenth of September. I need to get their senator choice and make arrangements to get the new senator on their way by the first of October. Winter starts around then this far south. It starts even earlier further north, so we are cutting it close. Not much happens in the winter season. Too much snow."

"Well, I best get cramming; that's less than two weeks from now," Governor Katrina replied. After thanking them for the dinner, the two departed for the spaceport, carrying a whole loaf of the nut bread with them.

Chapter 22 Acceptance

The next morning, both Governor Katrina and Carla visited Elegant Fashions Inc, where they met both Inez and Nadja. Lilly was also there and Nita joined them to help out. The first thing both women saw was the enormous bosoms of the three older women, along with Nadja's giant lip plates. After introductions, Inez asked, "So Katrina, Carla, exactly how can we help you today? Isabella said you wanted some of our fashions."

"I am so honored to meet you, Nadja! I've studied all the literature about how you and Governor Konrad worked so well with other worlds. I agree completely with your theories on how best to achieve mutual understanding between peoples. I insist upon following in your footsteps, if I possibly can."

Nadja laughed. "I see. Well, I must caution you at the onset, it can be a most difficult and challenging path, but as you know, it works miracles. So that we are clear, you wish to appear as the other noblewomen do when you first meet them in a couple of weeks?"

"Right. I hope I can manage it. I've never done anything quite like this before, but it simply must be done, if I have any hope of mending fences," she replied.

Inez took over. "Well, let's get both of your measurements, and then let's go over some of my fashion catalogues. As we go along, you can make your decisions and choices. The elegant men and women of Tierra are overly fashion conscious, in my opinion. Three quarters of the women go all the way, while the remainder takes a more conservative approach. Oh by the way, in case no one has told you this yet, if you live on Tierra for about six months, yours will become melons like ours. Unless you want to be bothered with frequent dress alterations as yours grow, we could use the medical machine to enlarge them to what is likely to be their final size. Later, if needed, minor alterations can be made."

"Well, yes, that does seem to be the most practical way

to proceed. I don't believe I'll have time to get the gowns altered every so often," Katrina agreed.

"Now then, the most conservative women wear the pipe corsets. Actually, most all the noblemen and women wear them. Plus, they wear this style of well-made heels. Yes, those are six inches tall. The vast majority of women and many men opt for one of the two styles of toe shoes or boots in the wintertime. Personally, I would highly recommend, if you wish to do this, go for the style that Isabella and Amy wear. At least you can stand up on your toes that way," Inez explained, pointing out various illustrations in the large, glossy catalogue.

"Does everyone wear such huge earrings?" she asked.

"Yes, even the most conservative women wear them. In my opinion, the biggest choice you have to make is to go with the lip plates or not. As I said, three quarters of the women and a similar ratio of the noblemen wear them. However, as you might expect, they can be a *real* pain to live with."

Nadja added, "Quite true, but already I've uploaded speech patterns into the ULAT system so it can handle anyone speaking with them and in any of four dialects, three from Tierra and Imperium Standard. So everyone will be able to understand you, if you choose to go this route. Plus, that modification can be undone at any time, should you desire. Caution, once your feet are altered to fit either of the two toe shoes, that change can only be partially undone. Afterwards, you will have to always wear the six inch heels, like Inez here has to wear."

"This is going to be quite a challenge. I've never worn such heights before," Katrina pointed out.

"Yes, give yourself plenty of time to get used to them," Nadja suggested.

"Well, I need the works, that's for sure. I simply must make a very good impression on the majority. I have to help end the hostility between both sides. Showing them I appreciate your culture and dress will help create an affinity between us and reality too," Katrina volunteered, but then wished she hadn't. She just remembered Nadja had helped define this new method.

"Correct," Nadja replied. "How about you, Carla?"

"Well, I ought to wait for the really drastic ones until Elfe gets back. The oxfords, corset, and earrings will be fine for me right now, if that's okay with you, boss. I simply don't have the funds to pay for such elegant things."

Inez laughed. "Carla, Governor Katrina, everything that you get today, including at least six outfits, is on the house."

"What?" both echoed each other, quite surprised.

"Precisely. You see, when Nadja was the governor's wife, she became an instant fashion model for all the noblewomen, who just insisted upon emulating her appearance. When Neva became his second wife, she too became something of a trendsetter, though Nadja still remains a powerful model. So I am expecting you too, Governor Katrina, whether you wish it or not, are going to be setting fashion trends. All that generates business for the company. Just keep in mind whatever you wear to the meetings, the noblewomen will shortly come to me asking for similar outfits. So I'm not so altruistic after all." All chuckled.

"But I've never been a fashion model," Katrina pointed out. Carla nodded her agreement as well.

"You are now, whether you like it or not. Noblewomen will tend to emulate you, unless of course you dress down compared to them. In that case, there goes your attempt at generating affinity and reality between you and them," Inez pointed out.

"That said," Lilly spoke up, "we should look over the many styles of gowns. I'll take Carla, mom. You do Katrina. Mom, what about their hair?"

Inez grinned, "Old age strikes again. Forgive me. Yes, as you probably have noticed, all women of Tierra prefer very long hair. In the Easterlings, for example, it is taboo for either sex to cut their hair, not ever. Westerlings women like theirs rather long too, but there is no taboo on it there. We can lengthen yours, if you like." Both agreed to that small detail.

An hour later, the two women had decided on six outfits; three were various shades of red; three were various shades of blue. Additionally, Katrina chose the design for her lip plates, two people shaking hands, a symbol of mutual unity. Everyone praised her design, pleasing her.

Inez then explained, "Okay, time for the modifications and the medical machines. However, I must be honest with you both. You will believe there is no pain with any of these procedures."

"Oh yes, that is correct. Imperium medical technology has become totally painless for centuries now. Marvel of modern medicine," Katrina volunteered. This was one thing she knew among so many strange things she was facing.

"Unfortunately, that is not true, Katrina. It does *appear* to be utterly painless. However, the trauma and pain lies buried beneath the anesthesia that's used. Here on Tierra, a woman called Benjamina developed a therapy that actually uncovers and erases the trauma. I'll get in contact with those that deliver the therapy and see if I can't get you both scheduled for some later this winter. Now then, shall we begin? I'm going to let Lilly run the machines. I'm getting too old for such things, a little forgetful too."

"Mom! You are only fifty-eight," Lilly pointed out. "We want you around a lot longer." Inez grinned.

Carla was finished up first. "Oh, I can't breathe!" she exclaimed, as she was helped up from the medical machine. "It's way too tight!"

"Shallow breaths, easy does it. You'll get used to it; just takes a little time. Let's get you dressed in your new outfit, the red one?" Lilly suggested.

"Look at my breasts! Oh, I wish Elfe could see me now. Look at my curves. My hair — so long," Carla gushed. "I do look gorgeous, don't I? I've never worn such fine clothes before. How can you walk in these heels? My ears are being pulled off."

"Small steps. Come on; Nita will help you practice some, while I finish up with Katrina. You'll probably need to help Katrina with her walking for some time, until she gets used to everything."

Sometime later, Katrina awoke. Her reactions were quite similar, bringing a smile to Carla's face. By now, she was getting the hang of walking in such extreme heels. After getting Katrina to a sitting position, Lilly showed her how to operate the latches on her new lip plates.

"How utterly clever. Yes, I see. In order to eat anything, they have to be raised up, but down at other times. Clever."

"Yes, that was dad's invention. He's very clever," Lilly explained, rather proud of Peter's contributions.

After getting her into her new red satin gown, Lilly helped her to her feet. "Oh, I can't even stand up!"

"Don't worry; you'll soon get the hang of it all. We always allow folks time to get used to the changes before we let them leave here. Have a look at your new look, Governor Katrina," Lilly suggested.

"Oh my! I look so different! What a change. I can't believe my figure, such curves," Katrina said, turning slightly this way and that.

Lilly allowed Carla to help lead her boss around the office area, while she and Nita packed up their many new purchases and arranged for them to be transported down to their electric car. Before she allowed them to leave, Lilly made very sure Katrina knew how to handle her lip plates and was able to walk reasonably well, as she did for all beginners.

On the way out, she overheard Katrina say, "Carla! I am going to need your help getting around for the next few days, please."

"You got it boss. If I say so myself, you look stunningly sexy. If I weren't married. . ." Her voice trailed off, and Lilly grinned to herself.

After helping her boss into her apartment and then hanging up her new outfits that were brought up by a Rigel-3 man, Carla decided it would be best for her to stay with Katrina to help her better manage, much to Katrina's great relief. She visited her own suite, storing her new prized outfits before rejoining her boss.

"I guess I have so much to learn. You might as well learn with me," Katrina suggested. Together, they began looking over the voluminous reports, a task on which they spent the entire time before the High Council meeting. She wanted to know as much as she could before meeting these rulers.

On the fifteenth, the many kings, queens, aides, venerados and veneradas arrived, though many were grumbling about coming so late in the season. Down south, harvests were underway. However, Queen Isabella observed they were all dressed for the occasion. Plus, she sensed a current of ambivalence towards meeting this new governor.

Right on time, Governor Katrina entered to a short fanfare, clinging to Carla for support. She whispered, "Oh my. So many! This place is packed. I'm getting nervous!"

"You'll do fine, boss. Small steps, shallow breaths," Carla whispered back. The fanfare ended. All eyes turned to the two blonde women making their slow, careful way towards the throne. When she finally stood beside Queen Isabella, she was nearly out of breath.

The queen began the formal meeting. "Kings, queens, venerados, veneradas, aides, it's with great pleasure that I get to introduce our new governor to everyone. This is Governor Katrina Lutgard and her computer technician, Carla Childa. Governor Katrina wishes to take this opportunity to introduce herself and explain a few things. Governor Katrina," Queen Isabella said and leaned slightly towards her, the best gesture she could make. Hernando helped her get seated.

Katrina was glad she'd listened to the language disks every night for nearly two weeks. "Hello kings, queens, venerados, veneradas, and aides. I'm Governor Katrina Lutgard. I know. I'm awfully young. Actually, I just graduated from our Academy. So yes, I'm inexperienced, though I hope you'll not hold that against me. First, I want formally to apologize for all the recent bloodshed and criminal acts the former governor committed against your people. She has been arrested and will be tried for her crimes in due time, I'm sure."

"It's my job to see that nothing like that *ever* happens again. To that end, as you know, Tierra is now the thirty-seventh world in the Ataro Empire of the Twelve Sacred Planets of the Wasp, somewhat a misnomer, since there are thirty-seven planets in the empire now."

"Just what does this mean for you and for me, your governor? That's the most important question we all should be asking ourselves right now. First, it means Tierra will remain a Closed World. Your cultural development will not be drastically altered by the whims of the Imperium. Second, it means from now on, kidnaping of your people will be a high crime. The Emperor will investigate any such incidents, and the guilty punished severely. Third, it means a general amnesty for any and all actions either side committed is in effect. No one will hold you responsible for any damages that Tierra may have committed nor will the security guards be held accountable. They were following the orders of Governor Mc Greggor and would have been shot for treason had they disobeyed her."

"Yet, this change also has a much more far reaching impact on both yourselves and on me. You see, no longer do I have to answer directly to the Imperium and follow *their* orders. Rather, my immediate boss is the queen of Tierra, that is, a duly trained queen of Ataro. At the moment, this is your Queen Isabella Valen Gervasi. Queen Amy is her heir designate, should something terrible happen to her. Further, if I do not like a ruling that Queen Isabella has made for me, I'm to appeal it to Emperor Kino Sango directly. Thus, any Imperium orders to me that impact you directly must be Okayed by Queen Isabella and/or Emperor Kino. This is extremely important to you and to me. The governor of Tierra can no longer issue orders, for example, to kidnap some of your people. For me to issue such an order, it would have to be okayed by both Queen Isabella and Emperor Kino, which they certainly would never do so."

"So you see this change is going to protect your culture, your way of life, insulating you from the whims and decisions of the Imperium. We all know how terrible some of those have recently been."

"On a more personal level, I hope to meet with each of you rulers and tower leaders to discuss the problems and issues that you face. I'll endeavor to assist you as best I can, always subject to the approval of Queen Isabella, that is. I know I'm young and lack experience, but the young often bring new ideas to the table."

"The former governor has done one thing that is beneficial to some of you here today. My geologist is out in the field conducting the first ground survey of the Goza Mountains. He has already located some new and substantial ore deposits, including three copper, two tin, three silver, and one iron. When he returns, he and I will meet with Queen Isabella and identify in whose kingdom each lies. I apologize for not yet knowing kingdoms and their borders. We'll then be contacting those rulers and outlining in detail where these new and valuable deposits lie. In time, I hope Jaques will be able to visit all your kingdoms, assisting each to discover additional unknown resources for your kingdoms."

"In closing, just so the air is clear between us, I'm twenty-one and not married. Inez has also told me to expect to be a fashion model. I'm flattered by her declaration, but between us, I've never thought of myself in this way. I've always liked fine dresses, even though they are terribly expensive out there in the Imperium. So ladies, before you decide to copy my look, check with me. I could well be making a horrible mistake in fashions. I'm new to these incredible styles of yours. Still getting used to them, if the truth be told. Thank you for allowing me to address you today." She stepped back, signaling she'd finished.

Bernardo was clever. He began a slow clap. One by one, others joined him until the whole room was applauding, somewhat embarrassing her. She'd not expected such a reaction. Be gracious, be gracious, she kept telling herself.

With Hernando's aid, Queen Isabella then rose. "Thank you all. That's all we have for you today. I would like those of you who wish, come on up and meet personally with our new governor. Share your ideas with her and get familiar with Governor Katrina. I've arranged for some light music and plenty of food for the rest of the day. Thank you all for coming, even though I know some of you have had to take time away from harvests and other important work." Diego and Hidalgo began playing their guitars, creating a soft ambience in the huge room, as many chats began.

Almost at once, Katrina found herself at the center of attention, though Carla kept a steadying arm around her. "Welcome, governor, I'm King Arthur Wye of the Kingdom of Wye, some fifteen hundred miles east of here. We all loved Governor Konrad and his wife, Neva, and of course, Nadja. You seem to be following in their footsteps."

"Pleased to meet you, King Wye. Yes, I've studied his pioneering methods, and I'm doing my best to follow them. I believe that this way, we all can so much better understand and respect each other. So is your kingdom a farming one? Forgive me if I am not fully up on what's where. I've only been here on Tierra a very few weeks."

"Yes, Wye is at the northern band of the breadbasket lands. So, are you serious about not following Imperium orders, such as might come from the president himself?" he asked pointedly.

"If those orders should impact the people of Tierra, then yes, I'll be getting Queen Isabella's okay on them before I do anything. If she rejects them, then I certainly will not follow them. That's the great benefit Tierra now has by being a part of the Ataro Empire," she replied politely. She suspected she might be asked this again, and she was right. Throughout the day, she was asked this in many different ways, at least sixty times or more.

He smiled, but it was invisible behind his giant lip plates, which sported a wheat field design. "Excellent, Governor Katrina, I do believe we'll get along just fine. You asked about things that we need. Well, I would like to see an Imperium medical center in Wye, where any of my people, who get sick or injured, could come for expert care. Also, we'd like to see a school in Wye, like Nadja has going here in Exchange City. My son Bill is going there now, and he raves about what Nadja is doing."

"Ah, those do sound to me like most worthwhile projects. I'll certainly see what can be done about both of them as soon as I can," she replied. "Mind if I quickly jot those down so that I don't forget?" She pulled out a paper and pen from her purse and wrote them down.

"Excellent, governor. I hope to hear from you on these later on. Mind if I ask you a personal question?" he asked rather coyly.

"Not at all, King Wye."

"You said that you are single. Do you have a boyfriend? Someone as attractive as you will likely be rather sought after," he suggested.

She knew this topic would inevitably come up. "Sorry, no boyfriends. I am more interested in the fairer sex, if you follow me," she replied politely, wondering whether these people would pick up on her subtle clue without her having to be very explicit. In the past, being explicit was often rather embarrassing for both parties. Further, throughout the Imperium, acceptance of same sex alliances ran the gambit from utter hatred to complete acceptance. She chided herself for not having explored this in greater depth with Queen Isabella.

"Ah alas for we men," he said disarmingly. "Perhaps you will find love here on Tierra as Nadja has."

"Dear, how about letting us women have a chance to meet our charming new governor," his wife interrupted him, taking this digression of his as her opportunity to make herself known. "I am Queen Ruth Wye. So very pleased to meet you, Governor Katrina, Carla. You look just fabulous, and I do so love your design on your plates. Hands across the universe is it?" she asked. Katrina noticed that both the king and queen wore similar lip plates; both wore pipe corsets, though his accentuated his robust frame, and toe shoes. She had the long earrings as well. Her gown was far more daring than Katrina's, a pink satin strapless gown that hugged her curves to below her knees and had a tiny walking slit.

"Why yes, how observant of you. It reflects what I'm trying to do as governor, reach out to everyone, and become understanding friends. You look very well yourself, though you're far braver than I am. I'm too scared to wear a strapless gown, though Inez and Lilly did try to get me to."

"Oh I know just what you mean. Risky. But with our monster bosoms and Inez's fabulous fit, I'm quite secure." She leaned forward and whispered, "It does drive Arthur mad with lust!" She giggled and Katrina smiled, not fully realizing yet just how invisible her facial expressions had become. Nevertheless, Ruth picked up her reaction.

She then asked, "So if alien travel is no longer as restrictive as it has been in the past, we would dearly love for you to come and visit our castle in Wye. Come and spend a few days with us. I would be delighted if you could."

"Well, thank you very much for the invitation. Right now, I am terribly busy trying to learn all about Tierra, almost overwhelming. But later on, I certainly will try to come for a visit. Thank you, Queen Ruth," she replied, again jotting down the invitation on her paper.

"Ruth, are you dominating our lovely new governor?" another man pushed his way closer to her. "I am King Rusden. Most pleased to meet you, Governor Katrina." His apparel and ornaments looked very much like King Wye, only his finely tailored suit was brown suede, and he wore matching toe boots. His drooping large plate showed a farming scene of a man reaping wheat. Ruth backed away, joining Rusden's wife and chatting to her, probably about Katrina, the governor guessed. She wasn't surprised to hear him asking pretty much the same questions as had King Arthur. Once more, she received an invitation to come to Rusden Castle and spend time with them.

Standing on her toes and in one relatively small location for so long began to take its toll on her feet and legs. As soon as one pair of rulers finished chatting with her, another pair nudged their way through the crowd to Carla and her. She quickly realized each of the kings and queens wanted to ask her similar questions. Katrina got the uncanny sensation they were somehow trying to detect if she was being honest with them in her answers. Perhaps, this was another aspect of their many gifts, though she noted many did not have the requisite yellow eyes.

She also sensed some disappointment with some of the kings, when she divulged she was not interested in men. During one small break, Carla whispered, "I heard some of those kings were trying to interest their older sons in you. I think they are disappointed they cannot send their sons to court you. Now, I suspect they'll be thinking about sending their daughters to you."

Both women giggled, and Katrina whispered back, "That's a relief!" Both giggled again.

Now others who did have yellow eyes began making their way towards her through the crowd. Quickly, both women discovered there was definitely a pecking order to these "visits." An armless woman with very long black hair, wearing a strapless red satin form-fitting gown with matching six inch heels like Carla's, was escorted up to her by a man wearing a black camelhair suit. Both also had the large lip plates. Hers had an image of a tower on it, while his pictured an eagle or similar bird.

"Hello. I am Venerada Maricela Wait, leader of Brom Tower and my charming husband, Theo. He raises and trains eagles. I'm very pleased to meet you, Governor Katrina and am very much pleased with how you have been handling this most critical first meeting with all these rulers. I'm also a katalyein telepath; hence no arms, born this way."

"Very pleased to meet a leader of the towers. I know so very little about them, but I intend to learn as much as possible for an outsider. I take it the rulers are to meet me before the tower leaders?"

"Yes, observant. We exist to support the elected rulers. Brom is home to the only Trauma and Spiritual Rehab Center on Tierra. I would like to invite you and Carla to visit Brom as soon as you are able to get the trauma of your body modifications erased, along with any other traumas you may have suffered in the past. You'll not regret it, that I can assure you. Queen Isabella insists this be done as soon as possible for your own mental health."

"But we didn't feel anything," Katrina protested slightly. "But if Queen Isabella insists, then we'll come as soon as things get settled down some. I've met a charming young teen, Drina. Is she related to you?"

"She's King Emilio Bolivar's daughter; she's a niece of mine, a katalyein too. But she is sure an adventurous one! She insisted on being in Nadja's first class of students some eight years ago. Quite a precocious young woman, which is to her credit. We have a far more difficult time with most normal activities, as you probably can imagine."

"Yes, she is a very bright and pretty young woman. I was very much impressed with her and with Lena. I can't imagine how hard it must be for all of you and Lena, and even more so for Isabella."

"True, dressing up like this is particularly hard on us.

We use our feet where you use your hands. Dressed like this, I must depend upon Theo here for nearly everything. Still, it comes with my position, so I endure these meetings. Just don't set new fashion standards that make it even harder for us," she teased. Both women chuckled.

"I've never thought I'd ever be setting fashion standards, not in a million years."

Venerada Maricela laughed. "I can imagine. No, when Konrad and Nadja were here, it was his wife Nadja that all the noblewomen emulated. I suppose if you find love and get married, you can shift the fashion modeling off to your wife."

Both laughed, including Carla. "Hey, that's a really good plan!" Katrina suggested. "No wait, then I'd have to dress like a man." All three laughed heartily.

"Come, let's get you off your feet. By now in those toe shoes, your feet must be aching. Mine are in these too. They are only a bit more comfortable," Venerada Maricela suggested, much to Katrina and Carla's great relief. After finding some seats, a small circle of other venerados and veneradas joined them and began chatting as well. Questions flew by, as did the time, but Katrina was far more comfortable now, and relaxed, enjoying the friendly attention she was receiving.

Several aspects began to present themselves to her analytical mind. "Might I ask you," she indicated to the rather large group around her now, "it seems the rulers are somehow elected by the citizens of their kingdoms and hardly any have your special gifts. I know to be in a tower, one must have the gift. So I can understand that you cannot be 'elected.' That would make no sense. But what is bothering me, and forgive me if I'm sticking my nose where it doesn't belong, but, if you all possess or command such unimaginable powers, how come some of you are not the leaders? Within the Imperium, those with such powers would most certainly be found in positions of power and influence."

Several looked at each other and Venerada Maricela decided to answer this one. "In our distant past, the towers did rule Tierra. I hate to say this, but they darn near destroyed our world. Queen Isabella has a powerful point. Great power must have some form of limits, either physical body ones such as she has or some system of checks and balances, such as she has set up with our Senates, rulers, and the courts. Without some limits, unchecked power is modified only by the sense of ethics the wielder has. We all know how often personal ethics can be corrupted by unlimited power."

"That makes sense," Katrina admitted, filing this vital information for future study.

"Aye, but that was then, Venerada Maricela, not now. Today, many of us feel quite differently about it," Venerado Arturo Valen broke in. "Our ancestors were blinded by immense power. We have learned from past mistakes and will not repeat them. Yes, Governor Katrina, some of us do not like the way that some of our head blind rulers are managing our kingdoms. We know we could do a far better job of it. After all, we do have immense powers that they do not."

"Excuse me, venerado, head blind? I've not heard that term before," Katrina asked, baffled by this new phrase. It sounded derogatory.

"Our term for those who do not have the *mentales* gifts, those who do not possess telepathy. Head blind," he explained, though several including Maricela visibly grimaced. The implication was obvious. Katrina and Carla were head blind.

"Well, I simply cannot imagine what it must be like to have telepathy. That ability is so utterly rare throughout the Imperium," she replied politely. She sensed this was somehow a major concern, perhaps a dividing factor among these tower leaders. Though she couldn't put her finger on the undercurrents, she knew that they were there and were quite significant. She made a mental note to follow up on this with Isabella later on.

Venerado Arturo went on, "You see, we are quite powerful. I do believe we sent a clear and unmistakable message to the Imperium, when we brought down their spaceships and that tanker. I'm glad they learned to treat us with more respect than that bitch Rae Mc Greggor did. Some of us have always tried to have excellent relations with you aliens. Indeed, some of us are strong supporters of bringing valuable Imperium technology to Tierra. Lord knows how badly we could use the central heating that you have, to say nothing of your electricity."

Venerado Domingo Bolivar-Brom countered him, giving Arturo a very nasty look. "Yes, but *only* when we ourselves acquire the knowledge of how to create and use those ourselves. That is why we need education. We don't need to become Imperium puppets." Arturo glared back at him. Katrina took note of this dichotomy, which plainly was a very significant factor among these tower leaders.

Based upon what she'd been hearing repeatedly today, Katrina volunteered, "Well, now that you are a part of the Ataro System, I should think I'll be able to make a very strong case to begin to get more schools and education established on Tierra, as well as many local hospitals, making Imperium medical facilities more readily available. It would be criminal for Emperor Kino to not at least allow them here." That seemed to please both men.

Just then, the dinner gong sounded, and the small conference broke up. Drained and exhausted, Katrina and Carla took their leave, heading back to the spaceport. However, after the many attendees headed home, Queen Isabella and Venerada Maricela met privately, along with the Gang of Ten in Isabella's private study.

"Well, I invited them to come to Brom for therapy, but I think you'll need to give her a little push in that direction. She seems a perfect match for her position here, in my opinion," Venerada Maricela suggested.

"Yes, amazingly she does. Well done on the clapping, Bernardo. That really solidified her outreach and their acceptance," Queen Isabella praised her son, who smiled.

"Just how much are we going to share with her, Isabella? The Underground? Madiera? The mermaids? Our knowledge of *mentales* gifts and their nature? Should we trust her?" Maricela asked.

"Very good questions, Maricela. In some ways, the more she knows, the easier her job will be and the less trouble I'll have with her on her future queries and orders. She likely has access to much information on the gifts from previous governors. Let's keep Madiera and the mermaids out of this for the time being. Give her a chance to study her records about our gifts on her own and let her ask questions."

She continued, "The Underground is trickier to handle, since many of their 'actions' could well be considered illegal in her eyes. Piggy-backing on their technology is not something she would likely go along with. Still, I'm supposed to be getting my own set of Imperium comm equipment along with that Deep Space Transport. Perhaps at that time, we can reveal some of the Underground's activities to her. I think she has more than she can handle just now."

"Agreed. Well, Theo is waiting patiently for me. Best get going. Let me know when she is ready to come get her therapy," Venerada Maricela advised, and their brief meeting broke up.

Chapter 23 Of Dust and Loss

Following the meeting with the rulers, Katrina dove into her records, comparing her notes from the meeting with her records. She began memorizing the names and locations of the many small kingdoms, placing rulers with their kingdoms, and with their mentioned needs. She knew she had much to learn and swiftly.

Carla returned to her many computer duties. Several systems needed long overdue upgrades. She sighed; these would occupy her for at least a month. Mundane work. Still, she threw herself into the project, keeping her mind off Elfe's long absence. Her heart ached to see her mate once more. Why had she gone off for such a long time?

Both women were continually bothered by the bluish dust, which seemed to be everywhere in their apartments, in Katrina's top floor office, and now inside some of the computer systems Carla was refurbishing. Well, both knew the dust had come from the massive cleanup project Katrina had ordered shortly after her arrival. When they arrived, the entire plateau was covered in the bluish dust. Clouds rose when ships landed. Their first excursions in their electric cars had sent up trailing plumes of dust.

Governor Katrina had ordered six Rigel-3 workers to clean up the mess. For many days, these men had been using their suction vehicles to vacuum up the dust, making snaking passes across the plateau. Of course, their passage near the Admin Complex of buildings had stirred up the dust considerably. Some of it had been sucked into the air filtration system. Unfortunately, that equipment was nearly three centuries old, and in dire need of replacement or refurbishing as well.

The intake lines sucked in some of the dust. While filters were supposed to remove the tiny particulate matter, several holes allowed the dust to enter the buildings. Unfortunately, the initial out take lines were in the ceilings of the top floor of the two adjacent buildings. Hence, the daily buildup of the dust in Katrina's twentieth floor office and the top floor of the housing complex, where Katrina and Carla had their suites. From there, the incoming air entered the cooling systems of the massive computer networks into which Carla crawled while performing the necessary upgrades to the equipment. From there, the pipes led further down into the complex, though most of the dust had been deposited in these three areas.

Both women found the daily dust rather annoying, but thought little of it. Dust was always present on any planet, giving maids and housekeepers steady employment on all worlds. The first of October, Governor Katrina was interrupted in her studies by an urgent call on her intercom. "Doctor Becktold. Governor, you best come down to the infirmary at once! One of our maintenance men has just died rather mysteriously! Five others are quite sick."

"On my way, doctor." She cursed her incredibly slow pace in her toe shoes, nearly losing her balance several times. She entered the infirmary only to discover a hive of bustling activity.

"Ah, you're here. That one has died. Those five are in very critical condition," the harried doctor spoke up.

"What's the matter with them? Some virus? Infectious? How come you haven't gotten them cured?" she asked.

"Don't know what is wrong with them! We've used every damn medical machine in the place! According the stupid machines, there is nothing wrong with them. They are supposed to be perfectly healthy, but any damn fool can see that they are dying. They are all running a very high fever and nothing we've given them has brought it down in the slightest. They are all unconscious too."

"Are others coming down with this mystery illness?" she asked.

"So far, no, we are lucky for the moment. I'm not yet ready to issue a formal quarantine of the station. Not enough information on it."

"That's wise. We don't want to cause a panic. So did they perhaps catch it at their workstations?" she inquired, trying to remember the protocols she'd been taught just for such events.

"These men were running the cleanup of the dust out there. I think that their supervisor said they finished that up yesterday. Long project. Dust everywhere."

"Well, that's something. Been having tons of dust in my office and quarters. Guess that'll improve."

"True. What bothers me is the dead man. Come here; take a look at his eyes," Doctor Becktold requested. She moved over to the corpse and watched as his latex gloved hands pried an eye open. It was yellow. She gasped. "Right. My thoughts exactly. I am leaning towards some kind of local pathogen. Combine that with these five." The two moved back to the beds on which the five men lay, tended by nurses. Again, he gently pried an eye open. "Definitely a color change is happening to these five too. Almost conclusive this is a local pathogen of a most virulent variety. Worse, they are not responding to any treatment in the book. I am afraid we'll lose them too."

Katrina thought quickly. "Let me check with Queen Isabella about known local diseases. Keep them alive until I get back," she ordered. "And have someone check on everyone else on the base for similar symptoms."

"Right boss. My thoughts exactly," he replied. She left as hastily as she could manage safely. Instead of going back to her office, she headed to the ground floor and checked out an electric car. Fifteen minutes later, she walked slowly into Queen Isabella's private study just as Hernando led Isabella there.

"Came as quickly as I could," Isabella said. "What's the emergency? Let's sit please."

Both women sat down, relieved. "Six of our maintenance men have contracted some unknown illness. One has already died. All are running a high fever, but our medical machines keep saying the men are healthy. Obviously, they've contracted some kind of local disease our machines and doctors have never encountered before. I was hoping you might have some ideas. The dead man has yellow eyes, bright yellow. The eyes of the five who are still alive are pale yellow, varying shades. My doctor showed me. Can you help? Is this a plague? Ought I quarantine the base? How is it spread?"

Katrina coughed a little.

From the symptoms, Queen Isabella had a very good idea what their ailment actually was. "I am no doctor. However, I think I know what it might be. Can I send over our best, most knowledgeable people to check on them? If it is what I think it might be, they can hopefully cure them."

"Please do. How soon? They are not doing well at all," Katrina replied, coughing again, rather annoyed with herself for perhaps getting a cold right now. Well, the weather was certainly changing.

"She's on her way here now," Queen Isabella said.

"But how? You've not left to — oh! Telepathy. I forgot." Katrina said rather embarrassed.

"Yes. Her name is Rafaela. She, Misty, and Misty's twins, Jane and Sara, are on their way. Ah, here they come now." All four materialized a few feet from the two women and the ever present, but usually silent, Hernando.

She introduced the armless Rafaela to Katrina. "She's our resident expert and has trained Misty well, who in turn has trained her twins. Oh yes, Rafaela is far, far older than she looks. Rejuvenation." Katrina saw a woman wearing the six inch heels and a blue satin gown. Her long black hair was rather curly. The other three were all carrying small backpacks. She tried to hide her surprise about the rejuvenation machine. Time later to inquire about how that was possible. Perhaps, there was more about such things in the massive pile of computer records that she'd not yet seen.

"Hello, very pleased to meet you at last, Governor Katrina. I've heard many good things about you. Let's save the formalities for later though. We need to get to these ill men as soon as possible. Time is our worst enemy."

"Right. One has already died. Come. I've an electric car outside," Katrina replied. "Sorry, I walk rather slowly." To her surprise, Jane, who like the other three women, all wore warm leather tops, pants, and boots, slipped her arm around Katrina's waist.

"I got you," she replied. Sara did the same with Rafaela.

"Thanks, this is much easier."

"Of course, we need a little assistance," Rafaela replied.

"I had the misfortune to once have worn shoes like yours. After I lost my arms when I nearly froze to death, I had my feet partially repaired. Now, I have no choice but to wear these. Ah, here's your car. Nice."

Fifteen minutes later, the five walked into the bustling infirmary. "Doctor Becktold, this is Rafaela, their best healer, and her associates, Misty, Jane, and Sara."

"Pleased to meet you. Sorry about your arms. Have you seen anything like this before?" he asked worriedly. "Nothing that we do seems to help them at all."

"Where were they working?" Rafaela asked, while her three companions began lifting up eye lids and touching the sick men's grey heads, almost as if Rafaela was telepathically telling them what to do, Katrina mused as she watched, coughing twice.

"They were all working to clean up the mountain of that bluish dust covering the spaceport. They finished yesterday, but reported here quite sick. That one died not long afterwards. Is this a local pathogen?" he asked.

"They've all got the Verge Sickness that some of our people get," Rafaela answered. *Bart, get the teleport ready. I think I will be bringing five Rigel-3 men back to Brom for treatment of Verge Sickness.*

You got it. Are you going to tell them what this could mean? He sent back.

Don't know. Prepare some rooms in the basement of Brom Tower.

Katrina coughed again, but her mind was working overtime. "Wait, I read something about Verge Sickness. Isn't that the disease that some young people get when they are about to get the *mentales* gifts? Did I say that right?"

Cat's out of the bag. Doing containment actions now, she sent. "Yes, Katrina. That's basically it. These men are somehow beginning to manifest having just such gifts. However, they all have some form of blockage that's causing their bodies to reject the transformation. We need to get some *bacal* tea into them at once, and then get them to my infirmary, where I can care for them, and get some katalyein to see if their blockages can be removed. If we don't, they are as

406

good as dead men. Doctor, we need a pot of boiling water immediately. Misty, you and the twins know what to do. Try getting a half cup into their systems as soon as possible."

"Okay. I will arrange a shuttle. Where do we take them?" Katrina asked, worried.

"Brom Tower will teleport them up to Brom, where I'll care for them personally."

"Okay. That's faster, right?" Katrina asked and coughed again, clearing her throat.

"Yes, time is critical, if we want to save them."

"Let me look at you, boss. Sounds like you are coming down with a cold too," Doctor Becktold ordered.

He hooked her up to one of the machines, while the tea was being prepared. "Hum. Strange, boss. No signs of a cold. Guess you are okay."

"Probably all that darn dust that's been coming into my office and suite. Carla's had it all over her place too, and it's gotten into the computer's cooling system too. Probably an allergy," Katrina answered.

"Hardly. Allergies would be detected by the medical machine and cured," he replied.

"Let me examine you too, governor," Rafaela said softly. Katrina felt her body tingle, but the armless woman apparently had not done anything to her. How could she, Katrina thought.

"I'd best see Carla too. Could you have her come down here, please?" Rafaela asked politely.

Ten minutes later, a rather dusty Carla came into the infirmary. She was covered in the fine bluish dust. "We have a serious medical emergency. One's already died. This is Rafaela, one of their best healers. She says they have a local disease called Verge Sickness. She's taking them back to her place in Brom to heal them. I don't know why, but Rafaela wanted to see you too. I've come down with a cough. This darn dust anyway."

"Me too. Dust has infiltrated the computer's cooling system, but it's all cleaned up now. Back to normal," Carla replied. "Too bad about the men, though."

Rafaela said, "Okay, Carla, you and Katrina are also coming with us. Both of you are also in the very early stages of

Verge Sickness. Doctor, keep watch on everyone else on this base. If any more show these symptoms, contact Queen Isabella immediately. Time is critical. If we get to them in time, they can make a full and complete recovery. Now then, they are ready to teleport us."

"But," Katrina tried to protest. It was cut off by the teleport activation.

She and the others arrived in the basement of Brom Tower, where Drina, King Emilio's wife Anita, and Venerada Maricela were waiting for them. "Oh my, this *is* bad," Drina commented, getting her first look at the five men, being lifted onto some beds by several of the tower's men.

"I'm not sure I know what's happening here," Governor Katrina said to Venerada Maricela. "Are Carla and I going to get as sick as they are? Is this contagious? I have the base security to consider."

"Let me defer to Rafaela on this one. I can do more for these men right now than I can for you two. She can explain it far better than I can," Venerada Maricela replied, nodding to Rafaela, and deftly passing that hot potato.

"Okay, let's step into the next room, shall we?" Rafaela suggested. The two very worried women followed her, though Carla quietly slipper her arm around Katrina's waist steadying her. Rafaela pushed a pair of chairs out for the two and then tossed her hair to the front and sat down. Dutifully, the two followed suit, but looked rather nervously at her.

"Verge Sickness usually, but not always, happens to some people on Tierra, whose bodies are beginning to adapt to the possession of the *mentales* gifts. It happens because, as the gifts begin to fully mature, the person has severe mental blocks that fight against having those gifts. Another way of looking at it is that they have suffered some severe trauma in their past. Let me give you an analogy. Suppose a woman was severely beaten and raped by a bunch of men. Later on, when she was around a bunch of men, would she not thereafter be very leery at best?" Both women nodded, that seemed quite reasonable.

"Yes, I knew one poor young woman who had something like that happen to her," Carla volunteered. "Afterwards, she was terrified of ever being alone with a man."

"Precisely. Now that they've been given *bacal* tea, which temporarily blocks all *mentales* gifts, what the katalyein will be doing is to attempt to disintegrate those mental blocks," Rafaela explained.

"What's *bacal* anyway? What does it do?" Governor Katrina asked.

"It is a local herb that temporarily suppresses the pituitary gland's operation. You see, the *mentales* gifts are tied closely to the pituitary gland. In the *mentales* gifted, our glands are more than three times those of ordinary people. The herb stops temporarily one side of the ongoing war within their bodies, hopefully allowing the katalyein to get the true source removed, that is, their mental blockages."

"You know about pituitary glands? Amazing," Governor Katrina exclaimed, then coughed.

"Whatever you think of us, we're not as ignorant as many believe. Anyway, as you're suspecting, if we can save those five, when they revive, they will be telepaths, men with the *mentales* gifts. Just what their gifts will be, who can say. Once they recover, they'll have to spend a couple of weeks here getting trained. We have an ancient saying here on Tierra. An untrained telepath is a danger both to himself and to others."

"Oh my! Telepaths!" Governor Katrina exclaimed. "But what about us?"

"I believe you both are in the early stages. I want to have you both thoroughly checked out by tower healers, who are very experienced in these matters. Will that be okay with you? If there isn't anything wrong with you, I'll have the tower teleport you back right away. If there is, let's talk about it then. I would rather error on the side of caution," Rafaela answered rather conservatively.

"Well okay. That's best. But I'm sure it must just be a reaction to all that infernal dust. The whole base is long overdue for maintenance and upgrades. There's a hole in the air intake system," Governor Katrina said.

"Yes, but I finally got all the dust out of the computer's cooling system. What a mess that caused," Carla added.

Just then, ten men and women, all wearing warm leather clothing, entered. "This is one of the tower's Circles.

They will be examining you both. All you have to do is just sit still. It won't hurt." The ten proceeded to sit on the floor. The two noticed each wore a crystal around their necks that began to glow in a pale blue light. Katrina and Carla realized all the tower folks and *mentales* gifted that they had met or seen, also had such a crystal. While they wanted to ask about them, they decided now was not the time. Eight seemed to have a vacant stare on their faces, while one sat outside the circle and observed the other nine. The last man then rose and stood before Governor Katrina and closed his eyes, joining with Rafaela as well.

She felt her body tingle with energy. Somehow, she seemed to sense every cell in her body. Is that even possible, she thought. It did feel incredibly relaxing, though. Then, that wonderful feeling left her. Carla now felt it too. Five minutes later, the "spell" ended. Quietly, the ten rose and left the three alone.

Rafaela cleared her throat. "Well, that is a relief."

"Are we sick too?" Carla asked worriedly.

"You both are about to have your own *mentales* gifts appearing, probably within a day or so. There are no signs of blockages to it in either one of you, so with luck there will be no Verge Sickness for either of you. However, once your bodies have adjusted to the gift, you'll both have to be trained here for a while. You see, if you don't, you'll automatically be picking up the random thoughts of everyone around you. At the crowded spaceport, it would be like hearing hundreds of voices in your head at the same time. Also, your own thoughts would be broadcasted everywhere, and anyone on Tierra with the gift would be overhearing your thoughts. Not good at all. The first aspect of your training will be to learn how to block the thoughts of others and to keep your own thoughts from being broadcasted to everyone around you. Then, we'll determine what other forms your gifts will take and assist you in mastering them. Finally, we'll give you one of these special crystals. They amplify your mental powers a hundredfold. You see, each day a person only has so much potential psi energy to use. When it is exhausted, you will be head blind until you've gotten a good meal and a night's sleep."

"What? Are you saying we'll become telepaths? Like all of you? How can this be?" exclaimed a very surprised Katrina.

"Yes, it has happened to other aliens who have come to Tierra. No one can predict it. Konrad and Nadja both became telepaths, as you already know."

"But I need to be in communication with my base, my people, daily," Governor Katrina protested slightly.

"Hey, I need to be there when Elfe calls me each night. I don't want to miss her calls. She'll get terribly worried about me," Carla complained. "Besides, I just discovered someone has hooked into our computer system illegally, boss. I was going to tell you about this once I finished my back trace — that is, locating where the guilty party was at so you could have them arrested or something. At least, I know their handle: Sly Fox. Can't this wait a while?"

"What? Someone has hacked into our computer network?" Governor Katrina exclaimed.

"They have total access to damned near everything! Even the geo-sat too!" Carla added with emphasis.

"Good god. And on my watch! Well done, Carla!"

Rafaela sent, *Jan, Bart. Carla is very bright. She's found your hack into the base's computer system. Sly Fox, you've been discovered. Jan, join Bart. I've got no choice but to bring Governor Katrina and Carla in on the Underground. They are both shortly going to have the mentales gifts anyway.*

She then said, "Okay, I need to show you something right now. Carla, would you like to meet Sly Fox?"

"Yes, he's the best hacker I've ever come across!" Carla exclaimed. "I got to meet this guy! I did some Net searching. Sly Fox is one of the most wanted system hackers in the entire Imperium!"

As Rafaela led them out of the small room and entered the tunnel complex beneath Brom, she explained, "Ever since the time of the Emperor and Empress, over a century ago, we've had an Underground, who has been charged with monitoring everything that goes on at the spaceport and in all the towers. More than once, they've been able to keep disastrous catastrophes from occurring. Only a handful of people know about the Underground, formed by Emperor Amy and Empress Jan, the grandparents and great-grandparents of many of the Underground members today. I must swear you both to secrecy. Do not reveal the existence or presence of the Underground to anyone. We give you our sworn word they do not ever interfere with any of your spaceport's operations."

She went on, "These tunnels connect to them. Please don't be too shocked at what you are about to see. Besides, once you have gotten your *mentales* gifts, you both can make full use of the Underground to assist you in running your base. Ah, here we are in the master communications room."

"Jan? Jan, you are involved?" Governor Katrina gasped.

"Carla, I'm told you wanted to meet Sly Fox? I'm Sly Fox, well, rather that was my handle over a century ago when I was Empress Jan and set all this up," Jan explained.

"You? Sly Fox? Now I've seen everything! Sly Fox is one of the most famous Imperium underground hackers ever!" Carla exclaimed, very much impressed.

"Yes, but I've been mostly dormant of late. I must say, you are the first person to discover my hack into the spaceport's computer system. How did you ever figure that one out?" Jan asked. "Oh, this is Bart, his wife Anita, and my twin sister, Lilly, and little brother Tom. They usually run all the electronics here. Got our own teleport pad, all powered by disguised solar cells above ground. Totally self-sufficient system, though it needs quite a lot of maintenance and parts replacements that I am going to have to get to doing one of these days," Jan chatted away. Soon, Jan and the Bellweather family became involved with Carla on all manner of technical details.

Governor Katrina stood there flabbergasted. Never had she suspected there could be such a large amount of Imperium technology on Tierra. They didn't even have electricity. Rafaela said, "Come on. I'll show you some more things." Further down the hall, she pointed out their four medical rooms. "Got some of the latest medical machines here, four of them, plus two rejuvenation machines, though they hardly get any use at all. You see, Governor Katrina, you have the Underground watching your *back* now. We can tie into any place on Tierra. Actually, Bart brought you and the sick men here a bit ago. Using him was faster than waiting for a Circle to teleport them."

"I think I've a million questions now. Does Queen Isabella know about all this?" she asked.

"Yes, she does, and we've helped her several times now. She backs us fully and trusts us with her life," Rafaela explained. "Once you have your gifts and have been trained, from your office, you can contact anyone of us about anything. No need to have to hop into that electric car of yours to visit Queen Isabella to ask about the sick men."

"This is all too much to believe, to grasp. Incredible doesn't begin to describe this. And the Imperium doesn't know about all this?" she inquired.

"Nope, they haven't got any idea the Underground exists. A long time ago, one of the governor's heard rumors that we existed. We made the mistake of becoming too visible above ground. We very nearly got exposed. All this equipment has been quietly smuggled in here, mostly Jan's doing. The main thing to realize is that you now have some very powerful allies on Tierra, Governor Katrina. Call on us anytime. That's our purpose here, to help preserve peace and prosperity on Tierra."

All Katrina could do was keep repeating, "Incredible!"

"Now, let's get you both settled into one of these rooms where I can keep an eye on you for a few days. Bart will make a connection to your base so you can issue orders through the intercom in your office or bedroom suite. Pretend you are temporarily unavailable. Plus, Jan will fix up the system so Carla can get her nightly calls from her mate, Elfe."

"Incredible," she repeated and coughed.

While Carla stayed with Bart and Jan continuing their lengthy discussion that now focused on what new equipment the Underground needed, Rafaela and Katrina returned to check on the five men. Venerada Maricela took them aside. "Touch and go. I've had a Circle come and help out. Drina, Anita, and I have knocked out their mental blocks. If they survive the night, they should recover fine, and be ready for training in a couple of days."

"Well, that's good news. What about us, Carla and me?" she asked.

Rafaela answered instead, "By tomorrow you should be able to detect some changes. Let me know if you start hearing voices in your head. Your eyes have already begun to change color."

"Wow. Can I see?" she asked.

That evening, Jan and Carla sat beside the comm center waiting for Elfe's nightly call. Carla commented, "Jan, what's strange is I've not heard from her for the last three nights. It has me worried. Thanks for staying up with me. She's always been checking in each night. So has Jaques; he is supposed to make daily reports. Both have been reporting in daily as ordered, until three nights ago when they stopped. I haven't been able to raise them. Now, I'm starting to get worried about Elfe. It's not like her to not call me."

"Hum, where were they last at and where were they going?" Jan asked.

"I've got that info in my logs, but I'd have to go back to my office to get them."

"Hah, not with Sly Fox on duty." Bart chuckled and watched, as Jan soon brought up her logs. "You can enter your password. I don't really want to hack it if I don't have too."

Carla grinned and typed in her long one. Her logs came up. "Now what?"

Bart spoke up. "You are using geo-sat coordinates, right?" She nodded. "So we bring up the geo-sat overlay. Tom, bring them up on that monitor. We can compare them."

Not wanting to be left out, Lilly added, "We can plot them, make a daily progress image, and see their trail. That ought to get pretty close to where they were when you stopped hearing from them."

"Cool! That saves me a lot of work." Carla was impressed with their efficiency. As they set about their various tasks with Lilly making a large scale map of red dots indicating their nightly call locations, Jan looked at Bart. Both grimaced. Their last known location was on the western side of the far northern Goza Mountains! It was winter there already, almost inhabitable now with frequent blizzards and bitter cold.

A bit later, Ken, Crystal, Katrina, and Maricela, had joined them, and been fully briefed on the situation. Ken exclaimed, "My god! That Mc Greggor woman sent them into the northern Goza in the middle of the winter! She's sent them on a suicide run!" He explained what the conditions would likely be that far north.

"But it's only October," Katrina complained.

"That far north, winters are exceptionally bitter and start in September, unless they made it even further north, where the snows almost never melt," Crystal explained.

"I'll order shuttles to go out and try to find them," Governor Katrina responded to the emergency.

"I wouldn't do that unless you want your shuttles destroyed. The winds and crosswinds up there are fierce. Tell them Jan, you know more about their shuttles than I do," Ken suggested.

"He's right. They can't take the torques without cracking up. They'll be tossed about like a kite in the wind. Not even our gliders dare fly there," Jan added.

"You have gliders here?" asked Governor Katrina.

Ken smiled and nodded. "We'll have to go overland, but even that is fraught with perils," Ken suggested rather worriedly.

Carla moaned, "It's all my fault. I should have said something the first night that Elfe didn't call me."

Ken countered, "Carla, it's doubtful that only a few days would have made the slightest difference. We're going to have to mount a rescue party."

"I have to go with you. She's my mate. I have to go," Carla insisted.

"But you have no training for such harsh conditions," Governor Katrina pointed out, unwilling to sacrifice her computer technician on apparently such a dangerous mission.

"If it was your wife out there, you'd go too, and you know it," Carla said defiantly. Katrina flushed; she knew she would and relented.

Ken took charge. "Okay, we are going to need to form up a rescue party."

Jan quickly spoke up, "I'll bring Bernardo, Henry, and Ben with me. But we'll need the best possible guides. Carla, we can get you some proper gear too. Ken, you see what you can find. Try the Sisterhood in Hilliard Heights. Amy's suggestion. I just told her about this mess."

"Okay, you head back to Exchange City and get the heaviest winter gear possible. Try Jack's Outpost. He's always got good winter gear. I'll get a hold of Hilliard Heights. From their last known position, I don't know how you can get there from this side. Probably have to bring everyone from here over to the western side. Bart, start working out reasonable teleport locations. We don't want to land them on an isolate ledge somewhere."

"On it boss. Lilly, Tom, lend me a hand with this one," Bart barked, rather excitedly.

Rafaela spoke up, "Jan, I'll send along some *bacal* leaves in case Carla develops Verge Sickness. I don't believe she will, though. I want to play it safe."

Chapter 24 In the Land of Ice and Snow

Elfe had made one startling discovery, the ruins of the ancient Portillo Tower. While she wanted to stay and make a proper survey of the site and perhaps begin some test excavations, she had to continue on northward with her party. This was a geological survey after all. From here, Jaques led them into the outer range of the Goza Mountains proper, leaving the foothills behind.

One packhorse carried his surveying gear; a second carried their camping gear; a third carried their food supplies. The five Rigel security guards were bored out of their minds, continually wishing they were anywhere but here, riding on these awful beasts of burden. Jaques, in contrast, was in heaven. He was discovering mineral deposits right and left. After her big discovery of the tell that was now Portillo, Elfe was hopeful of discovering more such ancient sites or tells.

Then, it began to snow. "We're prepared for this," Jaques convinced everyone, and they pressed onwards, deeper into the Goza. However, they did not know of the existence of the fierce predatory cats, the Montaña beasts. That evening as they began to setup camp in the snow, one of these giant cats jumped them, killing two of the security men, before making off with a pair of horses. Jaques didn't know the cats were dining voraciously, preparing for the long, harsh winter. Foolishly, he decided to press onwards, ordering Elfe not to mention this in her nightly report. Under his control, she obeyed.

The next night, the smaller group made a fatal mistake. "Hey, there is a natural cave up there. Good place to shelter for the night," Jaques pointed out. On his world, that may have been a wise decision. However, lacking intimate knowledge of Tierra, he had no way of knowing they were walking into the lair of one of the Montaña beasts! Worse, the cat was out on the hunt at the time.

As they set up camp in the cavern, Elfe asked, "Jaques, what is all this matting here? Do bears live in here?" She grew more and more nervous about this place. All her training suggested they'd entered an animal's lair.

"I'll post guards all night, Elfe. Nothing to worry about. We'll be safe and warm in here," he replied. Elfe began to heat up their rations on her small cook stove, while the men prepared the camp and fed the horses. Their grain was getting low, but Jaques didn't think that would be too serious a problem. He figured tomorrow he'd make a call and have a shuttle drop them more via parachute. Already the winds had picked up enough that he doubted the shuttle could land safely. He didn't want his excursion to be tainted by the crash of a shuttle.

Elfe had just finished eating when it happened. The great cat returned to its lair, only to find food had very conveniently placed itself there. Two guards went down before anyone knew what was happening. The lanterns were smashed and total darkness fell. D-gun shots flew right and left, until Jaques screamed for them to take care and not shoot themselves. Screams from the horses were hideous. Jaques and the remaining guard fired blindly toward the horses. Elfe felt her right arm being ripped, and she screamed out, terrified. If only there had been light! Jaques felt hot breath on his face. He fired at the same time the cat tried to pounce on him. He dropped his gun and rolled. Play dead, he told himself. Quiet. Eternal quiet.

Then, he heard a low moaning. Elfe. He lit a match. The giant beast was dead. He dropped the match, crying, "Ouch!" He lit another and managed to find one of their lanterns they'd not yet lighted. Now he could see the carnage. The cat was dead, blaster hole in its head. The Rigel man was headless. Their horses, dead. Elfe was bleeding from a claw cut down her right arm. He acted, found their first aid kit, and began to clean her wound, wrapping it in a sterile bandage.

"Well, now I'd best radio for help, Elfe. You were right; this was a lair. Incredible beast. Look at the size of that cat!" He began rummaging for one of their radios. A bit later, he came back and sat down beside Elfe. "We're in trouble, Elfe. All the radios are smashed. We've got no way to call for help."

"What — what are we going to do? I don't want to die in

this cave," Elfe fought hard to keep from crying. Don't get all emotional, she told herself. *Fear is my enemy now.* "How are our food supplies?" she tried to think of something useful.

Jaques rummaged around. "Looks good on the food. We can melt snow for water. Guess we're going to have to walk out of here tomorrow."

The next day was a white-out blizzard. They had no choice but to hold up in the cavern. The following day, they packed up what they thought was the most vital for their survival, dividing the load. Elfe carried about a third of the weight; her arm throbbed and was not healing properly yet. A few minutes in a medical machine, and she would never know her arm was sliced.

"We've got more problems, Elfe. The compass is broken. I have no way to tell directions. Plus, I know we came up that way," he pointed to a huge snowdrift far over their heads. "We can't go back the way we came. The only way out of here is on up that way. It looks sort of like a path. Perhaps there is a small village somewhere near here where we can get help."

"Can't we stay in the cavern? They'll be able to locate us via infrared scans from the geo-sat," she suggested.

"Nope, inside the cavern, our body heat will be totally blocked by the mountain. We could stay out here, but we'll freeze long before they find us. Our best chance is up that way. Pray for a village soon," he suggested. The two began trudging through the knee-high snow, heading on up, ever deeper into the northern Goza. All the d-guns were destroyed; they felt defenseless, hoping and praying no more of the cats would appear.

Day by day, they trudged every upwards, deeper into the mountains. Steadily their strength began to diminish from the strenuous effort to plow through the deep snow. Twice, they slept through the entire day, waiting out other blizzards that whirled around them. Their small camp stove was their lifeline. Elfe's arm became infected, but there was little Jaques could do for her, except continue pushing on, praying the village would soon appear. It just had to be here, he thought. This had to be some kind of path, well-traveled at one time. He didn't know that had been nearly two hundred fifty years ago.

Feverish, Elfe called out, "Jaques. There, openings. The village." They increased their pace and entered what was obviously a man-made entrance to a cavern complex. Just as soon as Elfe entered it, her spirits rose. This was another archaeological site! Jaques was wholly depressed. No help was here, and he was the limits of his endurance, as was Elfe.

Elfe knew that she had stumbled upon a huge site, but she was too sick and too exhausted to do anything about it. She slumped onto the ground, which was covered in a thick layer of pale bluish dust that had blown into the complex. It was all Jaques could do to set up their meager camp before he too collapsed from sheer exhaustion. He figured they were doomed now. There was no hope of their ever being found. His dreams consisted of a futuristic archaeologist stumbling upon their skeletons and subsequently trying to figure out who they had been and how they had died. Over and over, he kept trying to tell them he was not from Rigel-3, but from Ettine-3.

"This is nuts! A rescue in the dead of winter in the northern Goza! Impossible!" twenty-five year old Mary Tribe e Hays exclaimed wildly. "This is suicide." She looked at the others who had gathered in her Sisterhood house. She was all set to sit back and relax through the long winter. Her free mate Jean Hays e Tribe nodded in agreement.

Jan, Bernardo, Henry, Ben, and Carla were there and had just explained what they needed: a guide to get them over the mountains, unless Bart could teleport them there, and then to track the party and rescue them, if they were still living.

"Please, Elfe is my mate. I must find her. She's out there I just know it. I have to get to her," Carla pleaded with the woman.

Jean sighed, "Missa, she has a point. If you or I were out there, you know nothing would stop the other from trying."

Mary sighed too, glancing at her mate. "All right then. I will do this but only because Carla and Elfe are like us. If it was her husband, forget it."

Bernardo breathed a sigh of relief. "You are the very best guides in all Hilliard Heights. If anyone can find Elfe, it's you."

"Well that may be, but you all will never make it dressed as you are in those southern garb. You'll be an ice cube the first night out. Jean, take them to the boss and get them properly prepared. I'll see to the reindeer and the supplies," Mary said quietly. "I still say this could well be the end of us all. I won't take any responsibility, if you fall off a cliff." She added, "We'll take ten reindeer with us, using three as pack beasts. If we are lucky and find them, she can ride one back with us." She ignored the possibility that they could also find the other men.

A few hours later, Mary, bundled up in a very heavy, fur lined parka and pants, tied up the ten reindeer, eight with saddles and two with pack frames, loaded heavily. Jean joined her, leading the now parka-clad five. "All set here, you ready love? Going to be quite an adventure, donna ya think?"

"Suicide mission is more like it, but she's her mate. We have to try. Okay, Bernardo. Get us teleported to their last known location. Mind you, don't drop us on a cliff or something equally bad," Mary barked.

Ten minutes later, Bart and Anita finished the last of the five teleports, dropping them off at the last known position of the party. All around them, the winds swirled, whipping up snow. The world was white or dark grey, where the stone of the mountain could be seen. Bitter cold chilled their faces. Carla's hopes began to sink. How could poor Elfe survive in this?

Mary poked around in the snow for a time. "Ah, they are fools after all. They headed deeper into the Goza! This way, mount up and never, *ever* lose sight of the rider in front of you. If you do, yell out at once! Jean, bring up the rear will you? Men, you lead the pack reindeer." She led them off into the white, frigid world of the northern Goza.

Yet, Mary was no fool. Bernardo convinced her, if they ran into any serious trouble, Bart was standing by to teleport them to safety. With four telepaths along, Mary finally relaxed, though she doubted very much that they'd find the missing party, let alone alive. They were going the wrong way to safety.

Bernardo followed single-file behind her. He called out, "Mary, how can you tell they went this way? Snow is everywhere."

"They are on horseback. That might be fine in the summer, but it's suicide now. Even reindeer might not make it. Horse shit. Leaves warm piles. Melts the snow over it. Sunlight is also more readily absorbed over the piles, which also melts it some. Look for dimples, Bernardo," she explained. *Honestly, these tower kids don't know anything about the real world.*

Bernardo thought about sending her a response. If the weather wasn't so bad, he was ornery enough to do it. Just now, the winds whipped his face, and he thought better of it. On they rode, climbing ever higher.

"Ah, halt here," Mary barked. "Keep a sharp eye out for Montaña beasts. Something happened here." She dismounted and lunged her way through the snow. Then, she began moving snow around some. One by one, the others filed into this large open area.

Jean called out above the wind, "Camping spot?"

"Yes, cat got them. Trying to figure out how bad it was," Mary yelled back. While she continued her examination, Bernardo explained about the Montaña beasts to Carla, whose face became white as the snow.

She said, "Governor Mc Greggor said nothing about there being predatory beasts on Tierra. My god, Elfe! Is she dead?"

Mary moved back to the group, who remained mounted. With her back to the chilling wind, she yelled, "Old campsite. They were here. Found the remains of two Rigel aliens and a horse. They continued on into the mountains, fools. Mount up; we are going to push it some. I feel a blizzard coming."

"What? You mean this isn't a blizzard?" yelled Carla.

"No, this is just a normal winter's day up here in the north." She turned and got back on her reindeer and headed off again. Around noon, the sky cleared and the orange-red sun poked its head out, nearly blinding them all. Mary stopped, and had them all don their protective lenses, crude sunglasses as far as Carla was concerned. "We should push it some and try to find shelter before the blizzard hits."

"But the sun's out," Carla protested.

Jan called out, "Weather's really weird on Tierra. Pole shift caused it. Trust her; Mary knows what she is doing, Carla."

They rode on upwards until late afternoon. They were on the western slope, and dark came later than it did in Hilliard Heights on the eastern slopes of the Goza. "Ahead. Shelter, unless there's a cat in it. Can you check it out, Bernardo?" Mary asked.

For a moment, his crystal glowed a pale blue. "No signs of any life," he yelled. The winds had started to pick up. As they reached the cavern's entrance, giant snowflakes began falling, whipped by the winds.

"Oh crap!" Mary yelled. "It's awful inside. Brace yourselves; we don't have any choice but to stay here." She rode on inside and lit a lantern. Soon, Jean entered and got her lantern going as well. The others stood stunned at the grizzly sight. Hastily examining the signs, Mary added, "Two more Rigel alien bodies. No sign of Elfe or Jaques. Lost all their horses though. The fools make camp in a Montaña beast's den. Cat probably returned to find its supper waiting for it. Looks like they fired an awful lot of blasters. Look at all the circular holes in the walls and cat. Here, they gathered up all these things in one pile. Over there, it looks like they sorted through all their gear. I'd guess at least one of them got smart and packed just what they needed. They are on foot now."

"Those are portable radio communicators. No wonder they couldn't call for help. Oh Elfe!" Carla cried out. "She's out there in this blizzard!"

Mary didn't want to tell her she thought Elfe was probably dead now and that in a day or two, they'd find her frozen corpse, unless the Montaña beast got it first. Instead, she set about issuing orders, having the men drag the corpses off to one side, while she and Carla set up their tents and Jean took care of the reindeers.

Jean returned with a load of nicely chopped resinous pines. Soon, she had a crackling fire going, and Mary began warming water for tea. Outside, the winds howled, occasionally blowing a wave of snow into the cavern. Soon all gathered around the fire, warming themselves, while chewing on their dried food. Carla was never so glad for a cup of hot tea in her life. "It'll warm you from the inside," Mary commented. "Tonight, we all sleep close together, wrap up in all our blankets. With a bit of luck we can ride it out."

"How long will it last?" Carla asked.

"Probably til dawn," Mary replied, "that is, if it follows the usual pattern. Hard to tell this far north."

Carla shivered. She whispered, "There isn't much hope is there?"

Mary glanced at her mate, Jean. "I can't pretend it's not really bad out there. If they got to some kind of shelter," she paused, and then changed her mind. "Look, they survived this attack and went on. Jaques and Elfe must be very strong people. She must be a fighter."

Carla grinned, "She is. She's always been the strong one. I so depend upon her, you know. Ever since she's been gone, that's become so real to me, just how much I need her. I guess that's why I've been trying to pay it back, helping Katrina when she's needed me — what with all her body changes." Mary and Jean understood what she meant. Everyone turned in and tried to stay warm. Their reindeer merely chomped away on the dried grasses Jean set out for them.

Still, cold and shivering, the group rose as dawn's light filtered into the cavern, highlighting the grizzly sight. Jean made only a small fire for tea, while the others saddled the reindeer and broke camp. As they again chewed on their dried rations, Mary looked outside. One by one, the others came to see the results of the blizzard. The path they had come up yesterday was buried in an enormous drift. Yet to their right, the high winds had blown a winding path clear of its previous drifts.

As Carla joined her, Mary commented, "If they got caught in the previous blizzard and were on foot, they most likely headed up that way. We know they didn't return the way they came."

"Where does that lead?" Carla asked. The path looked dangerous to her. It was only about five feet wide and rocky. A sheer cliff lay to the left of the path, while an unclimbable mountainside lay to its right.

"Been up here once in the summertime. There is an abandoned complex not too far up there. If they could have possibly made it that far, there is some chance we might find them alive. We best get moving. It's going to snow in a few hours."

"How can you tell that?" Carla asked.

"Clouds. See they've broken now allowing a bit of sun through. That means by noon, it'll be cloudy again and likely snow. No blizzard though, not until tomorrow. Come on; let's get a move on it before the snow makes the path slippery."

Again, they rode single file up the path with Mary taking point, as always. The path seemed cleverly laid out, wandering ever upwards like a snake, but taking the gentlest gradient available from the surrounding mountainside. The blizzard had cleared the snow off the first five miles, but then it turned eastward again. Here they hit heavy snow, but the reindeer were perfectly suited for it. Their biggest problem was that their animals wanted to stop and lick snow rather frequently.

Mary was right, just after lunch the sky was overcast once more. Gentle, pure white, giant flakes began to descend from the sky overhead. The eternal stillness was only broken by the labored breathing of the ten reindeer, as they continued trudging upwards, gaining elevation by the hour. Carla had not noticed it, but they left the tree line far behind them.

Around four that afternoon, the flakes began falling heavily. Even Carla knew they had to find shelter soon before darkness fell. She could not imagine trying to continue traveling in the dark on such a narrow trail. Then, Mary cried out, "There it is. The western entrance. Come on everyone. Shelter ahead."

Mary led them up to an entrance. One didn't need to be an archaeologist to recognize the entrance was manmade. An arch of stone blocks held in place by a key stone beckoned them to enter. They rode on inside and halted while Mary and Jean lit their lanterns.

"What is this place?" Carla whispered, as if ghosts of

former inhabitants might be roused by her voice. She felt shivers down her spine, and she heard voices in her head. "Do you hear the voices? Elfe! That's Elfe." She cried.

Mary looked at her, her head half-cocked in disbelief. "Voices? I don't hear anything at all, Do you Jean?"

"No, ghosts? Is this place haunted?" Jean whispered, growing worried. Men, those she could and did fight, but not intangible ghosts!

"Can't you hear her? Elfe! Elfe! I'm here," Carla called out.

Bernardo looked at Jan, curling his eyebrows as if to say, "Has she lost it?"

Jan had an idea. *Do the voices sound like this?*

"Yes, exactly, Jan. Can you hear her too?" Carla asked.

"You are in telepathic contact with them," Jan explained. "Carla, focus, see if you can sense which direction they are coming from?"

"That way, further inside." Mary and Jan handed their reins to the boys, along with Carla's. The three moved forward, a lantern held high. This was some kind of entrance chamber. Four exits led deeper into the complex, but Carla headed down the third one. It quickly narrowed. About fifty feet ahead, it opened into another room, filled with dust and the two missing aliens!

Jaques was unconscious; his body temperature was dangerously low. Nearby wrapped in several blankets was Elfe. Carla ran over to her mate. "She's sick, wounded. Fever. Help me, please!"

Mary took charge. "Jean, get a fire going. Bernardo, Ben, Henry, get the reindeer unsaddled and get all our lanterns going. Carla, let her stay covered up, until we get the fire going." She headed to her pack and began foraging for tea and her first aid kit. Within a few minutes, the room was well illuminated, a fire crackled, and both patients were now moved as close as they dared bring them to the flames. Jean tended the tea, while Mary and Carla began to examine Elfe.

"Her arm. It's her arm," Carla exclaimed. The makeshift bandage was blood soaked. The odor from it indicated infection, as did her fever. Jan took this opportunity to glance at Carla's eyes. Bright yellow. Her suspicions were confirmed. As Mary examined Elfe more closely, she lifted her eyelids. Jan caught a glimpse of yellow eyes there too. She glanced at the floor. It was covered in a layer of germanium dust, probably blown in here by the winds. Elfe had lain on the stone floor for days, probably inhaling it, Jan theorized. Now she checked on Jaques' eyes. They were brown, showing no signs of having changed color — at least not yet. He was on his back.

Mary sat back and reported, "She's got an infection in her arm. Probably sliced by the giant cat in that last battle. We best get her back, Jan. Now is the time for Bart, if he can, while we're here inside this place."

"On it. Give him a few minutes," Jan replied. "Bernardo, you stick around until everyone's gone and make sure the reindeer don't get spooked. Bring the last lantern with you."

Mary and Carla lifted up Elfe and soon vanished from sight. Jean stayed with the reindeer until the end, along with Bernardo. Then, they too vanished, appearing just outside of Brom, where Henry and Ben were frantically trying to calm down the ten reindeer, which were spooked by suddenly appearing elsewhere than where they'd been. Under Jean's masterly hands, the beasts calmed down quickly, and the teens led them into Brom Tower's stables and bedded them down. Later, they joined the others in the medical rooms. Both Jean and Mary were quite surprised to see the Underground. Both had heard rumors of its existence and were very honored to actually be in it.

Rafaela and Katrina were standing beside one doorway. Misty and Jane were just finishing up with Elfe. Carla sat by her mate's side. In the next room, Jake was handling Jaques. After stabilizing him, Bart teleported him to the spaceport's infirmary, where Doctor Becktold was expecting him, thanks to Governor Katrina's call to him. He was also asked to keep an eye on the possibility that Jaques too might get the Verge Sickness. He did not and days later, Rafaela theorized he had not inhaled much of the dust, while Elfe had. She was found lying on her side with her nose on the floor.

Misty pronounced, "That's that. I've got her infection

cleared up, and her wound healed. It's pinkish now. I don't think there'll be much of a scar, but if there is, the tower healer can work on it some. Now, Rafaela, it's your turn. She's got the gift too."

"So she's going to be all right then?" Mary asked, holding Jean's hand firmly. Her eyes were watering.

"Yes, you found her just in time. Another day or two and she might not have made it. Certainly not Jaques," Misty answered honestly. "Very well done, Mary, Jean!"

Jean's eyes watered, too, as she saw how much Carla cared for Elfe. She continued to sit beside the bed, stroking Elfe's forehead, whispering to her. At last, Elfe roused and squeezed Carla's hand. Mary and Jean quietly backed out of the room to wipe their eyes together.

"You found me? I thought I'd never see you again, Carla. I cried so hard. It was so cold, so cold," Elfe whispered.

"It was my time to be there for you, my love. Rest now. You are safe and healed," Carla whispered back, still squeezing her mate's hand tightly.

Neither realized Rafaela was examining them and their mental states. Both had fully developed *mentales* gifts now and would need to be trained as soon as Elfe regained her strength. Rafaela quietly stepped back to report her findings to Katrina, who was very relieved to hear the good news.

All three women returned to the spaceport near the end of October. They had received both their basic therapy and their mandatory *mentales* training. All three women were highly enthusiastic about the therapy, each felt a renewed vitality of life. While they all had telepathy, of course, and their own germanium crystal, the forms of their gifts varied. Elfe had an uncanny ability to "see" what had happened around a certain area in the past. This she found highly useful in her archaeological work. Carla was now able to pervade all manner of "machines" and diagnose what was wrong with them, though she put this skill to work more often on computer systems. Governor Katrina's gift lay in knowing whether or not a person was telling the truth. She preferred this description to being able to detect if a person was lying. Either way, this was perfect for her work.

Chapter 25 Finding a Senator

During September, somehow Queen Isabella had to get an acceptable senator to represent Tierra in the Imperial Senate. That this new senator would be staying with and seated with those from the Ataro Empire mostly alleviated her fears that whomever they sent would not be abducted and mistreated, as she and her wives had been by Senator Carlos. True, that was no guarantee something similar could not happen, it was just far more unlikely.

She was facing the first of October deadline. At that time, Emperor Kino was sending a group to Tierra, bringing her necessary electronic communications equipment and her own deep space transport ship. On the return side, they would take the chosen senator to Proxima Prime. Thus, while the others were handling Katrina and later the rescue mission, she focused on this serious problem. While the giant crystals actually posed a far more serious threat, that one could be delayed. The choice of a senator could not be. She kept in near daily touch with the various leaders of the kingdoms.

At Valen, King Alano met with his Pentagram of Power. "Look, Isabella has been hounding me nearly every day about this damn senator issue. I'd love to do it, but I would rather be king. How about you, Concepcion? I could nominate you."

He didn't expect her retort. "You do that and I'll have to kill you, Alano! Good god, I don't want to end up like Isabella! We both know out there in the Imperium, our yellow eyes are a dead giveaway that we are telepaths. You couldn't even walk to the market without being terrified that someone would come up behind you, knock you out, and then mutilate you just as they did to Isabella and Lena and Amy and Jan. I've no intention of ever putting myself in that position! Find some other sucker." That ended the conversation dead.

When Queen Isabella contacted King Alano next, he replayed his wife's diatribe for her. *No way does Valen want to be involved in that. Find yourself some other moron who wishes to become a victim.* She sighed. Over and over, she heard relatively similar expressions from the other rulers.

In desperation, she finally began asked the rulers, "Do I have your backing to pick someone myself? If so, don't criticize my choice." By the last week of September, she had the majority agreement that she should go ahead and appoint the next senator from Tierra.

Over dinner, she confided in the remaining Gang of Ten members, "Well, I have at least gotten the majority of the rulers to consent to my choosing our new senator. Wonderful. Now it is in my lap. Who can I possibly suggest for this position? Originally, we thought it best to choose someone who had lived off-world and had a lot of experience out there. If it weren't for Jan, I'd probably still be Senator Carlos' slave telepath. I can't send someone with no off-world experience at all. My god, that would be tantamount to a death sentence."

"Calm down, mom," Amy countered. "This time, they will be under the protection of the other Ataro senators. It's not likely they will try again. But I can see the great benefit of having a senator who had lived off-world, I won't deny that point."

Zarita began thinking. Originally, she wanted to get back out there in the galaxy and begin her destruction of all-powerful men. After they had murdered her Neva body, she wanted revenge, particularly on President Snarry, who she still held responsible, even though at this time, he seemed blameless. Fifteen years had passed since then. She had made powerful new friends. Her new life on Tierra was full of promises, particularly with all the great crystals of power she now possessed.

She began to ponder the whole issue. *Look, these crystals make me incredibly powerful! But Isabella is on a rampage to get them all turned into the towers. That means in a little while, only the towers will possess these power crystals. The rest of us will be powerless against the towers. They will take over, and I'll be a peon yet again! I simply will not be usurped of my power. Not ever, not again! So what do I do? Join a tower? Hell no! And be subject to the venerados? Ha. The tower technicians are also mere peons, carrying out the will of the venerados. No way, not this woman! But what do I do? I'm scared that any day now, Isabella is going to demand I turn in my crystals. I can't let that happen.*

She thought some more. *If I stay here, the best thing I can do is to seduce Governor Katrina. I think she'll be easy prey, especially if she gets the gift too. We all know she is a lover of women. I can seduce her and get her to marry me. I'd have dual citizenship then and could travel anywhere I want. No, Katrina would want me here with her. While I would be the second most powerful woman on Tierra, I'd always be trapped here, unless I could somehow get Katrina transferred to some other world. But that's no good either. I don't want to be stuck on some backwater, primitive world like Nadja was. If I can't come up with anything else, seducing Katrina is at least something, though. What good would having all that power if I can't do anything but suck up to a bunch of natives going uba guba?*

Her mind roamed even wilder. *Well, maybe I should be the new senator. I'll be back on Proxima Prime again. I could get at Snarry from there. I'd be protected, at least Isabella thinks so. I'm sure she believes that'll be the case. Senators are not the brightest fellows, so I doubt it. If I can take my crystals with me, then I might well be invincible. Hey, Isabella said that senator's ID cards allow them to travel almost anywhere with diplomatic immunity! I like the sound of that. But I'd need lots of credits. They have this huge fund set up for Neva's heirs. Maybe out there I could somehow get my hands on that money. After all, I'm Neva. They killed me. That money is rightfully mine.*

Now her thoughts continued exploring this avenue. *Jan is always saying that the fatal flaw of the Imperium is that computers control everything. But I don't know squat about computers. I could learn. If I knew half of what Jan knows. . .* She didn't finish that thought. Possibilities flew past her far too fast to vocalize. Then, from some dark corner of her mind, something that Amy had once said floated back into her conscious thought. *All mentales gifts could be learned. Yes, that's it. I can learn to do other things, especially since I've got all these power crystals! A senator has access to lots of secret information. This is my ticket out of here and back to the power that I truly deserve!*

The next morning, she visited Queen Isabella. "I've been thinking about the senator position. None of the kings and queens wants anything to do with it. You can't send a head blind person out there, that's far too dangerous. No *mentales* gifted wants to take the chance on being mutilated as you were, and Lena, Amy, and Jan. So I've been thinking about it, Queen Isabella. You know how I hate my folks, and that I've disconnected my life from them. I've given this a whole lot of thought. I'd like to be Tierra's senator. I'm young and bright. I'm not worried about being kidnaped. I've got my fine jewelry," she hinted. "I think I can learn a lot quickly and be able to fairly represent all Tierra, though probably not Valen's. But Valen's one small kingdom now and not worth much," she justified, playing on Isabella's dislike and distrust of Valen.

"Honey, are you sure about this? The galaxy out there is a dog-eat-dog place. You would be so on your own out there. I had Amy and Jan to protect me. You have no one," Isabella countered, though Zarita saw she was considering her offer. What other choices did she have? None at the moment.

"That's not quite true. I would have all the senators from the Ataro Empire looking out for me. I am sure they would help me learn what I need to know very quickly. I have my fancy jewelry, which neither you nor Amy and Jan had. I should be safe enough. Please. This way I can make a valuable contribution to Tierra," Zarita pleaded.

Why is it that each time we need a senator there is only one choice, one candidate? Isabella thought. *She's so young, but who else could I possibly tap? I can't hit Jan, she's about to marry Amy and would totally refuse me. She is so young too.* "I will give your request some thought, Zarita. How old are you now?"

"Sixteen," she lied convincingly. "I ought to get some body adjustments from Inez so that I look a bit older, don't you think so?" Zarita had picked up on Isabella's remaining negative consideration.

"You would be an awfully young senator. If anyone asks your age, tell them eighteen, dear," Queen Isabella advised the teen. "Let me make sure no one else is coming forward, okay?"

"Sure," Zarita replied and left. She knew Isabella would come around soon, and she had some preparations to make. She'd found a few more of the giant crystals around the Exchange City markets and acquired them. She took all them to her jewelers. "I would like this one cut up like the others into smaller polished stones. I want a belt studded with them, black satin with a leather underlay, please. The rest I want polished into spherical balls. Can you do that?"

"Why certainly, miss. It will take me a week. Come, let's pick out your belt design," he said, once more seeing a fair amount of gold coming his way, especially if he didn't report this to Queen Isabella's court.

Why spheres? Zarita could not exactly put her finger on that detail. She knew the crystals were not easily recognized for what they really were, when polished up as those in her jewelry had been. In the back of her mind, she recalled once reading about some mystics or other who used crystal balls in their profession. If pressed, she would have probably mentioned that as her inspiration.

Two days later, Queen Isabella gave her consent for Zarita to become their next senator. "If you get your breasts further enlarged to those of an adult and your hair a bit longer, that will significantly alter your appearance, Zarita. Are you absolutely certain that you want to do this?"

"Oh yes, very much so."

"Okay then. I don't know how long your term will be as our senator, but probably quite a few years. I'll have a comm system here so you can chat with me anytime. I'll keep you posted from here, and you keep me abreast of Senate developments."

"Absolutely. You can count on me," Zarita exclaimed, very proud of her achievement. *Now I am heading back into a position of power!*

Queen Isabella then began a very lengthy chat with Zarita, outlining all she knew about the Senate and its operations. She asked her to check up on several other Closed World senators for her. In short, she did her best to get the teen hatted up on what to expect. "The worst part of daily living was those giant twelve inch finger nails that the women

434

senators are expected to have, though those huge skirts were quite an annoyance too."

"Well, perhaps I can see if Inez can lengthen my nails some so I can get used to having such long talons," Zarita suggested. Once Queen Isabella finished with her, she headed back to her room at Elegant Fashions Inc and found Lilly. The two discussed further body modifications. An hour later, Zarita underwent some minor alterations. Her thick, slightly curly, black hair now fell to her ankles, impressive, she thought. Her nails were six inches long so that she could get used to them before she had to get their length doubled once she arrived on Proxima Prime. In addition, her bosom was now that of an adult Tierra woman, monster melons.

Next, she and Lilly picked out more gowns for her to take. Lilly also arranged to have her existing tops altered to fit her much larger bosom. Zarita then began to pack her things into two shipping crates, leaving room for the new spherical crystals to be hidden in the middle of the crates. She planned to put half in each, just in case a crate got mislaid. She left nothing to chance.

The third of October, two deep space transports arrived from the Ataro Empire. One ship was brand new and was christened the Tierra Transport. Now Queen Isabella had her own ship she could use to travel to the Ataro system whenever the need arose. One of the arriving ships also contained a substantial amount of electronic equipment, along with a small power plant to provide the electricity needed for all the new communications equipment.

The technician from the Emperor set up her comm center in one unused study. He gave lessons on the proper operation to Queen Isabella, Hernando, Gabriella, and Amy. Gabriella became the full time operator of the Imperial Comm Center, as Isabella christened it, very much pleasing her youngest daughter. Now Gabriella had an important place in the queen's court.

Once that installation and training was completed, the second transport prepared to depart, taking Senator Zarita Valen along. She had her dozen spherical crystals stowed in individual pod silk bags and carefully packed in the centers of the two crates. Wearing a light blue satin gown that highlighted her shapely form, yet showing enough of her black stockings and her tiny toe shoes, she adjusted her butterfly hair clasp, allowing her ankle length hair to drape down her back. Next, she fastened her tiara securely and made a small adjustment to her new belt with its eighteen oval shaped, polished blue stones. Zarita felt personally armed to the teeth.

Already her two crates had been taken over to the spaceport. She fastened her ID card to the top of her gown, noticing its stripes indicating she was a senator and thus the diplomatic stripes. Freedom was hers. She stepped out of her room at Elegant Fashions Inc for the last time. There she gave her farewells to Inez, Peter, Lilly, and Nita, thanking them for everything. Nita followed her down the elevator and lent her a steadying arm as the two walked over to the Imperial Castle, chatting away.

"I do love having these long nails, Nita, and my hair too. Best changes yet, but I'm going to miss all of you guys."

"I know; we're going to miss you too, but maybe you can come back for visits sometimes. You'll probably get some chances to do that, I would think. I love your nails too. I've been thinking of having mine done too. They look really great on you, Zarita."

"Thanks, Nita. You'd look good in them; I just know it. I'll send you all back some fashion catalogues, if I can find them. Isabella said that the Ataro Empire makes shuttle runs between Proxima Prime and our home worlds several times a year. So keep your eyes open for a package, Nita. And do get your nails done. I just know that you'll love them too. Maybe you could even convince Amy and Jan and Adrianna to get theirs done as well. Oh, here we are. I have butterflies." Nita giggled.

Inside the gates, everyone, who was still here, gathered to wish their senator well and see her off. First, Zarita came up to Queen Isabella and gave her a hug. "Thanks. I won't let you down."

"I know you won't. Be careful. Stay alert and try to enjoy yourself," she replied.

Zarita gave Amy, Gabriella, Drina, and Adrianna hugs

as well. "When the others get back, tell them I said goodbye and that I'll miss them," she asked of Amy. Then, she shook hands with Hernando. Finally, he helped her step gracefully into the waiting electric car. The Rigel-3 security guard whisked her out of the castle gates. Once rounding the corner, they passed the security gates; he opened it up, and they shot across the plateau to her waiting transport ship. Meanwhile, the teens dashed up to the top of the castle and looked towards the northwest. A short while later, Gabriella pointed out, "There she goes!" The sleek, silver, deep space transport slowly lifted off from Tierra, on its way to deliver Senator Zarita Valen to Proxima Prime.

"Well, Hernando, that's finally done. All the emergencies are finally handled. Now comes the real problem," Queen Isabella said. The two were now alone in her private study where she spent most of her free time.

"Yes, you've done much to be very proud of, but this one still remains. I surely don't know how you can solve it. Even Zarita believes she needs many crystals. Perhaps she does," he sighed.

"You know my love, I've done my work. First as a senator and then as Queen for another fifteen years. Perhaps it is time I hand off the throne to Amy," Isabella sounded out Hernando.

"Well, you have tried to set term limits for the other elected officials, though the current crop of kings and queens haven't quite followed it. Would this help set an example do you think?" he asked.

"Perhaps so, dear, perhaps so. If Misty isn't too busy, I want to pay her a visit. Can you get our Circle to schedule a teleport for me please?" she asked. Later, she postponed her visit; they had their hands full with the governor and the others.

It was not until mid-November that Queen Isabella met privately with Misty and Rafaela in the Underground. "I want to end this life of torture. I've spent nearly fifteen years on the throne, and I ought to set an example and retire. Perhaps that will spur some of the other rulers to pass their torches as well."

"Honestly, Isabella, I don't know how you managed to

survive as hobbled as you are. But what did you have in mind?" Rafaela asked.

"I've lived over a hundred years without finding love. Just when I expected never to find it, along comes Hernando. Now, I don't want to lose him. I am not like Amy, Jan, and Benjamina. If the body dies, well you know what I mean. I was thinking, Rafaela, about what happened to you when you used the rejuvenation machine. You rolled back the years, but when your body rejuvenated to where it was when you were twenty-one, you again had no arms because you didn't have them when you were twenty-one. Right?"

"Well, yes, that was the gamble that Andres and I chose to take. It's not that bad; we're quite used to dealing with it, like the katalyein are. Why?"

She didn't directly answer that. Instead, she took another direction. "You know I'm nearly a hundred nineteen years old. I've used the old type rejuvenation machines a number of times. They have finite limits. Each time they are used, fewer and fewer years can be restored. But these new ones that Jan brought back don't have those limits. Is that correct?"

Misty answered this one. "Yes, they have made significant strides in the rejuvenation process. The process goes in and removes the buildup of bogus information on some of the DNA genetic strands that are responsible for the aging process and the overall degeneration of the body. Those old limitations are by and large removed now. Why?"

"I'd like to try to rejuvenate this body all the way back to when I was fourteen in hopes that my neck, arms, and feet would be restored to what they were back then. I could then have a new life, free from this terrible one and not lose Hernando. If it worked, he would join me. We can change our names and move somewhere and start a new life together, free from this never ending nightmare that we face constantly. You can't imagine how hard it is to not even be able to turn your head."

Rafaela cautioned, "But what happens if it doesn't work out that way? What happens if your neck remains fused? What happens if your arms are still gone? What then?"

"If my neck is still fused, then I will attempt Benjamina's route. Die and try to remember all in my next lifetime. Hernando will go along with whatever I decide. If it fails and I die, he will accompany me, and together we'll try to find each other next lifetime. Perhaps, we can get Benjamina to help us make it happen properly."

"I see you've given this considerable thought. Have you discussed this with your children?" Rafaela asked rather pointedly.

"No. Not a word. We'll tell them when and if we do this. If it works, Hernando and I will move to a warmer climate. We've our eyes on Arabella."

"So you mean to try this soon?" Rafaela asked.

"If you're willing to help us, then yes. We'll make a formal announcement that we are retiring, and that Amy is now in charge. I'll wait a while to make darn sure the transition is accepted. Then, we'll do it in secret. We don't want anyone besides you two and our children to know what happens to us, either way. We are stepping out of public life and finally having our own personal lives."

"Very well Queen Isabella. You've given us more than anyone could possibly ask. Make your arrangements. We'll be ready on this end," Rafaela replied. "Misty will operate the machine. I can't, obviously."

"Thank you both! I'll make the arrangements very soon." Queen Isabella thanked them, and Bart returned her to her castle.

That night over supper, Isabella made her announcement. "Kids, as of the last day of December, I'll be retiring as Tierra's Queen and head of the Supreme Court. Queen Amy will take over for me. I'll make a formal proclamation to that effect tomorrow."

"Mom! Why so soon? You are only thirty-one," Amy protested. She'd hoped to have many years of freedom before assuming the throne.

"Dear, life like this is just too hard on me. Poor Hernando has to care for me constantly. What we're going to try to do is use the new rejuvenation machine that Jan brought back with her. I'm going to try to remove almost a hundred years, and see if I can get my body back to my very early teens. I'm hoping my neck, arms, and feet will be restored. If so, Hernando will undergo it as well, and we'll retire to the warmer climate of Arabella. We'll change our last name and begin new lives. On the other hand, kids, there is no guarantee that this will work. I'm basing my attempt on what happened to Rafaela, when she used it to make her body twenty-one again. Of course, you know what happened to her and Andres. So I am hoping that works for me."

"On the other hand, kids, if my neck is still fused, I simply don't want to live like this any longer. Both Hernando and I will die, and we're going to have Benjamina help us get new bodies and remember everything, so we can begin a new life together. Either way, he and I want a real life together, free from this horrible nightmare that I face all the time."

"Damn, I wish we could somehow get our hands on that top secret cloning process that they used on us," Jan declared. "That would give you third option."

"Cloning has been declared illegal in the Imperium, so let's not consider that one," Isabella countered. "So do we have your backing and support?"

Gabriella began crying. Amy said, "Mom, of course you have it! If you are successful and move to Arabella, can we stay in touch, secretly of course?"

"Sure dear. We would love to one day see our grandchildren, if it can somehow be explained to them. If not, we can pretend to be some of your distant relatives. As I am now, I sure as heck cannot be much of a grandmother. Hernando pretty much had to raise you kids by himself. That was almost unbearable for me. I so wanted to hold you three, when you were babies. Perhaps, now I'll have a new chance at life one way or the other."

The next day, she did issue her proclamation. Shortly after that, many dropped by to pay their respects. Many did thank her for all that she'd done for Tierra. When asked where she would be retiring to, she said that they didn't know yet, but perhaps Brom or Hilliard Heights — some out of the way location where they could relax out of the limelight.

The teens helped the two pack their things into

shipping crates. After saying their farewells to the Imperial Tower members and their staff, Bart teleported them to the Underground. Amy, Bernardo, and Gabriella were quite worried. So many things could go wrong. They waited patiently outside the medical lab, where Misty and Hernando began their work on Isabella. First, he very carefully removed her neck rings. Together, they lifted her up and placed her in the machine. "Last chance to change your mind," Misty said softly.

"Do it," Isabella answered determinedly. Misty shut the lid and darkness covered her. Soon, she fell unconscious as Misty began the operation. She planned to make every attempt to make this work out. She adjusted the controls for body age fourteen and hit the Execute button. Now they could only wait on the machine. If this didn't work, she was going to try thirteen, and so on down to childhood, if need be, before she gave up and allowed them to die.

Hours later, the process finished, and the two took a look before rousing Isabella. Hernando said, "Take another half-year off. Senator Carlos turned her back to fourteen when he did this to her. I should have thought of that sooner." Misty nodded and complied. This time, they only had to wait a few minutes before checking on the process.

Hernando stepped out of the room, where Bernardo, Amy, and Gabriella were waiting anxiously. Tears streamed down his face. Amy panicked. "Dad?"

"She's back. It worked. She's thirteen and a half. It actually worked!" he exclaimed, hugging all three children at once. Amy exhaled as much as she could, greatly relieved!

Just then, the young teen Isabella came waltzing out of the room. "Look at me! I'm free at last!"

Amy grinned and said, "Mom, you better put some clothes on, don't you think?" Everyone laughed. She ducked back inside, followed by Hernando. He'd decided that he ought to be sixteen so he would be better able to protect her. Plus, she decided to have her bosom turned into an adult's size to help mask her apparent age. A little over an hour later, the young teens emerged from Misty's care with enormous grins on their faces. Their bodies were as normal as could be.

At dark, Bart teleported them back to the Imperial Castle, where Lena and Jan waited patiently. Only these other two of the Gang of Ten knew what was happening. They had the wagon loaded with their crates and ready for them, when they materialized before them in the courtyard. While it was winter, they were prepared for this. After farewell hugs and kisses, in three stages, Bart teleported them, their horses, and their wagon down to the coast road that led into Arabella, Westerlings. Amy made sure that they had a sizeable fortune with them, along with a giant crystal for each of them.

Now the master of the castle, Amy and Jan moved into her parent's large suite. Gabriella took Amy's old suite, because it was larger than hers was. Finally, the next morning, Amy and Jan headed over to Elegant Fashions Inc so that Amy could follow the orders of Emperor Kino. They returned around noon, with Jan holding on to her. "Well, it's back to being armless once again. That sure was short lived."

"Yes, but now you are officially Queen Amy, as far as Emperor Kino is concerned. Dear, we ought to get you an heir soon," Jan teased.

"What do you mean, dear?" Amy said coyly, but she knew darn well what Jan meant. They would make use of the latest features of the medical machines, designed for couples like themselves.

Jan replied, "If we do it now, in fourteen years, you can retire too." Both laughed.

As the new year 1292 began, Tierra had a new senator, a new queen, and a new governor. It was now a part of the Ataro Empire and had its Closed World status re-enforced. For the most part, youth had replaced older rulers. However, the enormous problem of the giant crystals of power loomed on the horizon. What would their fourteenth century bring?
The End.

Other Books by Vic Broquard

Without Warning (fantasy)

The Trident Series: (fantasy)
    Volume 1 The Trident and the Book
    Volume 3 The Trident and the Scepter
    Volume3 The Trident and the Resurrection

The Adventures of Elizabeth Stanton Series: (science fiction)
    Volume 1 The Evolution of the Path
    Volume 2 The Great Messiah
    Volume 3 Of Kings and Queens and Troubadours
    Volume 4 Chaos in the Aftermath
    Volume 5 Power Plays
    Volume 6 Age of Exploration
    Volume 7 Abducted
    Volume 8 The Emperor and Empress
    Volume 9 A Job Worth Doing
    Volume 10 Degradation
    Volume 11 The Second Crusade
    Volume 12 When Worlds Collide
    Volume 13 Dark Ages

The Lindsey Barron Series: (fantasy)
    Volume 1 The Rod of the Apocalypse
    Volume 2 The Board of Governors
    Volume 3 The Crown of Moses
    Volume 4 Dominus for President
    Volume 5 The National Health Care Program
    Volume 6 States Justice
    Volume 7 Cross and Double-cross

Zoran Chronicles Series: (fantasy)
    Volume 1 A Dragon in Our Town
    Volume 2 Dragons, Power, Courts, and War

Planet of the Orange-red Sun Series: (science fiction)
    Volume 1 When Kingdoms Fall
    Volume 2 Dark Ages
    Volume 3 Age of the Towers
    Volume 4 Difficillis Exitus
    Volume 5 Age of the Lords
    Volume 6 The Renegade Tower
    Volume 7 Rebellions
    Volume 8 The Aliens Return
    Volume 9 Power Struggles
    Volume 10 Guilds, Genetics, and Gods
    Volume 11 Magi, Witches, Swords, and Superstitions
    Volume 12 The Voyage of the Eagle's Seed
    Volume 13 Justifications
    Volume 14 Responsibilities

The Return of the Wizards: Twelve Companions – The Making of Wizards (fantasy)